CW00957522

Dead Game

Claire Kinton

GHOSTLY PUBLISHING
QUALITY INDEPENDENT CHILDREN'S BOOKS

First published in Great Britain in 2012

Ghostly Publishing, 34 Bakers Close, Plymouth, PL7 2GH

Published in Great Britain by Ghostly Publishing –

Visit www.ghostlypublishing.co.uk for more information

Connect with the author at
www.ghostlypublishing.co.uk/ClaireKinton/

ISBN-10: 1-909587-08-7
ISBN-13: 978-1-909587-08-3

For Gareth, George, Gracie-Jean & Joe

In the night of death, hope sees a star, and listening love can hear the rustle of a wing.

(Robert G. Ingersoll 1879)

In loving memory of Charles

ACKNOWLEDGMENTS

I owe this entire story to my cousin Charles. He was a soldier, one of our heroes, but as fate would have it, he became a dead hero. To me he remains one of my best friends.

I would like to convey sincere thanks to the Benevolent Fund and SSAFA Forces Help, who supported my family and who do fantastic work with our service personnel and their families.

The initial secret of this book writing was broken no further than three chapters in, when my great friend Sarah Davies charmed me into sharing it with her. Sarah and writing were, without doubt, my Prozac during my time of mourning and baby blues. It seems an eternity ago that we both sat in my tiny living room with very small children playing at our feet whilst we immersed ourselves in words. I typed as she read and between her and her husband Al, they gently coaxed me to finish the job.

I would like to thank my Mum and Dad, Auntie Gill and Cousin Sam, Jan and Nic as well as my amazing friends Katie, Vicki, Sandra and Jo, for all your honesty, faith and help. It's been a long road and without their support I never would have made it.

Jo Field, my writing mother and phenomenal editor, truly brought 'Dead Game' alive and gave me hope beyond belief that my manuscript would one day make it into print.

A huge thank you to my beautiful sister Nicola, whose afar and constant longing for the next chapter also forced me to keep going. Masses of appreciation to my brother

Matt, whose fine hand drew Dead Game's map of Transit – you missed your vocation big bro.

And last but by certainly no means least I thank my faithful husband Gareth. Although he has never read a word of Dead Game, he remained my silent anchor, fighting the world against evil on his play-station, night after night, as I, ignoring all his ovations of success, continued to write. With him and his heightened scepticism for my ambition, my feet remained firmly rooted in the ground whilst my head wafted a thousand miles away in the stars.

Prologue

23rd June 1992

Dear Sarah,

I can't believe at fourteen I'm writing you this letter! I hope you stuck to your part of the deal and are reading it after 20th July 2003. You'll probably be twenty-five now. You will be – but I won't.

I haven't gone loopy! What I'm about to tell you may come as a bit of a shock. Try to understand. It's about me - and you in a way - in fact it's about us. We've talked about weird stuff in the past, I know, but this may just blow your mind. Sit down.

Do you remember, at Nanny's house this Easter, (1992 - eleven years ago now, for you) when we played Dead Game? Well something happened. Something I've never told anyone. I think I'm going to die, Sarah. That is, I'm going to die young. I'm not afraid and I don't know how it will happen. I met someone who told me. I'm going to die on 20th July 2003! I know... our birthday. You probably think I'm daft to take any notice of a stranger I met on the mountain, but honest, he was creepy and there was something about him made me believe him.

I want to tell you so much, but I know this isn't what you want to hear, especially when you're tucked away in that private boarding school you detest, so that's why I am writing instead – a letter for your future, so you'll know I'm still out there somewhere. Hey - maybe I might even be able to fly. I've always wanted to fly.

Have you ever wondered where we've come from? Why we're here?

There's one more thing and it's important. One day, after I've gone, I need you to tell my story? I'll help you. God, I feel like I'm giving up on life just writing this. I feel like I'm breaking a deal, but at the same time as sealing my fate, I feel oddly like a new journey will begin. You are the one who must narrate my journey, Sarah. It's a massive and bizarre ask I know, but you must remember you'll never be alone. I'll be with you every breath of the way.

Love Archie

PS. How I know all this doesn't matter either, you'll find out soon enough.

CHAPTER ONE

20TH JULY 2003
FLYING INVOKES BOREDOM AND TERROR

Archie Fletcher's eyes flicked open. The contents of his stomach shot into his mouth as the plane delved downwards, the sudden descent into Kuwait putting an immediate end to his dreaming. Bring Me To Life, Evanescence's new number one single screeched in his ears. He ripped out his headphones, clutched his armrests firmly and swallowed hard.

The commotion in the cabin was quite different from the music that lingered in his head. Automatically he clutched for his St Christopher, muttering under his breath. He was never sure to whom he was praying or if it would help. It just seemed the thing to do when hauling oneself through the air at 800 miles per hour in a giant hollow hunk of metal headed for a warzone.

The Field Support, Second Company, REME were finding it difficult to remain calm. It was an unnerving flight for the hardiest of flyers. Archie forced himself to relax. Well rested after his sleep, his natural appetite for adventure overcoming his fear, he grinned hard at the chiselled soldier beside him. James mustered a nervous smile in return.

Peering out of the small airplane window Archie could see the rumbling storm the pilot was attempting to avoid. Streak lightning lit up dense black cloud that threatened to engulf them. It was a losing battle: quick as thought they were in the thick of it, thunder exploded around the aircraft blotting out the sound of shrieking engines. Lightning struck them over and over again. To those inside it felt as though the supreme hand of God had taken hold of the plane and was shaking it to see what was inside.

Overhead speakers crackled into life. "This is your Captain. We've lost an engine. Prepare for an emergency landing."

Archie sucked in a short breath and turned to look at James. This time neither man smiled. Their eyes locked momentarily, verifying each other's fear, then both leaned forward to stare out of the window at the majesty of the merciless storm. The lights in the cabin flickered as the lightning struck again and again and again, each time throwing into stark relief a blur of tense white faces.

"I'm sorry…" The panic-stricken voice of the captain shouted through the tannoy. "We've lost power and we're losing fuel. Ready a life jacket; under your seat, adopt brace position. We've overshot our landing… we're heading into the Persian Gulf. When we hit it's -"

He was cut off. The cabin plunged into darkness. The plane jerked suddenly downwards.

Seconds later, at five thousand feet and falling, Archie's Commanding Officer, Major William Clift unbuckled his seat belt. Madness had erupted and was rippling through his Company. Cries reverberated around the cabin reaching a crescendo of hysteria. Men were clambering out of their seats attempting to smash the tiny windows. Others fumbled frantically for their mobiles desperate to phone home. Some simply remained strapped to their seats and with an air of fatalistic acceptance mumbled the Lord's Prayer. Archie and James were two of these men.

Clift yanked at the pilot's door; it was locked. Helplessly he looked down at the flight-attendant secured to a flip-down chair. She stared up at him, eyes wide, face soaked with tears. As a massive strike of fork lightning hit the side-door of the aircraft bursting it open, she screamed. A gale ripped around the interior of the plane. Bodies flew helplessly between seats and were dragged towards the open door; overhead luggage compartments flipped open, tossing bags and debris into the chaotic equation. "JUMP… Get your life jackets on now… GO, GO, GO," Clift yelled, holding on for dear life.

People struggled to move, grappling under their seats for a life jacket. The plane was now nose down heading flat out for the ocean. Archie unbuckled and lurched to his feet, his fingers splayed reaching out to grip the seat in front of him. His eyes bulged at the nightmare playing out before him, lightning flashing relentlessly. It seemed insane that Clift wanted them to jump, yet as he watched, Archie knew nothing could be done: the engines were the plane's heart and the pilot was certainly its soul. Without them they were doomed; jumping was their only chance of survival.

"NOW, NOW, NOW…" ordered Clift, standing back as the plane began to empty. Some colleagues leapt, others were sucked out of the gaping doorway into the darkness, all plummeted for the frenzied sea that smashed treacherously far beneath them.

This is suicide, Archie thought. What am I doing?

Reluctantly he released his grip on the seat and staggered sideways into the almost vertical aisle. It was hard to breathe, never mind stay upright. Someone shoved his shoulder and a body swollen with an inflated life jacket pushed past him. It was James.

"What you waitin' for? Get moving!"

Losing his footing, Archie grabbed at an armrest, watching as James wrestled with the elements and toppled forward out of the hole. "No!" Archie lunged forward.

Lightning illuminated James's face as he fell. Then he vanished into darkness.

Clutching the cold metal doorframe, blood rushing to his head, Archie looked up. There seemed to be no end to the sky and no beginning to the sea, they had merged in broiling fury. "DAMN YOU," he screamed, "I WON'T DIE TODAY."

His adrenalin-fuelled rage giving him strength, Archie hauled himself back into the cabin.

"Jump, Fletcher, for God's sake jump," Clift shrieked, struggling towards him.

"I c-c-can't, sir."

"It's your choice. Either way we're done for," and letting go, Clift threw himself out of the aircraft.

Archie leaned forward hoping to see his Commanding Officer hit the water. He stared down hard, desperate for signs of life but everything was black; there was not even a splash. The elements had fused and it was impossible to differentiate between them. Exploding with intense frustration, in the last few moments left to him he swung round into the empty cabin. Too late now to search for a life jacket he wedged his leg behind a seat, grabbed hold of his head and curled his body to the floor.

"Ah," he roared, "what's the point of this, God? It's a useless end. It's not my fate. I WILL NOT DIE TODAY," he chanted. Momentarily he focused on his watch, 23:23 flashed back at him. Why was that so significant? He couldn't think; just knew that it was.

As he waited for the end, Archie became aware that the surviving engine had cut. The shattered plane was hurtling towards the sea in comparative silence. Beyond the rush of wind and screech of stressed metal he could hear the swell of the ocean. Time seemed to stop. Entranced, he shifted his position, stretching out to clutch what was left of the doorframe so he could see out. In the pitch black of night lighting flashed and for a few seconds it was as clear as day. The sea was coming up to meet him. The plane hurtled towards it, faster and faster and yet everything was happening in slow motion. This was not a new experience for Archie: he had been close to death once before and now as then a kaleidoscope of images haunted his brain; images of the years he had lived and the people he loved. But this time he was not trapped under the ice and drowning. This time there could be no guiding light to save him, no voice to say, follow me.

The angry sea was very near now. Archie blinked, staring in disbelief as he caught sight of something protruding above the waves. It looked like an almighty trident, rusted and draped with seaweed. Transfixed, he stared at it, feeling the tossing spume wet his face. Taking a deep breath and wishing he had on a lifejacket, Archie braced for impact, shut his eyes and surrendered.

***

Like a ragdoll hitting a brick wall the aircraft smacked into the water and broke up. Submerged, winded and disorientated, his heavy uniform weighing him down, Archie kicked and struggled against the torrential sea.

Still conscious, lungs bursting, he fought to see through the murky water and glimpsed a shadow disappearing beneath him as he battled upwards, pulling, pushing and driving to the surface. Breaking through, fit to explode, he gulped in a deep breath of cold night air. Unable to focus, he felt something clutching at his legs, as though a giant hand had grabbed him and was wrenching him downwards under the water.

Thrusting and twisting, grabbing and heaving at whatever had him trapped, Archie wriggled free, kicked out and once more began his fight for the surface, but the hand caught hold of him again, this time hauling him fast, upwards and out of the water. This could not be happening! But it was. In that moment, gasping for air like a landed fish, Archie knew that what he thought he had seen from the plane was real: it was a trident, and someone, or something had hold of it – and him.

Hanging upside down above the waves he saw the monster that held him captive. Half-man, half-fish the creature towered over the ocean, its long brown hair thick with seaweed and shells, its face streaming with water and livid with anger. Clutching the trident in one enormous hand and Archie, a miniature helpless figurine in the other, the monster held him there for a moment longer then dived, smashing him back into the sea. Stripped naked by the brute force of the impact, Archie knew no more.

***

When he came to, it was daylight and he found himself tied tightly to a large piece of debris floating on the water. As it rolled on the swelling waves he went with it, completely submerging over and over again. He had no idea how long he had been there or whether it was night or day. He knew he was alive because his head ached abominably, but strangely he could feel none of his limbs. As he slipped in and out of consciousness time passed and the sun rose higher, beaming down on his naked body.

Archie's hearing kicked in first, to waves crashing on a distant shore. Squinting, he tried to look about. In the few seconds before the sun blinded him he glimpsed a blue cloudless sky. Tears streaming, he shut his eyes against the glare and attempted to change position, but a severe throbbing in his head forced him to stop. Flat on his back, the waves lapping around him, he strove to make sense of what had happened; he had no memory of lashing himself to the debris. How had he got here? Was that Poseidon Sea God a bizarre nightmare during his fight for survival? What other explanation could there be? At least his limbs seemed to be coming back to life again and apart from a headache and a raging thirst, Archie was not aware of any injuries. To make sure, he quickly scanned his body, starting with his feet and working his way up: 'Legs, fine, torso okay, arms - ahh!' A spike of excruciating pain struck his right shoulder as he moved it; he immediately stopped and it subsided to an ache. Only then did he realise he had no clothes on and that what he was attached to was the aircraft door. He panicked, tried to sit up, but the pain was so intense he gave in and lay still.

After a time, soothed by the soporific warmth of the sun and the gentle motion of the water, Archie felt strangely at peace with the world. He was out in the middle of nowhere, mother-naked and unable to move and yet the sensation was not unpleasant. Lulled into a doze, it came to him that above the lapping waves he could hear a strange fluting sound. He strained to listen; yes, what he was hearing was without doubt music, but not like anything he had ever heard before. It became clearer and more defined as though an orchestra was playing something classical; it had to be coming from a boat. Help was at hand.

Elated, Archie turned his head, tears of pain blurring his vision. He could make out where the sea met the sky, but could see no boat. He moved his head up and swivelled round to the other side. All he could see was a deserted shore, yet the music played on. 'It must be in my head,' he concluded, sick with disappointment and gripped again by panic.

"The curses of the night have been dispelled, Archie."

Archie's eyes flicked wide open, to be blinded immediately by the sun. He screwed them up against the glare and ignoring the pain in his shoulder pushed himself onto his elbow and called out, "Who said that?"

"Have no fear. I will do you no harm. I can help you plan for the future," the soft, male voice whispered. Backed by the music it sounded almost hypnotic.

"Where are you? I can't see you," Archie looked around at the empty ocean.

"You can see me, but you cannot look at me. My light shines too bright. I am the sun."

"W-w-what do you want?"

"I want to help you return home safely."

Forcing himself to relax Archie lay back down; clearly this was a figment of his imagination. He must have sustained a head injury, which would account for the appalling thumping behind his eyes. In the circumstances it was hardly surprising his mind was playing him tricks. All things considered he was lucky to be alive. Unless... Oh God! The thought stopped Archie in his tracks. "Am I dead?"

"No, you are not dead."

"Okay, let me recap. I've recently fallen out of the sky, had an almighty battle with Neptune, I'm now naked, tied to an aeroplane door and floating on an open ocean. And as if that weren't enough, I am being serenaded by a phenomenal orchestra whilst having a full-on conversation with the sun, and you are seriously telling me I'm not dead?"

"No, you are not dead. You are what we call 'in Transit'. I have pulled you into an island tide, you will be ashore fairly soon. This, Archie, is the game of your life, so listen to me carefully. To return home you must let Hope guide you, and should you be so unfortunate as to meet my bewildering and evil sister, you must be vigilant. Keep your mind focused or she may take it from you. She can confuse any fool at a mere glimpse. Remember, I am always here for you. Be wise, Archie. Trust the foresight I have given you and go quickly."

The music stopped as suddenly as it had begun and Archie's reality became once more the sound of the sea cascading around him. He could hear waves breaking on the shore more clearly now. Iridescent droplets of water clung to his skin, trembling with tiny rainbows. They reminded him of his mother's story about his birth. Strange to think of that now when his life was hanging by a thread. "Mum," he whispered, "help me. I do not want to die; not like this."

CHAPTER TWO

1978

BABIES DON'T KEEP...

"20th July, 1978; time of delivery...?" Joanna Fletcher's buxom midwife lifted her nurse's watch, "Eleven twenty-three a.m. Weight: seven pounds and three ounces," she announced, scribbling in Joanna's maternity notes. "Congratulations Mr and Mrs Fletcher, your baby boy is beautiful. Do you have a name for him?" She closed Joanna's notes and popped them at the end of the bed.

"Not yet," Robert Fletcher answered, sounding wheezy and harassed. He puffed hard on a blue inhaler then dropped it back into the gaping pocket of his yellow flares.

Understanding his tone the midwife bustled to the door. "I'll leave you with Master Fletcher for a while. I'll be back in half an hour to take you for a bath, Joanna," she said with a smile, leaving Robert and Joanna alone with their brand new baby for the first time.

For several minutes in that small yet private hospital room the new parents remained silent, transfixed on the sleeping child that lay swaddled in Joanna's arms. Baby Fletcher was perfectly content, full of colostrum, hushed and utterly worn out after his entrance. The only interference of the peace was a slight crackle from the black and white television set on mute in the corner of the room.

Robert broke the silence, looking across at the red blanket folded neatly on the bedside locker, the crochet pin sticking out of the ball of wool beside it. "You've finished it then."

Joanna followed his gaze, "Not quite, it's nearly there though." Smiling she added, "Is there any news on Patricia?" Robert's eldest sister had fallen for her first baby at much the same time as Joanna and the two women had shared the toil of pregnancy, both due within a few days of each other.

"Yes, Jack phoned earlier. You aren't going to believe it," Robert grinned, "Pat went into labour just before breakfast, so we should hear something soon."

"Oh, they'll be like twins! I wonder if this freakish weather set her off like it did me." Joanna glanced up at the window remembering the tremendous thunderstorm that had been raging when they'd dashed to London City Hospital at three o'clock that morning. "At least the rain's easing off a bit now. It's more than can be said for Hurricane Fico..." Joanna turned her attention to the flickering television screen. "Can you turn the volume up? They say it might hit Hawaii."

"Mm," Robert agreed without looking up, his gaze firmly on his son.

With a fleeting grimace of pain, Joanna leant forward and offered the swaddled bundle to his father. "Here, you hold him."

"Are you sure? I might drop him," Robert's face creased with anxiety.

"Of course you won't," she smiled.

He stuck out his hands and took the bundle from her, fumbling a little, his eyes filling with tears as he held his son, "He's so small," he whispered.

"Small and perfectly formed," Joanna giggled, kneeling on the end of her bed to tweak the television volume. "He looks like you," she added settling back down.

"He certainly has my hair." Still buzzing with adrenalin Robert combed a huge and shaky hand through the baby's mop of jet black hair so much like his own but without the lengthy sideburns.

"Not mine, that's for sure!" Joanna laughed patting her white-blonde hair, which during her labour the midwife had scraped back into an elastic-band. It felt tight and was making her head ache.

"He looks slightly Oriental don't you think?" Robert said, tilting his head slightly. "A bit like my Great Uncle Archibald."

Behind her large, national health glasses Joanna's eyes widened. "Archibald, Archibald," she muttered, reaching for the baby book on the locker and riffling through the pages until she found the one she wanted. "That's it! It's a perfect name for him."

"What?" Robert frowned. "I'm not sure..."

"Here, look," Joanna pointed at the page. "It means 'true and bold', it's the perfect name for our little soldier," she repeated. Her eyes bloodshot with tiredness she looked at her husband, desperate for his approval.

Robert shook his head, "Archibald... hmm, I don't know."

Disappointed, Joanna sighed. Her husband had found names hard to discuss; he'd insisted on meeting their baby first, said it seemed wrong to name a child without at least looking at him. Yet, having finally met his son, Robert was clearly none the wiser. She supposed he now had to believe he would know their baby's name when he heard it.

They were silent.

"This is the longest-lived hurricane the Pacific has ever seen," said the sombre voice of the TV newsreader. "It started on the 9th of July. Hurricane Fico has developed from a tropical disturbance off the coast of Mexico. It moved north-westward and then quickly westward, with winds reaching 140 mph on July 12. Today, 20th July 1978, Hurricane Fico is still moving westward towards Hawaii. It has intensified from a Category 1 to a Category 4 storm over a period of eleven days, with winds peaking at 140 miles per hour. Six people aboard..."

"We don't need doom and gloom today," Robert said switching off the set, babe still nestled in one arm.

Lost in thought, Joanna gazed out of the hospital window. The midwife had left it ajar to let in the fresh air. As Joanna watched, the clouds broke allowing through a shaft of sunlight and with it transpired an almighty rainbow spanning the entire window view. She gasped, "Oh Robert… look... how beautiful!"

"Wow, that's awesome." With exaggerated care Robert got up from his chair and carried the baby to the window. "Look at that, my son," he whispered to the sleeping newborn. He frowned, turned back to Joanna, "There's a bit of a draught. Should I shut it?"

"No need, it's good to have some fresh air," Joanna said, but as she spoke, a strong breeze sprang up from nowhere. It sighed and whistled through the window, flurried the floral print curtains and blustered around the room ruffling the bed sheets and sending a shiver through all in its path, and as it sped by a whispered voice seemed to follow in its wake. "I give you this child… take care of him… he is yours… for a time…" Then it died down, leaving an uneasy stillness as though it had never been.

Robert and Joanna turned to each other, their eyes frozen wide open. "D-d-did you hear that?" Joanna asked, white-faced and trembling.

Abruptly, Robert moved to the cot by the bed and laid the babe down, gently teasing the honeycomb blanket up and around him. Satisfied, he moved over to the window and shut it firmly. Only then did he turn back to Joanna.

"Hear what?"

"That voice... it said-"

Robert cut across her, "It was just the wind."

"But didn't you hear…?"

"It was the wind," Robert insisted. "You're tired, darling."

Perplexed, Joanna frowned at her husband and drew in a deep breath about to argue. The words she was certain she had heard still ricocheted in her ears. But maybe Robert was right; she was exhausted; so desperately needing to sleep. She must have imagined it after all. With a shrug and a concealed yawn she refocused her thoughts on baby naming. "Well if not Archibald, let's call him 'Archie', he'd only end up being called Archie if we named him Archibald."

Robert swung round to her and laughed out loud, "That's it!"

Joanna pushed herself upright and almost bounced with joy, her face lighting up as she watched her husband's expression change: he knew as well as she did that 'Archie' was their baby's name.

"Well done you and thank you my beautiful Jo." Robert leant over the cot to gaze once more at his son, "He'll be called Archie. He's perfect. I know in time he and I will be the greatest of friends." He kissed the baby's forehead. The infant let out a muffled grunt and started to rummage.

He squirmed and squinted trying to open his eyes then he seemed to gaze knowingly straight into his father's blue ones as if to say, 'You're right, Daddy, we shall be the best of friends,' and for a split second, Archie's tiny mouth parted and he smiled.

"Oh look, Jo, he's smiling at me!" Lost in his son's face Robert beamed back, positive the infant's smile was meant solely for him.

"How lovely, darling." Joanna knew it could only be that the baby needed burping, but she was not about to dent her husband's joy. Outside, she noticed, the sun had gone in and the rainbow had evaporated. It was raining again.

***

A few days later Archie was taken from the hospital to 23, Eversely Avenue, the 1930's pebble-dashed, three-bed end of terrace to which the Fletchers had moved during Joanna's third trimester of pregnancy. It stood directly opposite the park on a busy cut-through to London's city centre. A wide tarmac driveway swept up the right hand side, framed by a low stone wall.

Robert and Joanna's lives were transformed. Their days revolved around their newborn who made his wishes known in no uncertain terms. A hyperactive baby, Archie, it seemed, liked neither bath nor bedtime and each evening his cries of protest could be heard three doors down. There was no in between with this little boy: when he cried, he howled, mostly claiming he was hungry. A very greedy and stubborn infant, nothing would suffice until his needs were satisfied. Nevertheless, when Archie reached the age to laugh, oh how he laughed, he could illuminate an entire room with one giggle. A whole-hearted roar would generate meltdown in seconds, contagious yet pure, so much so that sometimes it was hard to breathe. This child brought joy to everyone in his life. Robert and Joanna became like children again, always singing, dancing and storytelling, completely absorbed by every precious second of parenthood.

Life was not easy for the Fletchers in the late seventies. Joanna, a devoted and besotted mother, insisted on staying at home to look after their baby. Robert, as the sole breadwinner, found his fear of failure and will to succeed almost overwhelming. A trained geography teacher, he searched in vain for full-time work, but it was hard to find in the capital and he was not prepared to work away from home. So he either had to take supply work whenever and wherever it was available or change his occupation completely. With no set amount of money coming in, a mortgage to pay and another mouth to feed, any job would do. He took on door-to-door sales, advertised as a local handyman in the local newsagent and at one point even found himself selling ladies underwear; anything to bring in the pennies. Fortunately, neither he nor Joanna were materialistic, they never truly wanted much for themselves. They got by with 'make-do-and-mend' and were blissfully happy just the way they were.

Baby Archie had homespun toys and a homemade cot. The table where they ate had been handed down the family line and was considerably well used, as were the set of hard-backed chairs. Beyond the ancient gas oven and equally ancient fridge-freezer – both acquired from a charity shop - there were no modern gadgets in the kitchen to help ease the load. There were no carpets on the floors; in the living room they had no lounging sofas. They did not even have a television, they would simply sit on homemade cushions on the floor and play until Archie's bedtime and then read or fall exhausted into bed. Their one inessential item was a camera, which had been a gift. Saving every spare penny for film they recorded each precious moment of Archie's development. Instead of pictures, their walls were adorned with row upon row of photographs millimetres apart: in their hall; above the mantelpiece; up the stairs, even in their bathroom. These were far more precious to the Fletchers than priceless art could ever be. Quite literally, all that the family had were the roof over their heads, a subsistence ration of food and each other. And within this loving, committed cocoon of devotion young Archie thrived.

One evening six weeks after his birth, when the evenings were still light and the distant smell of barbeque lingered on the air, Robert and Joanna were as usual absorbed in Archie. "There's nothing quite like the smell of a baby, I wonder what it is that makes you want to pick them up and sniff them. They are almost edible, don't you think?" Joanna sniffed her infant obsessively. "Oh God, you're just so gorgeous." She lay on her back in their double bed, nuzzling and kissing her son as he nestled into her neck.

Robert switched on the bedside light. "Come on Master Fletcher," he said, mentally preparing his eardrums. "It's your bedtime. Mummy needs her sleep." Picking Archie up from Joanna's chest he pulled him in close and whispered in his ear. "She needs to recharge her batteries before the two o'clock feed."

For once the expected onslaught did not come and Robert, grinning at Joanna and holding his breath, placed Archie gently in the cot that stood at the end of their bed.

"I'd get your head down, Jo, whilst he's asleep. You'll be shattered tomorrow if you don't."

"Are you sure you don't mind?" Joanna yawned, snuggling under the covers and cuddling a piece of used muslin permeated by Archie's scent.

"'Course not. I'm only going to be filling in those applications that came this morning. I'll do the washing up first though; you need to sleep," Robert whispered, covering Archie with the red crocheted blanket his wife had stitched religiously every day of her pregnancy. He picked up Joanna's empty teacup and bent over the bed to drop a hard kiss on her lips, "Love you."

"Love you too," murmured Joanna, already half asleep. She was physically and mentally drained. The colossal demands of breastfeeding her baby, which she insisted on doing, were taking their toll. She reached out to switch off the light and Archie began to rummage; a few seconds later he was snorting and kicking at his blanket. Joanna groaned, shoving her head deep under the pillow. It didn't help; she could not block him out; he started to whinge. Joanna, whose natural instinct was to get up and nurse him, forced herself to stay put and finally fell into a deep and necessary sleep, only to be rudely woken far too early by her now screaming baby.

Throwing back the covers, Joanna, padded barefoot and zombie-like over to the cot. "What is it, Archie?" she asked, attempting to soften the irritation that crept into her voice and reflecting she could well understand how it was possible to be driven over the edge of sanity by sleep deprivation. Picking him up, she sat on the end of the bed, drew back her floral nightdress and latched Archie onto her breast. His cries stopped, transformed instantly into satisfied slurping. Feeling as though her eyes were filled with shards of gravel, Joanna looked at the digital alarm clock on the bedside table: 23:23 shone back at her. Robert was still downstairs. She sighed, "Why don't you want to sleep little one? You've barely slept all day, you must be tired. Mummy's tired. Actually, she's past tired; she's completely exhausted. This lack of sleep is no good for her." Joanna refocused her eyes, looking down at her nuzzling infant, "Or you, come to that, Mister."

Joanna continued to mutter and hum at Archie for a good thirty minutes, trying desperately to stay awake and alert whilst he fed. Finally his sucking slowed and stopped, his little fists relaxing against her breast. "He sleeps. At last," she murmured. "Dare I burp you? Don't wake up again, God forbid!"

Then a thought popped into Joanna's head that had not occurred to her before. Seizing the moment, she placed Archie down on her own bed, surrounding him with pillows and cushions. Then she began to drag the cot out of their bedroom and onto the landing, shutting the door behind her and heading for the tiny box room at the top of the stairs.

"What are you doing?" called Robert, disturbed from his form filling. Joanna stopped pulling and took a breath, by which time her husband was half way up the stairs.

"I can't have another night like last night," Joanna explained, "or the night before or the night before that. I'm so tired, darling. I'm going to put Archie in his own room now. He's nearly seven weeks. It's silly him being in with us, all we do is wake each other up. I'm sure he will sleep for longer if he's completely undisturbed."

"Are you certain?" Robert's face was shadowed with concern. "I don't know, Jo. Don't you think it's a bit soon?"

"No I don't," Joanna snapped. "I'm his mother and I have decided he needs his own room. And that's that!" She continued to drag the cot, ramming it at the box room door. "I need to sleep… and I need to sleep now, do you hear me?"

"I don't think that cot is going through that door, honey, not unless you mean to bash through the door frame," Robert said mildly, raising his eyebrows at his wife to make it clear her lack of composure both amused and astounded him.

This irritated Joanna even more and she burst into tears of frustration. "It went through our bedroom door okay; the doors in this house can't be different sizes." She continued to slam the cot at the rigid door frame until forced to admit defeat. "Fine, he can sleep on the landing." Turning on her heel she headed for her bedroom.

"Don't be silly," her husband laughed, steering her back to the abandoned cot.

"I'm not being silly, Robert." Joanna stood, hands on hips, eyes closed. "You made the wretched cot so you can dismantle it and set it up in his bedroom. I can't." She tried to force her eyes open in an attempt to give her husband 'the look', but failed. "Please, Robert, it's either that or I'll go mad."

"Whoa, you really do mean business don't you? Okay, I'll sort this out. Let's see if we can get it through at an angle."

Together they edged and nudged the bulky homemade cot through the box-room door. "There now," Robert said smugly, standing in the open doorway of Archie's new nursery, the cot squeezed snugly into the corner by the window. He put his arm tight around his wife's shoulders, propping her up. "All we need now is Archie."

Joanna turned out the light and tiptoed along the landing to fetch her baby. Holding her breath she carried him back to the box room, placed him into his cot and tucked him up neatly with his red blanket. For a moment both parents stood looking down at their sleeping firstborn then crept from the room, Joanna closing the door softly behind them.

"What if we can't hear him cry," whispered Robert, worried.

"You are joking aren't you?" Joanna stared at her husband in utter disbelief. "Our little man has a mighty set of lungs on him and this is hardly an eleven-bedroom mansion, of course we'll hear him."

"Let's leave the door ajar," Robert ignored his wife's sarcasm.

Joanna was too tired to argue. "You do what you like; I'm going back to bed." She disappeared into the darkness of their bedroom leaving her husband listening at the nursery door.

After a while, satisfied that all was well, he snuck back downstairs to finish his paperwork.

CHAPTER THREE

LOSING HOPE DOES NOT ALWAYS MEAN YOU ARE LOST

Exhausted and drenched, Archie dragged the plane door out of the crashing rollers and crawled onto the narrow beach. He collapsed in the sand beside his anchor and for a few moments lay prone, overcome with relief to be out of the water. The relief did not last long. The sand shimmered with blistering heat and he could feel his rapidly drying skin beginning to burn. Dehydration was his greatest enemy now; he had to find water or die. Rolling onto his knees he struggled to free himself from the rope that had kept him from drowning, but now enslaved him. It was thick and wet and wrapped tightly round his injured arm. Crying out in pain Archie twisted and pulled at it tears drizzling from his swollen eyes. After a few moments he gave up.

"Hello?" he tried to shout, but his voice came out as a hoarse, broken whisper. He cleared his throat and tried again, "Hello?" His yell echoed back at him. He sounded different.

"James…?" He shouted. He sounded younger. "Someone... anyone?" With increasing despair he looked up and down the beach, then back out at the ocean. There was no one; nothing. Not even a speck on the horizon. He was completely alone.

"Oh God, please… there must be someone else." There was silence, but for the shushing of the waves on the shore. Tremendous cliffs rose up out of the sea on either side of the beach and gathered together behind him. They must be at least eighty-foot high and formed an insurmountable barrier. 'There's no way out,' Archie's mind pounded, 'unless I climb.' He gazed up at the cliffs in utter desolation. "What is this place?" Critically thirsty, he sat on the glorious white beach and for the first time in his life was besieged by paranoia and fear. He felt utterly helpless; he simply did not know what to do.

"Well one thing's for sure," he muttered attempting to bolster his courage, "I'm not going anywhere attached to this door. First things first: get out of the heat and into the shade." To his far left were a number of large and smaller rocks framed by a gigantic concave cliff that cast a huge shadow on the beach. From Archie's perspective it was quite awesome. The shape of the cliff was one thing, but the colour took his breath away: it was a stunning shade of amber, becoming paler as it rose up. Attracted by the cliff's beauty, he gritted his teeth and drawing on all his reserves struggled to his feet and set off towards it, hauling the door behind him through the sand.

He made slow progress. The sand blistered his feet as he trudged closer to his target. Excruciating pain where the rope cut into his skin, combined with his injured shoulder, triggered a stream of involuntary tears. It was all too much and Archie, brave soldier that he was, found he was sobbing like a child.

Reaching the shadow of the cliff at last, he perched on a smooth orange rock to rest. His mouth was dry and his tongue felt as if it had swollen to twice its normal size. The temptation to drink seawater was almost overwhelming, but Archie knew better than to give in to it. "I have to find fresh water… and quickly, so I must get rid of this door –

but how?" He spoke aloud, discovering that talking to himself somehow made him feel less alone. It was odd that he sounded so different, his voice not quite as deep as it had been. Must be the effect of the salt water, he decided. He scanned his immediate surroundings, his gaze lighting upon a piece of flint glistening in the sand at his feet. Edging towards it he crouched down, picked it up and ran his thumb along the edge. "It might just do."

Archie examined the rope: encrusted with salt it was almost dry now and somewhat frayed in places. Picking a spot, he started gingerly to saw at it and slowly the strands began to part beneath the flint. After several minutes the rope loosened its grip and the pain eased a little. Trembling with relief Archie took a deep breath, freed his arm and cradled it. His arm felt thinner, much thinner. His fingers strayed automatically to his neck to feel for his St Christopher. To his dismay it was no longer there; stripped away along with his clothes. It had been the one object of real permanence in his adult life. He had never taken it off since the day his 'twin' cousin had given it to him - not even when he showered. "St Christopher will protect you. He's the patron saint and protector of travellers," Sarah had said as she'd hung it round his neck. Without it he was completely naked in every sense of the word.

Looking up at the overhanging cliff, Archie's heart sank. Although his Army field training had included rock-climbing, he knew he was in no fit state to meet the challenge. Giving way to hopelessness once again he was unable to comprehend the fate he had been handed. He wished he could turn back time and abort the mission; snap his fingers and be teleported to the security of his parents' home. He saw it in his mind's eye: 23, Eversely Avenue, the house in which he'd grown up, his sanctuary, his family. They had always been there for him. Where were they now? Bizarrely he found himself blaming them for his misfortune.

Gazing out at the heavenly view of white sand and turquoise water, which looked like something out of a holiday brochure, Archie contemplated his situation. Shading his eyes, he looked up to see the sun still blazing high in the sky and was reminded of the strange voice that had seemed to talk to him. Had this, like the sea monster, been nothing but a dream after the nightmare of the plane crash? He knew one of the chief symptoms of dehydration was extreme confusion and hallucination. Maybe that would answer why he sounded and felt different. He had certainly lost a lot of weight. Was he going mad through lack of water?

"Talk to me now, sun. Help me. Show me the way home," whispered Archie, staring into the sky, fraught for a reply. His eyes watered, his sight becoming distorted. He closed them and looked away and as he did so he distinctly heard a familiar girly giggle. Startled, Archie swung round blinking hard to renew his vision. Aside from the flight attendant, there had been no female on his flight. Had she survived too? Was she here?

"Hello," Archie shouted, jumping to his feet, a surge of hope powering his lungs.

"Hello," replied a sweet, feminine voice.

Archie shaded his eyes, scanning the beach and spinning round to search the rocks behind him, but could see no one. "Where-?"

"I'm up here," interrupted the voice.

Archie looked up. "I can't see you."

"Yes you can, you're looking at me."

Following the sound, Archie caught sight of a small orb-like light coming towards him from the sun. The harder he stared, the bigger it got. Like the voice, it seemed strangely familiar, but his senses refused to give that familiarity credence. 'Oh great; I'm imagining things again. So what are you then - a fairy? I'm completely off my rocker,' he thought, 'and here comes Tinkerbell to prove it!'

"I am actually a star and I like to be called Felicity," trilled the voice indignantly.

Archie gazed at the ball of light that was speaking to him, rubbed his eyes, shook his head and winced. "That does it," he muttered, "I really have gone mad."

As the light drew nearer it began to take form: transparent at first, but becoming increasingly solid, transforming into a vision of such loveliness that Archie was struck dumb with awe. Wide-eyed and staring he suddenly remembered he was naked, but forgot to be embarrassed. His eyes stopped stinging, his wounds seemed to ease and his head ceased pounding. It was as though the creature's beauty had eradicated his pain and all he could think was: 'Wow! She's gorgeous.'

The star giggled again. "I know what you're thinking, Archie," she twinkled as her tiny feet landed on the sand in front of him, her hands cupped in front of her. She was dressed simply in brilliant white, her shimmering gown falling to her knees, her transparent wings, each as large as her body, folded neatly behind her back. Her knees bent in as she swayed towards him on one leg in a manner that was decidedly girly.

"What do you mean you know what I'm thinking?" Archie was horrified.

"You think I'm gorgeous," Felicity said.

“Oh God, you do know what I’m thinking,” he flushed and looked away trying hard not to think of anything at all. He was now overcome with embarrassment, mixed together with that indefinable feeling of déjà vu, which puzzled him. Then he had it; he was back under the ice. “It’s you, isn’t it,” he breathed.

She trilled with laughter. “Of course it’s me, Archie! And it’s okay, there’s no shame in being honest. I am gorgeous.” Felicity gave her wings a little flutter, propelling a pale white aura around her.

Despite himself, Archie was drawn to look at her again. Visually, Felicity portrayed herself as beautiful, pure and fragile, her soft features enhanced by her pale golden hair, which curled around her shoulders and fell in luxurious waves to the small of her back. It was obvious to Archie that behind this image of beauty she was mischief personified: she seemed idle, completely self-obsessed and her flirtatious giggle told him she was trouble. All the same, he liked her. In fact he really liked her; she was utterly alluring. Archie tried to stop thinking, panicked that she was reading his mind, but this time she seemed not to notice or had chosen to ignore him.

Suddenly, as though remembering why she was here, Felicity gently cleared her throat. “Now, let me see… looking at you… hmmm... you’re in a bit of a state aren’t you. This will help.” She stretched out her hand and a large glass of fresh, cold water appeared in it. Where it came from Archie had no idea and he honestly didn’t care. He took the glass, opened his throat and downed the contents in one ecstatic gulp then held the glass out for some more.

“Thanks… so much better now,” he gasped, revived and still staring.

"That goes without saying," Felicity grinned. "I'm here to guide you."

"So… are you Hope? The one the sun told me about?" Archie hoped he didn't sound like a complete moron, but she did not seem at all surprised he'd been conversing with the sun. Why would she? She was a star for God's sake!

"No, I told you, I'm Felicity. I've changed my name. Hope is what I represent, the name is far too old-fashioned for me, don't you think? It's a bit like the name Faith." Felicity screwed up her face disapprovingly and shook her head, her blonde hair ruffling around her face.

"Felicity's fine," Archie said. He was so in wonder of her he would have agreed to any name. Even so, he could not quite bring himself to believe she was real. Tongue-tied, he stood there gawping as he tried to think of something to say. "What time is it?" he asked eventually, noticing the sun had begun to dip from its zenith and reflecting that of all the questions he might have asked, that seemed to be the least important. He could have asked, 'What day is it? or 'Where am I?', but for some reason he seemed incapable of logical thought, as if he were in the throes of a living dream from which he was unable to wake and where nothing was as it seemed.

"Half the day is gone." Felicity pursed her lips, "You were asleep a long time on that plane door floating out on the ocean. Now then; I believe you were thinking about climbing the cliff?" She looked up at the rocks looming above their heads.

"Yes," said Archie taken aback. He had never met a mind-reader before, or a star for that matter, but he supposed in dreams anything was possible. Physically he felt fifteen again not twenty-four. 'I just wish I could read your mind too,' he thought.

"You are fifteen again Archie and it's a good job you can't read my thoughts. They would be too much for you so early on in your journey, but I pray you'll manage it soon enough," replied Felicity. "Just give it time. Everyone does it here. It's how we communicate, although we don't call it mind-reading, it's called telepathy. Usually you don't even need to think to express yourself, you just feel it.

He was about to ask, 'Here? Where is here?' but as he opened his mouth to speak, Felicity took his breath away by saying, "Would you like to fly with me?"

"Yes," Archie said instinctively, followed swiftly by a sane thought. "Where are you taking me?"

A slight frown revealed the star's irritation. "Don't be slow, Archie. To the top of the cliffs. Isn't that where you want to go?"

"Well, yes… but is that the way I should be going? You're the guide aren't you? Shouldn't I be following you?"

"I can give you hope when you find your journey difficult and guide you when you're lost, but right now, Archie, water has cured your headache and you know where you want to go."

"I do? Where's that?" He stared at her blankly.

"Home; so you're not lost, you know the way. Can I take you to the top of the cliffs now?" Felicity reached out a tiny hand.

"This is insane. You're a mind-reader and yet you're so vague. What's happening to me? Please, I'm begging you. How can you hear my thoughts? Why is the sun talking to me? I'm not in the world I knew. My plane fell into the sea and everything has changed, I've changed. Stars don't just fly down from the sky and offer hope to people at their wits end."

"Oh yes we do. People are just too ignorant to see us and we stars are too... er," she raised an eyebrow at Archie, "idle to care." He had the grace to blush and she smiled at his discomfort. "Any fool can get the gist of hope; it's whether their intuition can perceive the guidance offered that will keep them on the right path."

"That's too profound, I don't understand," said Archie, shaking his head and wincing with renewed pain.

"That is why some are foolishly guided by false hope. They perceive us wrongly." Felicity pouted and looked him up and down, taking in the sheen of sweat on his naked body, his swollen shoulder and bleeding arm. "Mm, you admittedly have a few problems, Archie, but nothing that can't be ironed out. You have good foresight and you also have some really great friends… remember that. Yes, I may be a little elusive, but like all stars I am simply a guide; just a glimmer in the midst of darkness - we cannot dispel it completely. You must find your own way. Now, do you want me to fly you to the top of this cliff or should I leave you here to climb it?"

"No! Don't leave me," Archie cried in sudden panic. "Let's fly." He reached out his good arm and took hold of Felicity's hand. Her touch felt familiar and cool and as she curled her fingers in his, Archie's body temperature started to drop. Hesitantly he smiled, not sure what to expect. The irony of the situation did not escape him: flying naked with a gorgeous star had not been on his agenda!

Felicity gave his hand a tug and he felt a sudden surge of energy rushing from his feet to his head. Every hair on his bare body stood on end as though an electric current was passing through him.

Spreading her delicate wings, which buzzed as her feet left the ground, Felicity hovered for a moment, pulling Archie into the air beside her. Gradually she gained speed and they rose higher and higher.

Looking down at the heavenly beach that had so torturously welcomed him and brought him to the pit of despair, Archie was not sorry to leave it. Feeling exposed and out of control, with his free hand he clutched at his neck forgetting he had lost his St Christopher. His lips moved in a silent prayer, 'Please God, keep me safe; please God, keep me safe.' He was horribly aware that the star was tittering under her breath.

Flying with Felicity was like a semiconscious, thwarted dream; one from which he would wake desperately thankful that it was only a dream, yet intrigued and possibly even a little sad that it had ended so soon. However, he did not wake. Instead they cleared the lip of the cliff and Archie's transformed reality continued.

Eyes wide he searched the desolate terrain below him and sighed with disappointment, not sure what he had expected. The land was immensely flat and really quite bleak with nothing to see but willowy burnt yellow grasses and distinctly trodden criss-crossing paths leading in different directions. It looked much fresher way beyond, greener than the sunburnt scrub below him and in the far distance he could see a ridge of hills.

With practiced grace, Felicity glided down placing her toes on the ground and allowing her feet to come gently to rest. Archie on the other hand seemed to follow the example of his plane by executing an incredible crash landing that ended in a triple army roll.

"Ahh," he screamed. "My shoulder… Why did you let go of me? I think I need a doctor."

Felicity giggled and arched her eyebrows.

"It's not funny!" Archie clung tightly to his arm, turning to see the star standing on the cliff edge. Behind her in the distance hovered two giant ravens flapping their ragged wings and filling the air with raucous squawking as if they too were laughing.

"I'm sorry but I have to go now," Felicity said, scowling up at them. "It'll be dark soon. I suggest you find shelter somewhere. You don't want to be out in this environment overnight." Chuckling at Archie's predicament she pointed to the open plain where it was obvious there was nowhere to take refuge.

"You can't just leave," he protested. "Did you not hear me? I need a doctor… I'm in agony. Where do you expect me to find shelter here?" His voice rose as he spoke, his eyes glistening with unshed tears. He was finding it hard to breathe and knew that at any moment he would be overwhelmed by sheer blind panic. Abruptly he stopped speaking and fought for control.

"You will, Archie. You have to," Felicity said, her tiny feet lifting off the ground once more, her white aura glowing brightly as she hovered near the edge of the cliff. The fierce looking ravens were now right beside her still crowing harshly.

"You can't go… I need your help. I'm injured. I have no shelter… no clothes," Archie pleaded as he chased her to the edge.

"I really am sorry, but I have to go. I have a job to do. I'll come and see you tomorrow," Felicity sniggered, "if you're still around."

"Would you stop giggling, this isn't funny," he repeated. "What do you mean if I'm still around? Where the hell am I going to go?" Archie watched as she backed away from him and began to fade. "Where are you going?" he called out in despair.

"To work; I'm a star remember? I have a sky to light up. Look for me tonight. I promise I'll see you tomorrow. I know it's hard but you must try not to worry." She winked at him, "I'm the gorgeous one, the third to the left of the moon." She turned to go, hesitated. The ravens squawked more loudly flapping around her, "A word of warning: always listen to the sun, never look at the moon." So saying, Felicity's form vanished into a ball of light and accompanied by the screeching birds sped through the sky and disappeared.

'Great; this is just great!' Archie cradled his injured arm and grimaced up at the sun, which was sinking towards the horizon flushing the sky a dusky gold. Doubled up with pain, he turned to inspect his new location. The still air was flooded with mosquitoes and in the rapidly fading light his surroundings looked eerily forbidding. More than a little depressed, Archie shivered; in the past he had always taken clothes for granted. What he would not give to have some now. Slapping at the biting insects he felt more vulnerable than at any time in his life. He was about to move when just beyond where he stood a clump of tall grasses began to rustle and twitch. He froze, the hairs rising on the back of his neck. Was some other strange being about to emerge into this nightmare? Conscious he was standing on the edge of a thirty-metre drop he repositioned his feet and looked warily down at the cliff. In the ocean far below he could see shadows of stingrays and sharks looming in the depths. No escape there then. He returned his gaze to the source of the rustling, thought, 'Get moving, Archie, left or right - anywhere but here!' As he shuffled quickly and quietly to the right the grasses swayed alarmingly and Archie heard the unmistakeable sound of heavy panting.

Sweating with fear he broke into a run, following the cliff edge round as far as it would take him. He seemed to have travelled for several hundred metres, his pounding feet stubbing on sharp stones and tangling in dried grass, when the cliff started to decline. Blistered, sore and bleeding, dropping with exhaustion, Archie stopped to catch his breath. He looked warily behind him. Nothing moved; for the moment there was no sound of pursuit. He scanned his surroundings looking for somewhere to hide. About three metres below him, cut into the cliff face beneath the overhang, was a wide, rock-strewn ledge. Heart thumping, he climbed down to it and found himself on the upper level of three similar ledges. Of equal width they descended like big steps in the cliff, each with a large cave entrance reaching deep into the rock. On all fours, he scrambled breathlessly down to the first one.

Breathing slightly more easily, Archie sat in the cave mouth and leaned his head back against the rock wall. He had little respite; something was snuffling on the cliff top accompanied by a lot of padding and pawing. He moved further into the cave and curled into a tight, cowering ball. Desperate not to make a sound nor give off any scent, he held his breath and listened. The scratching and panting, sniffing and grunting continued for a few moments then stopped.

Archie stayed still for as long as he could then lifted his head and breathed in the stale air of the cave. It smelt quite rancid, as if something was either living in it - or possibly had even died in it. He shuddered, wrinkling his nose. More than anything he wanted to leave but if he left where would he go? He may as well take his chances here than head back out to whatever beast was lurking in the grasses above. Whatever it was, it didn't seem too friendly.

In a kind of petrified stupor, Archie remained unmoving for quite some time contemplating his predicament. What was this land with sea monsters and fairies? Had the velocity of the plane crash somehow forced him into a different dimension? It happened in sci-fi movies, but was it possible in reality? And what had the sun meant about him being in transit? Archie felt tears welling. Aside from anything else, he was beginning to feel acutely hungry, his stomach was rumbling, his injured shoulder was aching abominably and he was stuck with no clothes on in a dark, stinking cave in a land that was totally alien.

As his limbs began to chill and stiffen, Archie risked crawling to the mouth of the cave. Shifting to a more comfortable position, he watched the red ball of the sun disappear beneath the horizon and the moon take its place. The cave was pitch black but for a moonbeam shining across the entrance. It was more than creepy and Archie had to clench his teeth to stop them from chattering. Even on training exercises designed to toughen up army recruits, nothing had been as bad as this; it was beyond his experience and as the shadows gathered and the air grew cold in the moonlight, Archie had never felt more alone nor so scared.

In an effort to stop wallowing in hopeless despair, he turned his thoughts to his lost family and friends. His mind was swimming. In the darkness he could almost see their faces, their smiles. He could hear their voices echoing around him and at one point he thought he could smell his home over the top of the rotten stench emanating from the cave behind him. Home: fresh cut flowers, furniture polish and the faint reek of burnt dinners, and underlying all of that, the scent his mother always wore. In that moment he longed for her as he had not done in years. Conjuring her image, Archie whispered to her in the darkness, "I'm sorry Mum. I'm lost, hungry, tired and cold and my shoulder is agony." Fairly certain now that it was dislocated, he attempted to get more comfortable, thinking that if he could just get some sleep he might feel better, but with hard rock pressing into his buttocks and back it was impossible, so he settled for watching the moonlight creeping across the earth floor towards him and tried to judge what time it was – as if that mattered!

"I'd move away from the opening if I were you, Archie," a resonant gruff voice echoed deep within the cave.

"Wha...!" Archie screeched, started backwards and banged his head on the hard wall.

"Get away from the moonlight," the voice said urgently.

Still hunched in a ball and cradling his shoulder, Archie shuffled obediently out of the moonbeam and into the shadows. After the initial shock he was not surprised by this random voice in the darkness; nor did it escape him that everyone around here seemed to know his name. Nothing about this extraordinary place could surprise him anymore. With a wry grimace he strained to pierce the gloom to see who or what was speaking to him.

"My name is Emrys. Welcome to my home and my temple," the voice boomed.

Archie remained silent. The silence dragged on. He was on the point of saying 'thank you' when it spoke again.

"I can help you with your shoulder if you like."

"Oh yes, please help me... I'm in agony." Archie's voice came out small with pain and fear.

"I will come forward so you can see me, but please don't be afraid. I'm like nothing you have seen before."

"Nothing's what I expect here. Please just help me." Archie heard a ruffling sound like something large finding its feet. Then he heard the clip-clopping of hooves on the stone floor of the cave. "Are you a talking horse?" he asked, searching the dark for a sight of it.

"No, I am half horse, half man. A centaur to be exact, some call me a 'Hierophant'."

Archie saw a shadow stop just before the moonbeam hit the floor. He could see a short white beard and behind it, a gentle human face, seamed with age. Around the old man's scrawny neck was what looked like a dog collar; a preaching horse? This was going beyond a joke! Archie could not see the equine section of Emrys' body, but aside from his collar his exposed torso and arms were as naked as Archie's own and considering the age of his face, his physique looked remarkably muscular and athletic. His expression was friendly but sad. There was something about it that was vaguely familiar and Archie had the strangest feeling he had seen this face before. He racked his brains, but try as he might he could not place where.

"I can feel your pain, Archie. You have a dislocated shoulder and if we don't get something on those open wounds you will have an infection by morning. Come here."

Without stopping to think why he instinctively trusted this warped being, Archie pushed himself onto his feet and walked towards Emrys.

"Stand against the wall."

Doing as he was told and knowing exactly what Emrys planned to do, Archie felt sick. The centaur was going to pop his shoulder back in and it was going to be excruciating, but it had to be done. He braced himself against the wall. His mouth felt dry; he licked his lips and swallowed, watching the well-defined muscles in Emrys' foreleg bunch and ripple as he lifted a large, cracked hoof and paused to take aim.

"Ready?"

Archie nodded. Seconds later: BANG! The hoof thudded into his shoulder. He screamed as the joint clicked into place, sinking to his knees, winded by the pain and the power of the blow. He tried to smile; barely able to breathe, gasped, "Thanks... better now." Amazingly, it was.

"It will feel even more so when I sort out those sunburns and wounds. Wait there a moment." Slowly Emrys turned, disappearing back into his cave. There was a lot of ripping and grinding from the void of darkness. Archie waited patiently somewhat relieved he had miraculously stumbled across this creature and his lair. He could hear Emrys' voice drifting back to him.

"It is not by chance that you are here, Archie. Hope guided you. She is mischief I know, but you must listen to her carefully, she is the only one who can take you home. There will be distractions that will lure you in the wrong direction, but you must stay focused and concentrate on your mission. Trust your guide, Archie." The creature reappeared from the darkness carrying a wooden bowl in fumbling hands.

In the glimmer of moonlight filtering into the cave, Archie, his eyes now fully acclimatised to the darkness, took in the appearance of the centaur. What he saw was a powerfully built gray horse of about seventeen hands.

Except that it wasn't a horse exactly, for above the powerful chest and shoulder muscles, where its neck should be, was the torso of a man; one whose sombre, authoritative face commanded instant respect.

"Rub this ointment on your arm, it will ease your burns and stop infection getting in the wounds. It is thick and will act as a barrier."

Taking the bowl the centaur handed him, Archie tried to focus on the concoction within, but the cave was too shadowy and dark. He bent his head and sniffed. It was not unpleasant and masked the stench of the cave for the better. It reminded him of his sister's bedroom at home. Helena had always liked to burn joss sticks in her room, he had often teased her about it. Archie stuck a tentative finger into the bowl. The contents felt tacky and thick like tar. Scooping some out he smeared it over his injured arm amazed when it provided instant relief. "This stuff is phenomenal, sir, what is it?" he gasped.

"A combination of herbs and aloe to control the burns and infection, mixed in with a lot of mental healing. It's good stuff."

"Mental healing?" Archie wondered if he'd heard right. Emrys smiled, but did not enlighten him. "My arm feels perfect; sticky… but I've no pain. It's brilliant; thank you. I-" He never finished what he was saying. Somewhere above the cave the sounds of snarling and scratching had returned, closer than before. Terrified, Archie shrank back against the wall and looked through the shadows at Emrys. "What is that? Do you know?"

"I don't. I have never been outside my cave… not once. I have remained in here since my time as a centaur began, but whatever it is up there it seems to be hunting you."

Speechless, Archie stared at Emrys in horror.

"You're safe here," the centaur said quickly. "It cannot enter my temple. My home is your sanctuary."

"Thank you." As though announcing exactly what hunted him an almighty roar bellowed through the cave. "I may be staying a while," Archie added with a weak grin.

"You must stay until your wounds are healed. Then, as I said, try to focus on making your way home." As he spoke, the centaur laid himself out on the cave floor beside the ashes of a fire that Archie had not noticed until now, closed his eyes and seemed to fall instantly asleep.

Taking his lead from Emrys, Archie curled up close by. It was hard to get comfortable on the beaten earth floor, but to be free of pain was such bliss it did not seem to matter and curiously he no longer felt cold or hungry. The beast remained above them, groaning and shuffling, reminding Archie that it was still out there, waiting. Unlike the centaur he could not stay in this cave forever. He was too confused to make sense of anything at all let alone plan what he was going to do, but his tumultuous thoughts kept him awake.

The night drew on. Utterly exhausted Archie listened to the fearsome noises penetrating the cave, his gaze fixed on the entrance and the cold light of the moon. The scent emanating from his arm evoked memories of home and he sought comfort by calling up images of his parents and his brother and sister, Stewart and Helena. Eventually he slipped into a restless doze, heard his mother shouting his name and smiled as he slept.

CHAPTER FOUR

1987

GRASPING THE HAND OF MORTALITY

"Archie, Helena, Stewart, get up… breakfast's ready." Joanna, her face and neck flushed from the heat of the frying pan, shouted up the stairs to her three slumbering children. Today was her busiest day of the week; she'd been up since six, battling the Saturday morning market for the weekly shop ahead of the crowds. She was now endeavouring to tempt the bed trolls out of their pits with the smell of frying bacon, but the sharp nip in the air on that crisp March morning was keeping their toes tucked safely under the duvet.

Helena appeared first, showered and casually dressed as usual in tracksuit bottoms and a hand-me-down jumper. Her thick blonde hair, identical to Joanna's, dripped with water and was scraped back into an uncombed ponytail. "Morning Mummy," she squeaked, jumping onto the booster step to reach the kitchen work-surface. She reached for the teapot and with great care poured a cuppa from the freshly made pot, watched closely by Joanna, who gently towel-dried her daughter's ponytail on a handy kitchen towel.

"Morning sweetheart," Joanna planted a kiss on the top of Helena's damp head, topped up the pot and was putting the kettle back on the hob to boil when Robert surfaced. Glancing up she blew him a kiss. His jumper, many times darned, was looking far too tight for his expanding waistline. She would knit him another, had she only the time. "It's a glorious morning," she smiled. Popping the cosy over the teapot Joanna carried it to the scrubbed pine breakfast table. "We should take the children to the park. The lake's still frozen solid. We could go skating like last week."

Robert grinned, raising an eyebrow at his beautiful wife of ten years, "Well, perhaps not quite like last week, eh?"

She giggled; she had gracefully wiped out half the local skaters with her rendition of figure skating last Saturday.

"Any sign of the boys?" Robert ruffled his daughter's hair in passing; she was peering under the grill watching the toast. "Silly question… ARCHIE, STEWART," he roared up the stairs, "BREAKFAST!"

Archie, nine years old, had been upgraded to a larger bedroom when Helena was born. He now shared it with his four-year old brother Stewart. As far as Archie was concerned breakfast could go hang; sleep was the main order of the morning. He and Stewart had spent most of the previous evening playing with their army figurines and building a Lego fort. A truly fierce and bloody battle had taken place in their bedroom and the conquerors were seriously into recharging their batteries.

Stewart threw back his bedcovers scattering half his army battalion across the bedroom floor and taking out the fort as he swung his legs over the side of the bed. "Ouch!" He scrambled over to Archie and jumped on him. "Wake up," he said, shaking his brother with all his might. "Daddy's shouting. Get up. Can you smell bacon?"

Groaning, Archie tried to open his eyes, his ruffle of dark hair sticking up in every direction. "Gerrroff Stew… five more minutes," he rolled over and stuck his head under the pillow. Stewart began to bounce from one bed to the other, landing squarely on his brother with each leap.

"Okay, okay, I give in." Archie sat up, rubbed his eyes, shivered and tried to focus on the day. Outside their window it looked as though the sun was shining. Stewart flew at him again, but knowing his brother's every move, Archie was ready for him. He bundled Stewart under the covers, sat firmly on top of him and began tickling his feet, ignoring the muffled shrieks for mercy.

Stewart never resisted this daily torture for long. "Stop, please stop, I need a wee."

Grinning, Archie loosened his hold and Stewart struggled free, jiggled out of the bedroom door, narrowly avoided treading on a musketeer and headed for the bathroom.

"I'M INVINCIBLE." Archie bellowed after him, bouncing off the bed and flexing his muscles.

In the kitchen his parents exchanged exasperated glances. "Prepare to repel boarders," Robert murmured.

"Boarders? Sounds more like a herd of baby elephants to me," Joanna arched an eyebrow at Helena, who giggled.

Moments later, still in their pyjamas, the boys raced through the kitchen door, swung around the table and sat down, tucking in like locusts to eggs on toast with bacon. "Thanks Mummy," they chorused mouths full.

"Can we go to the park now Daddy?" Helena, her plate empty but for a few unwanted crusts and a curl of bacon rind, scowled at her brothers.

"Absolutely," Robert said, gobbling his daughter's leftovers. "Hurry up boys. Last one on the driveway's a sissy. Throw on some clothes, we've a park to conquer, a lake to skate and a girly scooter kid to hunt." He winked at his daughter, whose pale face flushed a dusky pink.

Within short order, muffled in gloves, hats, scarves and coats and with Robert shouldering a large backpack full of skates and emergency supplies, the family stood at the park gate, their breath clouding the cold air. Helena had her scooter at the ready; Stewart his bike, minus stabilisers for the first time, and Archie his BMX – all second-hand and many times repaired by their father.

"Right; all ears listening if you please," Joanna called in her no-nonsense tone. "If anyone gets lost we meet by the bench." She pointed to the first seat along the main path. "Please stay together." The children nodded desperate to explode into the giant park. They knew the rules.

"Three, two, one, go," shouted Robert. They were off. Taking a swift pull at his inhaler, Robert ran across the grass after the boys while Joanna followed Helena at a fast walk along the tarmac path. "I'll meet you up at the lake," she called to her husband's departing back.

Well in the lead, Archie headed for the dirt track that led to the lake, weaving in and out of the undergrowth. From top speed he skidded to a halt turning to see where his dad and brother were. "Ha, miles behind," he chuckled. Jumping off his bike he found some thawed wet mud and smeared it on his face in large gooey stripes. Satisfied with his camouflage, he continued on his way up the track until he came to the fallen oak. Hiding his bike behind it, Archie scrambled into the dirt and waited.

Meanwhile, Robert helped his youngest wobble along the trail following in Archie's tracks. "Do you think he's at the lake with Mummy already?" Stewart asked.

"Most… like…ly," Robert wheezed.

"Let's go faster, Daddy," Stewart stood up on his peddles. "You can let go now, I won't fall."

"Are you sure?"

"Yes," said Stewart, pushing hard on the pedals.

"Okay, off you go." Robert gave him a gentle push and let go of the rear mudguard, reaching for his inhaler and grinning with pride as he watched his four-year old cycle unaided down the track. Moments later his grin was replaced with a frown as Archie leapt out from the bushes brandishing a stick and yelling, "TARGET DESTROYED!"

Inevitably, Stewart wobbled, lost his balance, keeled over the handlebars and burst into noisy tears.

"Archie Fletcher, stop right there," Robert snapped, bending to pick up his hiccupping youngest. Satisfied no harm was done beyond a grazed knee and a bruised ego, he turned to the mud-covered spectacle of his firstborn and keeping the twinkle out of his eyes with some difficulty, issued a stern dressing down that ended with the demand for an apology.

"Sorry, Daddy; sorry Stew; didn't mean to frighten you. I was only playing a game." Chastened, a crestfallen Archie discarded his 'rifle', retrieved his bike and with a last apologetic look at his father, shot off uphill towards the lake.

Brushing away his tears, Stewart got back on his bike, but his confidence was shattered and he raised no objections when his father once more grasped the rear mudguard and kept him steady as they made their way at a more sedate pace in Archie's wake.

"Tell you what," Robert whispered in Stewart's ear, "why don't we play a little game on Archie? Let's capture him on the ice."

"How can we do that, Daddy?"

"Well, you know how he hates ice dancing."

"Yeah, he says it's only for girls."

"Does he now; cheeky young pup. Anyway, he's sure to want to show off his speed-skating while we're practising our turns. How's about if we join hands with Mummy and Helena and form a ring round him so he can't escape. He'll have to dance with us then, won't he - what do you say, eh?"

Stewart giggled, his tears forgotten. The game was on.

There were only a few skaters on the lake this morning. Archie was bombing around on his BMX doing wheelies on a patch of grass by the coffee-shop. He played alone for a while, but got bored when he saw the others all having fun on the ice, so ran to put on his skates.

"Quick, quick, he's coming, Daddy," Stewart hissed, reaching for Robert's hand.

Archie looked across at them and grinned as he made his way onto the ice. He planned to do laps, skating as fast as he could and attempting the occasional jump. He had no sooner set off than he found himself in the centre of a revolving circle. His parents, brother and sister had linked hands and were gliding around him singing and laughing. Clearly they were all in on it.

"Hey, let me out," Archie demanded, frowning. "You know I hate dancing. It's meant for girlies," he made a face at Stewart and smirked.

"Shan't," Stewart stuck out his tongue. "TARGET DESTROYED," he yelled, mimicking his brother with a gurgle of delighted laughter.

Furious, Archie lost his footing. Out of control and teetering, his skates running away from him, he broke through the circle and slid for several yards across the ice, his arms going round like windmills. Legs splayed, he slipped over backwards and crashed down with a resounding thump. There was an ominous CRACK… then he vanished.

Helena and Stewart gasped and backed off as the lake began to crack around them. "Get back," Robert yelled at Joanna, marshalling the children away from the broken ice, never shifting his gaze from the hole where Archie had disappeared. "Take them back to the bank; hurry," he panted. "Everyone; GET OFF THE ICE!" Spinning round he screamed, "ARCHIE!"

Joanna, panic-stricken, grabbed the two children and hurried them to the bank, watching in helpless terror as Robert, repeatedly screaming his son's name, skated back to the spot where Archie had fallen.

There was no sign of him. Robert hesitated, his breath coming in short wheezing gasps. Cold with dread he dropped to his knees and down onto his front, lying at full length to spread his weight as thinly as possible on the unbroken ice near the hole. Cautiously manoeuvring his body forward until he was hanging over the edge he peered into the murky depths of the lake.

***

Beneath the ice the freezing water was like a million needles piercing Archie's skin. Winded from the impact of his fall, eyes bulging, his heart pounding in his ears, he flailed around desperate to breathe. He looked up, gripped by panic when he could not see the hole he had fallen through. He reached over his head, but his hands met solid ice. It was a moment of pure, unadulterated terror. He had no co-ordination or strength to break it or even push on it and his skates and waterlogged clothes were dragging him down into the darkness. The compulsion to draw breath was overwhelming; the pain from his lungs unbearable. 'I'm going to die,' he thought. Numb with cold, he stopped struggling and waves of blackness overtook his mind. Hours seemed to pass; he seemed to be drifting very slowly as he sank beneath the ice, as if everything was happening in slow motion.

Through his distorted vision there appeared a circular ball of light. The orb grew larger the more he tried to focus on it and in the centre he saw a figure. It had wings and a glowing white aura. Archie knew then that he was dying for it could only be an angel. Clear in his head he heard the words, 'Follow me,' and saw the angel stretching out her hand, felt her fingers curling around his. And then he lost consciousness.

***

Fighting his dread, Robert stretched his arm into the freezing water and felt for his son, sobbing with relief when his fingers met with something solid. The boy had been submerged for barely three minutes; it seemed like hours. Grabbing hold of Archie's coat collar, Robert slid onto his knees and pulled the limp body out of the water onto the ice. Praying it would hold he backed cautiously away from the hole, lifted Archie into his arms, struggled to his feet and skated to the bank. Thank God Joanna had had the presence of mind to call for an ambulance; he could hear the siren approaching as he laid his son on the grass. He covered Archie's blue lips with his own, breathing for him, weeping with relief when the boy coughed up a lungful of water and began to breathe for himself just as the ambulance screeched to a stop outside the coffee shop and two paramedics came running with a stretcher.

Pushing her way through the ring of ogling onlookers, Joanna, the two children in tow, ran back from the coffee shop where she had gone to call emergency services. Her face white and strained she was managing to keep it together for the sake of Stewart and Helena, but only just.

Archie, now conscious and in his father's arms, attempted to speak, but all he could manage was a whispered, "I'm okay..."

"Of course you are my brave soldier," Joanna said, her eyes swimming with tears as she bent to kiss him, "and I love you so very much."

The paramedics checked Archie over, wrapping him in a thick foil blanket. "You did that well," one said to Robert. "He's breathing normally, but his body temperature is dangerously low. We'd like to get him checked over at hospital. I doubt they'll want to admit him, but it'll best if a doctor has a good look at him."

"Of course," Robert gasped between urgent puffs on his inhaler. "You take the children home, Jo, I'll go with Archie."

"Call me when you know what's happening," pleaded Joanna, distraught.

"He'll be fine. Try not to worry, darling. We'll be home in time for lunch, you'll see." Robert directed his gaze to Stewart and Helena, who stood white-faced and tearful clinging to their mother's coat. "You two be good and help Mummy please. Will you be okay with the bikes, Jo?"

"I'll be fine love, the children will help me. You go… and don't forget to call."

All the way in the ambulance Robert kept a protective arm around his son in an attempt to keep him calm, reassuring him by talking about inconsequential, everyday things. Archie was shivering uncontrollably and his breathing was laboured. His eyes were unfocussed and his expression troubled as though deep in thought, and although his skin was no longer blue there was a sheen of sweat on his upper lip. As Robert paused to draw breath, trying to think of something to say that would keep his son from dwelling on the whole terrifying experience, Archie spoke.

"What happens when you die, Daddy?"

The question came out of the left field. Startled, Robert squeezed Archie's hand, "You're not going to die, Archie."

"No, but what happens?"

Robert opted for the simplest response, "You go to heaven."

"Where is heaven?"

Unable to think of an appropriate answer, Robert avoided the question. "I don't think you should waste your energy talking, Arch, just try to relax and keep warm, we'll be there soon. You need to be able to answer the doctor's questions. Concentrate on your breathing instead." He gave Archie's hand another squeeze.

"Yes, Daddy," Archie whispered, but inside his head the cogs had been set turning. What had happened under the ice was a blur. He could barely remember it, but he knew he had been drowning and that something very strange had occurred. Death was not on his agenda, he had never thought about it before, not even when his granddad died. He had been only five at the time and had not batted an eyelid. Thinking back on it now he could vaguely remember being told that Granddad was in heaven with the angels, but he had not wondered what it was all about, had simply accepted it. Now, facing his own mortality, his mind delved into the concept of death. He wished he had paid more attention at Sunday School, he was sure heaven had been mentioned there too.

"I wonder if it's like flying into outer space," he wondered aloud, "or will I be collected by fairies to travel to the Neverland? I hope people can come visit me if I do end up having to go."

"You're not going anywhere, Archie Fletcher; you're going to be just fine." Robert bent to drop a kiss on his son's hair, squeezing back the tears so that Archie would not see his distress.

CHAPTER FIVE

A HIEROPHANT'S PROPHECY

Drifting in restless sleep, Archie clutched at a beautiful moment of innocence, aware it was a dream and not wanting it to stop. He was nine years old, at home in his bedroom. The smoky scent of bacon was in the air and Stewart was leaping about on his chest, "Gerrroff Stew… five more minutes," he muttered. The rock hard floor beneath him impinged on his consciousness, the elusive dream fading as he stirred into wakefulness. Slowly opening his eyes, for a brief moment disoriented, Archie had not a clue where he was. And then full awareness kicked in and everything came rushing back. The smoky odour was rising from a crackling fire and he was lying in a cave in the company of a centaur - or was his dream of innocence reality and this just a dream?

Confused, Archie fisted his eyes and ran his fingers through his hair. "Good morning," he said, struggling to sit up. Emrys was by the fire crushing plants in a bowl.

"Morning? It's well past morning my friend. You've slept much of the day away. Sleep, however, is the best healer. How do you feel?"

"Okay, I think. I was dreaming, or at least I think I was. On the other hand, all of this," Archie extended his hand to indicate his surroundings and found to his surprise that his arm was almost fully healed and painless, "might be a dream. I can't quite decide," he managed a weak smile.

"Dreaming? That's something I don't do," informed Emrys.

"What's that you're making?" Archie gestured to the bowl of herbs the centaur was destructively hoofing.

"Lunch, are you hungry?"

"Starving!" Archie pushed himself straighter. "What is it?"

"Another of my herbal and plant concoctions; I have infused Thyme, Echinacea, Rosemary, Sage, Southernwood, Meadowsweet and Basil, they will all help keep infection at bay. Then there are marigold and foxglove leaves, all to add more flavour; they are delicious. In addition there's lady-mantle and golden-rod, along with creeping-jenny and viola to sort out any internal healing to your wounds. There's nothing quite like it. It'll fix you up for the rest of the day."

"I'll bet," remarked Archie, wishing he had never asked. A good, thick quarter-pounder and chips might have gone some way to satisfying the pangs gnawing at his stomach, but a bunch of leaves from plants most of which he had never even heard of? It seemed unlikely. "Where do you find them all?" he asked in an effort to be polite.

"I grow them in my garden at the mouth of my lower cave, these and as many more." Emrys kicked a large, hand-carved bowl of aromatic green stuff over to Archie. "Eat; take my word for it, you'll feel one hundred percent." So saying, he buried his head into a similar bowl of foliage and began to munch. He ate like a horse, Archie observed, watching the centaur raise his head to chew between each mouthful before delving into his bowl for another bite.

Archie stared down at his lunch with apprehension. It was the idea of munching through leaves like a rabbit that put him off. He had never been a great salad eater at the best of times, but if Emrys' miracle-cure on his arm was anything to go by he had every reason to believe it would make him feel great, could he only get it down. Since there was apparently nothing else on offer, Archie steeled himself to take a mouthful and began to chew.

They both ate in silence gazing out through the mouth of the cave at the ocean, sky and distant horizon. Beginning to relax, Archie found to his surprise that he was enjoying his herbal salad and soon emptied his bowl. Only then did it occur to him that if, as Emrys said, he was going to feel a hundred percent, he might be asked to leave. The thought brought a frisson of fear. He cocked his head to listen; there was nothing to hear but Emrys' munching and the crackling fire. It seemed the fearsome creature of the night had gone.

The centaur continued to stare out of the cave his expression one of unchanging melancholy. "Why are you so sad?" Archie asked.

"Am I? I didn't realise I was sad," Emrys shrugged, not shifting his gaze from the ocean.

There was a long, uncomfortable silence. Archie cleared his throat and tried again. "You never seem to smile."

"Since my transformation I've had little to smile about." The centaur turned at last to Archie. "I used to be a vicar you know, I guess the dog-collar gives it away? I do not remember my past nor can I leave my temple. I cannot even go near the entrance at night. If I do, the Moon will try to bewitch me again."

"Transformation? Bewitch you? The Moon?" Archie prompted, perplexed.

"I wasn't always half a horse, my friend. And yes; the Moon bewitched me. Be warned: do not look at her;

always take cover from her beams or she will boggle your brain and make you believe you are something or somewhere you are not."

"But surely that's-"

"Why do you doubt me?" Emrys interrupted, his gray eyes squinting at Archie. "I've told you the truth since you came to me, haven't I? Didn't I heal you and give you food and shelter? I'm your friend. You believe me, don't you, Archie? Tell me you believe me."

"Yes, I believe you," Archie said quickly, taken aback by the centaur's pleading tone.

"She's as wicked and deceiving as the sea that surrounds us. When dusk sets in, no matter where you are, be sure to shelter or she will trap you too. She will twist your mind so crookedly not one single innocent memory will survive and you will lose your past as I have done."

Archie thought for a moment. "The Moon is the Sun's sister isn't she?"

"Yes, what of it?"

"The sun...," he faltered, still unwilling to believe his encounter with the sun had been real. Suddenly he gave a self-mocking laugh. What was he thinking? It was no less real than conversing with a half-horse! "The Sun warned me about her; he too said she would take my mind."

"He was right to do so. She can make your worst nightmares your reality. On this island she is the wicked witch of the skies and the ruler of the night. Have your wits about you, Archie and be warned." Emrys lowered his head back into his food bowl. "Although," he said through munching, "I believe you have a more pressing battle before the Moon rises tonight."

"I do?" Archie gulped.

Emrys raised his eyes upwards, "Just because you can't hear the beast right now doesn't mean it's not up there waiting for you. You will have to face it sooner or later. Face it and overcome it."

"But how can I? Look at me, I appear to be fifteen years old again, I've n-n-nothing to fight with. How can I defend myself?" Archie knew he sounded like a wimp, but the thought of it was terrifying. He felt utterly helpless. "I need weapons," he said. "Without them I don't stand a chance."

"Take heart, my friend. I have sticks and flints. You could make a bow and arrow - or an axe maybe."

"I may need both," Archie shivered, discarding his empty bowl and wrapping his arms around his chest.

"Come with me." Emrys clambered to his feet and Archie jumped up to follow, sticking close to the centaur's swaying rump and glancing nervously over his shoulder as they made their way deeper into the cave. It was not as dark as he expected; light seemed to be filtering in from somewhere and Archie could see they were in a rocky passageway that sloped downwards. After a few yards it opened out into a spacious cavern. He looked about him. Water dripped from the roof and there was the same vile, musky smell. Against one wall was a large pile of stacked timber of various shapes and sizes and beside it an even bigger pile of stones. There were two passageways leading out of the cavern, one of them sloping up to an entrance. It dawned on Archie that the three caves he had seen yesterday were linked by tunnels in the rock.

Emrys slithered to a stop and pointed to the stones. "Help yourself. I would help you, but it takes me a long time to craft something of any use." He lifted his arms and looked ruefully down at his warped hands, which looked as though the fingers had at one time been broken and not properly set. "I may have these poor things, but my mind is so scrambled I sometimes forget how to use them. It took me seven days and seven nights to make one bowl. I had only just finished the second one when you arrived. Fortunate, don't you think?"

Archie nodded, looking past Emrys and along the tunnel that led to the third cave. Through it he could see a verdant floristry of herbs and a profusion of different flowers and plants. The sound of water gushing close by made it appear tropical and it was brighter, as though sunshine was let into the cave. A welcome and exhilarating scent wafted through on a light breeze and Archie breathed it in, deeply thankful for the fresh air. "Is that your garden?" Entranced, he stepped towards the tunnel.

"Yes. You can have a closer look later, but for now I think you ought to concentrate on making weapons," Emrys said.

Disappointed, but in full agreement, Archie turned back to the wood pile and studied it. After a moment he selected several long, straight saplings, testing them for springiness. Memories of childhood games with Stewart made him smile; he knew that bending wood stored its energy so that when it was released it sprang back to its original shape. Discarding first one length of timber and then another, he eventually found the perfect, ready-made bow. Now all he needed were some arrows.

"I'm a natural arrowsmith," he grinned at Emrys, who had sat down to watch. 'Hardly surprising with a name like Fletcher,' Archie reflected, wondering if his distant ancestors had done exactly what he was doing now. Perhaps they had fletched arrows for the Crusaders. He poked about in the wood pile until he found some smaller saplings. Pulling them out, he located a suitably sharp stone and used it to rip away the green bark, revealing the shiny white wood beneath. Kneeling on the cave floor, he stripped ten of them clean. Next he turned to the problem of arrowheads. Amongst the pile of stones there were hundreds upon hundreds of jagged flints, their edges razor-sharp; perfect. He created a notch in the end of each arrow and forced in a flint. They would need fletching in order to fly straight, but what with? It wasn't the only problem: what was he to use as a bowstring? First things first.

"I suppose you don't happen to know where I can find some feathers?"

The centaur squinted down at Archie from his perch on a large boulder and nodded. With a heave and a clatter, he disappeared down the tunnel towards his garden. Moments later he was back clutching a handful of black feathers. "I use them to cross-pollinate the flowers," he explained, "can't always depend on bees to find their way in to my plants."

Archie inspected them. The ravens, it seemed, had their uses. He smiled his thanks and scanned the floor, searching with increasing despair for something he could use to attach them to the arrow flights. Out of the corner of his eye he saw Emrys' twitching tail and his face split in a broad grin as the idea came to him: horse hair! He could use it to bind the fletching and what is more, if he wove enough strands together he could make a strong enough bowstring. He continued to eye the centaur's tail, too embarrassed to ask.

"I know what you're thinking," Emrys said. "You want some of my tail, don't you."

"Quite a lot actually," Archie said. "Would you mind?"

"Hurrumph," the centaur grunted. He swung round and presented his rump to Archie. "Help yourself. Ouch! Go gently now." Apologising profusely, Archie plucked at Emrys' tail until he had enough hair to do the job, at which point, Emrys muttered something about building up the fire and rubbing his backside, clopped back up the tunnel to the first cave, his tail noticeably diminished.

Sometime later, Archie had ten fully fletched arrows and a strong arched bow in his arsenal; now for the axe. It seemed to take a very long time to construct, but eventually he succeeded. The axe comprised a solid, smooth wooden handle and a whopping great flint bound with a rope of horse hair to one end. Testing it for balance, and satisfied that it was good and strong, Archie was pleased with his handiwork. He had been so engrossed he had not noticed the cave growing dim, the light filtering in from the entrance fading. He gathered up his weapons and carried them through to Emrys, who was resting by the renewed fire.

"Good work, Archie, you have been busy. How's the arm doing?" Emrys raised his head from his slumbers.

Afraid he would be asked to leave if Emrys thought he was fit, Archie stalled, "Better than it was, but weak and still aching quite badly." It wasn't true; in fact his arm was so well healed he had forgotten all about it.

The centaur gave him a long hard look. Archie flushed, he had never been able to lie convincingly. "I guess it might be psychological," he added with weak smile.

"I know it's psychological," remarked Emrys. "So now you must leave my temple and tackle your fear. As much as I have enjoyed your company - and without doubt I hope we meet again - you cannot hide here forever. You are fit and well and must face your hunter.

Archie flung his weapons to the floor and followed them, falling to his knees in the dirt. "I would have to be completely insane to go out there. You talk as if you believe I will succeed. How can I possibly conquer a ferocious beast with a few paltry bits of wood and stone?" He knew he was gabbling like a frightened child, but couldn't help himself. Making the weapons had been like a game and he had lost himself in it. Now, faced with the reality of actually using them, it defeated him. "Please, Emrys, don't make me go. I'm not ready."

"Archie, Archie," the centaur sighed, "your body may be back to that of a fifteen-year-old, but your mind and spirit is far older and wiser, where's your self-belief? I thought you were invincible. I have great faith in you; you must learn to have faith in yourself. We must all face our fears at some point or another. You are a brave and clever young man. Just look at your handiwork, it has taken you no time at all to craft those wonderful tools." Emrys sighed again, his gaze on the flickering flames, "Though what use they'll be I really don't know." With that he closed his eyes dismissively and nodded off.

"What?" Archie exploded. "I thought you said... What do you mean 'what use they'll be'? Why would you say that? It was your idea that I make them." Fists clenched, he directed a furious gaze at the centaur. "Now you as good as tell me I've been wasting my time!"

"As you may have noticed, Archie, everything is slightly different here," Emrys countered, opening an eye. "Not everything is what it seems. I have not seen the beast that hunts you, nor do I know what ability it has. It is logical to conclude - as you have yourself - that your primitive weapons might be useless against it."

"Then why did you tell me to make them?" Archie felt insanely irritated with this impassive, melancholy creature who had deliberately misled him.

"Not I," Emrys said. "You asked to make the weapons, my friend. You needed to make tools to satisfy yourself. I but showed you the way. What would you have done had I not helped you? You would have had to face the beast injured and defenceless. At least you now have some foresight and thanks to me you are fit and you are armed, though as it happens, I think your weapons are unnecessary. I believe you will come through the forthcoming battle with the sun on your back, killing your enemy with your bare hands."

"Huh!" Archie snorted with derision. "You're winding me up."

"Suit yourself." The centaur shrugged, yawned and focused on the fire.

It dawned on Archie that Emrys had meant what he said. "You're crazy," he retorted. "Being trapped here has sent you completely mad."

"You are right. My mind isn't what it was, thanks to the Moon, but you trusted me to heal you and you must trust this advice too. I say again, have faith. You can do this. Of one thing you can be sure: whatever awaits you up there, a lesson will be learnt. You will take something from the experience to strengthen your mission. There is a lesson behind every move you make." So saying, Emrys wriggled down to lie by the fire and closed his eyes again.

"What mission?" But the centaur was instantly and soundly asleep. Archie wanted to hit him. He was confused and frustrated, his irritation at boiling point, but he was not by nature confrontational and only rarely entered into an argument. His natural inclination was to leave, as he always did when he felt like this.

Standing, he shouldered his bow, grasped up his arrows in one hand and his axe in the other and strode to the entrance, surprised to find that it was still full daylight outside. He hesitated, looked back at the sleeping centaur then taking a deep breath he ventured from the lair.

Tense with fear, heart pounding, Archie scrambled back the way he had come along the ledge in the cliff face. Nearing the top he saw again the giant void of the open plain stretching as far as he could see. It looked completely empty. Fuelled with adrenalin he sprinted along the cliff-top, uphill and away from Emrys' cave, constantly looking back and forth for twitching grasses. As the ground levelled out he paused to catch his breath. There was no sign of the beast. He shaded his eyes and gazed out at the ocean beneath the great dome of the sky. The sun was quite low but still warm. Breathing deeply, Archie hefted his weapons and again broke into a run. He had been petrified leaving the cave, but as he ran he seemed to undergo a transformation: his fear dropped away and he felt an uncontrollable urge to become the hunter instead of the hunted, ready to face any foe and charge into battle. It was a strangely exhilarating feeling and it lent his heels wings.

He ran a fair way through the unchanging terrain, his bare feet pounding on the turf, his eyes seeking out the enemy. And then, there it was. Archie stopped dead in his tracks. A hundred feet in front of him was a male lion. A huge creature, it sat grooming itself facing away from him. Panting, he dropped to one knee, discarded his axe and in one fluid movement shrugged his bow off his shoulder, fitted an arrow to the bowstring, drew back the bow, aimed and fired. There was no time to think, he just did it.

The arrow flew past its target. The beast sprang up, swung round and emitted a spine-chilling roar, yellow eyes glaring, tail swishing with menace, four great feet planted firmly on the ground.

"Come on then," Archie spat through gritted teeth. "What are you waiting for?"

The lion started towards him, slowly at first but gathering speed. Archie remained focused, not taking his eyes off the giant cat as it bounded towards him. His palms were sweating as he fitted another arrow. This time he hit the lion's flank. The beast did not even hesitate; the arrow had bounced off its thick hide. Again and again Archie hit his target, and again and again the arrows failed to penetrate. The lion was almost upon him. He could smell its stinking breath, see the great snapping teeth as it gathered for its leap.

Dropping his bow, Archie seized his axe, ducked to one side and swung it at the lion. It was like striking a solid iron plate; the recoil ricocheted down his arm. Riddled with panic at this unexpected reaction Archie was thrown backwards, landing face up as the beast swung round to turn on him again. Nothing here is as it seems... the words came back to Archie as he took a firmer grip on his axe.

Furiously he smashed it down on the lion's face. Once again it was as though he was hitting solid metal, but this time the beast retreated slightly and Archie had a brief moment to find his feet before it charged again, its jaws wide, foam dripping from its beard. The attack was unrelenting and yet neither opponent was physically harmed. Archie managed to survive a third assault, but knew his axe had blunted and would soon be rendered useless. His weapons were proving to be as pointless as Emrys had said they would be. He refused to give in to despair. His blood was boiling, every muscle in his body tense and shaking. His mission was to the death. He had to defeat this beast and he had to get home.

After the fourth assault the lion retreated. It withdrew a short distance, sat down, opened its great mouth wide and yawned as if to say, 'I'm bored with this game.' Archie, still fuelled, did not know what had come over him, it was as though he had been injected with superhuman courage or insanity and in a moment of sheer madness he roared at the lion to provoke it, pressing for more. Panting, tail twitching, the beast continued to sit and stare, which infuriated Archie all the more. An unhealthy rage misted his vision as he stared back. It had become a battle of wills. The creature was only a couple of metres away; if he tried to turn away it would surely come at him again. Archie shuddered at the thought of those great claws gouging his back. And so he waited, axe at the ready. He was great at the staring game, never defeated throughout his entire life.

It took all of Archie's patience and self discipline to out-stare the lion. He tried to stay focussed, but his mind kept wandering back to what Emrys had said: a lesson will be learned. Was that was this was all about? Was the lion a figment of his imagination? Did it represent his fears: fears he had to face and overcome before he could go home? Feeling that he was somehow being manipulated by forces he did not understand, Archie, eyes watering, maintained an unblinking stare.

The lion broke down first. After several heart-stopping moments it blinked and looked away. Archie took his chance, covered the gap in one leap and dived onto the animal's back, dropping his axe in the process.

The great cat threw itself backwards, rolled and pounced, roared and snarled, bellowed and rolled again. There were some four hundred pounds of lion on top of Archie, but he clung on, his face buried in its stinking mane. With both arms wrapped fully around the beast's neck, he dug his fingers into its throat and squeezed. Eyes bulging, neck corded, sweating with effort he strained every fibre of his being until he felt his biceps would explode. The lion's struggles began to grow weaker. Archie could feel its gullet swelling; it seemed to cough, gave one last heave then dropped forward and lay still.

Exhausted, Archie felt the sun warm on his shoulders. He had defeated the beast with his own bare hands just like Emrys had said. He did not release it immediately, it was as though he could not let go. Lying full length on the great animal's back, he raised his head and shouted his triumph to the sky. He knew now that he could face anything.

Some minutes passed before doubts began to assail Archie and reaction set in. Trembling, he staggered away from the big cat and looked in sorrow at its lifeless form and lolling tongue. 'What have I done? It could have killed me, but it didn't. I am barely scratched. Would it have retreated to let me pass? How could I have known?' Archie's uncertainty was infinite. He felt as though he had committed a crime, yet he had simply reacted through instinct and the overarching need to survive.

The lion was a truly magnificent and handsome animal. Crouching down beside it, his fingers caressing its pelt, Archie whispered, "You were an amazing adversary. It was a fair fight and I'm sorry you are dead, but it seems I was your fate." He touched its coat surprised to find it was not hard like metal, but soft like velvet and still warm. He pressed down on it, not understanding why his weapons had failed to penetrate its hide.

Casting around for his axe and arrows, Archie found an arrowhead nearby. Overcome with curiosity, he pushed it into the lion's body. It punctured easily. Warm blood ran from the hole. He shook his head in disbelief. How could that be? He could not fathom it, but in the end it did not matter. He was triumphant and alive.

Archie stood and looked about him, shivering. The sun was sinking, the air growing cold. He stared back at the lion admiring the thick tawny pelt, and slowly his lips curved in a smile as an idea came into his head.

CHAPTER SIX

MAKING DO

Determined that the wild beast he had killed would clothe him, Archie was unsure where to start. The only animal he had ever skinned was a rabbit – and that only once and not very successfully. He contemplated dragging the lion back to the cave, but aware that he had misjudged Emrys he was now slightly embarrassed for his rudeness and abrupt departure. The centaur had been nothing but patient and kind. He had also been right.

Archie looked up at the sky, the sun was almost on the horizon already and lighting up a red pathway on the ocean. He was acutely conscious of being out in the open with nowhere to shelter for the night and he was weary; his muscles ached and his body was covered in bruises. If Emrys was right about the outcome of the battle, was he also right about moonlight? It was safer to assume so. In his present state, the last thing Archie needed was a confrontation with the Moon. He would have to move swiftly.

He recovered his bow and most of his arrows, but decided against trying to carry the axe; it was blunt anyway. He bent to take hold of the lion's front paws noting that the huge sharp claws were still exposed. Avoiding them he began to drag the weighty corpse away from the cliff top. Scanning the empty plain his eyes caught an indentation in the grass. He focussed on it and saw that it looked like a pathway. Veering inland it ran uphill for a way then crested a ridge and disappeared on the other side. He set off towards it buoyed with the hope that he would find some form of shelter in the dip.

After some minutes of trudging along the path, struggling for breath as he hauled the dead weight behind him, Archie realised he was actually covering the ground quite quickly. In fact his endurance surprised him as he'd had nothing to drink or eat for many hours – not since Emrys' bowl of leaves in fact, and yet he was neither thirsty nor hungry. It occurred to him that the centaur's concoction of herbs must include a magic ingredient. He could think of no other reason for this seemingly enhanced strength.

Cresting the ridge, Archie scanned the valley beneath him. In the bottom was a wide river and within one hundred paces of where he stood, a clump of trees growing on a steep incline. The path led straight towards it. Nearer, he saw that they were pines, tall and thick; creating a bushy canopy that would offer enough protection from any moonbeams.

Once on the downward slope he could no longer see the ocean, but Archie could tell from the deep pink colour of the sky that the sun had gone beyond the horizon. Descending on his night time hideout, he stared across at the river. The sweat on his skin from his exertions was cooling rapidly, 'I need to build a fire before I lose the light,' he thought. Dropping his bow and arrows, he let go of the lion's stiffening body and set about gathering dry tinder, dead leaves and kindling from under the trees. He had lit dozens of fires on survival expeditions with the Army, but then at least they'd had flint and steel. This time he had only what nature provided, but he had seen it done once at Scout Camp a long time ago and thought he could probably remember the technique.

He picked a spot well under the shelter of the trees, but not so close that he risked setting light to them, and cleared an area about a metre square. He found some flat stones near the edge of the river and with these he made a fireplace. Once he had built a pyramid structure inside the stones, it was time to make fire. With tinder and kindling at the ready, he gathered wisps of dried grass and set about creating the necessary friction, twirling and rotating a short stick between his hands and pressing the end into the dried grass. It took some persistence and it was almost dark before it at last began to smoulder. With infinite patience, Archie fed the tiny flame with dried leaves and twigs until at last the fire was blazing warmly. For the second time that day he experienced an exhilarating sense of triumph.

He moved on to his next pressing task: that of skinning the carcass. It was dark up on the incline where he had left the lion's corpse. Rigor mortis had set in fully now and the beast's legs stuck out rigidly before and aft. Archie dragged it forward into the light of the fire and laid it out on its back. Hesitantly, using his sharpest arrowhead, he started his incision at the tail. He slid the flint just beneath the skin and careful not to puncture any organs, gradually worked his way up one side of the body and then the other, loosening the hide as he went. Once this initial phase of the operation was done Archie felt less uncomfortable finishing the job. He cut round the animal's neck and then through each leg above the joints, using his fist to work off the hide and pull it free.

Gritting his teeth through the entire procedure, horrified at what he was doing, Archie promised himself he would waste no part of the carcass, but during the process of skinning it he had a battle with himself. It was not so much that he was squeamish as that it seemed all wrong to dismember and eat this magnificent creature, even though by removing its pelt he had reduced the lion to a lump of meat. He wondered briefly what it would taste like then put the thought from his mind and got on with removing the fat and flesh from the hide. He spent well into the night scraping the skin clean, removing every trace of tissue he could see. He then laid the hide out on some branches by the fire to dry. He had to be sure that all the moisture was drawn from it so it did not putrefy, but he also wanted it ready to wear as soon as possible - and somehow he needed to join it together in the semblance of a garment. 'How did cavemen manage?' he wondered.

Archie rested for a period, thinking about what he could use as thread. He paced over the ground that was illuminated by the fire, which was not a vast area and nothing even nearly suitable could be found. Lost in thought, he sat down for a moment and held his hands out to the flames. It was quiet under the trees; he could hear the bubbling and chuckling of the river. It suddenly occurred to him that there were sure to be tough reeds growing along the edge of the water. Maybe he could fasten the hide with some of those. It was worth a try. Jumping up he grabbed a stick from his gathered pile of firewood and held it into the flames until it caught then using it as a torch, he strode to the river.

He rummaged along the bank and into the shallows gathering reeds. They were tough to break and the water was cold but soothing on his sore feet. The river was deep and wide, flowing sluggishly with not a ripple on its surface. Sticking his torch in the soft mud of the bank, Archie dropped his bundle of reeds and proceeded to scrub the dried blood from his hands and legs then splashed water on his face. Feeling revitalised, he reached for the torch, but in that instant it flickered and went out sending a spindle of smoke and the acrid scent of pine resin into the still night air. Absorbed in what he was doing, only then did Archie realise how light it had become. He had been forewarned on three separate occasions of the Moon's spellbinding venomous snare. Too late he realised the error of his ways. Infuriated at his carelessness, he could not believe he had been so stupid.

She was reflected in the water, glowing in all her glory, a brilliant crescent moon, her gleaming white aura orbiting out in a wave around her. There was no avoiding her, she was enticing. Archie knew he should resist, get back to the shelter of the trees, but his limbs refused to move. Against his will, his eyes were drawn to the tantalising reflection that shimmered on the water. He tried to close them, but it was as if he were entranced. The reality of his surroundings faded into nothingness until there was just him and the Moon. Powerless to resist her thrall he gazed helplessly down at her reflection, felt her light engulf him, seizing hold of his mind and stifling all conscious thought. It was a suffocating feeling, one he had suffered in childhood nightmares. 'Please let me wake up; I want to wake up,' he cried in terror, but no words came out.

"Good evening Archie. I was beginning to think you were avoiding me." Her soft, sibilant tone was achingly seductive and despite himself Archie found he was straining to listen.

"Do you know where you are going, Archie?"

Archie's body was frozen he could not physically speak at all; his thoughts were the only way he could communicate and yet he did not feel he had control over them. 'Home - I am going home,' he offered.

"Home… ah yes… home… where the heart is. Would you like me to take you there now, Archie? It will take only a moment, less than that."

Gripped by a sense of longing so acute it winded him, Archie was thrown into a black void. He could no longer see and a cacophony of familiar voices filled his head. Blind, he grasped at them, tried to make sense of them, frowning in concentration as snippets of conversation threaded through his brain.

Helena was screaming, "Archie, stop messing about, it's not funny, you are really scaring me, wake up Archie; ARCHIE!"

"You did it, Archie," Stewart's voice chimed in. "You completed the final level without killing yourself. What do we do now? That's it, isn't it? It's game over."

"It's your choice, Archie," he heard his mother say. "You're a grown man now, more than capable of making your own mind up. It's a death sentence. It's not a game out there my love, it's a real and bloody war."

Tormented, Archie buried his head in his hands, "Stop, please stop," he cried, but there was no escaping the onset of disjointed memories colliding in his mind. He found it almost impossible to contain and understand them before the next voice came flooding in: his dad's this time.

"You need to fix it, Archie. No matter who created the situation, you must do your utmost to help. It is in your blood. If you get stuck, you can always call home."

Archie could barely remember the scenarios that went with the voices, it was all so jumbled. In the midst of the torment something sharp stabbed into his foot. The shock brought his sight back. He jerked his leg out of the ice-cold water fracturing the reflection that held him and for a brief moment loosening its hold on his mind, and in that moment he spied the star of Hope, three stars to the left of the Moon.

"Help me, Felicity," Archie begged, stumbling backwards.

In answer to his prayer it went suddenly dark. He looked up; a large black cloud was moving slowly across the Moon blocking out her light. Taking his chance, Archie, his teeth chattering incessantly, hauled himself out of the river and collapsed in a heap on the bank.

'Get up, Archie; move faster, I can't create you an entire eclipse you know,' Felicity's sassy voice rang in his head.

Forcing his numbed limbs to move, Archie crawled back to the shelter of the trees and the welcome warmth of the fire. Echoes of his loved ones' voices still chimed in his head making him feel lost, drained and utterly alone. His foot was throbbing where he had gashed it on the riverbed. Since there was nothing he could do about it, he turned his attention to stoking and feeding the fire, sitting close to it and drawing from its energy. And as his limbs began to thaw, so he remembered why he had ventured to the river. The reeds were still on the bank where he had dropped them and there they could stay, for there was no way he was leaving his shelter again until daylight.

Archie looked over at the carcass lying in the shadow of the trees. His thoughts ran to the lion's hamstrings and the main sinews of its legs. Cursing himself for not thinking of it before, he realised that once dried out they could be used as thread. Armed with his trusty arrowhead, he approached the remains and proceeded to cut, revealing the lion's strong, white, cord-like ligaments. Absorbed in his task once more, Archie was reminded of his intention to waste no part of the lion's body.

Having tugged the ligaments free and placed them next to the hide to dry, he turned back to continue dissecting. Wrinkling his nose, he removed the lion's stomach and bladder to use as water carriers. That done he attempted to joint the carcass, but the layers of muscle were tough and the flint increasingly blunt. He did not want to dismantle another arrow, so contented himself with removing the liver and slicing two good slabs of meat from the lion's rump, all of which could be dried into jerky. As he worked, he tried not to look at the beast's head which, still intact, appeared to gaze at him with unmitigated contempt.

Archie sat back on his heels and looked at his encrusted, bloodstained hands. He desperately needed to wash them. Could he risk going back to the river? The wind had picked up and he could see no moonlight through the trees. Perhaps there was enough cloud cover to protect him. But no, he dared not risk another clash with the Moon.

Longing for morning, he curled up close to the fire and attempted to sleep, but the pines were rustling above him and the wind gusting through the flames sent sparks onto the drying pelt. He got up, turned it inside out and moved it further back. Satisfied it was safe he tore up some turf to bank up the fire and lay down again, falling in and out of a fitful doze, his sleep disturbed by vivid dreams. Inevitably he drifted into the recurring nightmare of his childhood: he was confined in a box, struggling and screaming, trying desperately to get out. He could not see; it was black as pitch. He could hear dirt hitting the lid on top of him. "Stop… hello… HELP… I'm inside… I'm alive... I AM ALIVE." Archie slammed on the wood above him, choked by dirt falling in between the slats, but nobody heard him and he could not breathe.

Archie woke in a cold sweat, gasping for breath. The wind had blown into a gale and the tall pines were swaying alarmingly, the canopy of foliage parting above him revealed intermittent glimpses of the sky and the Moon staring down at him shedding her malicious light onto his face. Quick as thought, he rolled over and reached for the lion's pelt. With one hand he grabbed it and dragged it over his head then crawled deeper into the trees until he came up against a solid trunk. There he arranged the hide over him like a tent and burrowed beneath it. He felt completely protected. The wind did not penetrate the lion's thick coat, which was warm and almost dry. And it stank. Were it not for that, he could almost imagine he was camping again, in the tree house at home.

He settled down to wait out the remainder of the night, assailed by happy memories that dispelled the residue of his nightmare and made him smile. The stench did not keep him awake and after a time, muttering "Chocolate..." he drifted into an exhausted sleep.

CHAPTER SEVEN

JULY 1988
DOUBLE TROUBLE

"Chocolate, that's our fuel. It'll keep us running through the night." Clutching a box of Quality Street, Archie clambered up to the tree house and stuck his head through the hatch. "The purple ones are mine, Helena." His tenth birthday had finally arrived and his excitement was contagious. He grinned across at Sarah, who was cowering in a cobwebby corner of the den. She shot a nervous glance at Helena in the opposite corner and giggled.

"They're my favourite too," Helena pouted.

"You're just jealous 'cause it's my birthday," Archie said, rattling the box.

Helena's sun-freckled face flushed with irritation, "No I'm not."

"Well okay, but you'll have to earn them." Archie hauled himself through the dusty hole and into his den. The tree house had been painstakingly crafted by Robert more than four years ago and was the main feature of the Fletchers' garden. Lovingly maintained and added to over the years, it looked like a piece of contemporary sculpture. Raised high on supporting stilts and propped between two old oaks, it was painted camouflage style in bottle green and brown. On one side were a climbing wall and knotted rope and on the other, a slide. Accessed by a rope ladder, which dropped from a central hatch in the floor, there was also a hatch in the roof, which necessitated a more difficult climb. The structure transformed the garden into an adventure playground and was the envy of all the children in the neighbourhood.

Archie sat down cross-legged, a teasing glint in his eye. "I might share them. Then again, I might not. It all depends how nice you are to me today. Remember it is my birthday."

"Sarah's too, don't forget, know-it-all," Helena retorted, wiping sticky fingers on her grubby jeans. "You'll have to give her some too, so long as she doesn't mess up her oh so pretty playsuit."

"Shut up, Helena," Archie muttered. He hated the way she baited their cousin, who, though the older of the two girls, was petite and fragile-looking beside his sister's robust frame. Dressed in a pristine, candy-pink cotton jumpsuit, her tiny features framed by a blunt blonde bob, Sarah looked a bit like a Barbie Doll. Born exactly thirty minutes after Archie - the two cousins had always been referred to as 'the twins' by both the Fletcher and Walker families - she too was celebrating her tenth birthday.

"Do we have any crisps?" Sarah fluttered her eyelids at Archie, "I'm not really a chocolate fan. It makes me sick," she purred, seemingly unaware of how ridiculous she sounded.

Helena snorted with derision, but catching Archie's warning frown stifled the impulse to tell her so. "What! You don't like chocolate?" she said instead.

"I expect that's because you're never allowed to eat it," Archie bragged, offering his cousin the box.

Sarah shook her head, "I can't. Mummy says it sends me loopy."

"Well she isn't here today is she, and I think a loopy Sarah will be fun," Archie's eyes brimmed with mischief. "Besides, this is my den, so you have to do as I say, 'specially today." His aunt and uncle, Jack and Patricia Walker, had gone away for a Round Table weekend. It had clashed with their daughter's birthday and they had looked decidedly guilty when they'd dropped Sarah and her brother Dominic off with the Fletchers that morning. They need not have worried for, as Archie well knew, two whole days away from the watchful eye of their mother was paradise as far as his cousins were concerned. He rattled the chocolates again, "Go on; dip in."

"It'll make me sick and Mummy will be cross," Sarah pleaded.

"She won't know," Helena exploded. "He's not offering you the entire box, Sarah. One or two won't hurt you. Come on, it's your birthday. You eat chocolate at Easter, don't you?"

Crestfallen, Sarah gave in, "Okay, okay, just one then, thank you."

"Hurray," Archie and Helena sang in unison, fidgeting with excitement.

"We'll save the rest for after dinner," Archie quickly snatched the box away from his sister's questing fingers. Helena scowled, but Sarah sighed with relief.

"Let's go get our backpacks ready. Make sure you pack everything you need, there's no going back in the house later. Once we're out, we're out," Archie commanded, marshalling his troops.

"Right," the girls chorused in agreement.

"Where's Stew and Dom?" he added as an afterthought, clambering out of the den and down the creaky rope ladder. He'd not seen them since their earlier catastrophic water-fight. Dominic, who like Stewart was only five, had cut his knee falling out of the paddling pool and brought an abrupt end to all their wet fun.

"Dunno," Helena shrugged, added, "I think Mummy gave them a shower. They're probably in your room messing up your Lego by now," she teased, but Archie, in a generous mood, simply nodded.

Leading the way, he stepped over the guy ropes of their recently pitched tents and strode up the garden to the house. Smoke was billowing out of the open patio doors leading into the kitchen. Pushing his way through, Archie coughed, held his hand over his nose and peered through the fug.

Robert, dressed in T-shirt and overstretched shorts that displayed his white hairy legs, was helping his harassed wife to bring their wayward gas oven into line. Absorbed in the job at hand, neither parent noticed the flabbergasted children standing in the doorway, all mesmerised by the sight of Joanna slapping back flames with a wet tea-towel while Robert, his head almost inside the oven, was attempting to tong out a rapidly cremating chicken.

"Wow! It's like an indoor barbeque in here," Archie shouted, waving his hands about to clear the smoke from his route to the hall.

"Yes, well don't call the fire brigade just yet, it's all under control," Robert hollered, wheezing even more than usual and triumphantly brandishing the flame-seared bird.

Shrieking with laughter, Helena dashed after her brother. Sarah's mouth opened in a horrified, "Oh!" as she too scampered past, spluttering, "I think you need a new oven, Auntie Jo."

"Never," Helena hiccupped, "that's Mummy's best-friend; she won't part with it. Says it still gets hot and cooks the food and what more do we want? It's just slightly temper… err… temp..."

"Temperamental?" Sarah suggested.

"Right," Helena agreed.

Sometime later, in the breezy but now smoke-free kitchen, the five children, scrubbed clean and in their pyjamas, held out their hands like a scene from Oliver Twist to receive their dinner. Joanna handed them each a plastic plate piled with burnt chicken and soggy chips, accompanied by a picnic knife and fork set.

"Wait!" Robert commanded, bringing the stampede for the door to a jostling halt. "Before you leave there are three ground rules that will be obeyed." He looked at each eager face in turn, "Rule number one: Dominic and Stewart, you'll be back in the house, no questions asked, at ten o'clock prompt." Dominic gave a crow of delight at what for him was an unimaginably late curfew; Stewart a reluctant groan.

"Rule number two," Robert continued, "if anyone wants to come in during the course of the evening, no one," he paused, glared at Archie, "I repeat, no one is to try to stop them. Sarah, there's an extra duvet on Helena's bed. You'll have to share it if you both decide to come in." Robert glanced at his watch, "And last, but by no means least, rule number three: it is now half past six; I'm going to bed at midnight. At which time we expect you to be settled and soundlessly asleep - wherever you may be. Is that clearly understood?"

"Yes," they chorused, poised like greyhounds in the traps.

"So…" Robert twinkled at the expectant children, a huge grin spreading across his features. "What are you waiting for? Have a great campout!"

Cheering, the children raced through the patio doors and into the garden, Archie inevitably in the lead, Dominic forgetting to limp bringing up the rear.

Leaning in the open doorway Robert watched as they clambered into the tree-house passing up plates of food and chattering happily. "I've a feeling we're in for a long night. Did you see the look on Archie's face when I announced rule number two?"

"My money's on Helena coming in first," Joanna laughed, joining her husband in the doorway and passing him a glass of chilled white wine.

"Thanks. You think so? More likely Sarah I would have thought. Then again, she always sticks close to Archie so you might be right. Mind you," Robert chuckled, "with some of the ghost stories I've been telling him this week, he could be out there on his own by nine."

"Oh Robert, was that wise? You know he'll never come in don't you, no matter how scary it gets. I'll be up all night," Joanna sighed.

"Absolutely, he's a determined fellow our Archie, ghosts or not, his mission is to the bitter end. Ten years old... who'd have believed it? Ah well, let's get some peace and quiet while we may, eh?" He put his arm around his wife's waist and squeezed, giving a contented smile.

***

Archie was the last inside the den. Taking the hard route by using the climbing wall and rope, he crash-landed through the upper hatch straight onto Dominic's plastered knee. "Whoops! Sorry Dom." He placed an instinctive a hand on his tearful cousin's leg and looked him in the eye, "I bet a chocolate before dinner will put a smile back on that face." He was rewarded by a watery grin as Dominic reached for a gold-wrapped toffee. "In fact, let's all have one," Archie grabbed two purple chocolates and threw one to Helena. Stewart rummaged for a green triangle and Sarah chose a strawberry delight. "Told you… it works every time," the birthday boy grinned displaying a set of brown teeth.

Dominic pressed his advantage, "Can I have another one?"

"Not yet, its chicken and chips time now matey," Archie said.

Once all had been eaten and more chocolates demolished, the evening's adventure began in earnest. "Hide and seek?" Archie suggested.

Dominic and Stewart both squealed with joy. Helena rolled her eyes skywards and pretended to yawn. "Bit juvenile isn't it?" she murmured with all the maturity of her eight years.

"Okay, bandits then," Archie responded, stung.

"Yeah, yeah, yeah," Dominic and Stewart chorused. "We're bandits, you're our captive," and seizing Sarah's hands, they pulled her to the hatch. Protesting, she allowed herself to be forced down the ladder and frogmarched up the garden, looking back over her shoulder and mouthing 'HELP!' at Archie and Helena who were following close behind.

"Stop, you villains; bring her back," Archie shouted, catching them up by the garden shed.

"She's got to go in the shed," Stewart announced, wrestling with the door.

"Yes, she's our prisoner," Dominic chimed in, "we've captured her."

Archie looked doubtful, "Is that okay, Sarah?"

"I suppose so, if that's the game, but I don't want to be called Sarah any more, it's just so boring."

"What do you want to be called then?" Helena snorted eyeing her cousin's pink pyjamas. "Miss Piggy?"

"I don't know... something magical." Sarah, refusing to be drawn, put up a hand and swished back her hair.

"Um, how about… Rapunzel?" Helena suggested, meeting Archie's eyes with a defiant grin, her mouth falling open in surprise when Sarah nodded.

"Perfect!" Sarah smiled and with an air of self-importance stepped past Stewart and Dominic and into the shed, closing the door behind her.

"Not in there you don't!" Robert's voice boomed up the garden. "It's full of my tools. What will I say to your Auntie Patricia if Sarah cuts herself on the secateurs? Rule number four: the boundary lies at your tents. No higher please."

The shed door was flung open and the prisoner dragged out by the chastened bandits and bundled back to the den. The hatches were closed and Rapunzel was left alone in the gloom while outside an almighty sword fight took place in her honour, the bandits having transformed into King Arthur's knights.

The battle went on for some time and Rapunzel, bored and lonely, found the chocolate box. By the fragments of light filtering through the slats, she selected all the strawberry delights and then moved on to the hazelnut whirls. By the time Sir Lancelot came to her rescue, the damsel in distress had munched her way through at least ten chocolates and was beginning to feel very sick indeed.

Archie laughed as he lifted the upper hatch and spied the mess she was in. "Come on, up here, quick, they're climbing up the ladder," he whispered urgently, leaning down to take her sticky hand. As she grappled onto the den roof the lower hatch burst open and Stewart's and Dominic's faces peered up at them.

"They're getting away," Stewart squealed. "Get back down, cut them off!"

Helena waited at the bottom of the ladder ready to make her move and as she valiantly held off the two shrieking boys, Archie steered Sarah to the rope and climbing wall.

"I can't Archie... I'm scared and... I feel sick," she said, swallowing hard and edging backwards.

"Yes you can; you've just eaten too many chocolates," Archie insisted, taking her arm. "I'll help you. You won't fall."

Placing herself trustingly in her hero's care, eyes firmly shut and face a sickly shade of green, Rapunzel hung on to the rope and was helped down the wall. "When we get to the bottom, jump and run for the tents. We'll be safe there," Archie hissed.

"The game's up boys, we win, you lose," Archie bellowed moments later from the unzipped entrance of his tent.

"Never," both Dominic and Stewart roared, as they slipped out of Helena's grasp and kicking their steeds into a gallop, charged their foe.

Inevitably it ended in tears. In the ensuing struggle, Archie's heel caught Stewart's nose full force and it started bleeding profusely. Joanna and Robert were on the scene within seconds.

"I'm sorry, Daddy; it was an accident. Please don't send me to bed," Archie begged, fearing the worst.

"It's just a bloody nose, Stew," Joanna soothed, "let's get it iced then you and Dom can have some jelly and ice cream." She scooped up Stewart and rushed him back to the kitchen, followed closely by Robert clutching Dominic's hand. Concerned, Archie and Helena trotted along behind, anxiously waiting for the axe to fall.

At the patio, Robert turned to them, "You've got one more chance," he wagged his finger at Archie, "no more fighting games or it's game over." So saying, he closed the patio doors. Left alone in the garden, brother and sister exchanged stunned glances, both amazed by their parents' benevolence and very relieved that the party had not officially ended. Without a word, they turned and headed back to the boys' tent to retrieve the captive Rapunzel.

"She's gone!" Archie said ripping back the tent flap and peering inside.

"Gone where? I didn't see her go into the house, did you?" Helena stared at her brother.

Archie shook his head. "Well she can't be far. She wouldn't have left the garden on her own. She's probably hiding. Let's try the den." Calling Sarah's name they ran to the tree-house, but there was no sign of her.

"She might be lying ill somewhere," Helena said, beginning to panic.

"Oh cripes, yes, she said she was going to be sick – and she's probably gone loopy."

"Typical!" Helena said, exasperated.

"We shouldn't have let her eat those chocolates," Archie gazed in misery at his sister. "This could be the end of our party you know."

"We'll find her," Helena said, grasping her brother's hand in a rare gesture of sympathy.

Archie shivered. The evening was drawing in around them and though it had been a warm, sunny day, the air was cooling rapidly. He squinted at his watch, wiping a smear of chocolate from its cracked face onto his pyjamas. “It’s nine o’clock already.”

Slowly, brother and sister edged the boundaries of the garden, calling out every now and then. Disobeying their father, they homed in on the forbidden shed.

“We’d better check it, just in case.” Archie opened the door and poked his head into the dim interior to gaze at his father’s jumble of assorted garden tools. A mower took up most of the space, a wicked looking billhook and a large pair of pruning shears hung on the wall. “Sarah?” he called hopefully.

“I’m over here.” The frail reply came from somewhere behind the shed. Reversing rapidly and slamming the door, Archie bounded round the back with Helena on his heels.

Sarah was on her knees in the shrubbery, holding her hair back from a steaming pile of chocolate-coloured vomit.

“Ugh! Gross,” Helena cringed, peering at it over her brother’s shoulder.

“Helena, go and get Mummy,” Archie took control.

“No Helena, wait. I’m fine,” Sarah managed a weak smile. “They’ll make me go in and I don’t want to ruin the party.” Helena hesitated, looking at her brother for guidance.

“Really, I’m fine,” Sarah repeated holding out her hand to Archie.

He took it and pulled her to her feet. “Well if you’re sure. You look a bit green to me.”

“I’m okay, honest. Feel better now,” she said, wiping her mouth on the sleeve of her pyjamas.

“Too much chocolate,” Archie grinned.

“Don’t say I didn’t warn you,” Sarah said hoarsely. “What I really need is a glass of water.”

"Right; Helena, go and check on Stew and Dom and get Sarah a glass of water," Archie commanded, not removing his gaze from his cousin's pale face.

Unusually, Helena did not object to being ordered around. Peeping out from behind the shed to check no one was watching she made a dash for the house.

"I'm sorry, Arch," Sarah said. "I've spoiled everything."

"No you haven't," he put an arm around her thin shoulders and studiously ignored the pile of vomit. "Don't worry about the party, it doesn't matter a bit." It did, of course, but Sarah's welfare mattered more and Archie felt not even a twinge of resentment.

The sun's weakening glow bled across the garden casting shadows in the undergrowth. Archie looked up at the darkening sky: the moon was a tiny sliver, a few wispy clouds floating across it. He gave his 'twin' a quick squeeze and listened for Helena to reach the house and the door to close.

"I'm okay now," Sarah said, her teeth chattering. "Let's go back to the tent."

Archie nodded. Acutely aware that they were out of bounds, he looked cautiously round the corner of the shed. "All clear," he whispered.

As they reached the tents the patio doors opened and Helena came out balancing a tray of mugs and a large glass of water. "Stewart's nose is still bleeding and Mummy won't let him out till it stops," Helena reported, sticking out her tongue as she concentrated on not spilling anything. "I've got us some tea, Arch."

"Thanks. Is he okay?" Archie felt genuine concern as he took a mug off the tray.

"Oh yes, he's fine; just cross, he wants to come outside. Dominic's not bothered though; he's got hot chocolate and is watching telly."

"Ha, that sounds about right," laughed Sarah. "He'd never be allowed to stay up this late at home. He's in heaven, believe me," she said, taking the proffered glass and sipping her water.

"I didn't think you'd be up for the chocolate biscuits," Helena winced, remembering the chocolate vomit. Sarah grinned, her teeth clanking on the glass.

Safely under canvas in the boys' tent, the two girls settled down to listen to Archie's ghost stories, squealing with delight at the more macabre bits, much to his satisfaction. The dusk gave way at some point during this gristly saga, leaving the sky inky black and studded with stars. In the trees a pair of owls added their haunting cries to the ghostly atmosphere.

Pausing for breath, Archie switched off his torch and rolled to the open tent flap. "Let's see if we can find the Plough." Lying on his back, half in and half out of the tent, Archie studied the sky. Sarah followed suit and Helena, after a moment's hesitation, squeezed between them. Side by side, they gazed in rapture at the twinkling stars. Archie, assuming a hollow, ghostly voice, launched into his pièce de résistance: "This is a story about a man named Joseph, a cruel and angry man, bitter and twisted by jealousy, money and greed."

"I've never liked the name Joseph, it gives me the creeps," Sarah announced before Archie could begin.

"I do," Helena commented.

"You won't after this story," Archie said. "He was married but I don't know who to. Anyway, she was so desperate to get away from him she killed herself."

"That's awful," Helena butted in. "Do you think she killed herself in our house?"

"They didn't live here. They lived in a massive mansion somewhere in the country. Joseph had loads of dosh, you see. His problem was with his wife's guy on the side. Anyway, shut up Hels and let me start." Archie shifted himself into a more comfortable position and once more assumed his ghostly voice. "It was last Halloween, at almost half-eleven when I got up to go for a wee. I can remember hearing Mum and Dad downstairs, so I know full well I was awake. I was on the landing just outside my bedroom door when he appeared… a ghost in front of me… gruesome grey… completely see-through. I could see the bathroom door straight through him."

"Hey, did you see that?" Helena squeaked.

"Yes," Sarah answered.

"See what? Are you two listening or what?" Archie said, irritated.

"A shooting star; I've never seen one before." Sarah beamed up at the sky then looked back at Archie, "Hang on a minute, if Joseph lived in a country mansion, how come you saw him here at Eversely Avenue? That doesn't make any sense." She giggled, "You're making it up."

"No I'm not," Archie protested, "honest. It's because he's haunting… one of us…"

"Okay, now that's a bit freaky," Helena squirmed and wriggled closer to Sarah.

"What did he look like? Has anyone else seen him?" Sarah asked.

"Did he s-s-speak to you?" Helena gasped.

"Will you two stop interrupting and let me finish?" The girls stayed silent, waiting. "Thank you," Archie said, looking down his nose at them. "What do you think he looked like? Like a ghost of course; old fashioned. He had long hair tied in a pigtail and he had on a jacket with a high collar and his shirt was all frilly round his neck, only like I said, he was see-through. Well anyway, this ghost flew at me shouting and screaming, punching out at me like he wanted to kill me, but his fists blazed straight through me."

"And then you woke up," Sarah teased.

"No. I told you, I was awake."

"Okay, what was he screaming?" Sarah asked.

"I'm not sure… but it sounded something like… SARAH." Archie boomed in a quavering ghostly taunt as he fought off Sarah's playful beating.

Helena shivered. "I need a wee. Come with me, Sarah, please?"

"No way," Sarah moved back into the tent and snuggled down into Dominic's discarded sleeping bag. "I'm staying right here."

"Oh please, Archie?" Helena begged.

"Get serious Hels," Archie grinned. "Oooooooo," he quavered, "Joseph's coming to get youooooo...."

Helena's face fell, "I can't go on my own."

"Scaredy-cat," Archie chortled.

When neither her brother nor her cousin moved, Helena stood up and stamped her foot. "Fine… that's it… you horrid beasts. I'm going in. I'll sleep with Mummy and Daddy. I can't stand either of you a minute longer." She grabbed up a torch, ripped back the tent flap and without a backward glance ran full tilt for the house.

Having exhausted his repertoire of ghost stories and feeling a little guilty about Helena, Archie found his sleeping bag and wriggled down next to Sarah.

"I didn't much like that story, Arch," she said in a small voice. "Can we talk about something else?"

"Okay," he said, "what do you want to talk about?" Switching his torch back on, he started making shadows with his fingers on the tent wall.

"Um... what do you want to do when you grow up?"

Archie laughed and without a moment's hesitation replied, "Be a soldier in the Army. What about you?"

"I'm not sure. I wouldn't want to be a soldier."

"Well, you're a girl."

"So?"

"Girls aren't as brave as boys."

Sarah snorted with derision, "Says you!"

"Tell you what," Archie responded to the challenge, "let's play Double Dare."

With false bravado, Sarah nodded. "You're on, so long as you promise not to leave me on my own."

"Deal, let's shake." Archie recovered a hand from inside his sleeping-bag, found and shook Sarah's to seal the promise then flipped onto his stomach to think. "Got it; follow me," he said, squirming out of his bag.

"Wait, Arch, where are we going?" Sarah whispered.

"It's okay; a promise is a promise. I won't leave you, but I've always wanted to do this," Archie jumped to his feet, vacated the tent and shot off up the garden.

"Do what?" Sarah pleaded, wriggling free of her cocoon.

"You'll see," Archie said over his shoulder.

With considerable misgiving, Sarah followed Archie into the shadows, away from the light of the house. "What's the time?" she called softly, trying to stall him and hoping it was past the midnight curfew, which would curtail whatever it was he intended to do. Her hopes were dashed.

Archie paused, lifted his arm and tilted his wrist back and forth trying to see. "A bit past eleven," he said, dashing off again. Not wanting to lose him, Sarah broke into a stumbling run, wincing as her bare feet landed on the stony path.

When he reached the shed Archie waited for her. "Don't think about what we're about to do, just do it. This is a dare, remember. Ready?" He took Sarah's hand and gave it a quick squeeze. Ignoring her whispered "No", he turned to face the metre-high, chain-link fence that separated the garden from its neighbour. Taking a deep breath he ran flat out towards it.

Sarah watched him clearing the fence like a champion hurdler, gutsy and wild, and in that moment she would have followed him anywhere. He did not look back as he charged at the similar fence between the next two gardens and did the same again. In the blink of an eye he was four gardens up, his shadow racing before him in the moonlight. Sarah threw an anxious glance at the house then, without thinking of the consequences or remembering that she was some ten inches shorter than her 'twin', she began running towards the fence. She cleared it with a gasp of triumph, but ripped her pyjama trousers on the second and fell at the third, landing in a rose bed. She did not cry out as thorns punctured her legs, but rolled onto the grass picked herself up and ran on, beginning to enjoy the adrenalin surge of the dare. She cleared the fourth and fifth fences with inches to spare, ran for the sixth then noticed that Archie had stopped and was running back towards her, waving frantically, his face tight with alarm.

With no momentum to spring back, Sarah straddled the fence and yelped as it bit into her groin. She yanked herself over it just as Archie bombed past. There was a distant barking behind him. He grabbed her hand, pulling her across a neighbour's lawn and over the fence back the way they had come. "It's the Watts' Doberman," he said between gasps, "run as fast as you can."

Sarah stopped and bent double, "I've got a stitch," she moaned. "We can't out run a Doberman, Arch, let's hide." She tugged him by the hand towards some thick bushes.

Petrified they listened to the bark getting closer and closer. "Don't breathe," Archie whispered, crouching close to Sarah in the shadows. There was the sound of a door slamming, a light went on and pooled across a lawn. An angry voice hollered, "Oi!"

"We're done for," Archie whispered in dismay. "That's Richard Watt, he must've spotted us."

"BRUNO! Bruno, get back in 'ere," the voice yelled.

"He's not shouting at us, he's calling the dog back, we're okay," Archie squeezed Sarah's hand. There was a yelp and a whimper, the barking ceased and the light went out. Archie grinned, his fear dissipating instantly, "Phew! That was close."

Sarah sobbed with relief until a thought struck her, "What if your mum and dad heard? They might go and check on us and we're not there."

"Then we're in double trouble," Archie whispered, frowning.

"My mother's going to kill me," Sarah sniffed, wiping her nose on the sleeve of her ripped pyjamas.

Archie looked down at the bloodstains and then up at her face. Her eyes, full of unshed tears, glinted like twin stars in the moonlight. He felt a surge of protectiveness, "I won't let her. It's my fault, no one will blame you. I'll say I forced you. You're really brave," he added, "as brave as any boy."

For a moment they waited in silence, huddled together in the shadows, listening. "Have you ever felt like you're missing something?" Archie asked suddenly.

"Like what?"

"I don't know… I feel like I'm waiting for something amazing to happen, but it never does... like there's a hole... I can't explain it."

"No, I don't feel like that," Sarah said thoughtfully. "I just want to be me."

"You are you, what do you mean?"

"I want to be liked for who I am. You know, not for who my parents are or how I talk, or what Mum makes me wear. I guess it won't happen till I'm a grown up. But that's not the same as feeling like there's a hole."

"No," Archie agreed. "When I run like we just did or I do something else as crazy, I feel like I've filled the hole, but it doesn't last very long. I know when I get home it'll be back. Not in a bad way; I mean, I love my home, I just feel like something's missing, you know?"

"I love your home too." Sarah looked down, fiddled with a twig at her feet, added, "And I love being with you. You're the only one who makes me feel like me."

Faintly embarrassed, Archie stared at her, not sure what to say. His dilemma was saved by the sound of his mother's voice calling their names, high pitched and panicking. His eyes widened, "Oh God, they know we're gone. Quick, follow me."

Archie scrambled out of the bushes and set off in a hurry back to their garden. Sarah followed more slowly, Auntie Joanna's obvious distress bringing tears to her eyes and thoughts of what Uncle Robert was going to say constricting her breathing.

"Where've you two been?" bellowed Robert as his torch found the two children coming towards him.

Archie threw himself over the final fence, complete with a combat roll, then dashed back to help his cousin. "Sorry, Daddy," he said shamefaced. Sarah's echoing apology trembled on her lips as Archie launched into an explanation, "We got slightly carried away playing Double Dare and-"

"Slightly! I've had Richard Watt on the doorstep saying his Doberman was disturbed by a boy fitting your description. He lives eight doors down and it's after eleven-thirty at night. What were you thinking?" Robert's voice swelled in volume, his face ready to explode. "I'm disappointed in you, Sarah; I thought you had more sense."

"Don't blame Sarah, Daddy," Archie pleaded, "it was all my fault; I made her do it."

"I don't doubt that for a minute. There'll be no more campout tonight," Robert said, placing a firm hand on the children's shoulders and frogmarching them towards the house. "Tomorrow morning before breakfast you will both be on Mr Watt's doorstep to apologise. You have broken the rules Archie Fletcher, no Dandy for a fortnight - and as for you, Sarah, well…"

Joanna placed a calming hand on her husband's arm and mutely shook her head. Robert, shuddering to think what might have happened – the Watts' Doberman had not been known to bite, but who knew with an intruder in its garden - clamped his mouth shut. Fortunately no harm had been done and he knew all too well what punishment his little niece would endure should Patricia get to hear of this escapade. Pushing the children through the patio doors he settled for a gruff, "Get off to bed. And don't wake the others."

"Do you think they'll tell my mum and dad?" Sarah whispered as they climbed disconsolately up the stairs.

"No, but they'll be dead grumpy with us tomorrow," Archie breathed. "We'll have to be on our very best behaviour. No Dandy for two whole weeks, what a bummer!"

CHAPTER EIGHT

A REALITY PUNCH

The stench of rotting hide bounced Archie out of his dream and into his homemade tent. He could tell it was daylight by the glow filtering redly through patches in the skin where he had scraped it too thin. For a moment he lay there wrinkling his nose and longing for Sarah. She was the one person to whom he had confessed his innermost fears and dreams. What he would not give to have her here with him now. With a sigh he flexed his stiff muscles, threw off the lion's pelt and sat up. It was sunrise; the river ran pink reflecting the sky. Archie rubbed his eyes, which felt sore and were doubtless bloodshot. He was still fogged with sleep, but he urgently wanted to get on with the day. There was so much to do and ground to cover before he could get home.

Yawning, he took a deep breath and looked over at his campfire. 'I could get that going again,' he thought, his gaze moving on to his kill, 'and I must do something with that,' which reminded him that his hands were still encrusted with dried blood. He stumbled to his feet, grabbed hold of his would-be water carriers and staggered to the water's edge. Bending, he scrubbed his hands clean then cupped them and took a long drink. The water tasted peaty, but was deliciously cold. He looked down at his body: his skin was tanned and his muscles bulging, but his physique was slighter, as it had been ten years ago when he was fifteen - a time in his life when he had felt truly alive and happy. There was now no sign of the welts and bruises that had been so prominent after his fight with the lion and the scratches on his legs had faded - even his foot, though still slightly sore, was almost healed. That was odd. Were Emrys' potions still having an effect?

Feeling more awake, but no less bemused, Archie washed out the lion's stomach and bladder, taking a long time over it until they were completely free of gore. He knotted the bottoms then scooped them full of water, holding them up to check for leaks and giving a satisfied grunt when they appeared to be watertight. Finally, he selected a few of the reeds he had picked the night before, winding them round the top of each container and fashioning carrying handles.

Pleased with his resourcefulness, Archie was just about to head back to his camp when he sensed a presence. He looked around; there was nothing there. He peered across the river to the opposite bank, his ears picking up a low murmuring of sound much like a buzz of conversation, as if several people were talking. His skin prickling, Archie shaded his eyes and stared across the wide stretch of water, searching the bushes and trees for the source of the voices. He could see no one. Everything was still, there was not even a slight breeze to stir the grasses and yet he remained convinced he could hear talking. Archie continued to look this way and that when out of the corner of his eye he caught a movement. He swung round. A dark figure was walking upstream on the opposite bank, partially concealed behind a clump of bushes.

Archie could not make out if it was a man or a woman; could not even be sure it was human except that it walked with an upright stance. Nonetheless, he drew breath and shouted, "HELLO!" Making no sign it had heard, the figure carried on walking. "HELLO!" Archie bellowed again. He started running along the bank, calling out as he ran, his water carriers sloshing against his legs. "Hello... you… please… stop. Talk to me."

Still partially concealed by foliage, the figure stopped walking and turned slowly to face him. He now saw that it was clothed from head to foot in black, even its face looked to be covered. "Hello..." the word died in Archie's throat. The strange apparition neither spoke nor made any sign that it had heard, simply looked across the river then turned and walked on. Archie watched until it faded into the distance and vanished from sight and he was left staring at nothing. Conscious he could still hear the murmur of voices, Archie was flummoxed. There was no one in sight. Was the sound coming from behind the distant hill? Could sound carry that far? He considered his options: he could swim across the river, but it looked deep and the current strong and besides, he was not sure he wanted to meet whatever was on the other side; the figure in black had seemed hostile. Nothing here is what it seems, he reminded himself. He began to wonder if he had actually seen anything at all. Maybe he was imagining things. Seeing someone in this lonely emptiness might just be wishful thinking and the voices simply the chuckling and splashing of the river. Unsettled and feeling very much alone, Archie set off disconsolately back to his camp, determined to get on with making his clothes.

Thinking about how to set about it as he walked, he was jolted out of his reverie by the sight of Felicity. She was in his camp stoking up the fire. After the initial surprise it seemed bizarrely normal to see her there. He found he was no longer overawed by her beauty and the familiar sight of her made him feel much less insecure. "Hello," he smiled broadly, "where did you spring from?"

"Hello, Archie." Felicity dropped her stick and brushed her hands together, inspecting them for any signs of dirt. "You really went to town on that beast didn't you?" she threw a glance at the dissected corpse.

"Bar eating it, yes - and mind what you're doing with those," he indicated the pile of dried ligaments. Felicity screwed up her face in disgust accompanied by her trademark giggle. Archie grinned, "They're my thread," he explained, picking up Felicity's stick to poke at the fire. "I mean to make some clothes."

"Ah," she pursed her gorgeous lips and gazed into Archie's face. "It was a hard night wasn't it?"

"Not the best night's sleep I've ever had, it has to be said." He crouched to pick up a ligament, stretching it to test its strength. "Perfect," he muttered under his breath, reaching for another.

Felicity, who was watching Archie's every move, curled her fingers up and shut her eyes as he unravelled the lion's insides and tugged at them. After a moment she said, "You should have returned to Emrys' cave last night; he was expecting you."

"Oh, was he?" Archie said carelessly, retrieving the hide.

"Now who's being idle?" Felicity frowned.

He gave a nonchalant shrug, "He told me to leave, said I was fit enough to go home, so that's where I'm going. That's all I want to do, Fee. I just want to go home." Archie gripped the hide, ripped a large hole in the centre and stuck his head through it. He then cast around for his flint and began to saw around the bottom of the hide to create a knee-length tunic, wondering as he did so if he could fashion some kind of footwear from the pieces. Removing it, he punctured holes in the sides and began to thread through the sinews leaving gaps big enough for his arms. He was certainly no dressmaker, but it would do the job. Though absorbed in his task, he was conscious all the while that Felicity was watching him, a pensive expression on her face.

Eventually she spoke, "Emrys will help you in any way he can, Archie; it's his job. He is an amazing healer and teacher and I'm more than sure he's also your friend. You are cross with him for foretelling your future and sending you out to face your fear, but that is his gift and he used it to help you."

"That's as may be, but I couldn't bring myself to believe what he said. I thought he was crazy. I mean, who but a madman would imagine it was possible for me to kill a lion with my bare hands?" Archie did not look at Felicity as he spoke, his face felt warm and he knew he was blushing. "And now... well maybe I'm just too embarrassed to face him and admit that he was right and I was wrong. But I still think he's crazy," he added defiantly.

"He's not crazy; a little moon-mad maybe," Felicity allowed, "but you should not feel embarrassed when you've achieved so highly. Your accomplishment is astounding, you should be proud of your triumph. Emrys may have foreseen your fight with the beast, but it was you who lived his vision and made it happen. It's important you return to him, he has more to say to you."

"Like what? I can't backtrack. I told you, I just want to go home. What's more important than that?" Despite himself, Archie spoke without conviction. The thought of being safe and warm in Emrys' caves for another night was all too tempting.

"That is exactly what Emrys and I want for you too. We're here to help you get home – that's the whole point. We have helped you so far, haven't we? You need to hear what he has to say." Felicity reached up to take hold of Archie's face, gently turning his head to look at her. It was a gesture so like his mother's it brought a lump to his throat.

"Your run-in with the Moon last night was a close call. If she'd had you under her spell any longer there's no telling what state I'd have found you in this morning. Look at what she did to Emrys. You must talk with him, just once more… please. I can come with you if you like," she wheedled.

"He shouldn't have made me go," Archie said sulkily, aware he was being childish but unable to help himself. Felicity's gesture had made him feel like a child. "I wasn't ready. He should've said I could come back yesterday and he didn't."

"That's not quite true is it, Archie," Felicity removed her hands from his face. "You knew you could return to him at any time you wanted, he as good as told you so, and he didn't throw you out on your ear did he? He simply advised you to face your fear before sunset."

Archie looked down at his feet, mussing up the earth with his toes. Had Felicity witnessed their entire conversation from the sky? "Do you have anything to eat?" he asked hopefully, changing the subject.

"No, but Emrys does," Felicity smiled.

"I've got some meat to cook. I can do without more lettuce leaves!" It was a token resistance for despite the pangs of hunger he didn't much fancy lion meat and had already made up his mind to go back to the caves. Finishing constructing his tunic, he drew it over his head, pushed his arms through the holes and straightened it around his body. It felt damp and clung to his skin a bit, but he felt instantly protected.

Felicity put her head on one side, a critical look in her eye, "Mm, very fetching!" she chuckled.

"Maybe, but it's not quite dry yet," Archie attempted to pull it off.

"Here, let me help, hold your arms up." She hauled the tunic over his head, saying, "Skin a rabbit!" as she did so.

Archie smiled, transported back in time. His mother used to say exactly that when helping him off with his jumper. "Thanks," he said, emerging from the hide.

"I'm not a mother substitute, Archie, I'm a star."

He flushed; he had forgotten she could read his every thought. He turned the tunic inside out and carried it to the fire, holding it close to the flames to speed up the drying, pleased to notice that the smell seemed to improve the drier the hide became. "If I go back with you, once Emrys has had his say what do I do then? How do I know which way is home?" He tried to keep the note of pleading out of his tone, but Felicity just smiled at him. Seeing he was getting no answers he shrugged, "Okay, so you're not going to tell me. This is dry now." Turning away from her he put on his tunic, changed his mind about footwear – the soles of his feet were now like leather anyway - tied the left over ligaments round his middle, kicked earth over the fire, gathered up his water bottles, bow and remaining arrows and said, "Shall we go then?"

They walked back to the cliff and headed towards the caves. To Archie it seemed a thousand years since he had last come this way, so much had happened since. Trying to keep ahead of Felicity he forced the pace until he was almost running. But she was always at his side, her feet not touching the ground, her breathing no faster. From time to time she brushed her hand against his, which made Archie's stomach leap about. It was a feeling he had experienced only rarely and it came to him that Felicity was flirting with him. The thought excited him, but not for long: as they neared the caves his nerves started quivering until he was taut as his bow.

"Is there someone there?" Emrys' gruff voice echoed from deep within his lair.

"It's Archie and Hope," replied Felicity from the top of the cliff. "Can we come down?"

"Hope?" Archie looked at Felicity, confused.

"He can't get his head round calling me Felicity so I make it easy for him," she explained with a swift smile.

"Right," said Archie, depositing his water bottles and jumping down to the lip of the cave. Felicity beat him to it and led the way into Emrys' temple.

"You wear your trophy well, my friend," remarked Emrys, who was lying just inside the cave, his head raised to welcome them.

"Thank you." Taking a deep breath and looking the centaur straight in the eye Archie said, "I'm sorry I didn't believe you… you were right… I did win the fight. And I'm sorry I was so rude," he finished. It was the first time he had seen Emrys smile. It was only fleeting, but it reminded him of his father's twinkling attempts not to laugh when telling him off for one mischievous exploit or another. Archie found it immediately comforting and responded with a broad grin.

"Of course you are," Emrys said in a severe tone, "but you should be sorrier you did not return here last night. How foolish was that? Did you not hear me when I warned you? What were you thinking? It is imperative you do not fall under the Moon's spell."

"Foresight is a wonderful thing," Archie murmured drily. Felicity giggled from behind him and Emrys smiled again. It seemed that even he found it hard to remain sombre in the star's presence; her gaiety was infectious.

"Archie, come here, let me show you something." Emrys led the way outside onto the small ledge at the mouth of his cave and with a wide sweep of his hand indicated the ocean. He turned to look back into his caves and then at Archie. "Look at this. In front of you is my home, or for want of a better word, my prison. I am forced to remain here in these three hollow caves for eternity; eternity, Archie. My task is to heal those who pass by wounded and show them their way home, and all because I did not have Hope to guide me," Emrys glanced at Felicity. "Nor did I have the knowledge of foresight. You have been handed both on a plate."

"What happened to you, Emrys?" Archie asked, throwing Felicity a brief look of anxiety.

"It is painful for me to think about and I find it hard to remember," Emrys turned back to gaze out at the ocean, his distress clear to see.

"It's okay." Archie was filled with remorse. "I'm sorry I asked; I was just being nosy, you don't have to tell me."

"Yes, I do. You are at once too curious and too forgetful for me not to. Who knows what will happen to you next time you leave my sanctuary if I don't? Are you hungry?"

Puzzled by the abrupt change of subject Archie was appalled when he almost said, 'I could eat a horse'. "Yes," he nodded emphatically, while behind him Felicity gave a peal of laughter.

Emrys turned to her bemused. "Did I say something funny?"

"No," Felicity brought herself under control. "I was laughing at Archie's thoughts."

"Ah yes. Would I be right in thinking this young man wants something a little more satisfying than herb salad? Will you help me?"

Felicity, who had been busily braiding her hair, smothered a giggle, "As always, Emrys." She linked hands with the centaur and the two of them encircled Archie. "Close your eyes for me," Felicity instructed him. "Now think of your favourite meal, imagine it being set on a table in front of you. See it clearly: you are holding a fork, you can smell the food, your taste buds are watering for it."

Archie obeyed, mystified, imagining the first thing that popped into his mind. No sooner had he thought of it than a delicious smell of sweet and sour wafted past his nostrils.

"Interesting choice... for breakfast," Felicity giggled again.

"Now, open your eyes," commanded Emrys.

On the floor in front of them was a full course, Chinese meal, Archie's favourite aromatic duck and pancakes included. His slavering mouth dropped open. He looked from Emrys to Felicity in astonished disbelief.

"Believe it, my friend," Emrys smiled. "It's called the power of the mind: 'Nothing exists except atoms and empty space, everything else is opinion.' Democritus said that almost two-and-a-half thousand years ago. Eat, please, I don't like to see you dribbling."

Archie needed no second bidding. While he ate, Emrys talked. He spoke of the Moon and how she surveyed the world beneath her before descending to wreak her wicked mischief on the Earth. He described the catastrophic night of the accident when he and his beloved horse, Gareth, were attempting to find their way home.

"You had an accident? What happened?" Archie asked.

Emrys shook his head sadly, "I don't remember, I only know that I was riding Gareth and we were lost... and if you keep interrupting I will lose the thread of my story completely."

"Sorry, Emrys, but..." Archie caught a warning glance from Felicity and clamped his mouth shut.

"The Moon came down from the firmament and walked the land, tricking us both and forcing us into these very caves. My horse trusted me to guide him, but I was as lost as he. We were both trapped; the Moon took us hostage."

Emrys shifted his position, his hooves scraping on the rocky floor. "Then the Moon stole our thoughts, entwining them together. It was a slow and torturous procedure, taking us back to our conception and bringing us forward through unrelenting images of our lives, right up to our present, until our souls and bodies fused together and we were one being: half man, half horse."

Looking down at his fists, Emrys held them up to Archie, "Now, even a simple task like eating is confusing. My brain has a rift scored through it. Some days remembering how to use these poor hands is completely impossible and I find myself yearning to munch sweet-smelling hay and gallop across the plains feeling the wind in my mane. On others I am able to do dextrous things, like carve wooden bowls and grow plants. You see, Archie, I am neither one thing nor the other. At no time do I feel comfortable in my skin. It is as if our two parts, Gareth's and mine, are continually locked in mortal combat." The centaur fell silent, his eyes filling with tears.

"Are you sure you want to go on," Archie asked, suddenly losing his appetite and pushing his unfinished food to one side.

"I must, whether I want to or not. Your welfare is too important to me." The centaur drew a breath and went on with his story. "Even more painful than this, the Moon dragged our fused consciousness back to the home where we had once lived in harmony. She then proceeded to destroy and distort it so that all our innocent memories were twisted into horror and evil. After that I was unable to reminisce again, for once the Moon had finished her cruel torment she wiped our memories almost completely; turned them to stone. Finally she banished us under her evil curse to remain forever fused in the darkness of this lonely cave.

"Thanks to the grace of God, I was somehow spared my wisdom of His scriptures and my knowledge of herbs and healing – it is for that reason that I continue to wear this," he fingered his dog-collar, "to remind me that I once was a consecrated priest. But the moon poisoned the rest of my mind and my body. She is the Devil incarnate. To actually see her physically as I did that day would destroy anyone's mind, of that I am sure. Please, you must believe me. You are in peril if you do not take note of what I say."

"I do believe you, Emrys. I am truly sorry I doubted you. Forgive me I beg you. I promise I will never forget what you have told me." Archie fell silent.

Emrys nodded and getting up, he clopped back into the depths of the cave.

"How was your Chinese?" Felicity broke the intensity of the lingering silence.

"Great, thank you. Not much of an appetite now though," he responded automatically, his thoughts reeling with what he had heard. Emrys' story had brought back the horror of last night's torment. Archie could well believe he too would have gone stark staring mad had Felicity not answered his plea, hiding him from the Moon while he broke free of her spell.

"Why are you so concerned about me? You saved my sanity last night – and my life once before. It was you under the ice, wasn't it?"

"You know it was, Archie," Felicity said softly. "It wasn't your time."

They both looked up as Emrys re-emerged from the cave. He seemed to be his normal melancholy self as he sat down beside the star.

"And you," Archie said to him, "why are you being so kind to me when all I do is bring you pain?"

"I promised someone a long time ago that I would help you," Emrys said. "She told me how early you would arrive here and how determined and adventurous you are. You like to create escapades, my friend, whether it is in your imagination, at work or at play. Your journey home will be a tough one, for it is in your spirit always to find the hardest way, but I will get you there, I promise, if it is the last thing I do."

Stung, Archie was about to retort that Emrys made him sound like a prize idiot, but what the centaur said was true. All his life he had turned problems into almost insurmountable challenges. It was his way of filling the hole he had told Sarah about so many years ago. He swallowed, "Is that why you wanted me to come back? So you could tell me that?" he asked, beginning to feel agitated.

"No, there is more. I see a brutal battle ahead of you." Emrys paused closing his eyes.

Archie leaned forward, "This whole business is a battle, there's no two ways about it. I don't know what has happened to me - or you come to that - and no one I have met or spoken to will to give me a straight answer about anything. You and Felicity are as bad as each other."

"Who?"

"Hope - sorry - you keep telling me to find my way home, which would be great, but for some strange, gut-wrenching feeling, I don't think my home will be the same home I know and love. And it is that home I want to return to."

"That is the reason I asked you to come back," said Emrys. "It is hard for me to tell you this, but it will be even harder for you to comprehend." The centaur took a deep breath fixing his gaze on Archie. "Both the sun and I have told you that you are in Transit. This point in time for you is critical. You are crossing over to the next phase of life. You must stay focused."

Pinned by the centaur's gaze, Archie tried to keep calm, but panic was stirring in the pit of his stomach. Deep within him an understanding was growing, he wanted to ignore it; push it back down. Felicity reached out and gently took his hand. Her touch comforted him enough to face the answer to the question he must ask, even though he now knew what the answer would be because it made sense of everything that had made no sense, until now. "So you mean I am dead and I'm now lost in a place between Earth and heaven. That's what you mean by 'Transit' isn't it?"

"Nothing is lost in the eyes of God, Archie," Emrys fingered his dog-collar, "please try to remember that. Most people are aware that it is their time to die and they move on quickly. With others it is a little different."

"Others? Meaning me? So where are the rest of my Company?"

"They all accepted their fate as it occurred. Perhaps surprisingly, most people do. You, however, put up a fight from the moment lightning took out your second engine, right up until the moment your plane hit the water. Your last words, if you remember, were not 'please don't let me die', but, 'I will not die today'. There is a difference. For you, defeating death was another challenge."

Archie's mind flicked back to the plane crash. It seemed a world ago. "The sun and you both told me I was not dead," he accused, adrenalin surging through his body causing him to feel sick.

"Your shell may be dead, but do you feel dead?" Emrys smiled, his eyes filled with wisdom and kindness. "You can still feel pain, emotion, adrenalin. To say something is dead would mean they are cold and completely lifeless with no feelings. Your spirit is far from lifeless right now." Emrys spoke quickly, as though he could feel Archie's panic and wanted to assuage it.

"But my family, do they think I am dead?"

"Of course; you were all on national television and in the newspapers. All your bodies were recovered from the sea. Your parents know you are dead and will visit your shell."

Archie gritted his teeth as his eyes welled. The very thought of his parents made his heart pound. "So I am dead. You shouldn't have lied to me, Emrys." He gave up the struggle and allowed his tears to fall, scrambling to his feet and backing away.

"It's hard… I know, but look at me. I am half man and half horse. You have flown with a star and spoken with the sun, and you have killed a ravening beast with you bare hands. Where on Earth did you think you were?" Emrys' unaccustomed arms flew into action, trying to herd Archie back from the edge. "You must start understanding and believing, then and only then can you move forward. You have the strength now," said Emrys, indicating the hide on Archie's back. "You've proved it. Have faith in yourself, my friend."

"Well I have no faith in you! You should've told me the truth," Archie yelled, dodging Emrys' clasp. "I stand a better chance of getting home by talking to the Moon." As fear permeated him, his faith in Emrys collapsed. He stumbled, teetering on the edge of the cave lip. Way beneath him in the ocean the sharks circled.

"Don't be a fool Archie. I did not lie to you and I never will. You must try to understand. Think…" Emrys hollered. Archie, righting himself, turned his back on the centaur and ran up the ledge towards the cliff. "Remember what your father told you," Emrys called. "All your life you've known death isn't the end, you must have faith. There's more… I must speak with you more. Archie, come back," Emrys begged as Archie began to clamber up the vertical overhang.

"That went well," Felicity murmured drily. "Don't worry Emrys, I'll get him back." She spread her wings and flew to Archie, hampering his progress. "Where do you think you're going?" she snapped.

"Home," Archie spat, storming onto the cliff and setting off full tilt in the direction of the river, his eyes misted with hot fury.

"You can't leave, it's too dangerous," Felicity's voice shrilled with alarm as she came up against the full force of his obstinate determination. "You don't understand; the Moon will bewitch you. Don't speak with her, she'll trick you and take you back home, but it won't be your real home, it'll be an illusion. Please, Archie, listen to me, there are great perils out there. You cannot face them alone."

"I'll be fine."

"I'll come with you." Felicity kept pace with him.

"Go away; I don't need you. I'd rather be by myself."

"But you're supposed to follow me, Archie. You always follow me… I'm your guide," Felicity fought to take back control.

"You're a terrible guide, I don't want you with me," he cried, surging ahead.

The star stopped dead in her tracks. "Slightly harsh don't you think," she muttered, tears starting to her eyes. "I'm doing my best," she called after Archie's departing back. Too hurt to follow, she watched him storm off into the empty landscape.

Archie had not meant to hurt Felicity - or Emrys for that matter. He just needed timeout, time alone for this new reality to register. The centaur's words went round and round in his head as he fled: 'I promised someone a long time ago that I would help you. 'She told me...' he had said. Who was she? The question plagued him. He had been so wound up he had forgotten to ask. It must be someone who knew him well judging by what Emrys had said. Had 'she' also faced this terrible trauma of Transit? There was comfort in the thought that a person he knew might be here - wherever here was. He tried to think who it might be, using the puzzle to occupy his mind and stop him from thinking about his family, for that way lay madness. But inevitably their images crept into his mind: Robert and Joanna, Helena and Stewart, and especially Sarah. He saw them bereft and grieving, laying flowers on his grave, unable to accept he had gone from them forever. "I'M HERE," he cried out, shaking his fists at the sky. "I'M NOT DEAD!" His words echoed back at him hollowly. Acknowledging that he may never see them in life again, Archie plummeted into the depths of despair. His chest heaving, he faltered to a standstill, fell to his knees and wept until he was empty, drained and had no more tears left to weep.

The sun shone down powerfully, it felt humid and there were thick black clouds bubbling far away on the horizon; a storm was brewing. For a time he stayed on his knees swaying backwards and forwards, his arms wrapped around his chest. He could not understand why Emrys had not told him straight and explained everything at the start. What was the point in delaying the inevitable? Archie had been aware that his conscious reality had shifted; he was not a complete idiot, but he had thought he was having an extended nightmare or was trapped in a coma. He had truly believed Felicity would rescue him as she had so long ago. Truly believed she would guide him home to his family, to the point where he had half expected to wake up in a hospital bed, perhaps beneath the glare of lights in an operating theatre or attached to a life support machine. He would wake to see his parents' anxious faces looking down at him and he would smile up at them and say, "I'm back..." Thinking about this fantasy, which had kept him going from the time he had first seen Felicity's ball of light coming towards him on the beach, until now, Archie began to feel angry again, but this time with himself. He had been completely blinded by false hope, just as Felicity had warned. He was an almighty fool.

Pushing himself back onto his feet, he set off again, moving inland and widening his stride. "I'm a fool; I'm a fool; I'm a fool," he chanted to the rhythm of his pounding feet. Then he began to laugh. He laughed until he ached and his hilarity at the irony of it all turned inwards increasing his despair. His mind started spinning out of control and his body began to revolve, round and round, faster and faster. Arms outstretched, he spun like an ice dancer, the landscape a blur around him. When at last he stopped Archie was completely dizzy and disoriented. He had wanted to get back to his camp by the river, though could not have said why, but now he had not a clue where it was. He no longer knew which way to go. Paths criss-crossed in all directions and nothing looked familiar. Frightened, he ran his fingers through his hair as he always did when he did not know what to do. He started to shake uncontrollably, his breath coming in short, shallow gasps. As shock took hold, his legs gave way beneath him and he keeled over, curled into the foetus position and lay still, no longer capable of rational thought. An acute longing for peace overwhelmed him, translating into one overriding thought, "I wish I was dead. I'd rather be cold and completely lifeless with no feelings, than here."

"You have reached the crossroads now, Archie; it is time to make your choice."

The familiar voice washed over him, the strains of the sun's orchestral music filling his mind. "No, no, no," he screamed, wanting the disembodied voice to stop. "Go away! Leave me alone." He put his hands over his ears, but the voice was inside his head and he could not block out the sound. The sun continued to pester him until Archie had no choice but to listen to his words.

"You can either face your truth and move on to the next phase of your journey or you can remain here hiding in Transit. You must let Hope guide you. Remember, she and her friends are only here to help..." The voice faded and the music stopped just has it had before.

Archie remained where he was, sobbing, remembered voices threading through his brain. He searched them for a shred of comfort and found one: 'Nobody ever dies, Archie. Our spirits are simply energy and energy cannot be destroyed only transformed...' Who had said that to him? Emrys? No; not Emrys, but someone quite like him; someone in Wales...

CHAPTER NINE

1992

THE GAME

The long drive to North Wales in their battered old Volvo estate on a busy Easter Saturday morning took its toll on everyone, but by midday they were over the border into Conwy and at last nearing their destination. The squabbling in the back turned into excited cheers as each familiar landmark was ticked off. Driving slowly through the remote, sleepy village of Llangernyw, Robert passed the 4,000-year-old yew tree in the ancient churchyard of St Digain's and coaxed the car up the hill towards Woods Eves, his mother's house.

The children squealed with delight as Nanny Fletcher's giant Tudor house came into view and their father swung into the long drive. On the left was an expanse of lush grass mown short like a golfing green; perfect for games of pitch and putt or for pitching tents. Blossoms were appearing in the orchard and daffodils clustering under the fruit trees were still in full bloom. A moss-covered stone wall sheltered the deserted cobbled patio. To the right of the house was a tract of woodland and behind it a mountain, the crumbling ruins of a crofter's cottage clearly visible at the foot of the rocky escarpment. The woods looked mysterious and shadowy, a place where dark birds and foxes hunted their prey and where untrodden paths led to untold adventures. It was a garden waiting to be explored and the would-be explorers squealed even louder at the sight of it. Joanna, laughing, put her hands over her ears.

Nanny Fletcher was waiting at the top of her drive. Immaculately dressed in a pleated plaid skirt, her high-collared blouse fastened at the neck by a large brooch, a dark red cardigan draped around her shoulders, she looked every inch the genteel lady that she undoubtedly was. Her bobbed grey hair was perfectly set, chained spectacles perched on the end of her tiny nose and her arms were folded neatly behind her back as she waited with ill-concealed impatience to welcome her adored grandchildren.

"Mum looks well," Robert remarked.

"I hope she isn't taking on too much," Joanna murmured, smiling and waving at her mother-in-law. "It's such a lot of work having the entire family to stay all at once."

"You know she loves it and we'll all pitch in to help." Robert swung the Volvo round the back and brought it to a stop outside the coal house. As he pulled up the handbrake Helena and Stewart burst like birds from a coop out of the car and ran to greet their Nanny, overwhelming her with hugs and kisses. Archie and his friend James, a fellow Army Cadet who was staying with the Fletchers for the school holidays, followed more slowly until Archie, forgetting the dignity of his fourteen years, broke into a run.

Laughing and breathless, Nanny pointed to the back door, "Lunch is ready."

Needing no second bidding the four children charged into the house and ran whooping past the annex and down the long passageway to the kitchen. Within minutes they were sitting at the dining table in front of the window overlooking the back garden. Spring sunshine flooded into the room catching lost smoke escaping from the hearth and bouncing off the polished silver on the dresser.

"Save some pie for everyone else," Nanny said, setting down dishes of hot food and smiling at the children's expectant faces. She had lived in North Wales all her married life but her upper-crust tones were without a hint of Welsh accent. "There are plenty of vegetables and potatoes, help yourselves."

"When will the others arrive?" Archie asked, his adolescent voice pitching high then low.

"They won't be long." Nanny took her place at the head of the table. "You all left home at about the same time," she added, exchanging amused glances with Joanna as the children tucked into her legendary chicken pie as though they had not eaten for a week.

Archie was soon finished and on the edge of his seat fidgeting to get down. He had eaten all his potatoes and pie but as always, his green beans were left on the side.

"You'll never grow big and strong if you don't eat your greens," Nanny said. Archie grimaced, popped some beans in his mouth and pushed the rest around his plate hoping they wouldn't look quite so many.

"I can hear a car," said Stewart. The family fell silent.

"Me too," Robert confirmed. "Let's see who it is."

Everyone sprang from the table, dashed back down the passage and spilled out onto the driveway.

The Davies had arrived. Gillian and Sally Davies, Archie's cousins, were out of their car and running towards the house. Auntie Frances and Uncle Tom were rummaging in the car boot retrieving suitcases. The Davies had travelled from Ayr in Scotland: Tom's job in the Royal Air Force had recently posted him further than ever before from Wales, much to his wife's dismay.

"Jack and Patricia should be hot on your heels," Nanny beamed at Frances, the second of her three children. No sooner had she spoken than another Volvo estate, this one brand new, appeared in the driveway. Patricia, Robert's stern-faced older sister, was behind the wheel. Her scrawny husband Jack was beside her and Sarah and Dominic could be seen bouncing around in the back. The car had barely stopped before the doors swung open and the children piled out. Throwing hasty kisses to Nanny and their aunts and uncles, they shot off to join their cousins in a noisy game of Tag, leaving 'the olds' to lug cases and exchange grumbles about the journey before gathering in the kitchen for a catch-up over a welcome cup of tea.

Later, the four girls were sprawled on the lawn taking a breather while the four boys wandered off to explore. Helena watched them go, tempted to join them, but was irresistibly drawn into a discussion about sleeping arrangements - always a hot topic of conversation.

"I wonder which rooms we're in." Sally, who had just turned ten, sucked a strand of her blonde hair and gazed dreamily up at the rustic bedroom windows, her striking green eyes glistening with excitement.

"Do you think you'll be allowed to sleep in with us?" Helena asked Gillian, Sally's similarly green-eyed sister, who at twelve was closer to Helena's age but was far more girly, with curling blonde ringlets and an innocent baby face.

Gillian shrugged, "Well if I'm in the pink room bags I get the bed furthest from the door."

"Oh, I do hope we're all sleeping together," Sarah chipped in. At fourteen, she was regarded by the others as a bit of a grown up and almost as bossy as her ogre of a mother. "You know what'll happen, you guys will all be allowed to bunk down together and I'll have to share a room with Mum and Dad." Mortified by the thought, Sarah's gaze dropped to her gleaming patent shoes.

"No, I betcha it'll be us in one room upstairs and the boys will get the annex," said Gillian twisting a finger round a drooping ringlet. "It's so unfair."

"No it's not," Helena arched an eyebrow. "It's because Auntie Patricia is paranoid about keeping us separate from the boys. It'll just make it a bit more exciting," she directed a knowing look at her cousins. They all giggled, understanding full well what she meant. With or without parental acceptance, the bed allocation would change drastically several times in the night and would involve much clandestine activity; midnight feasts, ghost stories and pillow fights being the favourites.

With the topic of sleeping arrangements exhausted, the girls whiled away the remainder of the afternoon, ignoring the distant shouts of the boys and gossiping happily, mostly about school.

Before long the aroma of toad-in-the-hole wafted into the garden and by six p.m. everyone had squeezed round the table for an early supper. Under the watchful eye of Patricia, the children attempted to contain their excitement and attend to their table manners, from time to time receiving a conspiratorial wink from their grandmother.

"Thank you for your letters, Nanny, I love getting post," Sarah said, taking advantage of a rare lull in the conversation.

"And thank you for yours, dear," replied Nanny, "they're a delight, you write beautifully." She paused, "Which reminds me; I don't know if you are aware, Sarah, but I received a letter meant for Archie a little while ago. I read it by mistake and found it most… interesting. Do you want it back?" Sarah blushed and exchanged glances with Archie, hanging her head in embarrassment.

"That explains it," Archie came to her rescue, a sausage drenched in tomato sauce poised at his lips. "I got a letter meant for you, Nanny. It was all about Sarah getting into the lacrosse team. You must've mixed them up, Rap... err... Sarah." He looked quickly at Sarah's mother, who did not approve of 'Rapunzel', but she seemed not to have noticed his slip.

"That's wonderful, dear. Well done that girl," Nanny beamed across the table at Sarah then raised a quizzical eyebrow. "Your letter for Archie was not so informative; quite the contrary, it was rather forlorn." Nanny looked over her spectacles at her granddaughter, "I thought you were happy with your school?"

Sarah glanced fearfully at her mother. "I am, Nanny, I love it," she said hastily. Patricia had enrolled her at an expensive secondary boarding school almost a year ago and was not best pleased when her daughter appeared not to be enjoying it as she should. In fact Sarah positively hated it, but it was more than her life was worth to admit it. The only thing that kept her sane was her regular correspondence with Nanny and, of course, Archie.

Nanny Fletcher, being a wise old lady, always knew when something was adrift. Quickly she changed the subject. "Now that we've finished eating, I'm happy to announce the plans for the next two days." She paused, letting the anticipation build. "Tomorrow is Easter Sunday and I have spoken with my good friend the Easter Bunny," ignoring the older children's groans, she winked at Dominic and continued, "and I told him how well behaved you've all been so far this year. So there will be an Easter egg hunt first thing in the morning."

"Hurrah!" Robert, his eyes twinkling, gave a loud cheer and the children giggled.

"I was talking to the children, Robert." His mother admonished, her eyes brimming with laughter. "After that, we will all walk down to St Digain's for the eleven o'clock service." The giggles turned to a chorus of loud groans, which brought a slight frown to Nanny's brow.

"Children, behave," Patricia snapped, "or there'll be no Easter eggs for any of you, least of all you, Sarah. You're old enough to know better."

Sarah's eyes filled with tears; Robert quirked an eyebrow at Jack, who shrugged and looked sheepishly down at his plate; Tom hid a smile and Joanna and Frances exchanged wry glances. Nanny once more averted the crisis, "Who would like some jelly and ice-cream?" Everyone raised a hand.

"Where're we sleeping, Daddy?" Gillian asked her father quietly. She knew he wouldn't care where they slept so long as they didn't disturb him.

"Is this a trick question?" Tom glanced from one daughter to the other, their green eyes pleading a reply. "Ask Mummy."

Gillian groaned. Her jelly was placed before her by Auntie Patricia, who directly disappeared into the kitchen. Gillian took a deep breath and went for it. "Where're we sleeping Mummy?"

"Nanny's made beds up for you all in the annex," Frances said softly. "The boys are in the back room and you girls are in the front room nearest the bathroom."

There was a moment of stunned disbelief.

"Yessss...," hissed Sally, a customary strand of soggy hair trapped between her teeth.

The children all smiled at one another, wholly satisfied with the verdict but slightly apprehensive, not knowing if Patricia had been privy to this arrangement and would ultimately put the mockers on it.

"That said," Patricia's voice came from the kitchen doorway, "if there is any misbehaving whatsoever, you will be split up immediately, is that understood?"

"Yes Mummy; Yes Auntie Pat," came the subdued response entirely at odds with the glittering of suppressed excitement in eight pairs of eyes. Dominic almost let them down, his squeak hastily submerged by Archie's sudden coughing fit. "Must've swallowed something the wrong way," he gasped with an innocent smile at his auntie.

At bedtime the girls were ushered upstairs for a bath by a clearly irritable Patricia. The boys, shepherded by Jack, used the bathroom in the annex to get ready for bed. Once in their pyjamas, they congregated by the roaring inglenook fire in the sitting room to listen to a short story from Nanny. Then, with hugs and kisses all round, it was time for bed.

***

Next morning, like a swarm of buzzing bees, the children dashed around the garden unravelling clues and recovering Easter eggs. All too soon it was time to put on their Sunday best and walk to church. Although Archie would never dream of admitting it, he rather liked going to services in St Digain's, it was so ancient and felt quite spooky; even more so since Nanny had told them the tale of 'Angelystor', the spirit that haunted the church on the

Night of the Dead, its ghostly voice naming all the people in Llangernyw who would die in the next twelve months. Archie looked up at the east window under which in times gone by, so it was said, brave parishioners would sit after midnight on Halloween and listen in dread to see whose names were called. He shivered, suddenly glad it was Easter. Then, being Archie, he dared himself to creep out in the night to the churchyard on the off chance that Angelystor might be there at Easter too. Tucking the idea to the back of his mind, he joined in the enthusiastic rendering of 'Christ the Lord is Risen Today', his voice squeaking from bass to treble and back again on the 'Halleluiah!'

The rest of the day passed in a whirl of energetic play interspersed with breaks for the consumption of delicious chocolate eggs, and all too soon it was bedtime again. Tired out, having been awake for much of the previous night, the children went to their separate rooms and despite their best intentions stayed there prone till breakfast time.

On Easter Monday, after a lazy morning that culminated in a huge roast lunch – their last meal all together until the summer holidays - the children bundled into Tom's and Frances's bedroom to watch television. Nanny didn't hold with television, said it stifled the imagination, but Uncle Tom had brought a portable and said they could watch so long as they did not disturb the olds' afternoon nap and did not get chocolate on the bed cover. In fact, only Sarah had any left, the others having gobbled theirs up the day before, but being Sarah, she duly shared it out.

"I'm bored, let's go and play in the woods." Helena yawned as the credits rolled. They had been only barely entertained by an old war film that most of them had seen before.

"I've got a better idea. Let's play a war game in the woods," said Archie.

"Yeah," Stewart shouted enthusiastically. "How do we play?"

Archie had been insightfully structuring his game whilst they had been watching the film. "It'll be called 'Dead Game' because unless you win that's what you'll be: dead!" Archie grinned, pretending to slit his own throat. Arching his eyebrows at Stewart, he pounced, restraining his brother in a full-blown monkey scrub. Stewart squealed and squirmed and was about to call 'Mercy' when James came to his rescue, fists flying with mock punches.

"Okay, okay, you guys. Stop please. Are we going to play this game seriously or not?" Helena shouted, being the only one brave enough to call order. "Are there any rules, Arch?"

Detaching himself from James, Archie took charge as always. He sat on the edge of the bed and beckoned them all in closer, "Dominic, Helena, Sally, you're on my team. We'll go into the woods first. In ten minutes, the rest follow. We can hide in the woods or higher up the mountain but no further than the ruins. The house and garden are out of bounds. The coal-house is base. We've thirty minutes. James, you'll lead the other team. Synchronise watches," Archie set the digital alarm on his new multifunctional watch. "Okay, first on home wins."

"What will we do in the woods?" Sally asked with a puzzled frown, adding, "Can't we call it something else? 'Dead Game' sounds horrid."

"What do you think we'll do?" Archie shot a despairing look at James, who grinned. "We hide and hunt the other team and stop them from getting home, silly. After thirty minutes, if no one is captured, head for base. Is everyone clear?" He stared at his company, all of whom stared back attentively. "Okay, let the Dead Game begin. Let's go."

Archie and his team scampered up the earthy incline into the woods. "Spread out, stay low. Dominic, guard the base, don't let anyone through," Archie ordered.

"Right," Dominic agreed obediently.

"Keep well out of sight. I'm going up to the ruins to hide out. I'll give you a ten-minute call so you know they're coming. I'll hoot like an owl, okay?" Archie whispered. "Are you girls going to stick together?"

The girls nodded looking at one another. "We stand a better chance of capturing one of the others if we do," said Helena, grasping the role of hunter. She was used to playing Archie's games but only rarely had she enjoyed the privilege of being on his team.

Sally, still looking slightly confused, was sucking strands of hair from either side of her head and was clearly nervous. "Oh yes," she lisped, "I'll stick with Helena."

"Okay troops, scatter," whispered Archie. They all ran in different directions. Dominic stayed close to base, dodging in and out of the trees. The girls hovered on the woodland border by the edge of a rushing stream. Archie ran beyond the stream through the tall grasses of a meadow behind the woods and on up the mountain towards the ruined cottage.

It had turned out to be quite a hot and humid day and he was sweltering, wishing he had worn his shorts and t-shirt. He had joined the Army Cadet Force a year ago and taking his role as a cadet exceptionally seriously, wore his greens proudly day in day out until Joanna, tearing her hair, insisted they be given a wash. Now, sweating in his combats, Archie felt in his pocket for his recently acquired potato gun and ducking low scanned the area for any signs of pursuit. It was then he noticed the old man digging in what had once been the cottage garden.

The gardener wore a long, bottle-green overcoat and a flat cap. He was bending over a spade with his back to Archie; a hoe lay on the ground beside him. Archie crouched down, pulled out his potato gun and stalked the stranger cautiously, aware that he might be trespassing. When he was sure there were no 'Keep Out' signs he stood.

"Planting anything tasty?" he called, expecting the man to be startled and swing round, but seemingly undisturbed he simply carried on digging. Archie, thinking perhaps the mysterious gardener was hard of hearing moved closer and was about to try again when the man straightened, eased his back and without looking round, pointed at a gray horse grazing on the mountainside.

"Carrots for my horse over there, he's my best friend; riding that horse is like breathing to me. He likes carrots." Still without looking at Archie, the gardener bent and continued digging.

Somewhat bewildered by the man's odd behaviour and feeling slightly awkward, Archie noisily cleared his throat. The man put down his spade and at last turned to face him. "You aren't trespassing here are you young man?" He had a gruff voice with a slight Welsh accent, but Archie could see a twinkle in his dark gray eyes and was reassured that he was harmless. His face was seamed with age, worn and tired looking and his chin covered in gray stubble.

"I don't think so; my Nanny lives at the edge of the wood," Archie explained.

"Would that be Mrs Fletcher? Making you a Master Fletcher - son of Robert perhaps?" The old man scratched at his chin with an earth-encrusted fingernail and regarded Archie with a quizzical gaze.

"Yes, sir, my father is Robert Fletcher."

"Out for a walk are you?" The gardener removed his cap to smooth a hand over his head and Archie saw that his hair was thinning and gray.

"Playing a game with my cousins actually."

The man grunted, replacing his cap, "Creeping about more like!"

"Not creeping, sir, hunting," Archie gave a cheeky smile.

"What is it that you're hunting Master Fletcher? The birds and squirrels in the trees? You'll find a sheep or two if you tread on higher ground. What's that you have in your hand?"

Nettled by the old man's sarcasm, Archie showed him the potato gun. The man moved closer, the sun behind his head blotted out his features and the long overcoat covered his body completely. He seemed to stand taller towering over Archie, who felt suddenly threatened and took a step backwards.

"What are you hunting, Archie?"

Archie squinted up at him, "People. I would never kill birds or animals, sir. It is only a game." As he spoke, it occurred to Archie that he had not told this man his name, but under a barrage of rapid-fire questions he had no chance to ponder it further.

"Why are you hunting people?"

"Because they're the enemy."

"What made them the enemy?

"The game did, it's in the rules."

"How long will you play the game?"

"Until the end – I'll be the first one home."

"What then?"

"We'll play again."

"Ah...." the stranger nodded. He seemed to relax and as he did so, his coat fell open at the neck, revealing a white dog-collar.

Archie's eyes widened, "I know who you are," he accused. "You're the vicar of St Digain's! I didn't recognise you at first, sir." It was hardly surprising since he had seen him only rarely, but he knew Nanny Fletcher adored this old man. Nanny must have talked to him about her family, which was how he knew Archie's name. At once his anxiety dropped away, though he remained completely baffled by the weird conversation they were having.

"Yes, did I frighten you? Forgive me, my son, I didn't mean to."

"You didn't... well maybe, just a little," confessed Archie.

The vicar put a hand to his chest and hunched over, his eyes shifting about as though looking for something.

"Are you feeling okay, sir?" Archie asked, concerned.

"Not too good; I'm not a well man," the vicar paused, took a rasping breath. "You like your game don't you? There's a sparkle in your eye, boy. That shows you've got spirit and you're truly alive. It's your passion to play isn't it?"

"You seem to know me quite well," Archie grinned. "What's Nanny been saying about me?"

"I do know you well, Archie Fletcher, I'm your friend. I know a good deal about you: I know you love a challenge and that you always want to win. You'll never 'suffer fools gladly...' the vicar paused, added, "Corinthians 11, Verse 19," and broke into a hacking cough.

Conscious of the time passing, Archie stole a glance at his watch wondering how he could extricate himself from this situation without seeming rude.

"Your time's limited," the vicar continued, breathless.

"Ten minutes and five seconds," Archie announced.

"No; you have eleven years and exactly one hundred and five days left, my son, then your game will end and we'll meet again." The vicar coughed and spluttered as he spoke.

"Not sure what you mean, sir." Convinced the vicar was rambling, and wondering if perhaps he had dementia, Archie began to back off. "That's a really nasty cough you've got there. I think you need to see a doctor."

"Too late for a doctor, my fate is spinning on the great wheel of fortune. I have counselled and healed others all my life and yet there is little anyone can do for me now. I don't have long, I'm afraid. It is my time and knowing that makes me think deeply about the future."

"Future?" Archie murmured, confused, his compassion for this sick old man making him feel uncomfortable.

"I don't mean here, Archie, I have no future here, my illness is terminal. I have questioned my faith to the highest degree. Where do we go after this material life do you think? Do you know what awaits us over there on 'the other side'?"

"You mean after we die?" Not sure what to say, Archie lied, "No; never really thought about it, but you're a vicar; surely you know the answers better than me?" Part of Archie wanted nothing more than to run away from this unsettling conversation as fast as his legs could carry him, but the other part was intrigued. Uncertain he lingered, poised for flight.

"It is a different world over there I am sure. I believe it is in heaven where our passions really come alive no matter if we lived them here or not; our lessons never end. Your passion is the quest or the game you are playing, but you are merely a pawn playing it. Enjoy the thrill, Archie, but keep in mind you cannot live a life of adventure forever, the mission must end at some point, and then what? What of those you love?"

Humbled by the vicar's conviction, Archie felt a qualm of fear, "Are you trying to tell me in a round about way that I'm going to die?" His eyes widened, "You're not... Angelystor are you?" he blurted. For a moment everything around him seemed still as if it too waited for the answer, even the breeze had died away.

The old man gave a shout of wheezing laughter, "I'm no ghost, boy!" Recovering his breath he smiled gently, "Nobody lives forever, Archie, but nobody ever dies. Our spirits are simply energy and energy cannot be destroyed only transformed. This physical life can end in an instant or it can be a drawn out process, either way we will all find our own way home eventually," he paused, added, "and there is only one way home."

"I don't understand. Which way is that?" Archie did not like this turn in the conversation. Only once in his life had he considered life after death, but that had been because he had thought he was going to die. It was on the tip of his tongue to tell this kindly old vicar of his strange experience under the ice, but he had never spoken of it to anyone. Had never been certain that it had really happened, and so he kept quiet.

"The quickest and easiest route is to follow your heart… wherever it may lead you."

"Oh." Archie's interest in the conversation suddenly dispersed, it was much too philosophical and his attention span far too short. He searched for a change of subject, pointed at the horse, which had wandered closer and was sticking its head over the wall. "He's waiting for his carrots."

The vicar looked to where Archie pointed, "Ah yes, so he is. He's my best friend, aren't you, Gareth old boy." He turned his back on Archie and without another word, picked up his spade and resumed digging.

"Gareth?" Archie muttered, thinking 'odd name for a horse.' He glanced again at his watch, realised he had forgotten to give his team the owl warning and in less than a minute everyone would be on the same mission back to base. His attention was caught by a movement behind one of the gaping windows in the crumbling wall of the cottage. For an instant he saw a figure silhouetted against the light. He screwed up his eyes to see who or what it was, but the hot sun was shimmering on the stones distorting his vision.

Archie was wired, his heart thumped, adrenalin coursing through his body. He fingered his potato gun ready to charge into action. Stepping forward he accidentally cracked a dry stick beneath his feet. The shadow took a step back, turned and disappeared. Archie grinned and dashed behind the wall. James's mop of white-blonde hair had exposed his identity immediately. Archie's digital alarm broke the silence. Time was up; the chase was on. Sprinting flat out, side by side down the rugged mountain the two boys raced for home.

"One jump or two?" Archie laughed breathlessly as they neared the stream.

"One of course." James jumped first, clearing the stream in a single leap and running on down the mountain. Archie did it in two, coming down in a giant splash, soaking his combats and alerting anybody within earshot of his position. Drenched, he stopped abruptly at the tree line and hid behind the trunk of a large conifer to catch his breath. Scanning the woods for movement, Archie saw that Helena and Sally had done a good job in capturing Stewart. He was tied with Helena's belt to a nearby tree and the two girls were now stalking someone else, presumably Gillian, whom he spotted lying in the undergrowth guarding the base. Bother! He now saw she had captured Dominic. Typical! James, Archie noted, had completely disappeared. He looked around for Sarah; she also was nowhere to be seen.

Archie waited. Then he saw his target. She was right in front of him, no more than ten feet away sitting cleverly camouflaged halfway up a tree. All he had to do was wait until she made her move, then he could take her hostage. His patience was rewarded; it wasn't long before Sarah slowly clambered down. With her gaze riveted on Helena, she stood poised on the slope ready to pounce. Archie went for her instantly. Bursting out from his hiding place he tackled her to the ground. Sarah screamed in surprise and lay still with Archie lying full length on top of her. For a moment they beamed at each other, breathless; then Sarah tried to wriggle out from under him. Taken by surprise, Archie was momentarily unbalanced and began to roll. Sarah did the same; they rolled side by side, faster and faster, shrieking with laughter. A tree violently halted their tumble and winded Archie, who got the brunt of it. There was a now a lot of commotion around them: the other girls dashed by pulling their hostages, Stewart and Dominic, and ran screaming for base. Sarah giggled and jumping to her feet set off behind them, but Archie was no quitter. He recovered instantly and shot after her. Once again he tackled her to the ground and scrambled on top of her, pinning her to the wet, earthy woodland floor.

"Let's roll again," Sarah said, still grinning. It was an addictive pastime rolling down slopes.

Archie beamed back at her and raised his eyebrows. "Okay twin, but you do realise you're now my hostage?"

"Or are you mine?" Sarah grabbed hold of his collar and they were off again, bumping over tree stumps, rolling over pine cones and into muddy puddles, their clothes ripping, twigs getting stuck in their hair. They came to a stop by the coal house in Nanny Fletcher's back yard, both of them laughing hysterically and gasping for breath.

"That's the most fun I've ever had," Sarah panted.

"Me too," agreed Archie, scrambling to his feet and helping her up. Grinning, he put a hand on her shoulder, reaching out with the other to pick a leaf out of her hair. The gesture turned spontaneously into a clumsy hug. Lost in the moment, it was a while before Archie and Sarah became aware they had an audience: the entire family was gazing at them with expressions ranging from scorn to amusement, to dismay; the latter from Patricia, who was for once rendered speechless.

James broke the awkward silence. "I won the game Archie, I got home first.

Feeling his face grow hot, Archie stepped sharply backwards with an embarrassed laugh. "Well done mate, but did you bring any hostages with you? Sarah's mine!"

Sarah's giggle was lost beneath Stewart's yell, "Fantastic! Let's play again!"

Tom looked up from the boot of his car, having stowed away the last case. "Sorry kids, there is only time for the loo and goodbyes I'm afraid. We must get on the road now."

"Oh no," the children sang in unison, their faces a picture of misery.

"I don't want to go home," cried Sally.

"Half an hour more, PLEASE Daddy?" begged Gillian.

"'Fraid not, chick," Tom shut the boot.

"Sarah, just look at the state of you!" Patricia exclaimed, finding her voice at last. Sarah gave Archie a look, flushed and hung her head.

"Nothing that a good bath won't wash off, dear, once we get home," Jack said, attempting to calm his wife down while steering his daughter away from Archie and into the house towards the annex bathroom. "Let's get the worst off you," he murmured. "Don't want all that mud in the new car."

"Come along boys," Robert jingled his car keys. "Hurry up, Mummy's waiting." It wasn't quite true; Joanna, clasping Helena firmly by the hand, was doing the round of goodbyes.

The children, eyes welling, followed suit. Even Nanny had tears in her eyes as they all made their farewells. The Davies, Walkers and Fletchers drove away from Woods Eves in convoy leaving the forlorn figure of Nanny Fletcher standing waving at the top of her drive until they were out of sight.

When he could no longer see her, Archie ferociously plumped up his pillow and nestled down in the back seat, thinking of Sarah and their fall through the woods. He smiled, promising himself to cherish the moment. He had felt completely whole, a feeling he had been searching for all his life and knew he would never forget. As they passed the churchyard, he looked out of the window at the ancient yew and sighed. He had meant to sneak out to the church last night; ah well... maybe next time. It got him to thinking about his strange encounter with the vicar on the mountain. Their conversation was one he knew he would come back to again and again, but not just now. Blanking it from his mind Archie opted instead to think about Dead Game and eventually drifted into sleep.

CHAPTER TEN

AS TEARS STREAM A RAINBOW ENFOLDS

Water splattering on Archie's face woke him. Opening his eyes, he found himself lying curled beside a large, spreading puddle. He stared at it a moment, half asleep, mesmerised by the raindrops splashing onto its grey surface sending it rippling towards him. He stretched, his limbs aching and stiff, surprised to find he felt only slightly damp beneath his tunic. The thick lion's hide must repel the rain. Coming fully awake he stared up at the angry clouds, saw a distant flicker of lightning and heard a rumble of thunder. How could he have slept through this? And yet he knew he must have done for he had been dreaming, the images still gripped his mind. Had that really been Emrys and his horse on the mountainside all those years ago or had his dream distorted everything as they sometimes did? Realisation of where he was now and what had happened to him hit Archie with full force. The images receded and he gasped with misery, a searing pain around his heart.

With no sun as a marker he had no idea how long he had been asleep or when night would fall. Crawling onto his hands and knees he looked blearily through the driving rain at the unending, featureless landscape. He shook his head; looked again. Standing beside him in the mud was a sturdy pair of legs terminating in black lace-up shoes. Archie blinked, his gaze moving slowly upwards. A very tall and broad-shouldered stranger, clothed a bit like an

Ancient Greek in a white, calf-length tunic and with a long red cape hanging from one shoulder, looked down at him. The big man's long, dark curly hair streamed with rainwater, which ran down his face and dripped off the end of his Grecian nose. With one hand he leaned on a staff and in his other he held what looked like a sodden map.

'Maybe he's lost too,' Archie thought irrationally, getting stiffly to his feet and hugging his chest, his breath coming in short, painful gasps.

"Ah, you're up, Archie. Did you have a good rest? I hope I didn't disturb you. Shame about the weather isn't it?" The stranger looked up at the menacing clouds. "It appears to turn quickly round here doesn't it? Not quite as bad as the last storm we had though." Forced to shout over the noise of the thunder he added, "At least not yet."

"And you are?" Archie shouted back, noting that the stranger knew his name and presuming he had been sent by Emrys and Felicity. They were nothing if not persistent. Irritated, he waited for an answer.

"I'm sorry, allow me to introduce myself. My name is Kriss," the stranger smiled, reaching out to take Archie's hand. "I thought you'd like some company on your travels. Do you have any particular destination in mind?"

"I travel alone," answered Archie shortly, pulling his hand away.

"So do I usually. It was just a thought," Kriss shouted amiably, folding away his saturated map and tucking it beneath his cape.

Archie did not want to enter into conversation with this stranger, or anyone else for that matter, but aside from his weird apparel this was the first comparatively normal person he had seen in this unknown land. Also, he needed to find his way back to his camp before nightfall. Reluctantly he asked, "Can you direct me to the river?"

"Of course," Kriss pointed to one of the puddle-laden paths. "Follow that one over the hill and you will come to it directly."

"Thank you," Archie replied and ignoring the outstretched hand he turned and stormed off towards the path. After a few strides he became aware that Kriss was hot on his heels, but disinclined to be sociable he increased his pace.

Kriss had spoken the truth: once Archie was over the brow of the hill he recognised the lie of the land, but of his camp there was no sign. Rampantly out of control, the river was so swollen with rainwater it had flooded the entire area. Archie stood high on the incline contemplating. He had an irresistible compulsion, which he neither understood nor cared to question, to get to the other side of the river. He just knew in the depths of his being that it was the only way forward out of his current state of madness. He gauged the distance. It was a good fifty metres across, but he was strong and could swim it.

"I'd think a little longer before you jump, Archie," hollered Kriss in his ear. "It's a tough current to swim. Why not wait until it calms down or at least until the rain's stopped. We could talk?"

Archie shook his head, "How can I be dead?" he muttered. Everything was too real for him to be dead: the wild river in front of him, the rain pouring down, he was soaked through now and chilled to the bone. "Dead people don't feel. Not like this," he shouted.

"No? What did you think would happen when you died?" Kriss was leaning heavily on his staff, his wet cape flapping round his legs.

"I thought maybe the lights would go out… or I'd see a tunnel of light. I don't know. It wasn't something I dwelt on," Archie yelled. Dazed, he turned to look the stranger in the eye. "What role do you have in my Transit then? Are you here to help me or hoax me?" Not waiting for the answer, he turned back to the river. Then a thought struck him and the irony of it made him laugh out loud: 'What am I worrying about? If I'm already dead, I can't die another death!' Archie took a great stride forward, broke into a run and hurled himself into the water.

It was icy cold, but he could remember being far colder. The foaming rapids swept him away. There was no point in attempting to swim across to the other side, he could not even see it and it took all his strength just to keep his head above water. Tossing and turning like flotsam in the current he spiralled downstream, catching glimpses of the bank from which he had leapt receding into the distance. Time after time he rolled beneath the water to come up moments later gasping for air. Jagged rocks crashed against his flailing legs and tore at his feet. Archie began to tire and he knew he was losing the struggle. Just as he was thinking that maybe in this alien world of Transit is was possible to die more than one death after all, the rapids began to give way to calmer water. Rising once more to the surface, Archie saw that he was approaching the river-mouth and, chillingly, the open sea.

Treading water, he looked back at the distant bank he had hoped to reach, but the river was much wider here at its mouth and too far for him to swim in his present state. His only hope was to somehow make his way back upstream and try again, but he knew that even had he not been exhausted that was a challenge too far. The earthy bank on the side from which he had jumped was near enough to offer respite and he could see a line of low growing bushes that might afford him shelter from the rain while he recovered. Archie did not think twice - he knew what lived in the seas around here and dead or not, he had no wish to end up a shark's dinner. He struck out, forcing his bruised and battered body through the water towards the bank.

Pushing through the mass of lilies that floated along the riverside, Archie dragged his body and wet hide out of the water and sprawled in the mud. The sweet, honeyed scent of the white lily flowers was so overpowering it made him catch his breath. He eased himself into a sitting position and looked about him. The storm was passing, the rain easing to a fine drizzle and the dark clouds dispersing, he could see fragments of blue emerging between them. Archie shuffled backwards up the bank on his bottom until he could look out over the ocean. His gaze swept the empty horizon: the sun had reappeared and was hanging low in the sky. Turning his head Archie stared upstream then clenched his fist and slammed it down on his knee in frustration. Far from crossing to the other side as he had intended, he had been swept for at least two miles downstream and was still on the same side as before. Beginning to shiver, he toyed with the idea of stripping off his sopping tunic and wringing it out, but what was the point? Even if he spread it on a bush it would never dry in this drizzle. He lay back closed his eyes and concentrated on relaxing his body, but was unable to still his mind. The questions kept going round and round: if he was dead, why did he feel so cold? Why did everything feel so real?

For a while Archie lay unmoving, but he became aware of a presence and knew without opening his eyes that he was no longer alone. He sighed, said irritably, "Go away, Kriss. I've told you, I don't want company." He was met with silence. The feeling of being watched persisted until Archie could stand it no longer. He sat up ready to give the Ancient Greek a piece of his mind, but the big man was nowhere to be seen. "Who's there?" Archie called out. There was no reply.

The feeling that he was being watched was so strong that Archie got to his feet, looking back and forth, up and down, searching the area. He gazed out over the mouth of the river. Through the drizzle there appeared a shaft of sunlight, catching drops of moisture and turning them into a shimmer of diamonds. As if by magic a beautiful rainbow started to form until, like a vast multicoloured bridge, it spanned from one side of the river to the other. Archie gazed at it in awestruck wonder and as he did so, a figure seemed to rise out of the rainbow and glide over the bridge towards him. As it drew closer, Archie saw it was a woman. She wore a flowing chiffon gown in shades of multicoloured pastel, her spellbinding polychrome aura pushing itself ever outward. Her long black hair curled to her hips and she held two slender white jugs, one in each hand.

'I am Grace, Angel of the Rainbow,' rang a soft voice through Archie's head as she glided gracefully onto the bank, placing herself before him. Giant feathered wings, brilliant white and twice her height doubled back behind her, she ruffled them gently and Archie was captivated.

'It is not every day you learn what you have, Archie.'

Grace's lips did not move but he heard quite clearly what she said. Enchanted as he was by this vision of loveliness, Archie was also irritated that yet another apparition had come to haunt him. "How is it I can hear your words when you do not speak them, and how come everyone around here knows my name?" he blurted out.

Grace smiled and handed Archie a jug. He took it automatically and as he did so, she reached out a delicate hand and stroked his arm. Her touch was light as swansdown and the gesture so filled with tenderness that Archie felt faint. He swayed on his feet, barely able to breathe in her presence. The angel lifted her jug and began to pour a steady stream of clear water into the one Archie held. She went on pouring until it was full to overflowing and yet it seemed no heavier.

'The road of life has many detours,' she said, still pouring. Her jug was identical to his, but appeared to hold an infinite amount of water. Archie lowered his eyes and watched mesmerised as the water cascaded from the lip of his jug to pool at his feet. He was besieged by the angel's power; his chest ached and he felt tears welling, almost as if the pouring water was releasing grief from deep within his soul. Archie gave way to his intense emotion and sinking to the ground he wept. His fingers opened and the jug rolled from his hand. Grace ceased pouring and putting down her own jug, empty now, she gathered her gown about her and sat down beside Archie, enfolding him in her wings.

"I'm sorry, I'm so sorry." Deep sobs racked Archie's chest as tears spilled from his eyes.

'There, there, child, there's no need to be sorry, but crying will help. There are thousands more tears to be shed beyond those I carry in my jug.' She kissed Archie's head and stroked his hair, squeezing her wings tighter and creating a white cocoon of comfort around him. As he wept, Grace spoke softly into his mind.

'You are weeping for the people you have left behind, afraid that you will never see them again.' Unable to speak, Archie nodded. 'What of those who left before you? They are all elated and waiting for you to arrive,' Grace said. 'Poor Archie, believe me, you will see all your family again.' She kissed his forehead, her gentle kindness making him cry all the more.

"I'm s-s-sorry," Archie snorted through uncontrollable sobs.

'Your breakdown is completely natural. Grief cannot be shared. Everyone carries it alone, as his own burden, in his own way. Your feelings will be constantly changing, sometimes positive and sometimes negative.'

Archie held his breath attempting to control himself, only to inhale harshly letting out another painful cry. "It was the wrong time. I had… so much…. to do… before I…" he sobbed.

'You left at exactly the right time, Archie. It was the time and date you set before you were even born. You must look forward. You cannot live in the past.' She thought for a moment, 'How far would you get if you tried driving while looking always in your rear view mirror?'

Archie smiled through his tears at her analogy, "Not very," he agreed, wiping his face with his hand.

'You've earned the strength to see you through to the end of this level, Archie. But your heart is not balanced. You long for home and you cannot cross over while you are in a state of longing, and yet even at home you felt incomplete. Understand, Archie, it is vital… vital, that when you cross to the other side you go with a balanced heart. Yours is not a normal crossing.'

"Why not? Why me?"

'Largely, though not entirely, because you have enormous strength of will and you refuse to let go,' Grace said. 'It is time for me to return now.' She opened her wings.

"But I don't know how," Archie shivered as his safe cocoon moved apart and let Transit back in. "Please help me, please don't leave me here," he pleaded, frightened that if he so much as blinked, the angel would disappear. "Where do I go?" Archie begged. "What should I do now?" He clung to her hand.

'You must follow your guide, my child, she's your best friend and she will take you home.'

"What about Emrys?"

'The Hierophant in the cliff caves?'

"Yes; should I trust him?"

'You must help him, Archie, just as he has helped you. There's a long road ahead of you. You need all the help you can get. Know your enemy when it faces you. Do you truly think Emrys is one of them?'

"No, but I don't understand why he lied to me," said Archie quietly, bowing his head.

'You know he would not lie. He just did not say what you wanted or expected to hear.' Grace stood, retrieved her jugs then glided back towards the river where her rainbow waited. As she stepped onto it the colours intensified and though she stood facing Archie, she was so camouflaged in its potency he could hardly see her.

"Will I see you again?"

'Maybe. Don't be afraid, Archie. This ending to your material world is deceiving and in many ways unfair, but there is a lesson you must face. Once it is learnt, you must let go of your guilt and move forward to the next level.'

“I don’t feel guilty...,” Archie started to argue, but of course he did. He was consumed with guilt for choosing to live on the edge of life-threatening danger leaving his family in a state of constant anxiety. And he felt guilty for dying prematurely causing untold grief to those he loved. It tore at his heart and he could not imagine ever being able to let it go.

Grace lifted an arm high above her head and waved it as though it were a magic wand. Colour flew from her fingertips high into the stratosphere, each exploding like a firework in the darkening sky. As the colours came floating back down, Grace plucked out the colour yellow and propelled it over to Archie.

‘This pallid yellow I give to you as a gift. Although you will not be aware of it, it will stay with you, becoming part of your aura. It will give you clarity of thought and the power of persuasion. Ask your guide how to use it. You’re a strong man, Archie, but with this fresh clarity you will understand far more clearly the actions of others. As well as this, it will protect you against those who aim to hinder you. Use it as a shield to guard you from the Moon’s beam. You must go quickly, she will be rising soon.’

“Go where?” Archie got to his feet.

‘Back to the Hierophant’s cave, there’s no other shelter between here and there and no time. Look up at the sky, Archie. You must outrun her; run all the way.’

“Thank you,” Archie said, transfixed on the spectacular display of colour before him.

‘No thanks are needed. Now go, please....’

A strong wind blew from across the river and Grace’s rainbow dispersed, her voice was lost in the wind and in the fading sunlight she evaporated.

CHAPTER ELEVEN

THE MOON'S MALICE

For a moment or two Archie stood rooted to the spot staring in the direction of the rainbow not wanting to believe that both it and Grace had truly gone. Her warning echoed softly in his mind and with a qualm of fear he spun on his heel and set off running upstream into the wind. He came eventually to a fork where a tributary flowed into the river. Without pausing he leapt across it, jumping onto protruding boulders rife with rapids the white water gushing beneath him. On the other side he splashed through sludge along the eroding bank, mud dragging his bruised feet into swampy mire and slowing his progress. Moving away from the river he was soon on a rocky slope pounding uphill into drier but unknown territory. Now on level ground he was jumping over low bushes and hurdling bits of tree thrown randomly in his way by the buffeting gale. Fighting against the elements and at the edge of his endurance, Archie experienced a sudden feeling of euphoria, such as when he and Sarah had hurdled the garden fences all those years ago. It was a feeling that came to him from time to time when he pushed himself to the limit against severe physical challenges. And this sprint of his life to outrun the Moon was nothing if not severe. He was so filled with adrenalin he almost forgot to be afraid.

Archie had not a clue where he was, could think of nothing except reaching his destination. He visualized the caves hoping that by some alchemy his feet would take him there. So focused was he that he did not once look up to see the sun sinking below the horizon. He ran with all his might ignoring his burning lungs, the thorns and sticks piercing his feet. But even Archie's considerable strength was not inexhaustible and he had used much of it up fighting the river. Eventually his pace began to slow and his run became a jog. It took all his will power just to keep moving, but somehow he did. When finally he recognised features in the landscape he wept with relief his breath coming in great sobbing gasps. Not stopping to see if the flood waters had receded he jogged uphill above the trees where he had camped last night. At the top his legs almost gave way and he was forced to slow to a fast walk, doggedly pressing on across the plain until at last he reached the cliff edge where he had met Kriss. There he paused, gulping air into his overworked lungs and looking in the direction of the caves then out across the ocean at the sliver of red on the horizon. The sun had gone and the pale silvery light at his back told Archie what he most dreaded to know.

Breaking once more into a stumbling run he struggled towards the caves, which were now in his sights, but Archie was running on empty, there was quite simply no gas left in the tank. "I'm not going to make it," he gasped, sweat running down his nose as he keeled over clutching his chest. Behind him the Moon was fast climbing the sky. She was waning but her light took no time at all to spread out over the land creeping far and wide to craft her spooky ambiance. Archie could feel her beams fingering him where he lay. He pushed himself to his feet and swayed forward staring in desperation at the distant caves willing them to come to him.

"Arch, where are you going?" His mum's voice came through to him clearly, carried on the wind. Archie stopped dead, staring hard from left to right.

Another distant voice floated in. It was Felicity: "Keep walking, Archie, don't stop."

"Archie, come home, it's not the same without you." Mum's voice sounded nearer and stricken with grief; hearing it was agony.

"Remember where you are Archie," Felicity again. "Your mum's not with you on this island. It's trickery. Keep focused and get to Emrys' caves."

His mother moaned, "Tell me it's not true… it's a nightmare… I'll wake up in a minute." Archie knew she was crying. He began to sob.

"Put your hands over your ears and run, Archie, just run," Felicity's words were drowned by his mum's who seemed now to be standing beside him. Archie spun round, but there was nothing to see except sombre shadows cast by the Moon's light.

"It's all very well you gallivanting off my son," his mother sounded cross now. "Remember who you left behind. Come home a while and see the family. Helena's distraught; Stewart's behaving like a wounded bear and Daddy… well… Daddy is a broken man."

Archie's breath caught in his throat as a finger caressed his cheek. He knew his mother's touch instantly. Startled, he tried to grasp her hand, "Where are you?" he cried, "I can feel you, but I can't see you." Archie searched the air in front of him.

"I am right in front of you, Archie," his mum said sharply. It was a tone he had never heard her use before.

"I can't see…"

"Boo!"

Joanna stood barefoot before him, her hair loosely plaited and her dressing-gown blowing open in the wind to reveal floral pyjamas that were achingly familiar. "Come on Archie, let's go home," she said, taking him by the hand.

"Beware... it's an illusion..." Felicity's cry sighed in the wind.

At his mother's touch, Archie's awareness shifted. It was an excruciatingly painful experience. His body no longer felt solid. He dared not look at it to see what was happening to him. His mother squeezed his hand tight then suddenly let go.

"I've got you back now, Arch. I won't lose you again..." Joanna's voice trailed into a faint whisper. Archie screamed as her voice distorted and the whisper became a keening wail that completely overwhelmed him, drowning all his senses in a vortex of agony.

In the blink of an eye he was standing beside his parents' bed at 23, Eversely Avenue. They were sleeping and both looked pale and drawn. On the bedside chest, beside the Ventolin inhaler on Dad's side was an empty bottle of whisky. Archie frowned; Dad never used to drink spirits. He leant forward to touch his mum's cheek, but his hand had no substance and met with nothing falling straight through her body. He could neither touch anything nor speak, but it seemed he had retained a sense of smell for he caught the reek of whisky on her breath. He wanted to cry out; to weep, but all of his bubbling emotions were confined inside him. His inability to express them was unbearable. He felt like a swollen barrel ready to burst and it was more than he could bear.

Powerless to turn the door handle, Archie forced his mind through the bedroom door and out onto the landing. He saw Stewart in his bedroom, snoring quietly, his collection of bikers' mags strewn across the end of his bed. There was a pile of dirty clothes on a chair. A pair of muddy trainers had been thrown across the room and made a mark on the wall. An empty bottle of rum lay on the floor surrounded by squashed coke cans.

With increasing despair, Archie moved away. Helena's door was firmly shut. Gripped by an intense and inexplicable longing to open it he lingered outside. Someone was in there, but it could not be his sister, she was still in Australia. He tore himself away, backed off and glided to the stairs, there to gaze at the wall covered in his memories. Descending past photo after photo of happy smiling faces he reached the bottom and turned down the hall to enter the kitchen. There were dirty plates and wine glasses all over the place. Black sacks overflowed with leftovers and crisps and biscuit crumbs were scattered on the floor. Archie moved out through the back door to the patio; the light was on and moths flittered helplessly in its beam. Here too the chairs and tables had remnants of food and drink all over them. Piled on a long table by the house wall were layer upon layer of bouquets and wreaths, each with a card tucked neatly inside. He drifted over to them and bent to read the closest card, recognised Auntie Frances's handwriting:

'Dear Robert and Joanna, Helena and Stewart. Please accept these flowers in lieu

of the words we are unable to speak. We are so desperately sorry. All our thoughts

and prayers are with you in your grief. If there is anything at all we can do, just ask.

With deepest sympathy and all the love in the world, Tom and Frances, Gillian and Sally xxx

Appalled, Archie realised he was witnessing his family's bereavement: they were grieving for him. With no way of releasing his emotion he was in utter torment. He backed away from the flowers, 'Help me,' he cried in his head. 'Please someone help me… take me back… anything but this….'

"Very well, Archie, back we'll go," the Moon's cackling voice echoed around the patio. Archie felt his surroundings alter and with it so did his mind. He began to feel younger and more fearful, like a child. With dreadful clarity he recalled what Emrys had described - and then the memory was gone.

"Where're you taking me," he asked, petrified.

"Back… way back, Archie, to the beginning of your time." The Moon broke into hysterical laughter.

Archie felt his mind shrink further. He heard again the familiar voice of his mother, but this time she sounded young and excited. Archie felt himself a tiny baby lying in his father's arms. He could smell his dad's breath on his face and see Robert's huge face beaming down at him. He heard his mother say, "Well if not Archibald, let's call him 'Archie', he'd only end up being called Archie if we named him Archibald."

"That's it! Well done you, and thank you, my beautiful Jo," his father said. "He's perfect. I know in time, Archie and I will be the greatest of friends." Archie sensed his dad's kiss. He wanted to scream at him and with all his concentration he tried, but his effort was in vain; all he achieved was a squirming grimace. "Oh look, Jo, he's smiling at me," his dad said.

"I am going to move you on now, Archie," the Moon sighed in his head and the scene rapidly changed. He watched his life flashing before him in a splintered jumble of images and emotions. It was like the last time the Moon had tormented him, but infinitely more painful. Archie was in another eventuality now, running flat out up a Welsh mountain.

"NO… NO… NO!" the Moon shouted. "You are not stopping here, Archie," she said, her voice charged with anger. "I know your game, Emrys. You can't have him back. Only when he's as awry as you shall he return. I'll take him back further than his beginning if you interfere."

Archie thrashed and struggled in his astral form, utterly helpless, completely enslaved by the Moon's power. 'I'm sorry… I can't get back,' he screamed internally to anyone who could listen. Time seemed to stand still for a moment then at full speed his mind was again dragged backwards, blurred and muddled. As the years sped past him he could recollect only snippets of his life. It all ground to a halt on a day he really did not want to relive. He was in the centre of a revolving circle of ice dancers: Helena, Stewart, Mum and Dad, all laughing at him. Archie could hear himself speaking but was unaware of how he was doing it; he was trapped mute inside his own shell.

"Hey, let me out," he heard himself say. "You know I hate dancing. It's meant for girlies."

"Shan't..." Stewart was sticking out his tongue and shouting something else, but Archie's mind had raced ahead to the next scene: losing his footing, breaking through the circle and crashing down hard on the ice. He braced himself for what was to happen: 'Will it hurt as much a second time?' He felt no pain; he had no body so how could he feel? Nor did he panic or struggle to breathe; he was a ghost. He just let the darkness of the water devour him and waited for Felicity.

"Follow me," she beckoned. Archie forced his mind towards her outstretched hand. "Propel your aura, Archie," she whispered again and again. Archie was only inches from reaching her light, desperately trying to obey her but he had no idea how to propel his aura. Suddenly he was blinded by the wicked and brilliant white light of his tormentor.

"Ah, shame," the Moon teased, "did you think Hope would rescue you again? Further back we go. They're not doing you any favours are they Archie?"

'Where now?' cried Archie in his head.

"Somewhere Hope can't find you."

The Moon's cackle reminded Archie of the 'Wicked Witch of the West' and sent a shiver of terror straight through him. 'This is just a warped dream,' he tried to comfort himself. 'It'll be over soon.'

"And when it is, won't you know about it! You're going backwards again, Archie, back and back, tee hee hee," she screeched.

Once again Archie was propelled into a whirlwind of scenes, all his memories replayed in reverse and all without sound, until time stopped again and he was lying flat on his back in a dark place. His eyes were shut, but through his eyelids he could see a crack of light under a closed door. A low-voiced conversation was taking place behind it. Archie strained to hear.

"What are you doing?" It was his dad.

"I can't have another night like last night or the night before or the night before that," his mum said. She sounded tired and irritable. "I'm so tired, darling. I'm going to put Archie in his own room now. He's nearly seven weeks. It's silly him being in with us, all we do is wake each other up. I'm sure he will sleep for longer if he's completely undisturbed."

Frustrated by his helplessness, Archie tried to find the power of his aura; it was all he had to work with. In his mind, he pictured the calm pastel yellow Grace had given him, but nothing he did made any made difference. Apparently in a deep sleep his tiny body remained prone and his eyes closed. His efforts were interrupted by a strange dragging noise followed by a lot of banging and crashing outside the room, over it he heard his dad's voice.

"I don't think that cot is going through that door, honey, not unless you mean to bash through the door frame." Archie wanted to laugh and cry at his father's dry humour; it was so dear to him; so painfully pleasant to hear it again.

There was more bumping about and more talking. Archie waited for something to happen. 'Help; can anyone hear me? I need help. FELICITY, WHERE ARE YOU?' Archie tried again, thinking the cry as loud as he could in his mind while still attempting to push out an aura - anything to attract the attention of someone who might help him.

The door opened and a shadowy figure came towards him. It was his mum, Archie could smell her. Had he been able to weep at that moment he would have done so; the sweet, familiar scent of his mother was almost his undoing. He felt himself cradled in her arms, carried under bright light and back into darkness, being placed gently into his cot and covered with his special blanket, warm and soft and red. The door was pulled to and he was left alone. The last thing he knew of this horrific nightmare was his dad's whisper: "What if we can't hear him cry?"

As Archie waited in suspense for the Moon's next torture the blanket seemed to devour his body sucking him violently downwards into a whirling vortex the colour of blood. Was he being taken back into his mother's womb? Archie screamed in horror, 'God! Please no!'

A shrill screech of anger pierced his eardrums and the vortex faded. He was covered completely in heavy red material and being carried, jolted and thrown about in someone's arms. Archie tried to call out, to move, but his cocooned body was consumed with pain and he could hardly breathe. His fingers brushed against something solid. It dawned on him that his body had substance again and that what he could feel was his own leg. He was no longer a ghost, this was not a twisted memory, it was happening now. He became convinced that he was back in Transit, but whose were the arms that clasped so firmly around his body? He could hear feet thudding beneath him and a man's voice muttering, "Don't look back, just keep running."

Archie could hardly bring himself to believe he had escaped the Moon. The relief made his head swim and he felt numb with gratitude to whoever carried him. It had to be someone with incredible strength: the feet were pounding fast over the ground, stumbling at times. "She nearly had you didn't she," the voice panted. "You ran well though mate, certainly impressed me." There was gasping as the man endeavoured to control his breathing. "Not a pretty face on that one tonight. A silver sickle fickle witch is what she is." The voice was vaguely familiar to Archie; he tried to place it. The man kept on running. There was a sudden jolt and a thud then a terrifying sensation of falling. The arms released him and he felt himself lying on something hard and cold. The cover was whipped away.

Archie blinked and tried to focus. He was lying on the stone floor of the cave and Kriss, Felicity and Emrys were looming over him. Only then did he identify his carrier as Kriss and the red cover as the big man's cape. Archie could not speak, he was shaking uncontrollably and he felt sick.

"Is he okay?" asked Felicity, her voice taut with anxiety, her aura glowing so brightly it made Archie's eyes water to look at her.

Kriss, the red cape hanging over his arm, leaned in, "Archie, can you hear us?"

'You saved me,' Archie thought. He tried to lift his head and talk, but he had not the strength. His head crashed back to the stone floor and his vision blurred.

"Give him space," Emrys' hindquarters nudged the other two aside. "When I was caught by that witch I was sick for days. He'll need to sleep." He peered down, "You'll be okay, Archie; you fought against her well. I almost got you back on the mountain, but she was too clever for me. I'm sorry I could not save you. I thank God that Kriss succeeded where I failed. Rest now, you are safe among friends. We will talk when you wake."

Felicity had disappeared from sight, but as Emrys turned away he summoned Kriss forward to replace the cape. Archie closed his eyes, thought, 'Thank you,' and fell instantly asleep beneath the warmth of its heavy folds.

***

He slept for two days and two nights and when he woke he had a hunger that seemed to burn. It was daylight outside the caves and the sun was shining low in the sky.

Felicity sat close by, grinding something with a battered pestle and mortar.

"Hi," Archie's voice was croaky and hoarse.

"You're awake! Oh, thank goodness. Don't move, let me get Emrys," the star flustered, dropping her work and rushing out of the cave mouth. The centaur appeared in moments, followed by Felicity carrying a large wooden food bowl.

"Did you finish the grinding?" Emrys asked.

"Yes… here." Felicity floated over to where she had been milling and sprinkled three pinches of the mixture over an array of greenery in the bowl.

"Archie, eat and drink before you move or speak. You may even need to sleep again." The centaur sat down heavily beside his patient, staring at him intently as Archie tucked into another of Emrys' salads. It was as tasty as the last one but with a little more spice to it. The bulk of it was clover - he was eating clover!

"That's for your understanding of what's real and what can be imagined," Emrys said, reading Archie's mind. "Don't speak. The white roots are raw ginseng, which will help improve your memory. It's the king of herbs; it saved my mind to a degree. The yellow flowers are false dandelion, to help you understand the vastness of your consciousness. You look as though you are enjoying it." Archie managed a smile through eating.

"Felicity, water please," Emrys ordered.

By pure magic, Felicity once again produced a large glass of water out of thin air. It reminded Archie poignantly of Grace and her jugs of tears. He swallowed, smiled shyly at Felicity, nodded his thanks and took a few slow sips.

"I don't like to think what would've happened to you if Grace hadn't blessed your aura with yellow and Kriss hadn't been around to see it glow," Felicity blurted out, unable to contain herself any longer.

"Hope, be quiet; he must rest," scolded Emrys.

"I know, I know."

"I t-t-think I'm okay," Archie stuttered.

"I know you're okay, my son, but you must not speak until you're perfectly well. It's crucial to the healing process. I'm talking about the matter of remembering your past and not remembering it. Retain your strength please," Emrys insisted.

Archie sighed, lay back down. His hide tunic looked a bit the worse for wear; he pulled the red cape up over his legs. He had hoped his trials were over, but apparently not.

"Kriss will be along later," Felicity whispered. "He's very wily and playful at most, but boy is he good in a crisis!" She stifled her customary giggle and it came out as a snort.

"HOPE! If I have to tell you one more time I shall send you out. Be quiet," demanded Emrys.

"He doesn't have to answer does he? Felicity argued. "It must be nice to hear someone speaking when you've been asleep for over two nights." Archie's eyes widened at the length of time he had slept.

"Listen little Miss Twinkle, be quiet or OUT, do you understand?" Emrys' gruff voice echoed angrily through the cave. Felicity did not seem perturbed by his harsh tone, she simply hovered for a moment twiddling her hair, staring straight back at Emrys her eyebrows raised. Then she shrugged, flew to the cave mouth and disappeared from sight.

For the first time since he had lost his St Christopher medallion, Archie's fingers strayed to his neck. He almost expected to find it had been miraculously restored to him and was disappointed to find it was not there. It got him to thinking about Sarah, who had given it to him, and in that moment he missed her so acutely it was a physical pain. Shifting his position he gazed up at the roof of the cave and pictured her smiling down at him. After a time Emrys, who was watching him closely, "Hurrumphed". Archie took the hint and closed his eyes, and soon thereafter he slept.

CHAPTER TWELVE

1997

WAR: A BLOODY GAME BOYS INSTINCTIVELY PLAY

"It is a way of life. REME exists to keep the punch in the Army's fist!" The speaker raised his fist and punched the air to illustrate his point and the outgoing cadets, for whom this seminar was intended, gave a muted cheer. Not that they lacked enthusiasm, but Major William Clift was a tall, broad and fierce looking man with a chest full of medals and they were a little in awe of him.

This was the first time Archie had laid eyes upon the Major, though they all knew him by repute. The Army Cadet Force, which Archie had joined seven years ago at the age of twelve, had invited Clift to talk about career opportunities in the Royal Electrical and Mechanical Engineers, of which he was a leading member.

"Join REME and you'll live life to the full," he continued. "Adventure, responsibility and travel can all be part of your working life. Whatever your role, you'll be a professional; a highly trained expert in your field, with real responsibility for the safety and security of others. You'll be kitted out with the best weapons, equipment, transport, and information technology systems. You could take advantage of excellent training and earn practical and professional qualifications that will set you up for life."

The presentation continued in like vein for almost an hour, but Major Clift was preaching to the converted as far as Archie was concerned. His mind had been set before the seminar had even begun. REME was going to be his next adventure. He had been dreaming about real-life action almost since the day he was born.

"The nature of the job means REME often finds itself at the sharp end of an Army operation or close to the frontline, reacting to whatever situation arises," the Major said, winding up. "Army equipment is built to cope in the most punishing of environments, but breakdowns happen and it's REME that gets things moving again," he concluded.

When the applause had died down and the seminar dispersed, Archie and James made their way home in Archie's revamped Land Rover. James sat quietly in the passenger seat fiddling with the radio.

"How do you think your mum and dad will react when you tell them?" Archie asked. He was in some trepidation about breaking the news to his own parents, but he knew it would be a lot harder for James.

"Mum and Dad are too lost in grief over Mal at the moment. Nothing I say or do will match up to his death. Some days I'm sure they don't even notice if I'm there or not."

Archie could hear the raw emotion in his friend's voice. James's brother Malcolm had been killed in an unprovoked street knifing six months earlier and the family were still trying to come to terms with their loss.

"To be honest, I need to get away." James finally succeeded in tuning in to a music station. "It was Mal's dream you know, to fight for his country. I think he'd be with us in this... if he were still alive."

Glancing up from the road to look at his friend's taut face Archie was lost for words, all he could manage was a sympathetic smile.

"What're you going to say to yours?" James asked at length, clearing his throat and rubbing a hand across his eyes.

"I'm not sure. I suppose I'll just go with it when I get in. I'm worried about Mum's reaction most. She'll probably say it's great, but part of me feels really guilty. Being away so much and in hostile conditions at some point... well, you know." Archie drove on autopilot, his head spinning with a potent mixture of excitement and nervousness at what was to come.

"It's a way of life isn't it? Like Major Clift said. The job comes first," James drummed his fingers on the dash as they joined a queue of traffic.

"That's for sure. What're you going to say to Helena?"

"Do you think it'll break us up?" James dodged Archie's question.

"It's a tough one," Archie shrugged. Helena and James had been friends for years, but after Malcolm was murdered their friendship had developed. Helena's affable and sympathetic ear had transformed their relationship into a compulsive need to be together. Archie was finding it hard to swallow. From a purely selfish point of view his baby sister and his best mate were not the best combination. At the start he had played the role of protective big brother on the one hand, while maintaining the role of cool mate on the other, but it was taking its toll and to his disgust six months down the line his role seemed to have changed to that of gooseberry. He refused to allow he was a touch jealous that his sister had purloined his best friend. "I can't imagine too many relationships survive when you're away six to nine months at a time," he said, "but then again, some do. More importantly, what do you think?"

"I don't know. I suppose we're both still young, she's only seventeen after all. I guess if it's meant to be it's meant to be." James smiled, "We'll just have to wait and see."

Once the traffic shifted along Eversely Avenue, Archie put his foot down and soon he was pulling into the driveway and parking up behind Helena's old black Escort. "Hello, we're back," he roared from the hall, knowing his sister would most likely be upstairs hiding in her bedroom.

"Hiya," Helena's shout confirmed.

Wandering through to the kitchen, Archie threw his keys on the table and flicked on the kettle. "Cuppa?" he asked James, who had followed him in.

"Thanks." Clearly agitated, James leaned against the table fiddling with the keys. 'What am I going to say to her?' he mouthed.

"You'll be fine. Helena will be okay; just tell her," Archie responded in a loud whisper.

"Tell me what?" Helena, wearing an old pair of ripped jeans and crumpled t-shirt, was leaning casually on the wall by the open kitchen door.

"Whoops!" Archie grinned at his sister, "Cup of tea, Hels?"

"Tell me what?" Helena repeated, ignoring her brother and staring at James. He stared back at her, eyes wide, speechless. "You look like rabbit caught in the headlights," she smiled. "It can't be that bad."

Busying himself with making the tea, Archie looked up and nodded supportively at his friend. "Yeah, go on mate," he prompted, "tell her."

James dropped his gaze, mutely found himself a chair and sat down, apparently still unable to find the right words.

Exasperated, Archie blurted out, "We're signing up."

"Oh… right." Helena eyed James from doorway. "That's great," she continued coolly, walking into the kitchen, seemingly not at all put out by this momentous news. "I could've seen that coming a mile off. When do you start?" She elbowed her brother out of the way and took over the tea making.

"September, I guess," James spoke at last, a nervous smile lighting up his features.

Helena handed him his cup of tea. "The hat'll really suit you both," she grinned, defusing the tension.

"Gee thanks," Archie mocked. "Where's Mum and Dad – do you know when they'll be home?"

"I was going to ask you the same thing," Helena said. "I'm babysitting next door tonight. Are you going to be about James?"

"I've no plans," her boyfriend smiled broadly, his relief plain to see.

"Talk of the devil," Archie muttered as the back door banged open. "They're back," he looked at his friend and pulled a comical face.

"Good luck mate," James said picking up his cup of tea and following Helena out of the kitchen.

"ARCHIE," Robert's voice boomed, as he strode in the back door. "You need to nudge the Land Rover up a bit. The Merc's hanging out in the street."

The Mercedes was a fairly recent acquisition: Robert's job as a chauffeur credited him with a brand spanking limousine. It had every extra imaginable and looked bizarrely out of place sitting on the rugged tarmac drive of the Fletchers' humble home. Joanna, overloaded with shopping, struggled in directly behind him followed swiftly by the now acne-ridden Stewart and his gaunt and stumpy cousin, Dominic, both fourteen.

"Can I move it?" begged Stewart.

"No," came a chorus of voices from every corner of the room.

"Oh go on, please, it's not like I'm on the road or anything. It's a private driveway." He forced the same excuse on them each time.

"Which you need consent to drive on," reminded Joanna, who desperately disliked her youngest son manoeuvring the vehicles around. It almost always resulted in damage of one sort or another.

"Dad?" Stewart begged his easy target.

"Tell you what, you can nudge the Escort up beside the garage instead." Robert winked at Joanna, who frowned.

"Okay," whinged Stewart, disappointed. He shot off, waving the Escort keys disdainfully under Dominic's nose just as Helena and James reappeared with empty teacups in hand and their coats on.

"Where're you two off to?" Joanna dumped her bags on the table.

"We're going to the video shop. I'm babysitting next door at eight and James is helping me." Helena clasped her boyfriend's hand, "We're going to get some nibbles. Anyone want anything?"

"A movie with popcorn sounds like awful hard work, Hels. All hands on deck, eh?" teased Archie, grabbing up his keys and ruffling Dominic's hair on his way out of the back door.

"Oh, shut up," Helena called after him.

"Helena, don't say that please," her mother admonished.

"And don't you call your sister 'Hels', Archie, her name's Helena," Robert said, following Archie out of the door.

Waiting for Stewart to move the Escort, Archie sat deep in thought in his pristine Land Rover. He had been going to ask Dominic where Sarah was, but changed his mind not wanting to attract Helena's mockery. Uppermost in his mind was how he was going to deliver news of his career decision to his parents.

"You going to move this vehicle, or what?" his father asked, climbing in beside him.

"Waiting for Stewart," Archie said.

For a moment they both watched as Stewart revved up the Escort to create as much noise as possible and proceeded to reverse and straighten it up. "You okay?" Robert asked quietly. "You look a bit anxious about something. Want to talk, Buster?"

"Yes, I… I'm okay." Archie drew breath and went straight on the offensive. "I've decided to join the REME Dad... that is, I think so." Not wanting to see his father's expression, he stared through his steering wheel at the Escort, which despite the high revs moved forward only slowly, hazards and wipers going.

"You think so?" Robert turned to his son, "Why the uncertainty? I think it's a brilliant idea."

"You do?" Archie could hardly have dared hope for such a positive response.

"I always knew you'd follow in Grandad Fletcher's footsteps and join the forces one day. You're like him in so many ways – and admirable footsteps they are too." Robert put his hand on his son's shoulder and gave it a squeeze, tears welling. Archie smiled, a lump in his throat. He had not known what to expect from his father, but whatever else he had not anticipated tears.

"I'm proud of you, Arch, I think it's the best decision you've ever made. It means a lot to you doesn't it?"

"It's everything I've ever dreamt of," Archie struggled to contain his emotion, his voice wobbling with relief. "Vehicles on a mega scale, the action, the duty, the uniform and all for Queen and Country. It's everything."

"I'm really proud of you, son, really proud," Robert repeated, a tear rolling down his cheek. He dashed it away, his lips quirking in an apologetic smile. "Nanny and Granddad would be too and so-"

He was interrupted by a gentle tap on the window. Deeply preoccupied both looked up startled. Stewart was grinning cockily through the glass. "I did it!" he shouted, hopping from one foot to the other.

Robert gave Stewart the thumbs up. "It seems we have a budding Damon Hill on our hands," he murmured as he opened the door and climbed out. Archie was still chuckling when his father leaned back in, "I was only going to say Mum will be as proud as I am, but tell her gently, eh?"

As soon has Robert had closed the car door, Archie turned the ignition key. "Yes!" he shouted, drumming his hands on the steering wheel and bursting into involuntary laughter, thrilled by his dad's reaction. 'Now I just need to tell Mum,' he thought, sobering instantly.

Once he was perfectly parked tight to the garage Archie jumped out of the Land-Rover and almost fell on top of Sarah, who was clutching a great bunch of sunflowers behind her back. With her long blonde hair and slender, stunning figure she had developed into an extremely attractive young woman. Archie and his twin-cousin had maintained a close friendship even though Sarah had been sent away to boarding school. They phoned and wrote at least once a week and Archie was a regular visitor to her Saturday lacrosse matches. When they both left school and went to different universities their habit of regular contact had continued, interspersed with meeting up during the holidays. Today, as always, they were delighted to see each other and both beamed from ear to ear.

"Hi, how come you guys are here?" Archie nodded to the kitchen window where he could see Auntie Pat and Uncle Jack laughing about something with his mum.

"We've been visiting Nanny Walker in town. Just for the day - we're going home tonight."

"Great, so you're with us for the rest of the afternoon?" Archie beamed.

"Looks that way."

"What's with the flowers?"

"Oh yes, they're for you. Congratulations," Sarah threw the gorgeous yellow flowers at his chest. There were tears in her eyes and her bottom lip was quivering.

"What's this all about?" Archie raised a perplexed eyebrow.

"I bumped into Hels and James at the shops. They told me you're going to sign up. I just wanted to let you know I think it's great. You're the man for the job if ever there was one… but I've a request," Sarah paused looking Archie in the eye, "just don't be a hero, okay?" She smiled breaking the tension of her words, but her eyes welled further.

"You're a special girl, Sarah. Crazy, but special all the same. Come here," Archie grabbed hold of his cousin and hugged her hard. They stood entwined for some time, Sarah sobbing uncontrollably.

"God, I'm sorry. Forgive me," she said at length. "I don't know what's come over me. I really do think it's marvellous, Archie. I just can't help crying." Sarah, attempting to brush away her streaming tears with her shoulder, gave up and plunged her hand deep into the pocket of her slouching jeans to retrieve a tissue.

"You're so sweet," Archie said. "Nobody's ever given me flowers before. Thank you." He squeezed his cousin again genuinely thrilled by her gift.

"Ha, you're welcome. The wet patch on your shoulder comes with them. You need to put them in water," Sarah sniffed, wiping away the remnants of her mascara from her now blotchy red face.

"I may never have received flowers before but I've a rough idea of how to look after them," Archie teased.

"Have you told your folks yet?"

"I've told Dad and I've a feeling Mum will know by now. Do Auntie Pat and Uncle Jack know too?" Archie felt his angst heighten.

"I don't think so. I went to the shop to buy some fags. I haven't seen Mum and Dad since I found out, so I've not told them."

"Oh, Sarah, you're not still smoking! When are you going to give that up, it's vile." Archie rolled his eyes in disgust. "Aside from which, you'll never get to see old age."

"Hark who's talking! And anyway, Mum and I have a pact: when she gives up so will I."

Choosing to ignore her barb, Archie grinned, "You only do it to annoy her don't you? I'd put money on you giving up before she does. It's just not cool enough for you."

"Maybe. Shall we do the walk?" Lighting up a cigarette, Sarah walked slowly out of the driveway.

"Okay, but don't breathe in my direction. One second." Hastily Archie pulled open the car door again and leaned in towards the glove compartment retrieving an envelope. Shoving it into his back pocket he caught Sarah up and still cradling his sunflowers kept pace with her.

They walked in companionable silence for a while heading for the park, Sarah puffing on her cigarette. She inhaled deeply, letting the smoke out slowly, "How was Uncle Robert when you told him?"

"Good actually; he was really pleased… said he was proud of me."

"I'll bet he is. You'll be following in Grandad Fletcher's footsteps now then. He was a Para in the Second World War, wasn't he?" Sarah drew in another hideously long drag. "What do you think your mum's going to say?" Smoke came billowing out of her nose and mouth as she spoke.

Archie turned his head away, wrinkling his nose. "To be honest, I don't have a clue." They walked into the park and along their usual path leading to the lake, stopping when they passed behind the thicket of fir trees. "What do you think she'll say?"

"She'll be fine. She must've known it was coming, it's not like it's a surprise." Sarah grimaced, "I take it you're aware of the horrendous possibilities of war breaking out again in the Middle East? It's like a tinderbox out there," Sarah, a pacifist, sighed. "But don't let me get started," she smiled up at him. "It's a big thing, Arch, what you're doing, but like I said you're the man for the job. I'll feel safe knowing you're defending our country."

"Thanks," Archie returned her smile, his hand nervously fumbling with the envelope in his back pocket.

"You're welcome," she grinned, her eyes brimming with more tears.

"Hey, you, what's up?" Tucking the sunflowers under his arm, Archie rubbed Sarah's shoulders. "Nothing to cry about," he comforted. "I'll be fine."

"Of course you will; it's just that once you're gone I'll hardly ever see you."

"But it's not like we see much of each other these days anyway. I don't suppose you'll even notice I'm away half the time."

"I know. I just feel like..." Sarah paused, staring up at him and holding her breath as though searching for words. Sighing she shrugged and flinging down her cigarette ground it under her heel.

Archie cupped her chin, wiping away her tears with his thumb. "I didn't want to make you cry," he said softly. "So tell me, what do you feel like?"

"Nothing, it doesn't matter." She looked away and moved a step back from him. "You'll get to see the entire world you lucky devil. Here look, take this," she fumbled with the clasp of a silver necklace half hidden beneath her t-shirt, pulled it out and handed it to him. He held it up watching the St Christopher medallion revolving slowly on its chain.

"I can't take this; you've worn it for years."

"Yes you can. I want you to have it."

"Wow, really? Thank you so much, this is great. But won't you need him on your travels?"

"Not as much as you'll need him on yours. St Christopher will protect you. He's the patron saint and protector of travellers, invoked against storms and plagues, or so I read." As she spoke, Sarah took it back and helped Archie put it round his neck. "You may need to buy a longer chain but it will do the job for now. Mind those sunflowers, you're about to drop them," she smiled.

"Thanks," Archie fingered the medallion. The chain hung much higher on his throat than it had on Sarah's slender neck. "It's going to be quite an adventure. What were you going to say before - about how you feel?"

"No really, it doesn't matter… well, if you must know, I just had a silly dream last night that's all. It was really weird and vivid."

"What happened?"

"It was you and me. I think that's why I'm feeling so emotional." Sarah blew her nose on her soggy tissue.

"Well go on, tell me what happened," Archie persisted.

"Nothing happened as such, like I said it was weird. We were in a big black void and I was hugging you and sobbing 'please forgive me'. I didn't feel sad though; it was a happy sob, like you'd come home or something. It was just so vivid," she repeated. "Like it was really happening, you know?"

"Please forgive you for what?" Archie asked, perturbed.

"How the hell should I know, it was a dream. I haven't a clue how to analyse it. But it was like you were actually there. When I woke up I was still sobbing. Don't think I went back to sleep to be honest, so I'm tired as well as emotional," she grinned.

"I've had dreams like that." Archie pulled out the envelope from his back pocket and held it in two hands in front of him.

"You have?" Sarah searched Archie's face as though seeking reassurance, then looked down at the envelope.

"Yeah, really vivid, where you can physically feel another person and hear them like they're actually speaking, you know? Once it was so loud I woke up thinking someone was in my room. I thought I was being haunted..." embarrassed, his voice trailed away.

"Exactly," Sarah beamed. "They're more than just dreams. Maybe there's a parallel universe or something. Mine was much too real to be nothing." When Archie made no comment, she said, "Do you believe in all that stuff? I mean, do you think that possibly there could be another tiny me and another brave you out there somewhere? What about life after this?" Sarah questioned eagerly. "I don't believe death is the end. I just have this feeling there is more. What do you think?"

Archie shivered. "Sarah... listen," he looked her straight in the eye. "I need you to do something for me," he almost whispered. "I wrote this letter to you years ago... I can barely remember what's in it. I must have been about fourteen." Sarah took the letter out of Archie's hands. "Please don't open it. Promise me you won't." Archie's stare never faltered but bore harder into Sarah's with intense sincerity.

"I promise... but why?" Confused, Sarah looked down at the blank envelope.

"This is going to sound strange okay, but only in the event of my death should you open that letter." Archie found himself struggling to hold his own tears back.

"Oh Arch don't even think it, please," fresh tears sprang into Sarah's eyes as she shook her head at the mere thought.

"I know, I know. Just put it in a safe place, don't lose it. You'll probably be waiting a while yet." Archie chuckled trying to lighten the tone. Sarah's dream sounded like a premonition to him and it made him feel uncomfortable. "As for life after death... seeing is believing," he said shortly, cutting the topic dead.

Sarah was watching him closely, "You cold?"

"No," he forced a chuckle. "Someone just walked over my grave." Thinking he was punning, Sarah giggled.

"Are you still going to travel?"Archie changed the subject. In his younger and quieter moments he had often thought about the afterlife and pondered on the significance of psychic happenings, but rarely had he been tempted to voice his thoughts. It wasn't that he had no faith; he did - a very strong one at that, but mostly he kept it to himself. There had been that strange experience under the ice, which he could never quite forget but had told no one. His view about what happens after death stemmed, he felt, from wishful thinking and like many another's was delusional.

"Yes, of course, I can't wait." At the mention of travelling, Sarah's face lit up, her dream instantly forgotten. "I haven't started yet and I've got the bug already. I've even saved up enough for half my round-the-world ticket!"

"Wow! Where will you go?" Archie was relieved to be on safer ground.

"America, Australia, Hong Kong," Sarah reached for another cigarette, but with a glance at her cousin changed her mind. She turned away and gazed through the trees at the traffic backing up on the street outside the park, the fug of fumes polluting the air around them.

"Sounds good," Archie stared at the back of her head. "Who are you going with?"

"Me, myself and I," Sarah swung round and grinned.

"Really? You'd go all those places by yourself?" Archie was astonished.

"Yeah... Why not? It may be the only chance I get. It'll be a really big adventure," Sarah giggled at his expression.

Archie laughed, he could see she loved the thought of it. His twin adored being unruly and wild, defying all logic and commonsense. She was a bit like him in that respect. It had got them both into trouble on numerous occasions as children.

"You never know," Sarah arched a teasing eyebrow, "I may meet up with some gorgeous guy who wants to travel the world hunting for 'Stripy' in the jungle and swimming with 'Jaws' on the reefs," she chuckled.

"Now he would be a lucky devil," Archie said, putting his arm around his cousin and guiding her back along the path. "Let's go home and see what's happening shall we?"

Joanna was waiting in the driveway to meet them. Sarah pulled away from Archie's encircling arm, taking the bedraggled sunflowers away from him. "I'll pop these in some water for you," she said, throwing a piece of gum in her mouth as she marched towards the house.

"Did Sarah buy you those? She's so sweet," Joanna smiled.

"Yeah," Archie agreed, anxiously searching her face. "Dad's told you I-"

"Yes," Joanna interrupted. She flung her arms around her son and kissed him, "No need to look like that, Arch, I think it's great – really." She stood back to look up into his eyes, "It's a real hardcore decision you've made."

Desperate for her approval, Archie met his mother's steady gaze without flinching. "Do you think it's a good one, Mum?"

"Yes, darling, I do. I think possibly you were born for the job and I could not be any prouder if I tried." Joanna grinned up at her towering firstborn and he laughed with relief. "I want you to do whatever makes you happy." She stood on tiptoe, reaching up to touch his face, smoothing an unruly strand of hair off his forehead. "Just look at you," she said, her eyes brimming. "You'll always be my special boy, Arch. You're a grown man now, more than capable of making your own mind up, freewill to do as you please. I think you've made a really positive decision. You'll have a good trade and a secure job and what is more you'll love it. What else could a mother want for her son, eh?" she gave him a watery smile.

"Thanks Mum." He flushed, swallowed the lump in his throat and mutely fought back tears.

"That's not to say I won't miss and worry about you every second you're gone, mind - the perils of war should never be taken lightly. But that's what us mums do; it's our job!" With a wry smile, Joanna fingered the silver chain around his neck. "What's this?"

Archie pulled up the medallion to show her. "Sarah gave it to me," he said shyly.

"I'm glad. St Christopher will look after you when I no longer can." She put her arm around his waist and together they walked slowly back to the house.

CHAPTER THIRTEEN

HAVE INITIATIVE, COURAGE AND A READINESS TO HELP OTHERS

'Has another day passed… or is it still the light of the same day?' Archie wondered, waking to the sound of Emrys' raised voice. Felicity had returned.

"Another two days have passed, Archie," she giggled. He was getting used to her ability to read his thoughts and grinned up at her. "You must've been wiped out," she said. "Emrys and I have prepared you another meal." Felicity passed Archie a food bowl. "I've been granted permission to speak to you again by His Highness the Hierophant." She glanced over at Emrys and gave him a cheeky wink. "He gets bad-tempered sometimes but it's just frustration," she stared around the cave, "he's been trapped in here a long time."

"That's enough, Hope," Emrys shook his head at her. "Let's get on with healing the patient, eh? Archie, eat!"

Feeling ten times better than the last time he had tried, Archie sat up. "How many years have you been here, Emrys?" he asked, shovelling leaves into his mouth; he was getting a taste for them now.

"I could only guess, my friend, it seems like forever… but maybe twelve or so."

Nodding thoughtfully, Archie chewed in silence for a moment. The salad seemed to be doing its job. He looked up at the centaur and noticed the dog collar; it sparked a memory.

If the vicar on the mountain had truly been Emrys – and he was convinced it had - he could not have been here quite that long for their weird encounter in Wales was barely eleven years ago. But he guessed the imprisonment must feel like a lot longer to the centaur. Archie stopped chewing and eyed him closely, "Does the name St Digain's mean anything to you?" Emrys stared blankly back at him. Disappointed to see no recognition in his eyes, Archie prompted, "It's probably just a coincidence, only I think we might've met before."

"I do not doubt it," Emrys smiled. "You are obviously feeling better. To have gone through such an ordeal and still be capable of realising that is fantastic. I'm afraid it is irrelevant to me, but for you nothing around here is a coincidence. It is all happening for a reason: your every moment is relevant to you and your passing."

"But what if you're wrong and it's relevant to your passing as well?" Archie frowned with concentration, wanting to help Emrys to remember and perhaps find a way to escape being trapped forever in this cave.

"Never mind me. What we need to do now is find the bridge and get you over it," Emrys said, sidestepping Archie's question. "The longer you're in Transit the greater the danger of your becoming a lost soul. Most souls don't even realise they've crossed the bridge until they're over, but it is not so for you." Emrys squinted at Archie, "There's a tiny part of you that believes you're not ready to cross." His gray eyes widened and he nodded to himself, "It is because you hesitated, and now you must face that hesitation. You will be challenged and each time you will have to make a choice: do you stay or do you go? But remember, my friend, you cannot go back."

Archie listened intently, desperate to understand what Emrys was telling him. "You're right. I have to go, but you'll come too? Where is this bridge? Let's go find it right now." He started getting to his feet. Felicity moved quickly, hovering above him to stop his progress.

"Just wait a minute," Emrys said. "The bridge isn't hard to find, but as I've told you before, there's great danger. Your mind has conjured up some amazing obstacles so far. You must try to tame your imagination, Archie, find the part in your heart that wants to cross. You have to let go and stop behaving all the time as though you're charging into battle."

"You're saying that my mind is my obstacle?" Archie said slowly, striving for understanding, echoes of what Grace had said to him about letting go clicking into place.

"Yes," Emrys confirmed.

"You said I hesitated. When was that? Do you know?"

"Of course – it was when you lost hope."

Archie shook his head in an attempt to clear his muddled thoughts. He still did not understand his impediment. He hadn't lost Felicity, she was still here, fluttering above him and getting in his way. "I have to get you out of here, Emrys. When I cross that bridge you're coming with me, come hell or high water."

"Hell and high water it may be, Archie, but not for me. My hell is here. I cannot leave these caves, it is impossible. Firstly, I am physically incapable of climbing the overhang to the cliff top. Believe me I've tried. Secondly, even should I succeed, if the Moon catches me her curse will duplicate tenfold. In that case I would lose the precious fragments of knowledge I have retained and that would be Hell indeed. I'm sorry to disappoint you, son, I want nothing more than to cross with you, but I am indeed cursed."

"We'll reverse the curse," Archie argued in desperation.

"How would you do that?" Emrys said.

"I don't know, but someone must, even if I have to ask the Moon herself."

"Now you're being ridiculous," Emrys frowned.

Felicity buzzed with excitement, "I might know someone." There was immediate silence as two sets of enquiring eyes turned to stare at her.

"You mean there's a chance I can get out of this predicament and you've never thought to tell me so before?" Emrys, clearly annoyed, sounded even gruffer than usual.

"It's not something I can do for you myself, Emrys," Felicity looked as though she were about to burst into tears. "It is no place for stars, I cannot go there and there was no point in giving you false hope."

"Go where?" Emrys and Archie shouted in unison.

"To where the lilies grow by the river," Felicity hesitated, looking from one to the other, "at night ... if you dare," she whispered, as though afraid someone might be prying outside the cave. "There is said to be a girl there who knows the secret to every man's soul, its purpose and its destiny. Some stars call her the 'Keeper of Secrets' and it is said she is as powerful as the Moon." Felicity looked down at her feet, her voice hushed. "Many have tried to talk with her but I know of no one who has succeeded." She peeped up at them and looked so like a naughty schoolgirl that Archie almost laughed.

"Why? Is she mute?" he teased, playing along.

Felicity shook her head. "She is protected by monsters. It is said they attack anyone who tries to speak to her in daylight. It is also said they have the strength of ten bulls, they are green, have no faces and are armoured with invisible toxic spines."

Archie laughed out loud. "And I thought I was the one with the imagination round here! Anyway, aren't you forgetting I'm already dead? How could your so-called spiky monsters harm me?" he sniggered.

"You think I'm lying?" Felicity gave him a withering look and Emrys "Hurrumphed."

"You mean you're serious? I'm sorry, I thought you were joking.

"It is hardly a joking matter, Archie," the centaur shook his head.

Felicity frowned, "You think only in terms of life or death, Archie, but there is so much more. Unless you wish to remain forever in torment you must avoid these monsters. They are demons, but they cannot harm you after dark."

"But the Moon can. I dare not travel at night."

"You must journey to the lily grove in daylight then hide until it is dark. Once you're with the Keeper of Secrets the Moon cannot reach you. She has no power there," insisted Felicity.

Archie gazed at her in silence. He was still not convinced, though Felicity clearly believed this nonsense. "I was there before, you know, where the lilies grow. Why did I not see this Keeper of Secrets and her monsters then?"

"Perhaps because you did not know they were there. I expect you felt their presence though."

He nodded recalling the overwhelming sense that someone was watching him on the river bank. So enraptured had he been by Grace's appearance he had forgotten that till now. "If I go to her will she know how to reverse Emrys' curse?"

"Like I said, she's the Keeper of Secrets. She knows the path of every soul. She can help, Archie, I'm sure of it," Felicity looked up at him a spark of hope shining in her eyes. It was infectious and Archie grinned at her as he struggled to his feet, adrenalin beginning to pump in his veins.

"Now just hang on a moment you two," Emrys put out a restraining hand. "Archie, you are running out of time," he said urgently. "You must be over the bridge before dusk tomorrow. No soul who lingers in Transit manages to cross and you've been here eight nights already, it is far too long. There is no time to seek out some elusive lily girl - the risk of failure is too great, you will be lost. Besides, even if she could help me - which I doubt - I do not warrant it, and most certainly not at the expense of your soul." He moved to stand across the cave entrance ready to block any attempts to get past him.

"What do you mean you don't warrant it? Are you saying you deserve to stay here for eternity? Is that what you really think?" Archie snapped, locking his gaze with Emrys.

The centaur broke first, hanging his head and looking to the floor. "You'd go there… risk your soul for a deformed beast like me?" his voice wobbled.

"The Moon may have warped your physical form, but your soul is not deformed. Aside from which, my dad always told me if I could ever help another being, whatever their appearance, then I should. You helped me in my despair. You healed me, comforted me and shared with me your wisdom and as you once told me on a Welsh mountain – even if you don't remember it – you are my friend. Of course I'm going to help you."

For the first time since they had met, Archie reached out with affection to touch Emrys, grasping his shoulder and squeezing it tightly. "Please, my friend, just let me try."

CHAPTER FOURTEEN

A HIDDEN SECRET

At dusk the sky was crimson, the air sultry and the land perfectly silent and still. Archie calculated he had just over two hours before the sun disappeared. It would take at least one of those to reach the lily grove. He crept quietly towards the river, looking constantly this way and that and wishing he had Kriss for company, but Archie had not seen him since the day the big man had carried him back to the caves and assumed he had moved on.

Much of today had been taken up with lessons from Felicity on how to project and use his aura. He had found time in between whiles to plait the lion's dried sinews into a belt and had fashioned the bladder and stomach into a pouch to hang from it. He had also made another bow, a handful of arrows and thanks to the centaur's generosity, a horsehair strap to carry them on his back. Whilst Archie worked he had talked with Emrys about all manner of things, finding it suddenly easy to share his innermost thoughts in a way he had rarely done before. It occurred to him that he no longer saw Emrys as deformed. He was what he was; simply his friend.

Felicity had filled his pouch with fresh water and it bumped and sloshed against his thigh as he scurried along the paths heading for the river his feet thudding on the turf. Tired, yet focused, he was hit by a wave of nausea as memories of the last time he was here flooded back to him. Determinedly putting them out of his mind he came at last to the tree line by his former camp, pleased to see the waters had receded and the river in the bottom of the valley looked much less swollen than it had.

Turning downriver towards the estuary where he had waded through the lilies, it was not long before Archie once again caught sight of the dark figure on the opposite bank. Unnervingly, the masked stranger seemed to be keeping pace with him, moving swiftly behind trees and bushes, disappearing and reappearing through the foliage just as before. Convinced he was being stalked, Archie took cover, crouching down behind a low growing willow, bow and arrow at the ready as he watched and waited. Sure enough, the apparition turned and stared in his direction. Petrified he held his breath, his skin prickling into goosebumps. After a heart-stopping moment that felt like an eternity, the figure continued on its way downriver. No longer sure who was stalking whom, Archie kept it in his sights as he resumed his journey.

Soon he was running along level ground a few metres back from the river, once again having to hurdle various wind-strewn obstacles in his path. A little further on he negotiated the incline down to the bank his feet slipping and sliding in the mud. So absorbed was he in tracking the hooded figure he almost fell headlong into the rapids at the river fork. Leaping from one giant boulder to another he got across safely and scrambled down the rocky slope on the other side of the intersection. The nearer he got to his destination, the wider the river became until he lost sight of the stranger altogether. Soon he could see the distant ocean and knew he was almost there. The ground dropped away suddenly, causing Archie to lose his footing. He broke his fall with an army roll that took him almost to the lily patch.

Dusting himself off, Archie looked all around hoping he might see Grace, but there was no sign of the beautiful rainbow angel who had come to him at this very spot. The place felt creepy and sinister in stark contrast to the tranquillity he had experienced here before. Shivering, Archie tried to assuage his fear by putting into practice what Felicity had taught him, chanting under his breath, "Aura bright propel my yellow light; aura bright propel my yellow light." Concentrating hard he closed his eyes and visualised his aura. Pushing all his energy skyward he felt an uplifting sensation in his chest and in seconds sensed his aura radiating around him, warm like the sun. As the bright yellow shield encircled him completely his shivering subsided.

Feeling slightly stronger; protected and armed, Archie wandered despondently along the edge of the water all his senses attuned for any sound or movement. There was nothing; he was completely alone. He poked at one of the lily pads floating in the shallows. It was huge, its thick edges curving up towards the sky. 'It must be at least two metres in diameter,' Archie thought, prodding another leaf. There were dozens of them stretching way out into the river. He did not recall there being so many before, nor that they had been so big, but perhaps in his exhaustion he had not really noticed them. He did remember being overwhelmed by the scent of the white trumpet flowers. Dwarfed by their pads, these grew in abundance, poking up through the water and spreading amongst the river reeds that grew along the bank.

Fascinated, Archie thought the giant leaves looked exactly like big green stepping stones. They seemed almost to be inviting him to jump from one to the next. It was irresistible. Tentatively he put out his foot. The pad felt quite firm; he pressed down hard; it did not budge an inch. "What do we think? Could you hold my weight?" he questioned. Feeling faintly ridiculous to be talking to a plant, Archie pulled back quickly onto the bank and looked about him. There was still no sign of Felicity's monsters or the strange Keeper of Secrets. The light was beginning to fade and he knew he should find somewhere to hide, but the magnificence of the lilies mesmerised him. 'Join us on our cool pads and enjoy the evening air', they seemed to whisper into the silence, tempting him.

Apprehensive of their lure, Archie forced himself to ignore them. Thirsty, he sat down on the bank, reached for his pouch and found that it was only half full; he must have snagged it when he fell. Gulping down what was left he gazed out over the water at the sharp, unmoving picture in front of him. The sea was flawless: a mirror for the red ball of the sun to descend into. He watched it sink slowly beneath the horizon. Then, as though someone had switched out the lights, the sun vanished and the sky turned from crimson to deep purple.

Leaving his bow and arrows on firm ground with his now empty pouch, Archie got hesitantly to his feet unsure what to do next. His gaze was drawn back to the lily pads. His legs seemed to carry him of their own volition into the shallows. Deciding to take his chances, he tested another pad with his toes. Cautiously, he stepped onto it. His feet did not even get wet, the entire leaf stayed buoyant. A sudden breeze sighed past him, it seemed to penetrate his aura and felt cold on his skin. For a moment, feeling very much alone Archie stood perfectly still. Where were the Keeper of Secrets and her monsters? Perhaps there was another grove of lilies and he was in the wrong place. Or had Felicity been spouting nonsense and it was just a myth as he had suspected? "Something isn't right," he muttered uneasily. "The people round here are usually all too ready to make themselves known. If she exists, why isn't she showing herself?" It seemed foolish to attract attention by calling out, but Archie did not know what else to do. He drew breath and yelled, "Hello? Is anyone there?" The world lay still around him. Only the water under his lily pad moved, rippling outward.

It was not yet full dark, but the stars were beginning to appear one by one in the dusky sky. Archie was aware of a growing urgency to find cover. 'Once you're with the Keeper of Secrets the Moon cannot reach you,' Felicity had said, but just in case she was wrong about that too he propelled his aura out further. "Aura bright, propel my yellow light; aura bright, propel my yellow light," he repeated the mantra again and again, springing from one pad to the next, jumping impulsively onto whichever one seemed to call to him.

Breaking the hush with each leap, Archie splashed his way well out into the river. It was exhilarating and he was enjoying himself, each stepping stone carrying him further away from the riverbank. After a time he stopped to catch his breath and looked up. Strangely, he seemed to be no nearer to the opposite bank. He swung round to see how far he had come and gasped in horror, "Oh God! What..?" Each of the lily pads behind him had vanished into thin air.

Archie stared at the expanse of black, empty water between him and the now distant shoreline. He seemed to have travelled for miles. There was no way back; he had to go forward. Out of the corner of his eye he saw the Moon creeping into the sky. Seized by panic, he gathered himself to leap to the next pad, lost his footing and stumbled backwards into the river. The cold shock of the water made him gasp, but he did not go under. Reaching forward he grasped the edge of the next pad and pulled himself towards it. Kicking his legs hard he swung them beneath it in an attempt to grapple his way onto its surface. A sharp pain pierced his calf as though a knife was ripping through his flesh.

"Ahh," Archie roared, letting go. He bent under the water and with both hands grabbed his shin seeking the source of the pain. He wrestled to the surface again only to be pulled back down. Something was catching at his legs and stabbing them repeatedly, the wounds stinging as though he was trapped in a nest of angry wasps. Forcing his eyes open Archie could see fragments of moonlight filtering into the water between each lily pad. His aura had disappeared and he was completely unprotected. He peered down into the gloom of the river and knew he had found the green, faceless monsters. It had been no myth; he had been jumping on them.

The underside of each gigantic lily pad was covered in sharp, metre-long red spines. His flesh was being pierced by hundreds of needles, his body injected with their venom. In a whirl of pain Archie backed away from the malicious plants and with all his strength kicked out, forcing his body down and out of their reach.

Swimming deep underwater, his lungs bursting, he searched desperately for somewhere to ascend and draw breath. It was hopeless, the pads covered the surface and their red spines were everywhere. They seemed to beckon, taunting him. Excruciating pain began spreading from his legs into his body, paralysing his limbs. The saturated lion's pelt was heavy, pulling him down and the compulsion to breathe in water brought back terrifying memories of drowning under the ice. Sinking slowly to the riverbed, Archie began to lose the will to fight.

And as before, he caught sight of something floating towards him. Not a ball of light this time; not Felicity coming to his rescue, but a younger girl. She wore a diaphanous white gown and her jet black hair was piled half on her crown, held secure with two short sticks of crystal. The rest of her hair, which was incredibly long, floated wildly like seaweed around her tiny head. Her eyes were fixed wide open, her expression melancholy and her skin the whitest Archie had ever seen. Arms outstretched, she seemed to hang in the water and for a moment he thought she might be a dead body. Petrified, he tried to move, prepared to face again the venomous spines to get away from her. With a tremendous effort of will he swallowed his fear and stayed where he was watching the figure drift towards him, her wraith-like form transparent in the water like a dainty fragile ghost.

As she neared him he heard a whisper in his head, 'You found me, Archie. Well done.'

He stared at her lips; they were motionless yet her soft, lisping words were as clear as if she had spoken them. He was not in the least surprised that she knew his name.

'Most prefer their chances with my armoured pads,' her gaze flitted up to the lethal lilies. Archie's followed, his eyes flicking to the patchwork of light and dark above him. 'Panic grabs them you see. Most fight upwards instead of down, fancying the toxic needles instead of me. They will render you permanently paralysed if you're stung too greatly you know.' She smiled, 'But don't worry, yours is temporary. You did well to escape them.'

'Who are you?' Archie tried to say though he had a feeling he knew and wondered if, like Felicity, the ghost-girl would read his mind. She did.

'I am the one you seek. My name is Lillian, the Keeper of Secrets. Why do you need my help?'

'Surely you know?' Archie thought, his mouth moving automatically to form the words, bubbles escaping from his lips.

'I know you've come in an act of selfless aid.'

'I have to help Emrys out of his cave and over the bridge. He has never harmed a living soul nor done an evil act. He is a man of God and deserves to walk beside Him.'

It dawned on Archie that he was communicating telepathically and his lungs were no longer bursting. The stinging in his legs seemed to have receded too and he was able to move them again. In fact, bizarrely, he actually felt quite comfortable. 'Why don't I need to breathe?'

'You are breathing, Archie. You are a simple spirit. You have been taken back to your origin and given the ability to use your gills like a fish. You do not need to rely on gasping for air to fill your lungs.' She smiled, 'Is it not like a dream?'

Archie's mouth turned down in a wry grimace, 'I wouldn't describe my experiences here as a dream, more like a succession of nightmares. Can you help me… will you help me?' he beseeched.

'Yes, come with me.' Lillian turned, swimming effortlessly with the current, her long hair streaming behind her. To his surprise Archie found himself following with no conscious effort, his legs propelling him rapidly like a merman's tail through the murky water. At Lillian's side, he glided around whirlpools that churned up the riverbed, suspended particles of sand making it hard to see.

They swam on through jungles of clinging riverweed and eventually into clearer water. Here Lillian began slowly to ascend.

Looking up, all Archie could see was a forest of vicious red spines, but his guide rose unerringly to the only gap between the lily pads. Keeping close behind her he broke the surface and found he had emerged into a massive underwater cave. He had been chanting Felicity's mantra all the while and it seemed to have worked for his aura burned brighter than ever in the darkness. Following Lillian's lead he pulled himself heavily out of the water onto an open ledge and attended immediately to his legs. The wound that had first pierced his calf was deeper than the rest, the flesh around it angry and swollen. Wincing from the pain Archie looked about him. Lillian's white aura created vast light in the echoing black cave and he could see long glistening stalactites hanging from the ceiling. The walls reflected her light in a scintillation of brilliance that made his eyes water. Looking more closely he saw they were covered in clear, colourless quartz; each crystal seemed to have pale shadows of other crystals inside it. He stared at them, fascinated.

"It is called 'Phantom Quartz'," Lillian spoke aloud this time, her voice bouncing off the walls. Having brushed water off her gown she removed the crystal chopsticks from her hair and set about wringing it out, throwing it over her shoulders to tumble down her back.

Shivering in the damp cave Archie gazed at the wall, reaching out a hand to run tentative fingers along the jagged crystal. "It's b-b-beautiful," he whispered, his teeth chattering. "I've n-n-never seen anything like it."

"Nor will you ever see anything like it again, though it's not quite so beautiful when you have to look at it all the time. This is my home, a place where I am bombarded day in, day out by the calls of lost souls seeking me, searching for answers to their destiny. Few reach me telepathically from the living land, even fewer have found me physically. In fact you are one of only two." Lillian tiptoed beside him, propelling her warmth to him, "Welcome."

"Thank you." Archie looked up at her, "And do you have the answers, Lillian?"

"Yes, I do; every one of them." She raised her eyebrows and turned his attention back to the wall. "Look closer, past its beauty and mystical appearance. Deep within the crystal walls of this cave is written the history of the cosmos from the beginning to the end of time. It is known as the 'Akashic Record' and all knowledge is contained therein. My cave is a storehouse of answers. I am one of only very few souls bestowed with the ability to interpret them. I can tell you all that has occurred and all that will occur in the Universe."

"Wow, that's quite a burden!" Archie commented flippantly, staring in disbelief from Lillian to the wall.

"It is a privilege and it is my destiny." She spoke curtly, spun round and began humming to herself, tiptoeing like a ballerina out onto a nearby lily pad where she sat with her back to him. Archie noted again how tiny she was. The pad was like a huge raft to her rather than a stepping stone to him. The smoky white gown draping her petite figure looked as though it was already dry. His own thick hide tunic was sopping and clammy against his skin, he had no hope of getting it dry down here.

"I'm sorry if I've offended you," he said to Lillian's stiff back, "I didn't mean to." He thought for a moment, "But if everything is written and each soul's destiny is predetermined, isn't that the same as saying there is no such thing as free will? And in that case, it doesn't really matter what I do for I am not responsible for my actions?"

Lillian half turned to look at him and spoke into his mind, 'People on Earth have been struggling to get their heads round that one since time began. It is hard to explain and you will not really understand it until you reach the other side, but try to think outside the box – or in this case, outside the Universe,' she smiled. 'Each time you make a decision, all the different decisions that you might have made splinter into different paths. The path you follow is yours to choose. Each of them is written.'

"You mean like a parallel Universe?"

'Sort of, except that there is not just one but thousands... hundreds of thousands in fact.'

Archie ran his fingers through his hair. The concept made his mind boggle and his thinking was too muddled to take it any further. 'So will you help me to help Emrys?'

Without preamble Lillian said, 'A negative energy has intervened in your friend Emrys' path. You must take him back to the original purity of his intention.'

"Excuse me?" Archie raised his eyebrows, baffled and confused by her words.

'He has repressed memories that need to be put into context,' she explained.

'I'm sorry, but I think you've been in this cave on your own too long. I've no idea what you're talking about.' Archie stared straight into Lillian's big brown eyes as he concentrated on projecting his thoughts to her. 'Please speak in words I can understand.'

Lillian laughed out loud. 'It doesn't take long to get the hang of telepathy, does it? Soon you will do it without thinking. Now then, let me try again: negativity has wished misfortune on Emrys. You must help him to remember where he came from. Doing this will save him.'

Her conclusion was blunt and to the point, but Archie was still struggling to understand her meaning. He focused on his thoughts, slightly irritated by Lillian's enigmatic answers. 'Speaking plainly, do you mean the Moon's curse will then be reversed?'

'She is a nefarious sorcerer, the Moon. She has indeed cursed your friend and her power is irreversible.' Lillian's behaviour was completely blasé; she yawned and stretched, arching her back.

"What?" Archie gasped, horrified. "Great!" He spoke aloud, his voice echoing round the cave. "You just drop that statement in like it's meaningless. So there's nothing I can do?" His distress was palpable.

'Don't be so pessimistic, you can always do something. You can, if you say you can.' Lillian rolled her yoga stretch down to her legs and then relaxed. 'Before you died, what did you believe about the afterlife?'

"I don't know!" Archie exclaimed, flinging his arms wide in frustration. "What good is there in knowing what I thought before? I know what I am now and how I feel now. I know that when I was a boy Emrys was Nanny's vicar and he helped me. All I want to do is help a friend." Archie looked away from Lillian and fixed his gaze on the glittering crystal. His shivering was becoming hard to control and his throbbing leg even harder to ignore.

'I know, Archie, and when you met Emrys by the ruins in Llangernyw did you believe what he told you?'

"How did you-"

"Did you believe?" Lillian cut across him, for once voicing her words in a sibilant whisper.

"No, I don't think I did - I was only fourteen. But he was right, of course. I grew to believe it later." Archie frowned down at the floor, unable to make head or tail of what Lillian was trying to say.

"Curses have power only if you believe in them," she explained simply.

"Well, Emrys believes in his curse. How can he not? The Moon deformed him into a centaur for goodness sake."

"Physically there's nothing anyone can do for Emrys, which is why the Moon's curse cannot be fully reversed. Unless God chooses to intervene he will eternally remain a centaur, but he can leave his temple and he can cross the bridge. All the Moon has done is made Emrys believe he can't. She's drummed it into his subconscious, poisoning his mind with fear and erasing his memory. He is lost. At the age of fourteen, Archie, you were told you would die, do you think Emrys somehow cursed you?" Archie gulped; he had never thought of that. Lillian arched an eyebrow, "Then you his rescuer show up by chance? Is that just coincidence do you think?"

"Now you're really confusing me," he shut his eyes, shaking his head. "Why would Emrys curse me?"

"He didn't, he just foretold your future correctly that is all… to the day as it happens. Did he not say, '...eleven years and exactly one hundred and five days left, then your game will end and we'll meet again...'?"

"Yes, but-"

Lapsing once more into telepathy, Lillian did not allow him to finish, 'You could have construed it as a curse if you had been so inclined or if you had been told it was a curse could you not?' She stretched out her legs and dipped them into the water. 'What I'm trying to explain is this: you never believed you were cursed when Emrys gave you your exact exit date. It never even entered your mind. You dwelled on it maybe only half a dozen times in the remainder of your life. You were too busy; you had a life to live.' Lillian kicked her feet about in circles, causing the pads to bump into one another.

Archie watched the commotion from the damp ledge, listening to Lillian's whisper echo around in his mind and screwing up his eyes as he tried to remember the precise details of his encounter with Emrys on the mountainside.

'Emrys on the other hand,' Lillian continued, 'has had a real and major deformation occur: his legs end in hooves, he has a tail and he yearns to eat hay! He cannot remember his past - he has no security; no constant, if you like. Aside from remembered fragments of the Scriptures, all he has is what he knows now. In all the time he has lived in Transit before you arrived, he has lived alone, stuck and abandoned in the caves with time to completely absorb the Moon's curse. What else has he had to think about? He has made it stronger the longer he's believed in it; on his own he has created a self-fulfilling prophecy. But like I said, all you need to do is find a way to jog his memory. Remind him of who he was before and you will win.'

"I tried, he doesn't remember and he says the past is irrelevant," Archie explained.

'That's because he can't remember it, but nothing is irrelevant. Emrys may be a wise hierophant but he believes his life has taken on a different purpose. He heals wounded lost travellers and guides them in the right direction and he does a fantastic job. Few would've made it over the bridge without him. However, he is himself wounded. Subconsciously and desperately he seeks to be healed. If you like, you could say it was in his blueprint to stay and help here for a while, but as with all phases in Transit, he must now move on to the next and it seems you are the man to get him going again.'

"How, though?" Archie was finding the combination of the dazzling wall in front of him and the sound of Lillian's hushed whispers in his mind hypnotic. He shook himself and tried to concentrate. Seeing his dilemma, Lillian reverted to speech.

"You must have a positive attitude, Archie. The Moon attempted to scramble your mind but you fought her every step of the way. You have an honest and strong faith in yourself, and your capacity for unconditional love is immense. I believe you can make Emrys' curse a blessing." She raised her feet in the air and let them drip dry for a moment. "Imagine a child who believes there are monsters and snakes under his bed and you are the parent. What would you do to help your child?"

Archie stared at Lillian dumbfounded. "Pass; I never had children... maybe tell them monsters don't exist."

"Yes, but you don't want to crush their imagination do you? And you also don't want to make them feel silly. So you create a magic spell with them, to banish the monsters and snakes."

"You want me to make up a fake spell to convince Emrys I'm reversing the Moon's curse?" Archie struggled to snap himself out of his trance, staring from Lillian back to the wall, amazed by the simplicity of her conclusion. "He's too intelligent, he'll see straight through it."

"No, it will remove his fear. But remember; first you must make him recall who he really is. You're next challenge after that will be getting him out of the cave, which is far easier than your mind is making it."

During this conversation, Lillian had gathered together all her hair into an enormous pile on top of her head and was messily poking at it with her chopsticks.

"If you have all the answers stored here, Lillian, you'll know if I make it over the bridge?" Archie pried.

"Of course you'll make it over the bridge," she let go of the sticks. Some of her hair stayed put but most of it fell down her back onto the lily pad.

"So I don't need to worry then… about all of this?" Archie raised his arms, referring to his predicament.

Lillian gave up with her hair and focused on Archie again. "You'll cross the bridge when it's your time to cross." She sounded annoyed and he hid a smile sure her tone was harsh because she was upset with her hair. "That will be once you've learnt your lesson; the one you couldn't learn on Earth. Just how long that takes I cannot tell you. It's up to you. This is your journey and you must make what you want of it. Free will applies here too you know." Lillian was now back messing with her hair again and looking even more furious with it, frantically wrapping loose strands around the sticks on her crown. Archie wondered if he should offer to help, but on second thoughts felt it best to turn back to the original topic of helping Emrys.

"So the plan is: I go back to Emrys and once I've convinced him of who he really is, or was, and he has a real memory link, I have to make up a poem about reversing the Moon's curse and then get him out of the cave?" Archie summed up.

"Be wiser, Archie. If Emrys – or you come to that - were to fall into the beams of the Moon again, what do you think would happen?" Lillian rose to her feet and began to tiptoe towards him, her gaze never leaving his face.

"Very true, I never thought of that." Archie watched and listened intently as she danced closer and closer.

"Tomorrow night there will be no Moon," Lillian smiled, so did Archie. "Unlike the sun she does not present the same face every day. She waxes - grows larger - until she becomes whole. Then night by night she wanes, or shrinks, into a curved sliver until she vanishes altogether for one night only." Lillian was now standing directly in front of him. "You must take advantage of this."

"Brilliant," Archie beamed. "Giving us one night and two days to get ourselves over the bridge?"

Lillian smiled at his enthusiasm. "Remember; you've a lot to do before then. Helping Emrys find a memory will be the real challenge," she whispered, now circling Archie.

"Would you be able to tell me where the bridge is?"

"There's only one bridge to 'the other side'..." She leaned against the wall, running her fingers along the jagged crystals then pausing to lay her hands on them, pressing down as though absorbing knowledge into her palms. "And you will find it, but please do not think your journey is over, Archie," she said. Head down and eyes shut, Lillian continued to press herself into the wall. "You're an adventurer, your mind is conjuring up battles to be had every second. Listen to me, Archie, when I say it is true that every conceivable energy state really does exist. Be careful what you think of, your thoughts are your creator. We're all creatures of imagination; this Universe is really just one giant thought. Have you ever heard the saying, 'mind over matter'?"

"Of course," Archie said, wondering where God was in all of this, but afraid to ask. He peered closely at the wall, willing himself to see what Lillian could see until his eyes ached with the effort. Thousands of glittering crystals stared blankly back at him.

Lillian paused, breathing deeply and shaking her head. "Your mind is reeling relentlessly. I say again, be careful what you think."

"Why can't I just cross normally like everyone else? Why do I have to travel this tortuous escapade?" Archie knew he sounded petulant, but he was becoming increasingly distressed, his mind so full of Lillian's philosophising he felt it might burst open and come trickling out of his ears.

"Because, Archie, there's an enormous part of you that doesn't want to cross." Lillian lifted her head and turned blindly towards him her eyes still closed. "Every journey travelled is simply one of unconditional love. Your love is torn." Archie sighed, not understanding, but Lillian continued. "On the one hand, you've lost someone," Lillian turned her left hand over, revealing a lily white palm. "But it seems you have forgotten who it is you're looking for. Your soul is naturally seeking them out. And on the other hand," she exposed her right palm, "is the unconditional love you have for your family. Your spirit does not want to cross," Lillian spoke loudly shaking her head even more vigorously. "Therefore you're building impediments, which will only get bigger the closer you get to the bridge." Lillian at last opened her eyes and looked at Archie.

"Bigger," he flapped his arms around, "than this? Bigger than defying a legendary sea monster? Bigger than defeating the king of beasts? What about lethal lily pads, or having my brain scrambled by the Moon, or freaked out by some weird shadow on the other side of the river? Bigger than all of that?" Archie, his face flushed, gasped for breath at the end of this livid rant. Scared stiff at the prospect of his future becoming even harder his fear had turned to anger.

"Yes, Archie, bigger than all those things," Lillian said unperturbed, turning back to the wall. "I see you'll be building a team to help you with all that follows. It is a strong team." She paused as she stared harder at the wall. "Emrys looks to be a vital part of it." She glanced in Archie's direction, "Therefore you must not fail in freeing him."

"But I thought you said I would make it over the bridge eventually, so why does any of this matter? I don't understand."

"Oh, Archie," Lillian sighed. "You will just have to accept that what I tell you is true. It doesn't really matter if you understand or not. Focus your thoughts on your first ever meeting with Emrys. Try to remember everything that was said between you by the ruins on the mountain. Every detail is vital. The tiniest memory may well be his trigger. Who else do you know who can help you?"

"I don't know anyone else. I've met Grace, but I have a strong suspicion that our meeting will be the first and last of its kind as indeed will yours and mine."

"And you may be right. Not everyone is blessed with an aura of the colour Grace gifted to you. Nor to come face to face with the Mind of God, which is how the Akashic Record is known on the other side." Archie drew in a sharp breath and looked in awe at the scintillating wall. Lillian smiled at his expression, but continued with her train of thought. "You were allocated a guide whom you may have recognised. Usually it is someone who's been with you as a Guardian Angel throughout your life on

Earth," she paused listening to the silence. Archie was about to tell her when she piped up, "Hope, possibly?"

"Yes, 'Felicity' is what she likes to be called, but I don't recognise her," Archie explained.

"Not everyone remains the same externally. Possibly you can't identify her, but you would certainly have known her at some point in your history. She's a funny girl, very vain if I remember. Has she proved useful?"

"I think so," answered Archie, aggravated by Lillian's dismissive tone of his friend. He was about to launch into her defence but was cut off by another enigmatic whisper.

"She's broken many rules that one, going way beyond her boundary on more than one occasion. She specifically asked to guide you." There was silence whilst Lillian concentrated then she swung round and looked Archie straight in the eye, "She cares deeply for you; it is like you're two of the same." Archie remained silent, listening intently, wondering what she meant and to whom she could possibly be referring. It could only be Felicity.

Frowning, Lillian turned back to the wall. "She watches over you constantly - she's waited a long time for your return."

Archie clung to her every word, confused yet enthralled, an involuntary smile spreading across his face. "That's insane, she's a star! How could I possibly know her? Are you telling me I have lived before and met her in another life – or in one of your parallel universes?"

Lillian avoided the question, "Well you know her now. She wants nothing more than for you to remember her, for then she too can move on. It may come to you. But for now accept her love. She will lead the way. She's also part of your team."

"Can you see anyone else?" Archie was both intrigued and puzzled.

"I see only one other, standing very close beside you. A youngish man; he's wearing a red cape. I believe you would have known him before as well. He has also vowed to wait for you and to defend you."

"Wow, I didn't realise I had such an honourable reputation. I must have been someone really special to have people loving me and wanting to wait for me here. Who was I? Do you know?"

"Yes I do," Lillian snapped, "and I know who you will become: you are Archie Fletcher and Archie Fletcher you will remain. Now then; you've been in Transit for eight days and it is much too long. No soul has remained here for so long and not become irrevocably lost. Be warned: you must cross on the eve of the tenth night. Before if possible or you will end up a lost soul. That gives you two more days. There's a calling to fulfil and a time limit has been fixed on it; you must return quickly."

"But it's still night. Once I leave you, the Moon will find me."

"The sun will rise in less than an hour."

Archie's jaw dropped open, he had no idea he had been so long in this cave. Time seemed to have as little meaning here as everything else.

"You'll be back to Emrys before he wakes for breakfast. Remember everything you can about him. I will guide you back to the surface and when you get there you must head straight for the caves. Do not allow yourself to be distracted by anything. Your timing is critical."

He did not ask any more questions; he could not have coped with any more of Lillian's answers. His thoughts seemed to have congealed into a soggy mass of cotton wool and he was utterly drained. He was also chilled to the bone. He wanted to feel the warmth of the sun on his back and inhale the smell of Emrys' herbs. "Thank you, Lillian," he said. "Thank you for everything. I will not forget what you have told me."

"You're very welcome," Lillian beamed. "It's not often I get company down here."

"Do you ever go up?" Archie asked, raising his eyes to the ceiling of the cave.

"Never, it's just me and the big old book, I'm afraid. Wouldn't have it any other way, nice to have a guest every once in a while though." Their eyes locked momentarily, then without another word Lillian led him to the gap in the lily pads and slid into the water.

It was even colder than before and Archie automatically held his breath as the river closed over his head. Their route was much shorter than when he had arrived and it seemed no time at all before Lillian was signalling for him to ascend. Turning without so much as a wave, she disappeared into the darkness of the river and he was alone.

Emerging into the pale light that precedes dawn, Archie gasped in the damp air. Treading water, he located the bank and began to swim swiftly towards it. There were no giant lily pads in sight, in fact he seemed to be at a completely different section of the river. The only reminder of his meeting with Lillian was a single white trumpet lily laid on the shore he was heading for. Lined up neatly beside it were his abandoned bow, arrows and pouch.

He clambered onto the bank and picked up the lily; it was spangled with dew. Twirling it absently in his fingers,

Archie looked all around for any signs of life, relieved to see the moon had disappeared and the sun was rapidly putting in an appearance, his golden light flooding the sky. Laying the lily back on the ground, Archie stripped off his tunic and wrung it out then towelled himself with it and wrung it out again. Satisfied that both he and it were as dry as they were going to be, he put the tunic back on. As he did so there came an overwhelming scent from the lily on the ground. He picked it up and sniffed at the rich mixture of honey and musk.

"Each thought you have is an investment, Archie, invest wisely. Right now, time is of the essence," Lillian's voice whispered, "God speed." Archie looked down into the lily, not sure what to anticipate next or if he should reply. As mobiles went, it was unusual to say the least! "Thank you," he whispered into the trumpet, feeling faintly foolish. He retrieved the pouch, opened it up and gently placed the lily inside it, tying it back onto his belt. Slinging his bow and arrows over his shoulder, he looked around quickly then set off at a jog, moving inland in the rough direction of the caves, the journey now all too familiar. For a moment he sensed the black, hooded figure watching him from the other bank, but with Lillian's words fresh in his mind he chose not to look back. Instead he forced himself forward, the thought of becoming a lost soul rattling round in his head.

CHAPTER FIFTEEN

A DREAM INTERRUPTED IS LIKE A LETTER UNREAD

Head down, Archie almost bumped into Felicity on the cliff top just before he reached the ledge leading down to Emrys' caves. Her aura was low and her face taut with anxiety. Hovering at his head height she looked him straight in the eye, invading his space as he walked. "Did you find her?"

Archie stopped dead and felt the skin around his leg wound tighten. "I found her all right," he grimaced, bending to rub it and inadvertently knocking off the partially formed scab. Both legs were covered in deep scratches where the spines had attacked him and were extremely sore.

"You're hurt," she eyed the wound. "Ouch! It looks horribly painful."

"It's nothing," he said, putting on a brave face. Felicity smiled and reached out to touch it with a gentle fingertip. He felt a warm, tingling sensation and looking down saw that a new scab had instantly formed. "Thanks," he muttered, in awe of her healing magic.

"You're welcome," she grinned.

Striding forward Archie scrambled down onto the ledge. Felicity continued to flutter backwards in front of him, searching his face. "Did you see the monsters? Were they truly terrifying?"

"Yes and yes," Archie grinned. "I'll tell you all about it sometime, but for now I want to get back to Emrys. Will you stop fluttering in my face?"

"Did she tell you how to reverse Emrys' curse?" Felicity persisted.

"Yes." Opening his pouch, he revealed the crumpled lily head, "She is called 'Lillian'." Felicity peered at it, wrinkling her nose. Archie stopped walking, turning his back to direct the conversation away from Emrys' earshot. "She lives in an underwater cave beneath the river. She told me Emrys will remain a centaur; there's nothing we can do about that." Archie put his arm around Felicity and steered her gently round to face away from the caves, "But we may be able to get him out of here and over the bridge."

"How?" Felicity listened intently.

"By creating a memory link back to his previous life; something that's crystal clear to him. I've been wracking my brains trying to remember things about him, but I was young when we met so it's difficult. We only ever had one proper conversation."

The star turned her face away, her smile vanishing as she looked up to the heavens. A giant raven had appeared and was circling above them. "A lost memory is a wicked fortune," Felicity whispered, "but remember, Archie, the past is never dead. There's a secret door lost somewhere deep inside Emrys' mind that must be found. We must delve into the corridors of his forgotten past and help him find that door so he can open it." Her gaze remained locked on the raven. "We should take cover." Turning on her heel, Felicity headed to the cave, "Hurry; dark eyes are prying on us," she whispered urgently over her shoulder.

Archie stared up at the bird; it was the first one he had seen since the day he had arrived in Transit. He wondered about taking a shot at it with his bow, but it didn't look particularly threatening. He followed Felicity down the ledge, "There's no reason why Emrys can't leave the caves," he said, breaking into a jog to keep up with her. "The curse hasn't confined him, he's done that himself. The only problem I can see is physically getting him out of here. This is too much of a climb for him; he told us so."

"He can get out behind the waterfall in the herb cave. It runs straight out onto a skinny lip then it's a short jump up to the grassy plain. He could make it that way I'm sure."

Inside the cave Emrys was bent over the fire stoking it into a welcoming blaze. He gave one of his rare smiles when he saw Archie, but before he could speak Felicity was blurting out what she had been told, hopping excitedly from on foot to the other. "You have to remember who you were before you died."

"But I've told you, I can't remember anything. My memory has been erased." Emrys sat down by the warmth of his fire, looked up at Archie and shrugged.

"When I first met you in Transit, didn't you say someone had asked you to look out for me? Who was it?" Archie's first attempt felt like a good one.

"I don't remember. All I remember is your name. It's a name that haunts me night and day." Emrys' chin sunk onto his chest and he closed his eyes.

"I know that feeling," murmured Felicity, but no one was listening.

"Archie Fletcher, the boy who'd never grow up," the centaur continued, his eyes still firmly shut.

"No, that was Peter Pan," Archie joked.

"Who?" Emrys opened his eyes.

"Never mind - there must be something that'll rekindle a memory. Can't you remember anything about the day we met on the mountain by the ruins? You were planting carrots for your horse and I was playing a game with my cousins."

"Was it the game of your life again?" Emrys asked with the echo of a smile. "I'm sorry, I really don't remember you, your face, your cousins or anyone else."

"Okay, do you remember your church?" Archie was not about to accept defeat. Lillian had seen Emrys as part of his team. He was going to get him out; he had to. "It's called St Digain's and there's an ancient yew tree in the graveyard. It is world famous and over four thousand years old? Surely you remember that?"

Emrys frowned, looked up at the ceiling of the cave and back at the flames. He sighed and shook his head, "This is useless, it's all gone. My memories are simply not there to be found. They have been taken from me." He slumped down to rest his head on his hooves, ash from the fire smudging his nose. "What's a graveyard?" he asked wearily.

"It's a place where the dead are buried," Archie said impatiently. "Don't think I've come this far to give up after only two attempts. Can you remember your illness? You were constantly coughing. You told me it was a long drawn out illness." Archie searched Emrys' closed face for a glimmer of memory.

"By the sounds of it I don't want to remember that," the centaur replied, not stirring.

"Try, Emrys, you obviously had a horse," Archie smirked, glancing at Emrys' rear. "You remembered his name was 'Gareth'. Try to remember something else about him: riding him; caring for him. You loved him, you told me that too. What about the accident? How did you both meet your deaths? You must have been riding Gareth at the time."

Still shaking his head, the centaur gave a half-hearted smile, "I am Gareth and he is me. The Moon fused us into one, I told you that. I remember nothing about the time when we were two separate beings. Like I said, it's useless, there's no point in any of this." Emrys rolled his eyes, his expression reverting to his customary melancholy.

"Listen to me," Archie said speaking an inch away from Emrys' ash-encrusted nose. "I've the means to reverse your curse. If you really want out of this hole you need to start thinking. All we need is one link. It's that simple."

"I can hear what you're saying my friend, but it's all gone. There's nothing there."

Infuriated and helpless, Archie clenched his fists and paced the cave. Felicity was not much inspiration. Her gaze remained fixed on his face, willing him to keep trying. "Only you can do this," she whispered.

For a time no one spoke. Their energy was intense, all of them focused inward, thinking. The fire crackled into the silence and somewhere water dripped. Outside the wind had got up and was gusting into the cave making the flames dance and gutter. Finally, Archie announced, "I've got it! Emrys come with me," he stormed towards the tunnel. "We'll role-play our conversation by the ruin. We need to be in the garden."

"Oh goody, I love role-play," piped Felicity. "Can I join in?"

"No you can't," snapped Archie.

"Why not?"

"Because you weren't there."

"How do you know if I was there or not?" Felicity fluttered in front of him, sniggering.

Annoyed by her flippancy he frowned, "True, I've no idea if you were there or not, but I'm pretty sure this conversation was solely between Emrys and me." Despite his annoyance, Archie felt disoriented by the possibility that Felicity had been on the mountain all those years ago. "If you were there then you were invisible," he said shortly. Felicity giggled, but did not enlighten him.

"Okay, I'm game, young man," Emrys laboriously got to his feet. "Anything to say I've tried and get you off my back." He shifted stiffly towards the tunnel, muttering, "Let's face it; I've nothing else to do with my time around here."

"That's the spirit. We'll succeed. Like I said before, you're crossing the bridge with me come hell or high water." Archie shoved Emrys' rear end through to the next cave. Felicity hovered anxiously behind them both.

***

As the three would-be role-players moved into the darkness, the prying raven hopped down from its perch outside the cave from where it had been eavesdropping on the conversation within. It flew along the cliff face, alighted by a fissure in the rocks and listened intently, head on one side, beady eye glinting with satisfaction. Lifting itself back into the air it flew to the mouth of the third cave and perched on a boulder. Hidden from sight, the scruffy bird listened carefully to the voices drifting out of the cave, memorising what it heard to pass back verbatim to its sleeping mistress.

***

Emrys led them through to his inner sanctuary, the aromatic scent of herbs and flowers filling their senses. A waterfall gushed across the lower part of the cave mouth and around it grew an abundance of ferns and plants, their foliage a rich bright green. It was the first time Archie had taken a close look at Emrys' garden and he viewed it with interest before taking charge of the role play. "Right then: places," he shouted above the noise of the waterfall. "Emrys you were planting carrots. I crept up behind you. Go over by the cave opening and pretend to be planting. Feel the scene as I create it for you," Archie ordered, "you were bending over a spade, like so," he demonstrated.

Emrys did as instructed and Archie, clearing his throat, began, "It was a sweltering day. I was in my combats and holding my potato gun. You were wearing... err... I'm pretty sure it was a long, dark green overcoat. I asked you what you were planting." Archie waited.

"Well go on then," Emrys barked, "ask me. Let's role-play, like you said."

"Planting anything tasty?" Archie said instantly, his mind playing out the scene.

"Carrots, for my horse," Emrys shook his head and let out a long sigh. "You've already told me I was planting carrots for Gareth."

"Okay, what do you think you asked next?" Archie pressed, praying Emrys would not lose motivation.

"Oh…" the centaur sighed, his eyes closed, "I've no idea. Was it 'what are you doing here'?"

"Almost, that's really close. You actually asked me if I was trespassing. I told you I was the grandson of Mrs Fletcher who lived at the edge of the wood. You knew her well. She was a local member of your church and was in the choir." Archie paused to see if anything hit home.

"I'd imagine myself to be a popular vicar, ensuring I knew everyone." Emrys stared out of the cave, doing his best to role-play while Archie thought about what came next.

"What about the game?" Felicity interrupted, still hopping from one foot to the other. "Remember, Archie; then you told him about the game we were playing."

Archie stared at Felicity, his eyes narrowed. He could not understand why she insisted she had been there or how she could have been - it had been full daylight and she was a star. "Fee, what're you on about, you weren't there," he snapped. He bit his tongue before he overreacted and said something hurtful. Lillian had said Hope was probably his Guardian Angel and if so, presumably she had always been near him even though invisible. After what he had been through lately, he could believe anything was possible.

"Well go on then, Felicity said, cheekily twiddling her hair. "Tell me that wasn't what happened next."

"You're right, we did discuss the game I was playing," Archie said irritably. "Are you reading my mind, Fee?"

Emrys continued to stare out of the cave, but his low "Hurrumph," made it clear he was aware of the situation arising behind him.

"If I remember correctly your game was called 'Dead Game.'" Felicity spoke slowly, her eyes twinkled and the corner of her mouth lifted in a smug smile.

The accuracy of her words unsettled Archie, yet it seemed they rekindled no memories for Emrys. His face blank, the centaur appeared to be lost in the dark passageways of his brain trying desperately to navigate his way back through the maze to his life.

"Okay, Felicity, I give in." Archie frowned, shifting restlessly in his exasperation, "So you were there, but where were you?"

Grinning from ear to ear Felicity chuckled, "At last he listens! I was hiding, like the rest of them." She raised her eyebrows, "Sorry, don't mind me, you just carry on with your role-play... what do I know?" She continued to smile, but the corner of her mouth twitched and her bottom lip began to quiver.

Archie, his task forgotten, stared back at her speechless, his mouth dropped open, but no sound came out.

It was too much for Felicity. "I've looked over you, protected and guided you all your life," she burst out. "I know everything about you: your every move, game and conversation. On the mountain, off the mountain, wherever you happened to be, I was there."

Dumbstruck, Archie did not know how to react. It was true he had always felt protected, as if someone was guiding and watching over him, but he'd never really believed in Guardian Angels.

Felicity read his thought. "Why can you not believe in me? I've shadowed your every moment from before you were born."

Shocked and trembling, Archie stepped closer. He reached for her, his hands closing round her thin arms. At his touch she leaned towards him, her huge blue eyes glistening with tears. "There's not been one miniscule of a second I was not there wishing I could be with you in your reality; praying you were aware of me," she whispered, her voice wobbling.

It seemed to Archie that the cave in which they stood dissolved around them and they were drifting in featureless space. All he could see was the star. She filled his vision completely.

"I'm well aware you can't remember me," Felicity tried to smile. "I'm sorry, I thought I was prepared for this." Big tears spilled over and rolled down her lovely face. Her gaze remained locked with Archie's, her eyes begging him to remember her. "I've waited an eternity to be with you again. I've loved you to the point of madness," she sobbed, her voice dying away to a faint whisper.

A huge wave of déjà vu rushed over Archie. He searched his brain, desperate for any memory of Felicity in his life, but if there was one it eluded him. He shook his head with regret, "I'm sorry. When I saw you for the first time in Transit you seemed so familiar to me, but I knew I had seen you before. Under the ice. I remembered nothing else about you then, nor do I now."

"Ah well; all I can do is pray that you will in time," Felicity hung her head. "Just as Emrys cannot remember his past, part of yours is lost also."

"You've waited an eternity to be with me again?" Archie suddenly realised the implication of what she had said. "We knew each other before... in another life?" He frowned, "So Lillian was right?"

"Why? What's she been saying about me?" Felicity spoke sharply, pulling her arms from Archie's grasp and stepping back from him, clearly agitated.

"Nothing horrendous, she just mentioned that you and I had known each other before and that we were...," Archie hesitated, searching for the right words, "err... close, but I didn't really understand."

Felicity smiled through her tears, "She spoke the truth. But for now you must concentrate on Emrys. I'm sorry. I've completely distracted you. Please… give me a minute. I'll be back." Pushing past the centaur, Felicity flurried out of the cave and before Archie could utter another word she had disappeared behind the waterfall. He rushed after her, but she had gone. Searching the sky he saw a huge black raven flapping away from the caves.

"I think she loves you, Archie," Emrys said in his ear. Archie jumped, he had forgotten the centaur was right behind him.

"Why can't I remember her Emrys? I don't understand. Look at her, she's so beautiful. What idiot could forget her?" Archie remained staring at the water tumbling from the cliff overhang.

"It seems you and I have a lot more in common than we thought," Emrys said. "Tell you what… let's keep thinking over lunch. I'm starving. Grab a handful of that basil. And also, let me put some of my healing potion on that nasty leg wound."

The day drew near its end and Felicity did not return. Archie continued battling with Emrys and himself, desperate for any echo of either past.

"You will never suffer fools gladly, Corinthians!" Archie exclaimed. "Do you remember saying that to me?"

"No," Emrys paused thoughtfully, "I know the quote well of course, but Corinthians is not our link." Emrys shut his eyes tight then opened them again. "My brain's so lazy," he moaned, staring into his empty food bowl. "I don't believe it'll be an instance in conversation that'll trigger us, Archie. It will be a brief moment, a smell or a feeling, maybe even a sound."

"Do you think she'll come back?"

"Hope? We possibly won't see her again tonight. Dusk is settling."

Sighing, Archie searched the heavens for the first sign of a star. "I didn't mean to hurt her," he whispered.

"She knows that, she never really leaves you," the centaur said gruffly. "Even now as we lie here beneath the sky that she lights up, she is with you in spirit."

"But who is she, Emrys? Why is she with me?" Archie kicked out his feet in frustration, knocking the remainder of his uneaten salad across the cave floor.

"Go easy son, "Emrys watched the food bowl rolling to a stop. "We've all lived many lives before our most recent one; she's clung to you from long ago through all of them."

The dusk faded and night drew in. Still Felicity did not return to them. They talked well into the night, Archie throwing memory after memory at Emrys; Emrys throwing them back at him unopened. There was nothing more they could do except sleep. Every avenue felt exhausted and Archie longed for morning when Felicity would return. Eventually he dozed, her beautiful tearstained face filling his mind's eye.

Sometime later, he was awakened by the arrival of a visitor. Quietly jumping down the ledge into the cave, Kriss, draped in his red cape and clutching his staff, strode into the firelight and sat down between Emrys and Archie without saying a word. Emrys slumbered on, but Archie pushed himself onto his elbow. "How'd you get here? The Moon's out," he whispered, squinting at the silvery light he could see outside the cave.

"My cape protects me from her beams." Kriss did not elaborate. Speaking quickly and with urgency he said, "She's only a sliver tonight, she'll be gone tomorrow. Her eyes have been prying the realms today in preparation for her departure."

"Her eyes? You mean the raven?" Archie breathed, coming fully awake.

"Yes, but there's more than one, I promise you that. They're evil, deceitful creatures who'll stop at nothing to spy out information for the Moon, their mistress. Have you seen them?" Kriss was still speaking at top speed as though he had something more important to say.

"Yes, today; Felicity and I saw one just above the cliff, it was early afternoon. Then a bit later on I saw it flying away from the caves. We were in the garden cave discussing Emrys' past... or at least, trying to get him to remember it."

"Damn!" Kriss grimaced. "By now the Moon will know everything that was said. Why would Hope be so careless as to let you have that conversation after seeing a raven? She should know better. They are the Moon's eyes and ears."

"We thought it had gone," Archie said in Felicity's defence, sitting up. "Have you seen her? Is she okay?"

"Yes. I found her in a bit of a state over by the river. She said she had spoken about your past." Kriss poked up the fire with his staff, reached for two large logs and threw them onto the embers bringing the fire crackling back into life. He peered at Archie's anxious face, "Are you all right?"

Archie nodded, his thoughts in turmoil. "What did she say?" As he asked the question he was hit by yet another wave of déjà vu. It was the strangest feeling; he was certain in that instant that he and Kriss had done exactly this before and yet until a few days ago he had never met the man, he was sure of it. He studied the perfect symmetry of

Kriss's face and thought again how like a Greek statue he was. With his calm strong features and long dark hair curling to his shoulders, he was actually more like the painting of some biblical character. Was that why he seemed so familiar? Archie screwed up his eyes and thought hard, but nothing came to him. Even so, he felt sure the feeling was significant; it was so real. Maybe it was as Emrys had said, a feeling would take them back into their pasts rather than a conversation.

"I'll tell you, but before you start having any reminiscing moments of your own, listen to me carefully. Love is a bit like the wind, Archie, you can't see it but you can feel it. Hope - Felicity - is a star now, but she was once a person as are you. There's good reason for her being a star," Kriss paused, looked at Archie and waited for a response.

"Go on," Archie prompted.

"Sometimes when two souls meet they blend. For example your parents, they are soulmates, they think almost as one. Emrys and Gareth, who are quite literally fused together, were also soulmates and in a sense, of course, still are."

"I understand," Archie leaned forward watching Kriss's face intently in the firelight, wanting more.

"We only ever have one soulmate and it is not often they are found. They are tricky things to find in the realms of time and most souls will search forever without finding their mate. However, a long time ago - and I am talking centuries here - you did meet yours."

Archie stared unseeing at the flames that leapt in front of him. "Felicity," he muttered.

"That's right. Now then, the rest is going to be hard for you to hear and I'm not sure how to say it," Kriss gazed at the floor, his brow creased in thought. He scratched his head and looked back at Archie, his face shadowed in the firelight.

"Say what? Tell me everything, please."

Kriss sighed, "This is her story to tell, there are no two ways about it. I cannot believe I have the deed of unleashing this information on you," he fidgeted, shuffling his position to uncross his legs. "She asked me today in her despair to see if I could bring back your memories of her. To my way of thinking it'll do you no good remembering what happened so many aeons ago. But Hope... that is... Felicity, insisted I try, so here I go." Kriss cleared his throat, glanced quickly at the centaur. Emrys continued snoring quietly.

"Yours and Felicity's story could be described as an inequitable tragedy of good versus evil. Except, at this time evil has prevailed. It happened like this: a long time ago, in the days when men were at war and women waited, Felicity – that wasn't her name then, of course - was betrothed by family arrangement to a man of high status and wealth. It was an age where a woman was a chattel, her life was not her own, you understand."

Archie nodded tensely, "Go on."

"Well, you and she met one day in a cornfield just outside the town where you both lived. The two of you loved to wander the untrodden paths of the cornfields where you could get lost for hours. You met there every day for nearly a year and in that time you fell deeply and irrevocably in love. But you were a humble arrowsmith, your status much lower in society than that of Felicity's family – in those days, a marriage between you would not have been countenanced even had she not already been betrothed to another." Kriss glanced up at Archie, "Does any of this strike a chord?"

Archie shook his head and continued to stare down at the flames.

With another deep sigh Kriss continued with his story. "While you could never have married, your relationship was certainly until death as far as you both were concerned. Caught up in the rapture of your love neither of you believed the day would arrive when you would be forced to part. When it became apparent that this was inevitable you persuaded Felicity to run away with you, but on the very day you had planned to leave your affair was revealed by another. It sparked great anger and you only narrowly escaped with your life. You continued to hope that Felicity would find a way to come to you, but in the end, however much she wanted to, she could not turn her back on her responsibilities to her family. Knowing her path she refused you and because she was afraid for you, she lied and told you it was what she wanted." Kriss paused, added, "Felicity's punishment was far harsher than yours, I assure you."

At that, Archie looked up sharply. "What happened?" he asked softly, afraid and yet compelled to hear the answer.

"You were forcibly consigned to the army and sent thousands of miles away to fight in the merciless war against the Ottoman Empire, which was raging at that time. Heartbroken by what you saw as Felicity's betrayal you did not try to resist your fate, on the contrary, you deliberately courted danger and in a fit of impassioned jealousy vowed never to return to her. But what choice did she have? As I said, she knew her path. She was not allowed to promise herself to you. Forced against her will to marry her betrothed - an angry and violent man – she escaped her miserable fate in the only way open to her and not long after her marriage took her own life. And like you, she also made a vow."

"About me?" Archie whispered his face wet with tears.

Kriss nodded, "She vowed to watch over the one she would love for eternity: you."

Shaking his head Archie closed his eyes in an agony of despair. "No matter how hard I try I cannot remember her," he murmured.

"Of course you can't," Kriss said gently. "It was another life and as I said, a very long time ago."

Archie glanced up frowning, "But I can feel a thread, Kriss. Every time I think of her or see her I get a weird rush of déjà vu and I feel... I feel..." He could not find words for what he felt - and even had he been able to, they were feelings too personal to share.

Kriss smiled knowingly. "That feeling is your consciousness taking you back, letting you know you are on the right path," he explained, nodding his head shrewdly.

"What happens to those who commit suicide?" Despite his misery, Archie wanted to know the entire truth.

"Most of them will move on as normal, they are embraced by their families who wait for them on the other side, where they will continue to progress. But Felicity's vow to watch over you had her banished to the heavens," Kriss paused, a flicker of sadness crossing his features, "where she was sold to the Moon as a slave," he added bluntly.

Horrified, Archie burst out, "Who sold her to the Moon? Why would anyone do such a thing?"

Kriss coughed, glanced again at the sleeping centaur. At length he said softy, "You did, Archie."

"What? Why would I, how could I?" Archie spluttered, fresh tears springing to his eyes.

"She hurt you beyond repair it seems. You could not forgive her for refusing you. She shattered your heart into pieces so microscopic that a quark would look big beside them. You were completely and utterly broken by it and in your pain you hit out blindly. You then vowed you would never love again as you had loved her - and down all the centuries, you never have."

At the sight of Archie's stricken face, Kriss began to fumble nervously with his staff, poking it into the fire, stirring the ash. "Try to understand that selling your love to the Moon was not a rational act. It does not make you a monster. It is just what happens when soulmates deny each other. The intensity of the emotion is just too great to deal with. Why do you think there are so many stars in the sky? Most do eventually move on with their lives quite contentedly. It has happened before - and it will doubtless happen again."

Archie searched Kriss's face, the smoke rising from the fire stinging his eyes. "I do not want to believe you. I cannot believe I would do such a thing, nor can I understand how it could come about."

"When soulmates are united - which as I said is a rarity – and then parted, it is unheard of for them to ever meet again. Well, looking at the locality of it, it is actually impossible as one will always remain on Earth whilst the other resides in the vastness of the heavens. I have no idea how your meeting with Felicity can possibly have occurred," Kriss admitted. "She is positioned very close to the Moon, and the Moon keeps close wraps on all her stars. Even so, she must sleep each day and while she sleeps, Felicity breaks the rules. That is why she is often accompanied by ravens." Kriss paused and the shadow of a smile emerged across his features. "But being Felicity, she finds ways to evade them. She is always getting into trouble."

"What kind of trouble?"

"I am surprised you need to ask," Kriss said gently, "given your run in with the Moon."

Archie swallowed, his face drained of colour. "If it's impossible for parted soulmates to meet, how did Felicity find me again?"

"As I said, I have no idea." Kriss rested back on his hands, shaking his head thoughtfully. "She probably saw a window of opportunity and jumped straight through it. It would not surprise me in the least if she stitched up a few of the other stars to distract the Moon while she made her escape. She doesn't get on with them, never has; she would have no qualms about getting them into trouble." He fell silent for a moment, shrugged, "Or maybe it is simply God's good grace in allowing a miracle to occur. Whatever, Felicity has risked everything to encounter you again and she's in even bigger trouble than usual. Anyway, my friend, all I know for sure is this: it is a fact that what your heart once held your heart will never lose." He leaned forward and with his fist tapped Archie's chest, "She is in there somewhere, Archie, it's just a matter of you finding her."

"What happened to me when she died?"

"You had already been killed in battle and born again, still reeling, never settling and you have been living over and over for a long time, confined to the Earth with Felicity helplessly watching over you from the heavens. The lives you have led have all been happy lives, but they have never felt complete. You have always been searching for something without knowing what; always aware that something was missing: a hole that could never be filled. Your painstaking infatuation with one another seems to have destroyed all sense of time. To her you were entwined in the cornfield only yesterday, yet to you she was so long ago you cannot remember her at all. Her memories of why you parted have been washed away by her tears - she certainly has no fear that your love will ever end. You are all she can think about; everything that matters to her. She prays constantly that your memories of her will reawaken and you will know her again."

Frowning with concentration, Archie shut his eyes and searched his memories. After a time he opened them and focused on Kriss's face. "It's no good. I look at her and I do feel I should know her, but she's like..." he paused, choosing his words carefully. "She's like one of those really annoying dreams that captivate you; you know the ones I mean? The incomplete ones from which you wake too soon. You want to hold onto them, but you no sooner open your eyes than you can't remember anything about them. You are just left with a feeling that disturbs you for hours afterwards. I don't know... it's a bit like when you know someone's sent you a letter but it never arrives. You know the gist of what it probably contains, but you don't get to read it so you never really know. It's hard to explain," he looked up at Kriss, who smiled.

"I know what you mea-" Their conversation came to an abrupt end. There was an almighty rumble of thunder and with it came fork lightning, striking the ground with a loud bang just outside the caves.

Emrys woke with a jerk, "I was dreaming!" the centaur exclaimed. "I don't dream! I don't think I have ever dreamt," he gasped.

Archie and Kriss exchanged glances. "Times are changing," the big man remarked.

"What exactly do you mean by that?" Archie shouted over the noise of the thunder.

"Wait and see! What did you dream, Emrys?"

The centaur did not seem surprised to see Kriss. He looked from him to Archie and back again, waiting patiently for the thunder clap to subside. When it did he said, "I dreamed I was in a kind of garden looking at all these big stones with writing on them. I think it must have been a graveyard? I was reading them aloud as I passed them by and then I stopped at one on which was written, 'To die would be an awfully big adventure'. It was so strange..."

"What name was on it?" Kriss asked calmly, putting a restraining hand on Archie's arm.

"Archie Fletcher, 1978 – 2003," Emrys said without thinking. His eyes widening as if surprised by the words he had spoken.

"Is that our link?" Archie gasped eagerly.

"I don't think so," Kriss answered for the centaur who looked totally confused. "But you can't be far off." As he spoke, the storm clouds crashed together directly over their heads and rain came belting down, thundering against the rocks and rapidly forming a rivulet that streamed down the ledge to pool just outside the cave mouth. Lightning cracked, an instant of stark white light illuminating every deep shadow in the cave and revealing three tense faces, each one open-mouthed at the elemental power the heavens had unleashed.

"Wow!" breathed Archie.

Kriss cupped his mouth and shouted urgently, "You have slept enough, Emrys. Tomorrow there will be no Moon, we must work harder and faster on evoking your memories so Archie can reverse her curse. We have less than twenty-four hours to crack it and make our move." Whilst he was speaking the thunder rolled away and a little sheepishly he lowered his voice.

"How do you know that?" Archie asked.

"Do you really need to ask, Archie?" Emrys butted in. "Surely you know Kriss reads your mind in the same way Hope does - and me too to some extent. He is here to help us." The centaur turned to Kriss, "Do you not think that with sleep I may remember more, it seemed to trigger my dreaming?"

"You could be right. Maybe we should all sleep now so that when we wake we are refreshed. Hopefully something more will come to you, Emrys." Throwing his cape over his legs, Kriss closed his eyes and leaned back relaxing onto the cold stone floor. Emrys in his usual way fell instantly and deeply asleep, his mouth open, snoring.

Archie was exasperated his mind still whirling. "How can I sleep after all that has been said? I've never been one for sleeping through a thunderstorm at the best of times. I think I'd rather stay awake and watch it."

Kriss opened an eye, "I have a better idea. Maybe it is the time for you to reverse Emrys' curse - right now while the Moon is still covered by rainclouds. Do you remember what Lillian said about a fake spell? Why not try it?"

"Yes, but how did you know about that?" Archie eyed Kriss suspiciously, not sure whether to question him further. For how could he have known about the fake spell when Archie was sure he had not once thought about it since the big man had arrived? Maybe Felicity had said something, but there was more to Kriss than met the eye, of that Archie was convinced. Even so, he had to trust Emrys' opinion and Kriss had come to his rescue in his moment of need, so for the time being he let it go. Then he panicked, feeling unrehearsed. Searching his mind for words of inspiration he muttered something under his breath.

"Are you ready?" Kriss asked.

"I think so, I'm just… I need to… practise…." Maybe it was the fear of being put on the spot that seemed to hinder Archie's every thought. After a moment he said, "Do you really think now is the time for this?" hoping Kriss would say 'No'. His hopes were dashed.

"I certainly do, we must crack Emrys' block before the morning so let's get on with it."

"Shouldn't we wake Emrys first? I mean, it's for his benefit, isn't it. And he's got to believe it's real. It won't work if he thinks it's fake."

"Good point." Kriss nudged Emrys awake.

The centaur "Hurrumphed" grumpily, but sat up and looked from one to the other expectantly. "What?"

"I was going to wait until morning, Emrys, but Kriss thinks I should do this now."

"Do what?"

"The Keeper of Secrets gave me the words of a magic spell," Archie lied. "She said it would reverse the Moon's curse so you could leave the caves. Look at me while I speak it, and concentrate."

Giving the surprised centaur no time to react, Archie cleared his throat. He had concocted a rough sequence of words during his journey back from the river, but had not firmed up on them at all. Very hesitantly, he started to chant in what he imagined was a mystical-sounding voice:

"What was done was done, Let it now be undone

Let now any hurtful spell reverse and lift from Emrys this vicious curse

So he can leave this sacred space, return Emrys' spirit to its grace"

Archie paused, drastically losing momentum, he murmured quietly to himself then reluctantly continued:

"Emrys accepts apologies for what was done

I defuse the Moon's hex with the morning sun."

There was a moment's silence then Emrys chuckled, "Is that it?" he said in disbelief and lay back down.

"That's it," Kriss announced. "Now we must sleep," he smiled at Archie and gave a little wink.

Although not entirely sure what he had expected, Archie was keenly disappointed by Emrys' reaction. Clearly the spell he had concocted had had no effect whatsoever. He gazed with a worried frown at the once more slumbering centaur. Only then did he remember what Lillian had actually said: 'It will remove his fear. But remember; first you must make him recall who he really is'. Archie ran his fingers through his hair in frustration. Of course the spell had not worked for Emrys had not yet remembered who he was. His instinctive reaction to hold back on it till morning had been the right one. It was Kriss who had encouraged him to do it now. As Archie considered the significance of that perturbing fact, the big man's deep voice penetrated his thoughts.

"You must try to sleep, Archie, or tomorrow will be a painful day for all of us."

CHAPTER SIXTEEN

THE GREAT ESCAPE

The dawn propelled an eerie ambiance into the caves. Emrys and Kriss slumbered soundly as the sun slowly oozed his light into Transit. Archie had not slept at all. Lying awake on the damp stone floor he had listened to the storm passing, going over and over in his mind all that Kriss had told him. As soon as the Moon had set he went to sit outside and witnessed the first splinter of light appearing. He was waiting for Felicity, but still she did not come.

Kriss roused as the heat of the sun warmed his face. Archie did not notice; he remained transfixed on a distant point on the horizon and hearing his friends stir did not lift him from this view. He was lost in thought, attempting to link telepathically with Felicity and begging her to return to him.

"She will come back, Archie," Kriss announced behind him. "She'll be tired after her night in the sky and maybe she's a little anxious too. There's no doubt her mistress will have questioned her. A lot of information was spilled and the Moon will want answers. Hope is a very clever girl though, so don't worry. Have you slept?"

"Yes," Archie lied, his stare not shifting. "And her name is Felicity," he said shortly, thinking, 'what has the Moon done to her?' His mind was reeling, completely delirious through lack of sleep.

"That too," Kriss acknowledged, "and at night she is the Moon's possession and by day her own, but Felicity has boundaries set upon her. She is forbidden to talk to anyone who is in Transit, a restriction she has continually flouted and yesterday was caught red-handed by a raven for the second time. Her mistress will not be pleased." Kriss turned back to the stirring centaur, "How did you sleep, Emrys? Did anything come to you in your dreams?"

Archie recognised that Kriss seemed to be taking control of the entire situation again. Reluctantly, he pushed himself to his feet, walked back into the cave and sat by the dead embers of the fire. Emrys was barely awake and still trying to focus in on the day. Before Archie could greet him, Kriss spoke again.

"Emrys, have you anything to report? Come on, time is of the essence here." Emrys had a confused look in his eye. To Archie it was obvious that something had twigged.

"There was an annoying noise," the centaur said. "It was high pitched and kept sounding constantly like a warning bell or a distress signal. I don't remember anything else, I don't think. There could be more though, but it seems to be slipping away as I speak," Emrys continued to frown. "No, it is just a silence between each repeated noise. I've never heard anything like it before."

"Well you obviously have heard it before or it wouldn't be stored in that head of yours," Kriss raised his eyebrows at his friend. "See, your memory does work after all. What do think it was?"

"I know what it was, Archie chipped in. "It was a digital alarm watch." Two sets of eyes swivelled to stare at him.

"What's one of those?" Emrys frowned.

"A wristwatch that beeps at whatever time you set. I had one when I as a kid. I had it on the day we met. You had turned back to your digging just before it went off. I had set it to remind me when to run for base," Archie smiled at the memory. "It was part of the game and –"

"Yes, I've got it,' Emrys interrupted, "there was a shadow, a shadow on an old stone wall."

"My friend James! That's the link, you did it Emrys," Archie snapped, springing out of his nostalgic daze and onto his feet.

Emrys was concentrating hard, a pleased enlightenment spreading over his face. "I was the vicar; we were on the mountainside. I was thinking about my next sermon while I dug the soil..." the words tumbled out.

Archie laughed elatedly. He felt suddenly lifted, things were moving forward and he was glad to take some control back from Kriss. "We should move. We don't have much time."

"You are right, Archie, let's get out of this hole," Kriss turned to Emrys and waited for a positive response.

"How, though?" Emrys whispered, fear screwing up his features.

"It's easy, Emrys," Archie said as reassuringly as he could. "Remember the spell: I defuse the Moon's hex with the morning sun. Look outside; the sun is shining. The Keeper of Secrets told me the Moon's curse would lift as soon as you remembered who you were. Well, most of it at least. I'm afraid you will probably always be a centaur, but you no longer have to fear the Moon's power over you. You can escape and move on over the bridge."

Emrys' eager expression dropped to one of utter misery, "But how? There is no viable escape route for one such as I. I cannot climb up to the cliff top. That has not changed."

"You don't have to. There's a way out behind the waterfall, Felicity told me yesterday about a ledge there. Let's go and have a look."

They hurried through to the garden cave, Emrys gasping, overwhelmed by the speed at which his memories were returning. "I heard you and your friend running down the mountain, you were laughing, Archie," he said as they sped down the tunnel. "And then I heard a distant splash."

"That was me attempting to jump the stream. I didn't clear it, James did though." Archie thought back to the race he and his friend had run and the bet they had made.

"And your friend... James ... he crossed to 'the other side' in one swift leap, whilst you created a giant splash into Transit." Emrys' frown melted into a delighted grin at the play on words.

The mention of James's death had brought a lump to Archie's throat and he did not return the smile. "Can you remember hearing anything else?"

"No, I don't think so, there is just silence," Emrys replied, but I think it will all come back to me now. There are some things I would rather not remember. I had a pain in my chest..."

"Take it at your own pace, Emrys. Nothing from the past can hurt you now," Kriss urged. "You do not have to rush."

The morning sunshine lit up the cascading water at the mouth of the cave as the trio inspected their escape route. Behind the waterfall a narrow ledge curved round the cliff face, it looked green and slippery. "That must be Felicity's 'skinny lip'," Archie said, eyeing the vertical drop to the jagged rocks and the sea way below. "I'll go first... best to not look down."

"Are you two sure this is wise? It's no more than half a metre wide," Emrys took a step back. "We have made no p-p-plans, surely we need to p-p-prepare for this?" he stuttered.

"We'll have to plan as we go, we have limited time. In less than two days the Moon's power will return," Kriss replied. Emrys gasped with terror at the mere mention of her name.

Archie put a reassuring hand on his shoulder. "Don't be afraid, Emrys. Remember the spell. It'll be okay. As if he had not spoken, Kriss continued.

"And who knows what other dangers we shall have to face before we find the bridge. We have to move fast."

All three of them stared from one to the other. "I can't, Archie, I'm sorry," Emrys broke down, turning round to return to the upper caves.

"Emrys, stop. It will be okay," Archie said again, jumping in front of him and fixing his calm gaze on the centaur looked deep into his frightened eyes. "I promise. I've got you this far, haven't I? Please, just take it really slowly and follow my every footstep."

"What if I'm not meant to leave the caves?" Emrys gulped, glaring at Archie, still completely unsure and utterly terrified. "What if the spell hasn't worked?"

"Of course you are meant to leave," it all slotted into place for Archie now. "Why do you think I turned up? You told me of my fate a long time ago and then you waited for me - and thank God you did the state I was in. Can't you see how simple this story is? Now it is my turn to help you by getting you out of here. We cross together

– hell or high water, remember? Now come on," Archie insisted.

"What about Hope? Won't you wait for her?" Emrys begged, desperate to stall.

"I've been thinking about her all night…" Archie's voice trailed away. Felicity's story was not so simple. He had indeed been thinking about her constantly and come to no conclusion. Her sweet familiarity and the feelings she engendered in him were raw, as though an old and painful wound had been ripped open again. Her continued absence concerned him deeply, fearing that in the night the Moon had punished her. But for now Archie knew his path – as had Felicity so many centuries ago. He could not wait for her. It was all about making choices and accepting his responsibility to rescue Emrys. In fact the compulsion to do so was so strong it was no choice at all.

"Let's go." Archie forced Emrys round until he was facing the cave mouth. Resisting the urge to slap the centaur's backside, he grinned at Kriss who was waiting patiently leaning on his staff, his red cape flapping in the breeze.

Slowly, Archie edged his way onto the ledge while Kriss and Emrys waited, watching as he clung to the uneven cliff face behind the waterfall. One false move and the force of the water thundering down would send him plummeting to the rocks below. Archie knew his biggest enemy was fear. 'It's mind over matter,' he told himself. 'If you think "difficult", then it will be, so think "walk in the park".' It was easier said than done: the ledge was like an ice rink and he began to worry about how Emrys, always so clumsy with his feet, would manage without falling to his death. Except, of course, that he was already dead. They all were. Archie found it hard to get his head round this anomaly.

His fear was very real and only his courage and strength of will kept him moving forward.

Treading tentatively, inch by inch, Archie murmured under his breath his same little prayer, slightly amended, in the hope that someone might hear. "Please God keep us safe, please God keep us safe." And then he remembered his aura: "Aura bright, propel my yellow light, aura bright, propel my yellow light." As he neared the middle of the waterfall he heard the distinct screech of a raven somewhere beyond the streaming curtain of water. He immediately ground to a halt.

Breathless with fright, beads of sweat emerging from his forehead to mingle with the mist of the falls that soaked him, Archie peered through the water and saw a distorted black shadow. 'Has it spotted me?' he thought. For a moment he remained motionless pressed into the cliff face in the hope the raven would not see him, a huge wave of nausea making his head swim as he visualised the big bird attacking him, its wicked beak going for his eyes. He would not be able to fend it off. He would be blinded and would fall. He fought against sheer terror, his hands beginning to shake, his fingernails clawing and scraping on the mossy rock. The slippery ledge on which he was narrowly poised trembled from the wrath of the pounding falls. Archie could feel the vibrations in the soles of his feet and as he struggled to hold on they began to slide. "Get a grip Archie Fletcher," he murmured sternly, re-positioning his toes and edging round until he could see back the way he had come. Kriss was ushering Emrys onto the ledge and keeping close, supporting the centaur's rear end with one hand and holding his staff with the other, like a handrail for Emrys to cling to. Neither had noticed the enemy.

Archie looked back through the cascading water and panicked. The raven was more distinct now. 'If I can see it, then it can see me. God, I wish I was invisible.' He wanted desperately to signal to Kriss and Emrys, warn them to stop and stay back, but both were too engrossed on their feet to see him. He tried to project a thought warning to Kriss, but the big man did not appear to receive it. Archie dared not shout, it would only alert the raven. So he remained where he was, helpless, frozen to the spot. He watched as Emrys clumsily placed one hoof in front of the other. The centaur slipped, his hoof sliding to the edge. Kriss grabbed and steadied him. Archie could not bear to look; he closed his eyes and pressed his face into the rock. "This is no easy way out, Felicity," he murmured. "Please help us someone. We have to get Emrys out of here." There was nothing else he could do but pray and wait. It felt like forever and as Archie struggled to control his fear he could feel the 'Moon's eyes' fixing on his back. He clung on with every last grain of energy he had left and prayed.

Then, in a heartbeat, a brilliant blessing struck through the gushing waterfall: a flash of light of such incredible intensity it was as if a nuclear explosion was taking place. Felicity! Even in daylight, a star could create an astounding light. Archie, his face still pressed into the dark rock, was temporarily blinded so what Felicity's light had done to the raven's eyes, which were probably staring straight at her, God alone knew. It lasted only a moment, but it was enough. Felicity did not show herself or speak to him, but as Archie's sight returned to him he saw that the dark shadow beyond the waterfall had disappeared. Presumably the star had retreated and taken the blinded bird with her. 'Thank you,' he called out in his mind, hoping against hope that she would hear him. Archie felt slightly more comfortable knowing that Felicity, although not with him physically, was still watching over him, listening and guiding, helping to keep any foes at bay – as she always had done. He knew that now.

"What was that?" Kriss bellowed. "I can't see a thing." He and Emrys were both balanced and safe on the ledge.

Archie made the snap decision not to tell them just now in case it gave the centaur an excuse to return to the cave. "Nothing to worry about," he yelled, "tell you in a minute. Just wait for your sight to recover, it won't take long." Kriss raised a hand in acknowledgement and Archie, satisfied, edged himself back round to look along the remainder of the ledge. It seemed to widen and move upwards. Step by slippery step he moved forward, becoming aware that the power of the water was lessening as he progressed. Soon he could see beyond the ledge to a grassy knoll at the edge of the waterfall and just as Felicity had described, it was but a short jump. Flushed with success, he leapt and landed on the grass, turning immediately to see where the others were. They had started moving again and he watched closely, beckoning them on.

Soon all three stood on the knoll, their ordeal over. Archie spun round in a circle, scanning the open land and praying Felicity might be there waiting for them, but she was nowhere to be seen. On their left the river frothed and sparkled, rushing ever downward on its journey to the sea.

Emrys fell to his knees, "I feel so vulnerable," he gasped. "It's hard to take in. I cannot believe I am free." Kriss was by his side in an instant, lightly stroking his back.

"You did it my friend. Now all that's left is to get you and Archie across the bridge."

"The Moon knows," Archie announced, looking from one to the other. "I didn't want to say earlier, but I saw a raven watching us as we made our escape. I think it was Felicity who distracted it. It could only have been her light that blinded us all, but the bird will have come off worst."

Kriss frowned, "Then we have to keep moving."

"I can't, I need to rest," Emrys spoke weakly. "I don't have the strength for this right now."

"Resting is not an option, Emrys. Who knows what lies ahead of us? This land is vast and unbelievably dangerous. We haven't a moment to lose," Kriss insisted, rubbing his friend's back harder and almost pushing him onto his feet. "We will help you. Come on, get up. You are free, aren't you excited? Let's get moving."

"Okay, I'm up," Emrys said, forcing himself onto his painfully cracked hooves and looking around at the landscape. "I'm not used to such escapades. I've been trapped for too many years. But at least I have remembered how to pray – I was, after all, the vicar of St Digain's," a gentle smile crossed his weary features. "Which way do we go?" He looked at Archie then at Kriss. Both their faces told the same story; they did not know.

"Right," said Emrys, unusually taking the lead. "Let's follow the river downstream." Without more ado he set off at a fast trot. Finding his stride and stretching his legs he opened up into a canter and then a full blown gallop, his tail streaming behind him.

Left standing, Archie and Kriss stared after him, jaw-dropped as Emrys' shout of joy came back to them. It was as though he had only at that moment realised his liberty and was suddenly elated. Yowling and whooping as he went, the centaur jumped the boulders and driftwood strewn on the riverbank, kicked his heels and bucked, his hooves flicking great clods of mud at his friends as he careered away from them. Kriss rolled his eyes and smiled at Archie who grinned back at him, it was hard not to. "Let's go," he shrieked suddenly, spurting into a full sprint after Emrys.

They had to run a fair way before they finally caught up with him. Thankfully, Emrys had slowed to a fast walk. "What took you so long?" he asked as Archie came up beside him.

"Can we stop for a breather? I thought you were tired," Archie puffed, bending over and clutching his sides.

"So did I," the centaur smiled, his melancholy apparently a thing of the past.

Kriss caught up with them then, his eyes constantly scanning the countryside for any sign of danger. They set of again at a more sedate pace, making their way downhill following the river, their feet sinking into the soft, wet ground. The water was rushing by fast, but looked fairly shallow and was dotted with large boulders protruding from the surface. "We will reach a fork eventually where this river joins the big one," Archie announced, "I recognise the lie of the land. I think we should cross this one now and walk down on the other side until we get to the intersection, then work our way upstream."

"Are you sure? Why do you think it is right to cross it now?" Kriss asked from behind.

It seemed an odd question and the big man's tone was peculiar; there was a strange knowing quality to it that unsettled Archie a little and brought back his suspicions of the previous night, but aware that Kriss could read his mind he blanked his thoughts. "Yes, I'm sure. I've followed the river all the way to the sea in that direction," he pointed over to the far right, "and I'm one hundred percent certain there was no bridge." He lengthened his stride to keep up with Emrys, flinging over his shoulder, "Do you have a better suggestion?"

Nodding to himself, Kriss ignored the caustic query, "Fine. Then we cross."

Emrys plodded on, but Archie, astounded, turned to face the big man. He had expected an argument convinced Kriss would want to take back the initiative."

"I have the utmost faith in you, Archie. Please try not to question it."

"Did you just read me, Kriss?" Archie knew full well that he had.

"I sense you don't trust me even after all I have done for you. I know I may seem bossy at times and appear to want to take control of the situation, but that is just my way. It is my task to keep things moving and ultimately to help you cross the bridge safely."

"Why should I trust you?" Archie queried, still unsure of Kriss's role in Transit.

"Lillian told you there was a time limit to your journey, did she not? The clock is ticking, Archie, you have to trust me."

"I find it hard when there are so many unanswered questions. Who are you? How come you are here in Transit and yet you are not a lost soul? Or at least, you don't seem like a lost soul to me. Who allotted you the task of helping me? And how come you seem to know everything? I ask again, why should I trust you?"

"Because just recently I saved your life from the evil spell of the Moon and helped you free Emrys from his curse, is that not enough? Listen to me, I am here to help you." Kriss placed both hands on Archie's shoulders, maintaining eye contact, his tone softened persuasively and his expression was deeply sincere. "Believe it or not, a long time ago, back in your cornfield days when you went off to war, Felicity commanded me to follow and protect you during your treacherous worldly travels. She could not do so herself, not physically, so every one of your lifetimes she has passed the responsibility of protecting you to me." Kriss straightened himself with a look of pride, removing his hands from Archie's shoulders. "And every life you have lived I have done exactly that. I have done as she commanded and I continue to do so to the best of my ability. Believe me, my only motive is to keep you safe and get you across the bridge."

"Why do you follow Felicity's every command?" Archie questioned, trying to block his thoughts from the big man, but unable to stop his astonishment.

"Because that is my job, please do not question me further, just trust me, I beg you."

Archie shrugged and resumed walking, his mind as busy as the tributary that rushed by them, the water frothing white around the boulders and creating miniature whirlpools. Still on the move, Archie said, "Over there, look."

Emrys and Kriss looked to where he pointed: a succession of huge flat boulders broke the surface creating perfect stepping stones across the river. Emrys did not speak. His previous spurt had caught up with him and he was still breathless. He simply nodded and moved sturdily onto the first boulder, teetering there for a moment before moving on to the next.

Without another word, Kriss began to wade through the bubbling water, leaning on his staff and choosing to ignore the boulders. "Well, are you coming?" he called to Archie.

A few metres ahead Emrys had halted on a stepping stone and was looking back at them quizzically. "Is anything wrong?" he called.

"No. You go on Emrys," Archie summoned a reassuring smile, "I'm just coming." As Archie watched the centaur resume his cautious journey across the river, he could no longer conceal his teeming thoughts. He was staggered by Kriss's revelation, but it did not answer his questions. Who was this larger than life man who had so neatly avoided revealing his identity? There was something strange here that Archie could not fathom, and yet knowing that Kriss was here at Felicity's behest made him feel less suspicious. He believed without a shadow of doubt that she would do nothing to cause him harm. He wondered briefly why he was so certain of that; after all, he still did not know her, not really - he just felt as if he did.

CHAPTER SEVENTEEN

A FIGMENT OF THE IMAGINATION

On the other side of the river the terrain was swampy and in places overgrown with waist-high stinging nettles and brambles. It became increasingly difficult for the three travellers to maintain their pace the further downstream they went. Since the crossing, no one had spoken a word. Emrys plodded in the lead stamping down brambles that were in their path, his hooves sucking and squelching in the mud. Kriss walked behind him, occasionally putting his shoulder to Emrys' hindquarters when the centaur got stuck. Archie, not in the best of moods, brought up the rear. Between the trees that clustered thickly back from the river bank he caught glimpses of a grassy plain stretching into the distance. After a while the trees thinned out to reveal a flat landscape devoid of a single interesting feature and certainly no bridge. Staring out across the dull scenery, Archie began to fear he was on a wild goose chase. To alleviate his boredom he let his imagination run free. Lost in a world of his own, he was in the middle of an exciting daydream involving heroic deeds when out of nowhere, Felicity's voice sounded clear as a bell.

"There is danger ahead, an enraged charioteer is careering this way completely out of control. His two wild horses are pulling the cart in every direction. You must get ready. He means to attack!"

They all stopped dead in their tracks. Kriss spun on his heel scanning every section of their surroundings. "Who is it?"

"A figment of Archie's imagination," Felicity proclaimed.

"What? Is this some kind of joke?" Archie, deep into his fantasy, had only just imagined a fearsome warrior charging across the plains in a horse-drawn, bronze chariot. He assumed Felicity had been reading his mind again, wherever she was. Before he had time to protest further she materialised before him, her face tight with anxiety.

"The ravens fly with him. He comes quickly, get ready," she shouted. "It's no joke, Archie, you have conjured him. The danger is very real." The star's arrival had been so unexpected and her stance so urgent that Archie completely forgot his anxiety about meeting her again. What he felt now was utter embarrassment for having thought up such a dangerous opponent and he was gripped by sudden, gut-wrenching fear. Too late, Lillian's words came back to him: '...every conceivable energy state really does exist. Be careful what you think....' He had thought she was just philosophising, had not realised she meant it literally.

"Aura bright propel my yellow light, aura bright propel my yellow light. Please God keep us safe, please God keep us safe." Archie had become so used to praying and feeling his aura rush out, he had not realised it had been continuously illuminated since the previous day. The vibrant light now spread out to encompass them all in a giant yellow shield.

The four friends moved into a circle facing outwards, back to back, surveying the land intently as they waited for the onslaught.

"Here they come," Felicity screamed.

The air was filled with the sinister rushing of hundreds of wings as flocks of giant ravens swarmed above their heads. The chariot appeared from nowhere; leaping through the air as though it had jumped through an invisible porthole. With it came dark, threatening clouds, the air growing cold as they covered the sun banishing the warmth of the day. Heading directly for the hapless foursome, snarling and roaring as he came, the charioteer was a fearsome sight. He wore a blood-red tunic protected by a steel chest-plate, his head encased in a bronze helmet. In one hand he hauled at the reins, in the other he held a long spear, which he swiped menacingly through the air. The two muscular horses, one black, one white, pulled in opposite directions, the chariot tilting alarmingly and jolting the warrior from side to side as he struggled for control. Their nostrils flared red, foam flew up from their snapping teeth and their eyes were wild and staring.

"Okay, what's the plan here boys and girls? Anyone got a plan… anyone?" Emrys panicked. All this commotion after his sedentary existence was proving too much for the unfit centaur. His legs trembled and his flanks were dark with sweat.

"Don't panic, stay focused," Archie said calmly, trying hard to maintain his composure.

"Don't panic, stay focused? Is that the best you can do?" Emrys hollered back.

"Emrys, you sent me out alone to kill a lion with my bare hands, surely between the four of us we can handle a loon in a cart," Archie hissed.

"Kriss, Hope, remind me never to travel with Archie Fletcher until his feral imagination is fully under control. This is ludicrous. Have you always had bronze war chariots rolling around in that battlefield you call a brain?" Emrys yelled.

"Only today," Archie said, trying not to react to Emrys' sarcasm. This horrifying situation was, albeit unwittingly, entirely his fault and he could hardly blame the centaur for being annoyed about it. "I'm sorry, Emrys, but this sort of thing seems to be becoming the norm in my present reality," he attempted to justify himself.

"ENOUGH!" Kriss bellowed. "Save it for the charioteer."

The horses were upon them. Kriss leapt in front of Archie, who leapt in front of Felicity, each trying to protect the other. It was Emrys who impulsively took action. As his friends cowered beneath the slashing hooves that pawed the air above their heads, the centaur reared, hurling his body forward. His front hooves landed with an almighty blow on the shoulder of the white horse. Thrown off balance it stumbled into its companion and the chariot veered off course. Red-faced and furious, the warrior hauled on the reins, gradually turning the stampeding horses until he was in position to charge again. The sky was dark with ravens swooping above them, their wicked talons stretched out ready to pounce.

Emrys did not take his gaze off the enemy. "Run," he bellowed. "Head for the bridge. This is my battle now."

"Stand firm," Archie shouted. "We can't split up. We cross together."

"No, Archie. The warrior is the Moon's fury. It's me he's after. This is my fight. I will catch up. Now run, for God's sake run."

The charioteer reared his horses and began his charge, focusing solely on Emrys. Kriss and Archie exchanged glances, no words were needed. Felicity was already away; they sped after her. "We should wait in case he needs us," Archie puffed, as he powered to keep up with Kriss.

"Emrys has made this his own battle now, Archie. Even if we return it would be discourteous to assist. You must trust me in this and do as I say." He spoke with such stern authority that Archie continued sprinting, but he had never been one to run from a fight, particularly when it involved a friend and he was deeply troubled, his guilt as intense as his concern. Turning occasionally to see what was happening behind them, all he could make out was a flurry of black feathers and a blur of rearing horses. And then he saw a lone raven; it had broken away from the fight and was coming after them.

Kriss had seen it too. He stopped abruptly. "I think we are out of harm's way now. I shall wait for Emrys here, you go on and catch up with Felicity."

"Why? Shouldn't I wait with you? What's wrong?" Archie gasped, catching his breath.

"Nothing; have no fear. Emrys is going to win this fight, but he will need me close at hand when it is over. It is his first battle since his plight with the Moon, he is sure to have some bragging to do. Aside from which, I think you and Felicity have things to say to each other," a slow smile spread across Kriss's face, "and I do not wish to play gooseberry."

Archie felt his face and neck grow hot and looked away. The raven was still there watching from the skies. Without another word he shot after Felicity.

She was beside the river, peeping out from beneath the weeping branches of a giant willow tree. He could see she was panicking, peering frantically behind him for the others. "It's okay," he called, running towards her. "Kriss is not far behind, he's waiting for Emrys.

"Is he surviving? Will he defeat them?" she cried her anxiety spilling over as she came to meet him, her aura unusually dim.

"He has to," Archie said simply, coming to a halt in front of the star. Her eyes flicked up to look at him then back into the distance. Archie's stare lingered on her lovely face, which was smeared with dirt and wet with tears, even her wings looked bedraggled.

"What?" Felicity snapped.

"He has to be okay because we are crossing together, remember?"

She scowled at him, "Of course I remember. I meant why are you staring at me like that?"

"Like what?" Archie's gaze slid away, his face getting hot again. "Sorry, I didn't mean to offend you. It's just that your light seems a lot less bright than normal," he said lamely.

"You haven't offended me," Felicity sighed, "I'm tense that's all. Emrys is my best-friend. I'm not used to such violent action and neither is he. I didn't mean to snap at you, Archie. Distracting the raven at the waterfall wiped me out. I'd been glowing all night, so whopping up the voltage like that during the day just about killed me - that's why my aura is low."

"I'm sorry; you did that for me, I know, and I'm truly grateful. Fact is, without you I would not be here."

Felicity dipped her head in acknowledgement, retaining eye contact, her glow increasing slightly. "This mission has to succeed, Archie, for you, for Emrys and for Kriss," she paused, her lower lip quivering, "...and for me." She squeezed out a tiny smile. "If you don't make it, I dread to think where we'll all end up."

"What do you mean 'if you don't make it'? You are all coming with me, aren't you?"

Distraught, Felicity gazed into his eyes, "I have longed to be close to you, I have dreamed of the day we would see one another again, face to face; eye to eye. I'm a star; stars don't dream, and yet I feel like I'm dreaming now." She looked down at her tiny feet, said in a small voice, "I can't come with you, Archie. Kriss did tell you everything, didn't he?"

"Yes; yes, he told me it all," Archie nodded.

"So you understand that we can't happen? Crossing over with you is impossible for me. I will be forever in your life, this I have vowed, but I am completely out of your reach."

She moved closer to him and he saw that her eyes were swimming with tears. "No, Fee, I will not have it," he barked. "You are crossing with me and that's all there is to it!"

Archie turned away from her, closing the subject abruptly. He did not know what had come over him to react in such a way. Normally he would assess a situation and see how to fix the problem. Here he was refusing to even look at it. Struggling for control, he glanced up at the sky then ducked under the canopy of the huge willow. "We should wait in here for Emrys and Kriss," he beckoned, settling himself down on one of the flat rocks that lay beneath the spreading branches. "There's a raven spying on us, it won't see us under here and you look as though you could use a rest," he patted the rock at his side.

After a moment's hesitation, Felicity followed, collapsing wearily beside him. "I do feel drained," she admitted. "The chariot coming at us like that was such a shock and I was already low. But it will not take long for me to recharge my batteries," she brightened, smiling up at him.

Grabbing up a handful of pebbles and manoeuvring himself in front of a gap in the draping foliage, Archie began to skim them one at a time across the water. Once again, although at ease in Felicity's company he fell lost for words, trapped in his thoughts. She sat silently beside him watching each pebble jump three times before it sank.

"Thanks for earlier," Archie broke the tranquil silence, "at the waterfall."

"You've already thanked me once," she giggled, her irrepressible humour returning. "You're very welcome. Those horrid ravens are everywhere. I could see it was putting you off your escape."

"Just slightly," Archie shuddered. "I could feel that wretched bird watching me. I thought it was going to blind me..." he laughed as the irony struck him, "but you did that instead!"

"It wouldn't have done. They only risk an attack when there's a flock of them. Individually they're cowards - merely spies. Be wary of them, yes, but don't fear them. Anyway, by nightfall we will be more than half way to the bridge. By this time tomorrow we should have found it and you will cross safely to the other side and be well away from the Moon and her prying eyes."

Archie nodded distractedly, "But what about you?"

"I've told you, my destiny is not the same as yours, but I'd rather not talk about that just now so please don't ask me," Felicity smiled, softening her bitter words. "I just want to sit here with you for a time. I deserve a moment's pleasure - I've waited so many centuries for this. Please,

Archie," she wheedled, "let's just enjoy being together." She jumped up from the rock and started snapping off twigs of willow.

He could refuse her nothing. Crestfallen, he nodded and continued in silence to play Ducks-and-Drakes, perfecting his throw and watching his stones skimming across the river. After a while he began to relax and as Felicity had asked, to enjoy the simple pleasure of their togetherness, chuckling when he saw what she was doing. Bringing back an armful of twigs to sit once more at his side she had begun to weave them into a circle.

Way above the shading tree, the sun discreetly serenaded them with his music. It was a warm, idyllic interlude: a moment to be treasured made all the more poignant because they both knew it would soon have to end. They had noted the giant raven perched high on the topmost branches reminding them the Moon was watching their every move, but with their backs turned and their minds preoccupied, they chose to ignore it and live for the now, knowing that life tomorrow could be so very different. The willow that sheltered them distorted the raven's view and the tree crafted rustling whispers with its swaying branches so that not a single thought could be divulged from their minds. Grounded by deep growing roots and with its widespread limbs stretching out over the water like a magnificent bridge of its own, the living tree cosseted Archie and his star for their all too brief moment of intimacy.

"The sound of this old tree dancing in the breeze reminds me of the cornfields. It makes me want to weep." A delicate tear spilled onto Felicity's cheek, but she continued to smile leaning her head against Archie's shoulder, her fingers still busy with the weave in her lap.

"Perhaps that's why it's called a weeping willow," he teased, yearning for a memory of their shared past. "The sound is hypnotic though isn't it?"

"Actually, it's because a young man once left his love under a tree just like this one while he went off in search of greatness and she was so unhappy when he'd gone she cried herself to death beneath its branches."

"That's a terrible story," Archie reproved. "And anyway, as I understand it, I did not leave you in search of greatness."

"No." Head down, Felicity focused on her weaving, bending to pluck some stitchwort growing at their feet and twisting tiny white flowers into the circle of willow, which now resembled a wreath. Sighing she said sadly, "You left because I told you to go. And in all this time you have never forgiven me."

Remembering Kriss's recent revelation, Archie raised his eyebrows. "Has everybody always done what you told them to?"

"They did back then, unfortunately. I was of noble blood, a bargaining chip doomed from birth to further my family's wealth and position in society by making a suitable match. How things have changed! To my parents I became a disgrace and in their eyes a vagabond to be forgotten." Felicity raised her head, tears welling once more. "I was forced to live a lie, Archie. Have you ever tried living a lie? Let me tell you, it's impossible. God knows I tried but in the end…" she shook her head. "Now, unbeknown to you all these years it has been me who has helplessly followed you." The star looked up at Archie, whose last shot at skimming flunked and sank.

"Can we fix this, Fee? Is there nothing we can do to reverse our curse?"

"It is not a curse that enslaves us, Archie, it is a promise I made to God."

"Surely God wants us to stay together this time, why else would He enable us to meet again like this?"

"Because He wants you to remember me - it is all part of your journey. I want you to remember me too. God has had this encounter written in the stars since we parted and in a very small way I have lent a hand to His plan by finding a way to be with you." Archie's eyebrow lifted in an unspoken query as he waited for Felicity to explain.

Looking faintly embarrassed she fiddled with her willow weave. After a moment she sighed and put it to one side. "Two other stars, Chara and Saiph, are in serious trouble with the Moon because of me. I locked them in a black hole. I did it to distract her so I could descend to Earth for your final life span. Intermittently you understand; I had to return sometimes so she wouldn't suspect me. She was too busy looking for them to notice my absences at first. When she did, I released them and told the Moon it was Saiph who had been walking the Earth. I also said it was she who had locked Chara in a black hole as a decoy. I made out I only knew about it because I had been accidently lost in Transit for a time."

"And the Moon believed you?" Archie gave her a worried look, amazed she had gone to such lengths and risked so much for him.

"Briefly maybe, but by now I'm sure Chara and Saiph have dobbed me in. I don't really care. What I was looking for is here and now and that's worth whatever punishment must follow."

"I can't bear for you to be punished because of me and if I can't remember you it's all been for nothing." Distressed, Archie drummed his fingers on his knees in frustration, "But how am I supposed to recall something that happened centuries ago?"

"Just as Emrys found his past so shall you. You have to or I shall be lost forever, this chance will never come again. I believe we are an experiment in God's great plan. If you can remember me we are free. If not I remain banished to serve the Moon for eternity and you will cross over to the other side without me."

"I will allow no curse or spell or promise to trap you in this land, Fee," Archie insisted wildly. "And I do not believe God means that to happen."

"I won't remain here, Archie."

"I know. You'll be up there. How is this fair? Emrys only had to remember what happened a decade or so ago, not hundreds of years."

"I know. It's impossible," Felicity said, springing off the rock and walking in circles, fluttering her wings in agitation. She threw the finished willow weave at Archie and started stripping more strands from the tree to make another.

"What's this?" Archie asked, catching the twiggy wreath.

"It's a willow crown. I made it for you," Felicity twinkled.

"Why?" Archie inspected it, gently spinning it on his index finger.

"Because… I just did, okay? God, you are just so insolent sometimes," Felicity teased.

"Is that how you see me? Have I always been like that?" Archie frowned; as far as he knew he was not normally impertinent. He had often teased Helena and Stewart, of course, and others with whom he had truly felt at ease, but that was not the same as being insolent.

Felicity grinned at his bemused expression, "Only with me. We jested constantly. You can with those you love," she lowered her gaze, a flush creeping into her cheeks. "Our banter back in the cornfields was how we dealt with our cruel reality. If we hadn't laughed we would have cried." Looking up she asked, "Why do you think I have made you a willow crown?"

"To wear?" Archie smirked, pretending to put it on, then tossing it up and catching it again.

"And why would I want you to wear it?" Felicity giggled, trying to grab the crown from him.

He held it out of her reach and grinned, "To make me look silly?"

Felicity glared up at Archie, a mischievous glint in her blue eyes, "Please will you be serious for a second," she teased crossly. "It is a symbol of affection. I used to make crowns for you out of corn." Her teasing smile disappeared and her lip began to quiver, "We used to pretend that we..." her words trailed away on a sob and she moved to sit on another rock away from him.

"Thank you," Archie said softly, he could see her distress and did not want to make her cry, so he put the crown on his head hoping to soothe her. Grabbing another handful of stones he skimmed them across the gentle flow of the river. "So you think we are an experiment? All of us, you, me and Emrys." He laughed with grim humour, "Emrys! Come on... if he isn't an experiment then I don't know what is, poor sod." Archie took another shot, "And Kriss, I mean, who on earth is he? None of this journey makes any sense to me, it's a paradox. All of it," Archie rambled on, forgetting he was talking aloud. Not that it made a difference since his thoughts were an open book to Felicity.

"So you don't remember Kriss?"

"Should I?" Intrigued, Archie turned to face her.

"Not even from recent lives you've led?"

He concentrated hard for a moment. "No, I cannot recall any previous lives. All I remember is the one I've just left and my family: Mum, Dad, Hels and Stew..." his voice softened, "and my twin-cousin, Sarah." Archie's eyes filled and he dashed a hand across his face. "And everyone else in my extended family and all my friends. I have no memory blockage of what has just passed. I remember everything, Fee. Even the smell of my home is with me still, it's part of me, it was my reality; where I was understood and where I made sense, you know? I can remember every feeling I had for each individual person in my life - and I never met Kriss, I'm certain of it." Archie shook his head still wrapped in thought, aware of the star watching him closely. After a time he sighed, "It's no good, Fee, if I am to remember you, won't you tell me more about the life we lived together? Maybe it might bring something back." Certain he was on the right track Archie pushed Felicity to answer him. Thinking of the digital alarm that had done it for Emrys he asked, "I mean, what was it like - can you remember the sounds we heard, for example?"

"Sounds? You mean like the church bells ringing or the curlews fluting over the fields, or the sound of marching feet taking young men like you off to war? I can recall everything, Archie, every second of our time together. I reminisce constantly, lost in the sky there is plenty of time for that," Felicity said bitterly, her expression sombre.

"Go on then, let's hear it," Archie pressed.

"Do you know how painful it would be for me to reveal, to you of all people, what we went through back then?"

Although he could see real terror in her eyes at the prospect of talking about it, Archie persisted, "You have to do this, Fee. If you want out as badly as I think you do, you are going to have to start talking. And fast, we don't have much time."

Felicity stared at the ground, tears now dripping onto her feet. "I can't," she whimpered, lifting her head to gaze up through the branches at the black ominous shape of the raven.

"Fee, what do you have to lose?" Archie followed her gaze. "You have already broken away from them. You have disobeyed the Moon's rules, deceived any friends you might have had, walked on Earth without permission and for what? Why trek so far to clam up now? You have put so much at risk for this, holding your heart out on a thread for me to clasp, but how can I if you won't talk to me. We don't have time for guessing games or waiting. You will just have to tell me straight like I did for Emrys."

"I'm not allowed to, Archie, it doesn't work that way for us. You have to remember by yourself. It is different for me," she said in a hushed voice. "I am a split soul. If I tell, I could lose you forever. I couldn't bear it, the agony is too awful even to imagine. That thread I put my heart on is frayed and battered, it could snap at any moment."

Aware he had opened the floodgates Archie's heart sank. Felicity's chest heaved and her tears streamed as she stared at him. The willow whispered around them, hiding her misery in its veil. "I'm s-s-sorry," she sobbed, "I'm ruining this p-p-precious time we have. I so didn't want to cry, but how can I pretend when every day for centuries I have looked down from the heavens and wished I could somehow feel you. Just a touch, a hug, yet knowing it could never come to pass. You were my friend and all that mattered to me. In the one life I lived, everything around me was so cold and calculated, so wrong. You were so warm, ingenuous and so unmistakably right." She hesitated catching her breath and bowing her head, "I made a really bad choice back then, Archie. I let you go and it destroyed my life and yours. I should have broken free, run away with you as you wanted me to, even though it meant my family would be ruined and you and I shunned as outcasts. When I realised my mistake and took my own life, I made a promise to God that with your every birth and rebirth I would watch and guide you from the heavens. A promise to God cannot be broken. It is not a case of 'until I change my mind', it is a promise made forever, never-ending. How can I break it, Archie?" Felicity's imploring eyes found his, "Please, help me. I don't know what to do. I feel like a dying star being swallowed into the darkness as if my broken heart is breaking all over again."

Her distress was heartrending and Archie leapt towards her, wrapping his arms around her and holding her close to his chest, rocking her as she unleashed her tears, "It's okay, Fee," he murmured, his lips in her hair. "Don't cry. I won't let you go." He closed his eyes, his heart pounding as he held her, his mind stammering, searching for something that would comfort her. "A promise is only words and words can be lost in the wind, they are made to be broken, it's an unwritten rule. If God didn't want us to find one another you would never have got this far. It is part of His plan, you said, so how can it be wrong? Anyway, you promised to guide me and you did, you guided me back to you and Emrys." He squeezed her tighter, stroking the long blonde hair that covered her tiny head. Déjà vu drowned him once again his head swimming to such an extent he almost overbalanced and had to open his eyes. "Were you on the mountain in Wales that day when I met Emrys?" he asked abruptly.

Felicity nodded, tears cascading, "It was one of the happiest days of my life. I have cradled that memory in my heart ever since." Her aura glittered as her mind went back in time.

"Where were you? Tell me, Fee, please." Archie pulled away from her, holding her at arm's length to look into her watery eyes.

"No, Archie, I can't. I'm sorry, I really cannot. I have already said too much. Please don't ask me." She removed his hands from her arms, easing herself out of his grasp. "I found you through pure defiance, but like you said, it would never have happened if it wasn't meant to. Now the decree is that you must find me, or the game is over. They win..." her gaze flicked up to the loitering raven, "and we lose," she declared, hovering backwards, tears still falling, "And then you will be a lost soul. I cannot let that happen." Without another word she drifted out from under the willow, the sun's orchestra faded as she floated over to the other side of the river. There she sat, out of Archie's reach and safe from his questions, to finish weaving her own willow crown.

With an enraged cry, Archie tore his own crown from his head and threw it into the pouch at his belt, frustrated and incensed at his inability to remember.

CHAPTER EIGHTEEN

MIND OVER MATTER

Emrys did not turn to watch his friends fleeing from the battleground. He stood at bay, facing forwards in grim determination to win his fight against the Moon's fury. The sky was black and the rain lashed down pooling into puddles around his feet. The ravens attacked first, swooping in on him, clawing for his eyes. Bending his neck, his chin tucked in against his chest, the centaur twisted this way and that rearing up to bat them away with his clenched fists and front hooves, crushing those that flew at him and beating off their attack. The ravens retreated, hovering in the air to regroup, ready to swoop again. Beneath Emrys' hooves the ground shook as the charioteer began his charge. The horses thundered towards him, their manes flying.

Teeth bared, the enraged warrior leaned forward aiming his spear. His first strike slid off Emrys' shoulder as he twisted away, but the warrior struck again sinking the wicked blade deep into the centaur's haunch. He roared with pain as the charioteer yanked out the weapon and hoisted it dripping with blood wheeling the wild horses in a tight circle to come in again.

With nothing to fight with but his hooves and bare hands, Emrys grasped the reins of the white horse and grappled in anguish for the spear in an attempt to dislodge it from the warrior's hand. The stallions reared pulling Emrys off balance. In desperation he lunged at the spear shaft, grabbed it, lost his footing and crashed to the ground, pummelled by giant hooves. The spear snapped in two, one half abandoned on the wet ground and the other still held in the stunned charioteer's hand as once again he wheeled away then turned to come in for the kill, steering his cart directly at the fallen centaur.

Trampled in the mud and severely wounded, Emrys, on the brink of defeat delved deep. He watched the stallions stampede towards him and observed the chariot wheels behind them spinning through the sludge. And then they were on him jarring against his body. Summoning an inner strength forgotten deep inside him, Emrys heaved himself skyward. The chariot toppled and the warrior disappeared, crushed beneath it. As the reins jerked the horses reared falling backwards in a flail of thrashing hooves, screaming as their backs smashed and broke on the upturned chariot, its wheels still spinning.

Emrys collapsed in an exhausted heap too weak to beat off the ravens that dived again and again, gouging him with their razor sharp beaks and outstretched claws, scraping at his broken flesh and tearing his pelt. The centaur, bleeding profusely, covered his eyes with his hands and waited for the end.

"Away, shoo, get off you vile scrawny creatures, get away from him." Kriss, having observed his friend's victory from yonder now felt free to intervene. He whirled around, whipping at the ravens with his staff, smacking them hard. Grabbing a bird by its wing he dropped his staff and wrapped both hands round the raven's neck. As it flapped and thrashed to break free; Kriss, enraged and merciless twisted his strong fingers. There was an ominous click as the bird's vertebrae snapped. "Let this be a lesson to you," he hollered flinging the dead bird away causing the others to startle and fluster squawking and screeching into the air; they did not look back. "Go tell your mistress that Emrys is free, freer than you'll ever be, you cowardly, repulsive, spying, scavenging vultures," Kriss called after them incensed, watching as they disappeared from sight. Once sure they had gone he knelt beside Emrys and gently lifted the centaur's hands. Beneath them Emrys' eyes were screwed shut. "You are safe now my friend," Kriss said. "They've gone."

The centaur opened his eyes, the stricken look on his face thawing to a smile as he looked up at Kriss. "I did it, didn't I? I won," his smile grew broader, "I've beaten the Moon's fury."

"You have indeed. I have rarely seen such courage. Where are you hurt?" Kriss looked down grimly at the centaur's gouged and bloodstained flanks and ran his hand along Emrys' back to his punctured haunch, examining the wound closely. He smiled back at Emrys, concealing his concern. "Are you injured anywhere else? That chariot rolled straight over the top of you; can you move all your limbs?" Kneeling in the thick, sticky mud, Kriss gently bent each of the centaur's legs in turn, murmuring, "How does this one feel?"

"Bit sore," Emrys winced, but continued to grin up at his friend, his teeth clenched. "I'm badly bruised, but nothing's broken. I'll live."

"Thank heavens for that! He was a scary looking chap that charioteer, but no match for you - though I'm sure his bark was far worse than his bite," he added teasingly, relieved the centaur had got off so lightly.

"I don't know, Kriss," Emrys flinched as the big man kneaded the flesh around the deep spear wound in an effort to close the edges and staunch the bleeding. "It's all very well for you to say that, you weren't on the receiving end. He meant business I can tell you." Raising his head, the centaur looked around in search of his foe, but the chariot, its horses and the warrior had vanished as though they had never been. The sun was high in the sky again and the threatening storm clouds had withdrawn into the distance with the ravens.

"This puncture is deep and you've lost a lot of blood." Kriss pursed his lips and thought for a moment. Removing his red cape, he wrapped it tightly round the centaur's croup. "We will have to catch up Archie and Hope and then you can rest." He folded a strong arm around his friend's shoulders, supporting him as Emrys found his hooves.

"So long as that careless, stupid, idiot boy hasn't thought up some other terrifying opponent for me," Emrys scowled, leaning heavily on Kriss and steadying himself.

"Now, now, my friend, don't think unkindly of him – he's not entirely to blame. Archie cannot help the person he is; he still has a lesson to learn and we are all part of his learning curve. We are here to help, remember? If we get it right..." Kriss puffed and panted under Emrys' great bulk, his eyes bulging as he heaved him upright. "If all of us get it right: you, me, Hope and of course Archie, his passing may well become the most eminent of all time." Still scowling, Emrys grunted but made no reply. "Are you okay?" Kriss removed his support and the centaur, his legs quivering, was left standing unaided. "Can you walk?"

"I think so, but I need some aloe to treat my spear wound and some aconite for the pain would be good - God, it hurts! – but I'm unlikely to get my hands on either round here." Emrys grimaced, wincing with each careful step he took.

"Come on then, I'll keep a look out. We need to get going." Kriss strode ahead forcing Emrys, who was very lame, into a shambling trot to keep up with him. "You just concentrate on moving forward as fast as you can. We have much ground to cover and we don't know how far the others have gone. We need to catch them up."

"Hope won't have moved on without us, they won't be far," Emrys insisted. "I can sense they are close. I can't keep this pace up, Kriss, I'm sorry, it's just too painful. You go on without me."

"I know you are suffering, my old friend, but you must try. I cannot leave you alone in this state, but I'm worried about what Hope may say to Archie. She has him all to herself right now, which I know is necessary, but I'm so afraid she'll say something she shouldn't. The star's emotions are in such turmoil and must be contained. Without us both there to restrain her, the temptation may be too great for her and I prefer not to contemplate the outcome."

"You're right. It would be a dreadful tragedy for both of them. I'll do my best," Emrys gasped, increasing his pace.

The two of them moved on quickly until they came in sight of the giant willow tree. When Kriss spotted Felicity sitting alone on the opposite bank and saw stones thrown from beneath the tree splashing into the river, he slowed and turned back to Emrys with a smile. "You were right, of course. They've not gone far. How's that leg? Do you want me to clean the wound?"

"Let's just reach that willow," Emrys grunted with pain, "the bark is an excellent analgesic and what's more it reduces inflammation - just what I need." He looked about him at the flat landscape his mind busy with healing herbs. "There's no chance of us finding aloe here, this land is saturated; we would need higher ground with better drainage."

"We are being watched." Kriss said in an undertone, nodding grimly to the top of the tree. Emrys followed his gaze. A lone raven perched on the uppermost branch, its beady eye looking down at them.

They both halted outside the willow's draping foliage and exchanged glances. "Are you sensing what I'm sensing?" Emrys asked quietly.

"Without a doubt," Kriss said, preparing to break the sombre mood permeating the atmosphere, "but I know of no herb that can fix a broken heart."

"True, my friend; best to take no chances and say nothing," Emrys' gruff voice attempted a whisper. "You don't know what's been said, we could be moving from one battleground to another."

Catching sight of Felicity on the opposite bank Kriss gave Emrys a nudge and exhaled a deep sigh of relief. "It's okay, she didn't tell him. You only have to look at her. Why else would she be sitting alone? She has removed herself from temptation in order to remain silent."

Looking across at the star's lonely figure, Emrys had to agree. "Thank God," he muttered, pushing through the hanging fronds of willow and into the shelter of the tree's canopy, followed closely by Kriss.

Archie had watched their approach with mixed feelings. He was glad to see them both and thankful that neither seemed to be seriously harmed, though he could see Emrys was in pain, but he was not yet ready to face them.

He was still taut with misery and frustration unable to understand why Felicity had refused to help him and hurt that she had chosen to put the river between them and now appeared to be totally absorbed in her weaving as if he didn't exist. In fact he was so thoroughly fed up with the entire situation he was more than ready to move on. Noting the bloodstained cape wrapped securely round Emrys' croup he frowned up at him with concern and guilt in equal measure. "Are you wounded, Emrys?"

"Just a scratch," the centaur beamed through his pain. "I gave that rugged-faced war god a good thrashing I can tell you." He leaned in close and whispered, "And by heaven, it felt good." It seemed he had forgotten how cross he had been with Archie for conjuring up the charioteer.

"I'll bet you did," Archie grinned with relief his guilt dropping away as Emrys shuffled past him to the willow's huge gnarled trunk, examined it closely, then proceeded to peel back the bark, stuffing pieces of it into his mouth and chewing vigorously. Kriss and Archie stared at him in amazement.

"Deadens the pain," Emrys explained with his mouth full. He looked down and suddenly shouted, "Eureka!" spitting bark chips everywhere.

"What?" Kriss and Archie said in unison.

"Puffballs! Look, see?" Emrys pointed at the ground beneath his hooves, "A godsend, thank you," he raised his head and winked up at the heavens.

Around the base of the tree, Archie saw a circle of puffball fungus that until now he had failed to notice. "What's special about them?" he asked the jubilant centaur.

"There are trillions of friendly spores inside these mushrooms," Emrys said, hoofing them gently. "They're exactly what I need. Dried they can plug, heal and prevent infection. They will sort out my wound in no time."

Archie narrowed his eyes, "I thought you said it was just a scratch, Emrys."

"It was an understatement," Kriss said shortly, shooting a doubtful look at the centaur, "I'm afraid they'll have to dry out en route. We can't afford to linger."

"That's fine. Just give me a minute to harvest them. I shall need more willow bark too; then we can set off. I'll be okay now."

"Let me," Archie offered, eager to make amends. He bent to pick the puffballs and placed them carefully into his pouch together with his willow crown and the crushed trumpet lily. "I can carry them for you."

"Thank you, Archie." Emrys proceeded to rip away more bark, murmuring a grateful apology to the tree as he did so.

Leaving them to it, Kriss walked out from under the branches and beckoned to Felicity. "We need to move on," he called across the river, a little surprised that the star had not come to greet them and congratulate Emrys on his victory.

Felicity had watched their return, happy that both appeared fit, but she was still warring with her emotions and had decided to stay where she was. With tears trickling constantly down her pale cheeks, she hummed quietly to herself while weaving her willow crown in an effort to soothe her torment. She was angry with Archie; she knew this was irrational and stemmed from her frustration that he could not remember her and the love they had once shared. It may be centuries ago, but to Felicity it felt like only yesterday and she found it hard to believe it was not the same for him. She could only assume it was because he was not really trying. When Kriss called to her, the finished crown was on her head and she was in the process of plaiting white flowers into her hair. She waved at him feebly and got to her feet.

Aware of the big man's scrutiny as she drifted towards him she could feel him attempting to penetrate her thoughts, but Felicity knew him too well and they were barred to him. She would not permit meddling when it came to her own tragic love story. Not acknowledging Kriss, she wiped away her tears, fluttered down to the bank and floated into the shelter of the willow tree, flinging her arms around the centaur's neck to give him a hero's welcome. "Is there anything I can get you, Emrys?" she twinkled, sniffing as she turned her back on Archie.

"I'm okay thank you, Hope. I have everything I need." Wholly aware of the star's deep and inner sadness, Emrys braved a smile at her and continued to strip chunks of bark from the tree trunk, throwing them in the direction of Archie's pouch, which was now stretched almost to the limit.

"Thank you for saving us from Master Fletcher's dangerously foolish and twisted mind, Emrys," Felicity said with a baleful look at Archie. She did not mean to be cruel, she merely wanted him to feel the same sad regret she did. In point of fact, the moment she saw him flinch at her words her traitorous heart melted and she wished them back, but it was too late. With her hands clasped demurely behind her back she began to sway nervously to and fro on one leg, knowing full well she had opened a can of worms and Archie was now in for a sermon.

"Yes, Hope, dangerously foolish certainly. 'Twisted' is a little harsh, but also a fair description of Archie's mind at the present moment." Emrys, now fully fuelled, turned his attention to Archie. The star's prompting reminding him that the painful battle he had just endured was almost entirely Archie's fault. "Hurrumph," he looked down his nose. "Please listen to me, young man, when I tell you that your mind needs weeding," Emrys said sternly. "Yes: weeding! It is completely overgrown with rampant imaginings. Do you hear me? You must remove all thoughts of heroic ventures. If you do not our cause will fail, is that clear?"

"I understand, Emrys, I'm truly sorry," Archie grovelled, snarling briefly at Felicity as Emrys' gaze diverted fleetingly. She opened her eyes wide in assumed innocence and hid a smile.

"So in future, Archie, be clear-headed. That means no enemies and no battles please," Emrys reaffirmed.

"Right," Archie agreed, but he knew the homily had not ended and was sure to be the centaur's perpetual lecture until they crossed the bridge. Felicity, who was only too well aware of the importance of Emrys' directive was even so attempting to make Archie smile, smirking at him from a distance.

Apparently satisfied that his message had gone home, Emrys turned and was ripping off another piece of willow bark when he felt the urge to continue. He turned back on Archie and leaving his medication glued to the tree for the time being, snapped, "And if you find a spark or a hot thought popping into that head of yours, you must zap it." He pulled at the bark, filled his mouth and with a sour look, began to chew again.

"Zap it?" Trying to keep a straight face, Archie frowned.

"Yes, ZAP IT," Emrys bellowed spraying woodchips in every direction.

"Exactly how do I zap a thought?" Archie questioned, removing a clump of half-masticated bark from his shoulder and ignoring Felicity's snort of mirth. "I know this is important, but my problem is when I think of something and then try not to think of that something, I can't stop thinking about it. It's like pink elephants…" Archie raised his eyebrows at Emrys, who in turn raised his.

"What on earth are you talking about?"

"Pink elephants," said Archie. Now you try not thinking about them. You see? It's impossible."

"NO, ARCHIE! Zap it," Emrys hollered. It was too late. With all their thoughts combined, a herd of elephants in every shade of pink trumpeted innocently past the willow tree.

Kriss poked his head through the branches, his expression one of bemused dismay. "Whatever's going on?" he questioned, but received no reply.

Felicity's giggles turned to uncontrollable hysteria and Archie dissolved into howls of delight as the elephants trudged harmlessly by. A close-roaming calf tugged on a willow branch, but that was the only disturbance.

Emrys turned on Archie, his face livid, "This is no joke Archie Fletcher," he roared. Archie's laughter stopped abruptly and he looked down at his feet as the centaur's furious voice reverberated in his eardrums. "You are what you think," Emrys hollered, shifting his head in the direction of the pink backsides that were now swaying out of sight upriver. "Look how just one naive and simple thought can generate pandemonium," he paused. "Look at me while I'm speaking to you!" Archie obediently raised his head and met the centaur's angry stare. "Now listen up and listen up good. I am going to give you one thing to think about until we find that bridge and I don't want you to take your mind off it, not for a single second. It is 'crossing the bridge'." His mouth full, whiskers quivering, Emrys emphasised every word. "You are to think of nothing else, see yourself there, envisage yourself walking up to it and putting your hand on the balustrade. It's not difficult. Please do not conjure up one more obstacle; not one. Do you think you can do that?"

"Yes, Emrys," Archie mustered meekly, fighting an almost uncontrollable desire to laugh in the centaur's face. He knew Emrys was right and that his thoughts must be contained. He had now seen at firsthand what they could do. It was just so hard for him to tame them. In warfare, for which he had been trained and had faced back on Earth, he had become so used to distorting the truth to hide his reality that he knew it would be hard to get out of the habit, but it must be do-able. "I promise I will try," he said, a little more subdued.

"Let's have a bet on how long it takes Archie to conjure us up another enemy," Felicity piped up her face still wet, this time from tears of laughter she could no longer hold back.

"Hope," gasped Emrys, "you of all people cannot doubt Archie. What are you saying? That he will deliberately sabotage our mission? Kriss, help me out here."

The big man had moved to stand by Felicity, but before he could admonish her the star glided forward and lifted her feet from the ground until she was hovering head-height with Emrys. Slowly she turned to face Archie and gazed deep into his eyes.

"I do not doubt him, Emrys, no… I do not doubt him at all. I know him so very well you see." Felicity spoke softly and slowly, the corner of her mouth lifting in a sly smile. She swayed hypnotically in front of Archie, twirling her hair with a delicate finger. "The thing about Archie is that he lives for the challenge and in his lifetimes there have been few if any he has failed to overcome. So, having now set him this task we must fuel him to succeed must we not?"

Giving Emrys no time to agree, Felicity moved closer to Archie. Her gaze locked with his, her movement so graceful and elegant he was dazzled by her. She was weaving a spell on him as deftly as she had woven his willow crown. "So, Archie Fletcher, let us see how long it takes you to be distracted shall we? We have set you a challenge, one that holds an almost overwhelming amount of responsibility." She arched her eyebrows, "Think of it as a dare – you know how you love a dare!" Felicity shot him a wry smile. "Are you up to it? It may be painful at times to keep your thoughts from blossoming, but you must. Keep every bud tightly closed until you are free from Transit and all its turmoil. This is your Transit, Archie, no one else's, not Emrys's or Kriss's or mine, but yours. Your thoughts are our fate; we can only try to help you, so please be kind."

Hypnotised by the star and humbled by the magnitude of his test, Archie was fired by an all-consuming determination to succeed. He bowed his head. "I understand," he said simply.

Kriss, who had been silent throughout Felicity's discourse, was itching to move. In his authoritative tones he summoned them all to him. "Let's gather ourselves and prepare to move. It is time we were gone from here."

No one argued.

***

Above their heads the solitary raven spread its wings. None of them heard the rush of feathers as it took flight.

Emrys pulled the red cape from his croup and handed it back, somewhat the worse for wear, to Kriss. "Best to let the air get to my wound," he explained indicating his haunch, which looked angry and sore but had stopped bleeding. "The willow bark is easing the pain and I will apply some puffballs as soon as they're dry."

"Well, if you're sure," Kriss took the proffered cape, shook it out and swung it round his shoulders. Taking care to survey the landscape vigilantly as they left the shelter of the willow, the four travellers resumed their journey.

His head erect, Kriss led the team in silence, swinging his staff with every stride and using it to usher his followers onward. Emrys limped behind him, still munching and occasionally spitting. Head bent, Archie followed Emrys closely and focused on the centaur's sparse tail, which routinely swished from side to side flicking at his wounded hide. Felicity brought up the rear, her face set in an expression of forlorn resignation, yearning to walk beside Archie, yet scrupulously holding back.

In single file they continued to follow the river upstream, each one silently anticipating what was to come. Archie kept his thoughts monotonously on the bridge, his one true destination. Every so often a raven would appear, diving low, head bent to listen, but meeting with silence it would fly away with nothing to report to its mistress beyond the team's precise location and progress. One, braver than the rest, swooped in on them and with its talons widely spread it tousled Kriss's hair in an attempt to scratch his scalp. Kriss ducked, swiping at it with his staff but missing it by inches. He shook his fist at the departing bird, but still did not speak. He simply looked back at Emrys, who in turn looked back at Archie. "Keep your mind free from obstacles Archie, we are what you think, remember."

Archie did not reply, nor did he fail them; his thoughts did not falter. With each painstaking step he visualised the bridge, the blessed bridge, constructing in his mind's eye a vast, sturdy, golden structure that soared high over the river in a huge gleaming arc, carpeted in crimson, its unblemished gold balustrade curving grandly round it. Then, laughing at himself for his presumption, he thought, 'Such a bridge should be used for royalty. Mine will be a slippery rickety old wooden thing trodden down by millions, rotten in places with slats missing and a limp rope to keep me balanced and I'll probably fall...'

Catching himself in dismay, Archie muttered, 'Stop it, Archie Fletcher; don't think about what it looks like, it's just a bridge, doesn't matter what kind of bridge, stop tempting fate by thinking.' Hastily amending his fantasy, he muttered, "I see myself at the bridge, stepping onto it with my new found friends beside me. It's going to have to be a wide bridge to fit all four of us side by side." Even now he could not bring himself to believe that Felicity would not be with them. 'If necessary I will lift her in my arms and carry her across and-' Archie's train of thought was brought to an abrupt end by the ominous sound of rushing wings.

This time there were four of them and their assault was aimed wholly at Kriss. Taken completely by surprise the big man ducked, swinging his staff at the vengeful ravens, "Get back you vicious-"

His shout was cut off by two exceptionally hefty birds, talons spread, mouths wide open to reveal serrated beaks and razor sharp tongues. Attacking in tandem they hurtled ruthlessly into Kriss's unprotected face, snapping at his features. One clawed at his eye, the other snatched at his lip ripping it open. Together the ravens screeched triumphant, as Kriss, screaming in agony dropped crouching to the ground and curled into a ball his hands spread over his face. Seeing he was down, the other two ravens joined in the attack, all four birds swooping to claw viciously at his back. It happened in an instant before his friends had quite realised what was going on. From a short distance, Emrys, Archie and Felicity charged forward yelling and cursing, Archie wishing for the second time that day that he had not left his bow and arrows behind in Emrys' cave. The birds flustered and flurried away still screeching in defiance, their vengeance incomplete.

"Are you okay? Put your head up. Look at me," Emrys insisted sharply, reaching Kriss's huddled body.

The big man remained where he was crouched in a ball, shivering and groaning, blood trickling through his fingers. Felicity blenched and knelt beside him. Placing her hands on his head, she propelled her aura over him and whispered into his ear. "My healing should help ease you. Now try to lift your head and look at me. Kriss… we need to have a look."

Slowly he raised his head, his hands still tight to his wounds. "Now take your hands away. Come on, Kriss, please," Felicity begged.

As he lowered his hands the blood poured, draining down the entirety of his ruined features, his face a ghoulish and horrifying mask of pain. Felicity instinctively withdrew a little, aghast at what she was seeing. She shut her eyes, swayed backwards and fell. Her aura dimmed and went out; her skin chalk white she lay like a wraith, motionless on the ground.

Kriss tried to speak, "…Can't breathe…" he rasped through collapsing airways. Emrys moved forward quickly, stepping over the fallen star, whilst Archie ran to kneel beside her clasping her hands and patting them, murmuring her name over and over.

"Breathe slowly," Emrys said to Kriss, "and try not to panic. You are hyperventilating. Slowly... that's right... slowly and deeply. In an ideal world, I would stitch these gashes," he murmured as soon as the big man was breathing more normally. "The best we can do for now is try to stop the bleeding. Keep your hands on the wounds and press down as hard as you can." Emrys swung round, called urgently, "Come and help him, Archie. Hope will be alright, she's just fainted."

Archie got to his feet and stumbled over to Kriss, doing as Emrys directed and holding the big man's twitching hands over the deep gashes. Kriss winced and cried out with the pressure, but he trusted the centaur implicitly and suffered his ministrations, obediently opening his swollen, bleeding mouth for the piece of willow bark that Emrys now placed gently on his tongue.

"Won't these help?" Archie fumbled in the pouch and proffered a puffball.

Emrys ignored him, his attention focused on his injured friend. "Just suck it or bite down on it, Kriss, I know it's bitter but it's all we have to help you just now and it will reduce the pain. We're both going to be munching on bark for a while," he smiled. Kriss nodded, lifted his hands and tried to open his bulging eyes. The damaged one, swollen and stuck up with blood stayed firmly shut. "No, keep your hands there," Emrys insisted, at last noticing the mushroom Archie was holding towards him. "Good thinking, Archie, but we need to clean his injuries first. Those vile creatures are riddled with germs and disease absorbed from the evil temperament of the Moon, they are like poison. We must help Kriss down to the river and let the clear water run through his wounds." Archie nodded, stowed the puffball back in his pouch, grabbed up Kriss's staff and wrapping an arm around the big man's waist heaved him to his feet, wincing in sympathy as Kriss gave a shout of pain.

With hesitant steps, his hands still pressed to his face, the wounded man allowed himself to be led towards the river. Archie walked at his side, his arm transferring to Kriss's shoulders as he cast an anxious glance at Felicity, still a crumpled heap on the ground.

Emrys limped along behind, reaching forward to support his friend's elbow. "Don't worry, Archie," he said gruffly, "she'll come round in a minute. For her this was the final straw."

Reaching the bank Archie helped Kriss to sit then tipping out the contents of his pouch he waded into the river and scooped up some water. The pouch still leaked but only slowly. He carried it to Emrys, who eased Kriss's hands away, "This is going to hurt, my friend, but it is necessary." Kriss nodded and gritted his teeth while Archie gently trickled the water over the wrecked face. "Pour it, Archie, pour it," Emrys said, still holding Kriss's hands away from the wounds. "It needs a strong flow to penetrate and cleanse."

Again and again Archie filled the pouch and poured, until Kriss could stand it no longer. "Emrys, please..." he gasped, pulling his hands out of the centaur's grasp. "No more… Archie…. Please, no more." He pushed weakly against Archie's wrist to make him stop. "It is clean now, for sure," he panted, his wounds seeping fresh red blood to mingle with the river water streaming down his face.

Archie looked to Emrys for guidance. The centaur nodded, "That'll do. Now for the puffballs. Place them on the wounds like so; Kriss, hold them there firmly. We can't wait for them to dry completely, they may sting but no more than the pain you have already endured. Archie, find something to secure them," Emrys ordered in complete control of the situation.

Staring around blankly, Archie remembered how he had used reeds before and was on the point of searching for some when Kriss mumbled shakily, "You can rip a strip off the bottom of my tunic, Archie."

"Wait!" Emrys pointed, "I have spotted something even better. Do you see that plant to your right, by the waters' edge, the one with the bell-shaped white flowers?"

Archie looked to where the centaur pointed, "Yes."

"That is comfrey and it is exactly what we need."

"Right," Archie lunged for the bushy herb, ripping it from the ground to expose thick black roots.

"Strip the leaves from the stalk and wash them. Quickly now," Emrys ordered, observing his patient closely. Kriss, sucking on willow bark and pressing two puffballs to his face, was clearly in excruciating pain. Hurriedly, Archie plunged the loose, hairy leaves into the river, swishing them about and running them through his fingers. Shaking the water off them he ran back to Emrys to await his next command. It came instantly. "Remove the puffballs and layer up three or four comfrey leaves to the wounds then place the puffball back on top. Together they will act as an antidote. That's it; now tear off a strip from Kriss's tunic."

"We have to keep moving, Emrys," Kriss wheezed, his fingers plucking in agitation at the centaur's hand.

"I know and we shall, but first things first." Emrys watched as his apprentice ripped two strips of fabric from the hem of Kriss's white tunic.

"Now bind it round his head," Emrys instructed.

Archie followed his orders precisely, crossing and tying the two strips in such a way as to leave Kriss's one good eye unobstructed. Emrys smoothed back Kriss's hair, all the while speaking in the reassuring tones of the competent physician that he was. "Your healing will be fairly instant with comfrey, my friend. It is a welcome find. I shall be doing the same to my own wound."

Kriss relaxed only slightly and as soon as Archie had finished, struggled blindly to his feet. "I need my walking stick. We must move on." Leaning heavily on the staff Archie passed to him he moved up the bank, Emrys limping in his wake.

"Archie," the centaur barked over his shoulder, "gather more of that comfrey and don't forget to bring the rest of the puffballs and bark."

"Will do," Archie called. He did as he was told; he even washed the comfrey before gathering up his belongings and stuffing everything back into the bulging pouch, fixing it firmly to his belt. As he jogged up the bank to rejoin the others he saw that both Kriss and Emrys were standing stock still, side by side on the spot where the ravens had attacked. Their backs were turned towards him, their stance rigid as they stared at the ground.

His heart thumping, Archie reached them in three bounds. Shoving both aside he dived between them, realising in that instant what he would see.

“She’s gone,” Emrys said.

CHAPTER NINETEEN

JUNE, 1686
A WOUNDED DESTINY CREATES A SPLIT SOUL

In the dust by the banks of the river Danube, a young English soldier lay dying. He had been mortally wounded by a Turkish arrow tipped with poison, shot from the walls of Buda, the city he and his fellow soldiers were besieging. It was yet another battle in the War of the Holy League; one that they were winning. But not he, for this soldier had welcomed death, indeed, had actively sought it, throwing himself at the enemy without thought or care, though he had hoped for a cleaner death than the drawn out suffering he now endured as the poison slowly did its work. As his eyes began to dim, the soldier lost all hope of respite and in his agony and despair he reached out for help to the stars.

Thousands of miles away, the woman who had broken his heart caught her breath as something touched her soul.

***

"Have you finished with that paper yet?" Joseph's harsh voice boomed from the top end of the parlour table, startling his bride and making her spill the fresh cup of hot coffee her maid had just brought her. It pooled over the polished oak table and spread onto the London Gazette she was attempting to read. She shot a nervous glance at her husband, her trembling hands and bruised wrists concealed in her lap.

"Now see what you've done," he bawled thumping his fist on the table so hard the dishes rattled and the cutlery bounced and fell with a clatter to the floor. "I do not understand why you wish to look at it. I will not tell you again, my lady. I do not want you filling that pretty little 'ead of yours with things you cannot possibly understand. Now give it 'ere."

His young wife bent her head to hide the sudden anger that blazed in her eyes. She ignored Joseph, as she did every morning, and getting up walked the length of the table without looking at him, throwing the soggy paper onto his plate. As she swept past his chair in a whisper of silk he grabbed hold of her thin arm and twisted. Still she did not meet his gaze. Without flinching, she tossed her head so that her golden ringlets fell to her shoulders, loosed from the immaculately dressed pile of glossy hair caught high on her head by a delicate band of sapphires, chosen to match her eyes. Focused on the door she waited. She did not need to look at him to know he was smirking as he pulled her roughly towards him. His cruel features were imprinted on her brain.

This profligate earl she had been forced to wed was tall and broad, with thick dark hair tied in a queue at the back of his neck and falling over his ruffled lace collar. Cold gray eyes surveyed her from his swarthy, handsome face, which despite his youth was already beginning to show the coarsened marks of debauchery. Wealthy beyond belief, he had haggled with her father as though she were a prize mare to be bought and sold and now, the price agreed, the documents signed and sealed, she belonged to him. She was his countess; a dazzling trophy to enhance his standing in society, for Joseph was not a cultured man. His earldom had come to him unexpectedly, inherited obscurely from the distaff side of his ancestors who had failed to produce male heirs. And what a prize she was: nobly born and stunningly beautiful and his to do with as he pleased. Always careful to hit her in places where the bruises would not show, he insisted that she dress in the latest fashions and adorned her natural beauty with gold and priceless jewels to show off his obscene wealth. He was the envy of the upper echelons of society in which he liked to parade her. As indeed was she, for my, they whispered behind their fans observing her darkly handsome beau, what a catch her noble but impoverished family had got for themselves.

And to the depths of her being, she despised him.

In her short life she had known love, a love that had brought her to an ecstasy of longing and given her a reason for existence. A love she had been forced to reject. And now her erstwhile lover was overseas fighting in a distant war, which was why each day she scanned the news sheet, hunting through the mass of gory reports on the dispatch of rebels in the aftermath of the Monmouth Rebellion, to glean whatever snippets she could find concerning the Pope's Alliance - the 'Holy League' as it was known. Thus she followed the victories and defeats of the Christian Army pitted against the mighty Ottoman Turks in the war to which her lover had been forcibly consigned. And each waking hour she prayed with all her being that he was safe, and every night she lost herself in the fantasy of his arms. Until a night six weeks ago, when she had woken from her dream with a sharp pain under her heart and the undying feeling that something was missing; had gone. Since then she had felt obscurely different, as though she had lost a vital part of herself and it consumed her with fear.

"Is 'e dead yet then, eh?" Joseph spat, lifting his fingers to her slender neck, sliding them into her cleavage and pinching hard. She closed her eyes, refusing to show any emotion. She had taught herself to blank out her husband's covetous ramblings, as she had his nightly attentions, drifting out of her body until she was barely aware of his sweating, heaving bulk on top of her. Knowing of her thwarted love affair and jealous beyond reason, Joseph's inability to engage her emotions rendered him impotent and frustrated him beyond measure. He could achieve satisfaction only by hurting her, devising increasingly ingenious ways to inflict torture on her unresisting body, incensed when she endured it in silence. Had he but known, the physical pain was as nothing compared to her inner torment.

He removed his hand from her breast, loosened his grip and allowed her to move on. "The carriage will be ready at three. You will wear that pink frilly thing I 'ad delivered last week; it reminds me of your mother," he guffawed. "And the rubies; wear them rubies today. They might bring a little colour to your cheeks. What's the matter with you? Are you ill? You look like a corpse this morning." He leered into her face, "I suppose it's too much to 'ope you might be breeding? Put some rouge on, for God's sake."

She fought to control her anger for no matter how much Joseph taunted her she would not give him the satisfaction of showing by even a flicker of her huge eyes that he had disturbed her. Indeed, Joseph meant so little to her she might as well be a corpse. She felt dead most days, apathetically wandering like a wraith around Hope Hall, the great mansion in which he had installed her. The only pleasure in her miserable existence came from the messages she received. They came to her infrequently and by devious means, not from her lover who was lost to her, but from her oldest and dearest friend, a courier in the service of the King's Secretary of State, who travelled widely carrying letters between the courts of Europe. He alone knew of her heartache and kept an ear to the ground for her, alert for any news of her beloved. It was a mixed blessing, for each time she breathlessly tore open his seal she dreaded what she might find written beneath it.

This morning, feeling even more drained and empty than usual, she lifted the latch on the front door and stormed out of the house into the pebbled courtyard, waving back her flustered maid. Slightly earlier than usual, she decided to divert along the stream that ran the periphery of the estate. Stooping to pick flowers, she tossed them angrily aside, drowning them in the stream or crushing them underfoot. It was unlike her to be so destructive, but a riotous breakdown was taking place within her. Everything she had been taught, every lesson she had learnt, every behaviour pattern in which she had been ruthlessly conditioned, was being erased to the point where nothing mattered to her. Impatiently she kicked at the trickling water, feeling sick and frustratingly incensed. Each morning since her marriage she had walked in the confines of the estate, sometimes accompanied by her maid, sometimes not, establishing a harmless routine to assuage the suspicions of prying eyes. On the days when she was alone she detoured to the old willow tree and there she loitered, apparently idly, outside its weeping branches whilst establishing that she was unobserved. Once certain, she moved beneath the tree and hidden by its foliage, pushed her small hand into the knotted cleft in its trunk, her fingers feeling for a fold of paper. Rarely did she find one, but hope kept her returning there week after week.

Today as she approached the willow, she knew a message would be waiting for her. She did not know how she knew; she just knew, and she was terrified of what news it might contain. Standing beneath the canopy of the draping branches, she closed her eyes, covered her face in her muddy hands and fell to her knees, "Dear God, please don't let it be true, don't let this emptiness inside me mean he is gone. I beg you, please, let him be alive." Then she ran her hands through her hair, causing it to collapse completely from its hold and blow wildly in the breeze. With her bedraggled silk gown now tarnished with fresh mud and grass stains, she got to her feet and felt inside the willow, her fingers touching and grasping what lay there.

Gazing down at the seal, she muttered to herself then looked skyward through the whispering willow. "My love… my heart… my soul… if you are gone then I know you can hear me. Listen…" she closed her eyes as though in prayer. The breeze seemed to answer, rustling the willow in reply. "I confess and with every fragment of my being I am sorry, I am so sorry," she sobbed, tears flooding down her pale cheeks. "I was so afraid when we parted, I did not know what to do. What could I do? You were gone; I could not go with you. Please, I beg you, forgive me." She opened her eyes, staring up at the weeping tree, a spark of defiance entering her mind. "But I will not be afraid today for I have been dead a while waiting… waiting for you even though I knew you would never come back to me." Then, as though chanting a spell, she murmured, "Our past is past; our now is distressing; what the future holds is our only blessing." And slowly she broke the seal and unfolded the note.

Sarah, my dearest friend,

He is gone. I am sorry.

In haste and with heartfelt

sympathy and love,

Kriss

What happened at that precise moment surprised even Sarah, for although her heart was sundered, she felt a wild urge to burst into manic laughter. At last, for the first time since he had gone away, she knew instinctively what to do. Once again she got to her knees, folded her hands and bowed her head in prayer. "Dear God, my heart is snapped clean into two pieces, so please will you also split my soul and I will make to you this solemn promise: wherever he is I will watch over him from the heavens and guide him, now and for eternity. And please, I beg you to allow me this, just let me live one more life with him so I can right our true destiny, Amen."

Feeling completely detached from her body and her surroundings, Sarah got up from her knees, thrust the note back into the tree and began to walk home, smiling as she walked her tears flowing ceaselessly. Picking up her pace she strode out as the house came into view her arms swinging powerfully by her side. Reaching the pebbled courtyard she broke into a run, sped up the stone steps and burst through the heavy, oak front door, brushed past her husband in the marbled hall and pounded up the main staircase.

Momentarily too stunned to shout at her, Joseph watched in angry disbelief as Sarah leapt up the stairs three at a time, her skirts caught up in her hand revealing bare, filthy but beautiful legs.

She flew across the lower landing to the next and the next, successive flights of stairs taking her higher and higher up to the top of the five-storey mansion. Her body felt like lead, her head spinning, but she was still smiling through her tears. Deaf to the entire world, she did not hear Joseph's bellow or her maid's fretful cries as they pounded after her. She did not lose momentum at any point, if anything she sped faster the higher she got. She dashed into the servants' attic bedroom and climbed out of the dormer window onto the roof.

Without a second thought, Sarah ran to the edge and launched herself into the air.

As her broken body dashed onto the ground below, her prayer was answered, her promise registered and her soul split out into the atmosphere.

CHAPTER TWENTY

FORGIVE AND FORGET

Archie, Kriss and Emrys stared at the deserted spot where they had last seen Felicity. One or two white flowers had fallen from her hair and lay in the grass. Were it not for these she might never have been there, for her body was too slight to leave an indentation in the ground.

Kriss broke the silence, grimacing with pain as he fumbled with his bandages. "There is nothing we can do. We shall have to move on without her."

Archie stooped to pick up the crushed blossoms, sniffing them absently and cradling them in his hands. "But where is she? What if she's in trouble? She was unconscious, the ravens or someone might have taken her. We can't just leave," he gabbled, spinning on the spot, searching for a glimpse of the fallen star.

One-eyed, Kriss looked a query at Emrys, who nodded but remained silent. "Okay, let's go," the big man turned away and ignoring Archie's dismay proceeded to walk haltingly upstream leaning heavily on his staff. Emrys followed, hesitated and cast a worried glance back at Archie, who was still staring around at the empty terrain.

"FEE!" Archie bellowed in despair, his voice echoing back to him in the surrounding stillness. "FEE WHERE ARE YOU? PLEASE, COME BACK. WE'RE MOVING."

Emrys returned in a shambling trot, waving his hands in agitation and clamping them on Archie's shoulders,

"Hush! What are you doing?" he hissed. "Stop it at once. Do you want the whole of Transit to know where we are? Come on, get moving." The centaur pushed his muscular chest against Archie's back, forcing him forward.

"Oh, come off it, Emrys, the Moon knows precisely where we are. What? Your punctured haunch is not enough of a reminder? She has her pitiless spies following us incessantly. What the hell difference does it make if I shout?" Despite his angry protest, Archie did not resist the centaur's urgings. Certain now that Felicity was nowhere nearby he set off, scanning the landscape constantly for the slightest sign of her.

After a time they moved further inland, losing sight of the river. The plain was giving way to more interesting countryside and to Archie it was a relief to see a few hills appearing and clumps of verdant woodland dotted about on their slopes, but it made it more difficult to see very far. From time to time he paused, shaded his eyes from the sun and peered into the distance.

"There's no point in looking, Archie. She'll catch up." The limping centaur had moved up to clop along at his side. "You know what she's like." Emrys sighed, "She's…" he paused as though searching for the right words and failing to find them. He sighed again, "Well anyway, she'll catch up don't worry." His concerned tone belied his words and it dawned on Archie that Emrys was actually as worried as he and had no explanation for Felicity's disappearance.

"You don't know where she is, do you?" he accused.

"No," Emrys said shortly. "But she disappears every so often, that's what she does. It's not unusual. She'll turn up when she's good and ready. I think we should catch up with Kriss before we lose sight of him."

Despite his extreme discomfort, Kriss, still clutching his face, had got into his stride and stormed ahead. The terrain, strewn with rocks and shale was beginning to rise quite steeply. Emrys broke into a trot and Archie put on a spurt keeping pace with him. He was determined to use this opportunity to source some answers. "Can you remember anything else, Emrys? From before when... well, you know," he puffed. "I mean, have any other memories returned?"

"Like what? I haven't exactly had time to dwell on it since my battle with the charioteer and the ravens' attack." Emrys' gruff voice was tinged with sarcasm, "So no, nothing has come to mind, but I can see you have a point to make so spit it out."

"Well, after the digital alarm went off and then the splash, can you remember what came next? Do you remember Hope being with us, for example?"

Emrys halted abruptly and grasped Archie's arm to make him stop, staring at him wide-eyed, a look of horror crossing his features. "What has she told you?" he snapped.

Remembering Felicity's panic and realising he might have dropped her in it, Archie quickly back-tracked. "Nothing; nothing at all, I'm just searching for answers. You know, trying to find the missing pieces of my own jigsaw. Is that too much to ask? Is it not my quest to learn who she is? I thought you might know that's all."

Before the centaur could reply they heard a muffled shout and both looked up. Kriss was nearing the brow of the hill and impatiently waving them forward. "We'd best get a move on," Emrys let go of Archie's arm and trotted ahead, wincing with every stride. "I'm sorry I can't help you find her, I only wish I could, but-"

"It's okay," Archie interrupted, keeping pace with him, "I understand. I have to be the one to find her."

"That's right, you and only you. You must tame your mind and go where your heart leads." The centaur gave a wry grimace and flapped his arms about pathetically, "Be sure to follow my advice and not my example, Archie. The unfortunate deformed creature walking beside you refused to take his own medicine and look where he ended up!"

Archie shot Emrys a sympathetic smile, but made no reply.

Panting, they reached the bottom of the hill. It was steeper than it looked and their climb soon transformed into a stony scramble. Sweat trickled from their brows as the sun beat down on them from the cloudless sky. Kriss waited edgily at the top, fidgeting with his face wounds and chewing willow bark. Archie stopped for a breather and looked back the way they'd come. From this vantage point he could see the fork in the river where the tributary gushed in. The water was swollen from last night's storm and overflowing its banks; it looked angry and mud-churned. Looking left he could see where it disappeared into woodland then re-emerged, widening to a stretch of calmer water that spread across to the other side. They were the same woods he had camped in on his second night in Transit. As he scanned the opposite bank, Archie caught a movement. Shading his eyes he peered across the water and saw lurking there the dark, haunting presence he had stalked on his way to the lily grove. The apparition was facing forward and seemed to be watching them. The hairs rose on the back of Archie's neck, "Can you see that?" he hissed, nudging Emrys.

"See what? What's the matter?"

"There look; over there, someone on the other side." Archie pointed, but even as he did so, the cloaked figure vanished.

"Where, I don't see it?" Emrys peered across the river to where Archie pointed.

"It's gone," Archie sank to the ground, his trembling legs giving way beneath him.

"Keep moving you two," Kriss called setting off down the hill. "Don't dawdle. We've no time for loitering. If we are to get within striking distance of the bridge before nightfall we have to move fast. We can't have much more than two hours of daylight left." He pointed vaguely at the sky his finger finding the sun. It was down from its zenith, dipping little by little towards the land.

"I agree, Emrys muttered, helping Archie to his feet. "Who knows what the Moon and her ravens have up their sleeves for us next."

They followed Kriss down the hill, sliding over the flinty ground and pushing forward towards the tree line. Once back beside the river they entered the woodland, their feet sinking into soft layers of shed pine needles, the cool mist of tall conifers sheltering them from the heat of the sun. Archie was preoccupied; he did not focus on the bridge as he had been instructed to do, nor did he wander into his usual trick of fantasising death-defying carnage. The one and only thought filling his mind was of Felicity, he couldn't help it. He chanted under his breath, 'Come back Fee, where are you? Come back Fee, where are you?'

The trio walked in silence weaving in and out of the trees, the light becoming dimmer as the pines grew more densely. Archie's mind remained focused on Felicity, making up little rhymes as he pictured her lovely face. 'You can't be far, you never are. Where are you Fee? Come back to me.' On and on went the mantra in his head, asking over and over again for her to return. He begged incessantly for a sign as he trudged through the woods, stumbling from time to time when he trod on a pine cone or his feet got caught up in twisted roots.

Kriss led the pace, his long stride lengthening as a distant verge came into view. The river had picked up speed as it flowed beneath the trees and a westerly breeze blustered, sighing through the branches. With a loud crack, a twig snapped above them. Startled, Archie glanced up as it fell, was this his sign? At that moment a mournful, elegiac voice wafted on the gusty air past his ear, softer than a whisper yet crystal clear, and at last he had an answer to his pleas.

"I won't be long, I hear your song. At this time I roam alone, don't worry though, I'll soon be home."

Archie grinned at his feet as the breeze passed him by. The relief was so intense it made him catch his breath. Emrys, limping just in front, had heard nothing. Still munching on willow bark he constantly rummaged and shuffled at the ground and in the undergrowth looking for any pain relieving herb he could get his hooves on. The rim of the wood drew nearer as they edged through the dark tunnel of pines towards the brilliant light of the sun. Beside them the river sang its own bubbling song and though it had turned slightly choppy it yet retained a tranquil ambiance. Spears of light intense as a strobe pierced the canopy of foliage and rebounded off the water, so dazzling it was hard to look at it. Averting their eyes, the trio marched on. Even the cries of ravens from beyond the trees did not make them falter, for every step taken was another closer to the bridge.

"We'll get to that clearing then rest," Kriss gestured to a section in the wood up ahead where the sunshine illuminated an open divide. The trees thinned out dramatically as they approached it. "Drink and eat what you can," he said. "There is watercress here and some berries on those bushes over there," he pointed. Crouching awkwardly by the river and easing his bloodstained dressing to one side Kriss took a long drink then rested for a moment, sitting back on his heels. "I think we should cross over today, before sundown," he glanced up at Emrys. The centaur nodded his agreement, stretching down from his lofty height to suck up the water. Kriss looked towards the tight curve in the river up ahead, his one eye glittering with suppressed excitement. "Just around that next bend we should see it. I can feel it, can't you? It is there waiting for us. Are you up for it, Archie?"

"We can't cross without Fee," Archie said adamantly, cupping his hands in the river and lifting them to pour a dazzling stream of water into his mouth then over his head, washing the sweat and dust from his face and running his fingers through his tangled hair. His lion's pelt tunic was filthy, but he had got so used to the smell he no longer noticed it.

"We don't have a choice, we cross as soon as we can," Kriss persisted. "You know Hope cannot come with us. She is merely a guide."

"I won't cross without her," Archie stood, outraged at the big man's apparent lack of concern, "And I wish you'd call her Felicity, it's what she prefers."

"Whatever. There is nothing any of us can do for her; her plight is here and will remain here. She is banished. Unless you can remember her, that is her destiny. And I fear it is a challenge even you cannot meet." They fell silent, everyone's thoughts on the absent star.

"Hi!" From the sun-drenched and glittering clearing behind them came an unmistakeable giggle. Taken by surprise they spun round as one to see Felicity perched on a tree stump. "Are you okay, Kriss?" she asked. "I'm sorry I had to leave when you needed me." Her aura glowed around her, back to its customary strength.

"I'm fine," Kriss lisped through his bandages.

"Fee, where have you been? I've been worried sick," Archie's fretful voice told no lies; his eyes sparked with unshed tears as he gazed at her, completely torn between anger and relief.

"Have you?" Felicity sounded delighted. "I'm sorry, I had to go. I'd have been no help. The sight of blood revolts me and destroys my aura. I needed to repair it." She tilted her head slightly to look at Kriss's makeshift bandages and the comfrey leaves and fungus peeping out beneath them. Again she giggled, "But I see you've patched him up beautifully."

"Let's keep moving," Kriss said flatly, striding out of the clearing. "We cross today."

The star's amusement died in an instant, her dismayed gaze turning to Archie, "Today? But…" swallowing whatever she had been going to say, Felicity floated off the tree stump and flittered into line to follow Emrys. Archie bringing up the rear stayed close behind her as they entered another long avenue of trees. Mightily relieved, Archie's thoughts now turned from finding Felicity to keeping her. If she could not cross the bridge unless he remembered her, he would just have to find a way, whatever it took.

"It must have been hard, marrying someone you didn't love - a difficult decision to make. Well, you would know," Archie blabbered quietly, almost treading on Felicity's heels.

"I didn't have a choice in the matter." She continued walking, snubbing his efforts to probe.

"No, of course you didn't. It's a real privilege to have the freedom to choose," Archie mused. "It doesn't matter anymore though because it was another life. You're not married to him now and we're here together, so..." his voice trailed away as Felicity slowed and turned to look at him.

"It doesn't matter? What are you saying? Are you forgiving me for not following you when you went off to war; for marrying Joseph?"

"God, yes, like you said, you didn't have a choice." Archie stopped walking and took hold of Felicity's tiny white arms, his fingers encircling them with room to spare. He looked into her eyes, propelling his sincerity into her mind. "Fee, I forgive you for everything. None of this was your fault. You were born into circumstances way beyond your control. I forgive you, do you hear me? I forgive you," he repeated, emphasising each word. It did not mean a great deal to him to say this since he had no memory of centuries past, but he knew Felicity desperately needed to hear it and he also knew that even had he remembered, he would still have forgiven her - anything. That being so his sincerity was not false. He slid an arm around her waist to hug her, but on hearing these long awaited words, Felicity's knees gave way and she stumbled gently to the ground. Archie, his arm tightening around her, guided her fall and sat down beside her. Oblivious to what was happening behind them, Kriss and Emrys marched on into the distance.

Archie squeezed Felicity's waist, looking at her in concern, "Are you okay?" Trembling she nodded, unable to speak, her eyes yet again filling with tears as she gazed into his. With a deep sigh she studied his face then leaned forward and kissed him on the lips.

In that instant a deep, forbidden secret was divulged, not from Felicity's mouth to Archie's ear, but tenderly, lip upon lip, her kiss telling of a golden cornfield and of rolling down a Welsh mountainside. But Archie did not hear it. Drowning in delight he knew only that something momentous was happening to him.

Gradually they parted, nose to nose, their breath still tangled as they smiled at each other. "We're half way there, Archie." Felicity's eyes searched his for a spark of recognition. Finding none her tears spilled over and tumbled to her chin.

"Please don't cry," his large hands cupped her beautiful face as he wiped away her tears. "Why did you kiss me?"

"I'm sorry; are kisses not like tears? When they are real they cannot be held back."

Archie's smile broadened, "Don't be sorry, Fee, I'm not," he murmured, returning her kiss to prove his words. For a while they stayed there, lip to lip, each utterly absorbed in the other. "We ought to move," Archie sighed after a time looking to where Emrys and Kriss were still forging ahead, barely visible now.

He helped the star to her feet and keeping hold of her hand ran to catch them up, Felicity floating at his side. Elated, Archie almost skipped with joy, unsure of what had just happened but certain it had helped. Everything would fall into place soon, he just knew it. A glance at his minders' stiff backs forced him to control the urge to shout and whoop. Slowing he whispered, "So, where did you go then?" guessing that if she replied at all her answer would be vague. For a moment she said nothing as they quietly resumed their places in the line a pace or two from Emrys' swishing tail. The centaur strode on seemingly unaware of what had taken place behind him.

"I told you, I needed to regenerate my aura." Felicity smiled, "And I had some business to attend to," she added in a low whisper.

"Business?" Archie snorted, leaning close. "What kind of business are you into?" She giggled and put a finger to her lips. "What," he hissed, "can't you tell me that either?"

Up ahead, Kriss halted, turning suspiciously to survey his team. Emrys also turned and directed a look of caution at Felicity. She shook her head, dropping her gaze demurely to her feet. Satisfied, he turned back, nodded to Kriss and they all strode forward once more.

"You know I can't tell you, Archie," Felicity spoke more quietly than a whisper, "but let's just say I made a very important choice today," she fluttered her eyelids at him.

"If I guess will you tell me if I'm right?" Felicity nodded, "Yes, but be careful what you think, they will read you," she breathed watching Kriss's and Emrys' every move.

Blanking his mind, Archie whispered, "Did you go back to the Moon and ravens?" Felicity shook her head with a grin. "Okay… did you go down to the Earth-plain?"

Felicity flinched and raised her eyebrows.

"Am I right?"

She nodded then winked at him.

None the wiser for this information, Archie struggled to keep his mind blank, his gaze fixed on Emrys' swaying rump. He was about to come up with another suggestion, when Kriss's pace began to slow and the group clustered more closely. Feeling Felicity's unease, Archie gave up and said no more on the matter.

CHAPTER TWENTY-ONE

2003

The Choice

The early morning sun shone through the large sash window of a converted apartment block in central London. On the top storey, just inside her front door, a young woman waited idly watching the motes of dust caught in its beam. Backpack at the ready, tickets and passport in hand, dressed in cut-off denim dungarees and a white t-shirt, Sarah Walker was still a rebel without a cause. She looked up at the hall clock yet again, drumming her fingers on the wall impatient for her once-in-a-lifetime long-awaited trip around the world to begin.

Her flat was desolate, almost empty, cleared of all her personal belongings in readiness for someone to rent. She saw that she had left a framed photo on the wall. It pictured a group of eight small children playing in a manicured garden - and had she room in her rucksack Sarah would have taken it with her. The clock ticked loudly, its big black hands pointing to six-thirty. Her flight to Kuala Lumpur was at twelve. She had been ready since five and up since three. In fact she had not really slept at all. She had tried, but the anticipation - or the apprehension - of the long-haul flight on her own had sabotaged any attempt to rest. Each time she had closed her eyes, all she could see was her plane crashing and plummeting into an ocean miles from anywhere. The image refused to go away, so persistent was it that Sarah had tried to flip her thoughts to the more positive image of being stranded on a desert island; not something she longed for, but all the same, better than being lost in an ocean.

Yawning, she looked down at her ticket and for possibly the thousandth time read it out loud: "First stop, Kuala Lumpur, heart of Asia, date, twelfth of June 2003, then onto sunny Sydney, date to be arranged and finally the Big Apple, return date to England to be arranged," she giggled, jigging from one foot to the other, her excitement irrepressible.

The mobile phone in her back pocket began to ring. Glancing at the name, 'Mum', Sarah chose to ignore it and instead examined the photo hanging beneath the clock. She, her brother and her cousins grinned out at her; it had been taken at Woods Eves years ago and it always made her smile. She raised a finger and traced the outline of her 'twin' and then of herself, and sighed.

At six–thirty-seven her mobile rang again.

"Oh Mum!" Sarah exclaimed, refusing once again to answer it. "For God's sake, woman; there's no need to keep checking up on me, I'm twenty-five, not five! There's not a hope I'm going to miss this flight." She put the phone onto silent and tucked it into the back pocket of her dungarees. Glancing back at the photo she lifted the latch on the front door. The cab was due in two minutes. Her phone began to vibrate in her back pocket. This time it read 'Dad'. Her father never called her; somewhat curious and a hint concerned she took the call.

"Hello," she tried to sound cheerful, but she was never very cheerful in the morning, even if she was going on the trip of a lifetime.

"Hi honey, it's only me," Jack Walker sounded drained. He was probably tired, but there was an edge to his voice, almost a crack in it that increased Sarah's unease.

"Hi Dad, what's up? You okay?" She sought to get right to the point, today was a very important and busy day for her and she desperately wanted it to go without a hitch.

"Listen… I have bad news. You might want to sit down."

Beginning to panic, Sarah reached up to drop the front door latch then crouched on the floor. "What? Is Mum okay?"

"Are you on your own?"

"Of course I'm on my own," Sarah snapped. "My cab for the airport will be here any minute, what's going on, Dad?"

"I'm sorry, love, there's no easy way to tell you this. Archie's and James's plane went down last night."

There was silence. Sarah waited. For what she did not know, maybe for some sort of outcome, but none came.

"Are you there?" Her father's quavering voice trembled in her ear. Sarah had never known her Dad fazed by words before, he was usually briskly confident and matter of fact, but he sounded so hesitant, his tone so childlike that it scared Sarah rigid.

"Yes," she whispered. "I'm here. What do you mean, Dad, 'it went down'?" Stunned, hoping and praying she had misunderstood, she listened intently.

"Down, darling… as in crashed. They overshot their landing in a storm, no survivors have been found."

As she tried desperately to comprehend the information Sarah's heart began to pound. She broke into a cold sweat, the mobile slipping in her wet hand, and although she was sitting on the floor her knees started knocking together. "Where are you, Dad?"

"At home at the moment, but we're going over to Eversely Avenue right now. Should be there in half an hour," he paused and Sarah heard a muffled sob. "Can you come?"

"Yes; yes. I'll be there." Wrenching her head back to gaze unseeing at the ceiling Sarah's jaw locked, tears of rage building in her eyes. A loud horn beeped twice outside the apartment. Struggling to speak she managed, "Cab's here. Meet you there. Thirty minutes."

Teeth chattering, Sarah pressed the off button. The mobile slipped out of her hand and skidded across the carpet. She fell onto her side, her head bumping on the floor. Darkness seemed to devour her. In that moment she felt as though one half of her had died. The pain was so intense it was as if she was being split in two. 'Please God, don't let it be true, it's a dream, let me wake. It's a bloody nightmare or a joke… a sick joke.'

Another four loud impatient beeps blasted from the street below. "Wait, I'm coming," Sarah whispered, pushing herself slowly onto her knees. She swayed on all fours for a moment, took a deep breath and got painfully to her feet. Grasping her backpack she flung it onto her shoulder and promptly dropped it, waves of nausea rushing up her throat. Hand to mouth, she dashed retching to the bathroom as fast as her trembling legs would carry her. Throwing herself at the lavatory Sarah vomited the contents of her stomach then hung shivering over the bowl. Head pounding, she reached up to pull the chain and dragged herself to the washbasin to splash cold water at her face. "I'm okay," she muttered, "just breathe." The cabby beeped again, one long angry beep. "Oh God, don't leave… please… I'm coming."

Sarah hurled herself at the bathroom window, throwing up the sash and hanging outside to attract the cabbie's attention. Her foot slipped and she toppled forward, grappling with her fingernails against the sill. One hand caught the blind, she grabbed it and hung on, looked down at the congested street way below where a cab was filtering back into the moving traffic. "No!" she cried helplessly, "Don't go."

In the precarious position in which Sarah now found herself, almost half her body hanging out of the window, a moment of serenity took hold as though she had been here before. Her world seemed to stop: the traffic hushed; her head stopped pounding. The fresh air cooled her sweating, blotchy skin and a summer breeze blew the smell of sick away from her nose and out of her hair. And as she hung there, she began to smile. "What's it like Archie?" she asked the air. "What's it like to die? I could just let go and join you." Still smiling, she looked down at the street. The pavement seemed to beckon. Her fingers began to relax their grip, loosening her hold.

A split second before she let go, Sarah's vision blurred and the concrete jungle faded, blotted out by a ball of bright yellow light. She heard a rush of wings and felt a strange pressure on her shoulders as though two tiny hands were pushing her back. A disembodied voice breathed into her mind, 'No. He'll wait. Your today is much fairer than your yesterday. You must live your life, Sarah; the world is waiting for you.'

The sensation lasted for no more than the blink of an eye and was gone.

"What am I doing?" Sarah gasped. Everything kicked back into action: the pavement swam back into view. The traffic roared, her head pounded, her body temperature rose and nausea bounced back in. Feeling giddy, Sarah pulled herself back into the bathroom, slammed the window shut and hovered over the washbasin, but nothing came. "I'm okay; I'll be okay," she murmured, staggering into the hall and almost tripping over her backpack.

She stopped in front of the photograph and yanked it off the wall, staring down at the grinning faces. She and Archie could only have been about thirteen or fourteen. None of them looked particularly organised, standing on the lawn outside Nanny's sitting room window pulling silly faces and poses at the camera, but they had been lined up strategically in height order. Stewart and Dominic were at the low end, Sally, Helena and Gillian came next; then she and Archie, tongues out, heads together, arm in arm. Beside them, striking a macho pose and using Archie's shoulder as a prop, was James Higgins. She read what was written in Archie's unmistakeable hand along the bottom of the picture.

1992, the year we played 'Dead Game' - best Easter I've ever had.

Looking long and hard, Sarah could see her mother and aunts and uncles messing around in the sitting room, pulling silly faces out of the window at the camera. Her father wasn't with them; he must have taken the photo. She had never noticed them before. It made her giggle; her giggle transformed into an anguished cry, "NO! Please don't be dead, Archie, please." Sarah's grip on the photo tightened as tears flooded down her ashen face. "Don't be dead, please don't be dead," she sobbed. 'Oh God... James... what about Hels, she's in Oz. I'm supposed to meet her.' Sarah's head spun, her grief spilling out as every thought struck home. 'I don't know what to do. Oh, Archie, please, please, please don't be dead.'

Sobbing uncontrollably Sarah leaned against the wall. An irrepressible feeling of rage surged into her chest. Clenching her fist she slammed it against the wall so hard the skin broke across her knuckles and left a bloody mark. The harder she thumped it, the easier she felt. It was as though the pain in her hand was easing the pain in her heart.

Above her head the clock ticked on relentlessly; it was seven-thirty. Drained and numb, Sarah cradled her bruised and bleeding hand, replaced the photograph on the wall, retrieved her mobile and called for another cab.

By eight she was on her aunt's and uncle's doorstep. The driveway was crammed with cars all gleaming in the summer sun. Archie's pristine Land Rover was tucked in the corner at the top of the drive next to Robert's Mercedes. The back door was slightly ajar. Sarah let herself in, propped her backpack just inside the hall and looked around flinching from the hush of sadness overshadowing the house. Not a thing had ever changed in the Fletchers' home. The walls were lined with clutter on the dated, homemade shelving, the handed-down ancient dining table was still tucked in the corner of the main room, the floor still uncarpeted and as she turned into the kitchen, Sarah spotted the prehistoric gas oven, which famously caught fire on her tenth birthday. On one side of it was her mother, green-faced and fussing and on the other, Auntie Jo, who was white as a sheet but with a calm look of resignation in her eyes. As soon as the pair saw Sarah, their arms opened.

"Come here, love," Auntie Joanna's arms wrapped around Sarah's tiny frame and Patricia's arms wrapped around Joanna. They clung to one another in disbelief, Joanna stroking Sarah's hair as they wept.

"I'm s-s-so sorry, Auntie Jo," Sarah managed, sobbing. "Is there any news? Any chance that-"

"Can I get you a cup of tea?" Joanna interrupted, breaking the embrace.

Looking into her aunt's bloodshot eyes, Sarah could see no spark of hope. No chance, then. Her shoulders slumped, "Would you mind if I had a gin and tonic?"

"Sarah! It's eight o'clock in the morning," Patricia exclaimed.

"Of course you can, dear," Joanna smiled reassuringly through her tears. "The bar is open. Robert's in the garage with your dad and a few others, he'll sort you out."

Sarah nodded and left the kitchen. She wandered through the patio doors out into the garden, squeezed past her uncle's Mercedes and slipped into the garage. Robert, her dad and two other men were sitting in a circle of deckchairs in the middle of the garage, a glass of whisky in hand and the bottle in the middle. Robert noticed Sarah and staggered to his feet; the others followed suit. She ran forward into her uncle's outstretched arms. No words were necessary; it was an embrace of mutual support and love.

"Now then, what'll it be? 'Fraid we've been at it some while," Robert slurred, indicating the almost empty bottle of whisky.

"G & T, please, I can do it, you sit down." Robert promptly fell back into his chair. Sarah, slightly shocked for she had never known her uncle the worse for drink, rummaged through the array of spirits scattered all over his workbench. She found a glass and mixed a drink heavy on the gin, downed it and mixed another. The alcohol hit the back of her throat and left a warm trail in her gullet. With a sympathetic smile at Robert she wandered drink in hand down the driveway to sit on the stone wall that framed the entrance of the Fletcher's home. Finding her phone and her airline tickets she began to dial the ticket cancellation number. She knew she couldn't get her money back but maybe she could reschedule her flights. It was hard to imagine a time when this day would end, but she knew that it must. And though life would never be the same again, she had to get away; she had to see the world that waited for her.

It was hot sitting in the sunshine. Sarah sighed heavily, wiping her brow with the back of her swollen hand, noticing for the first time how badly cut and bruised her knuckles were. "Jeez that hurts," she muttered under her breath, flexing and crunching her fingers to ensure nothing was broken. She dialled, connecting to an automated Malay voice; drearily she listened and was finally put through to an operator.

"Hello, my name is Sarah Walker. I'm due to be on flight MH001 at twelve noon today," Sarah explained to the female airline employee.

"How may I help you, Miss Walker?"

"I need to change my departure date."

"Your flight check-in is open, I am sorry, we cannot change your flight, Miss Walker," the operator said politely. Sarah bit her lip hard to stop it from quivering.

"It's a round-the-world ticket, I can change any of the dates," Sarah insisted, quite sure it must be possible.

"I understand, but we require forty eight-hours' notice."

"But I can't fly today. My twin was killed in a plane crash last night." Saying it out loud to a complete stranger made it so hideously real. Sarah's breath came in short, sharp gasps as she struggled to control her voice. "I've saved for five years for this. Please, there must be something you can do?"

There was an appalled hush on the other end of the phone before a soft, Malay voice spoke again. "So sorry; you give me phone number. I'll see what I can do. I call you back in ten minutes, okay?" In incoherent sobs Sarah gibbered her thanks to the benevolent Malay recipient. Once her number had been confirmed she hung up, dashing away her tears and turning away from the ogling stationary traffic just beyond the driveway. Downing her drink Sarah began to pace the drive, weaving in and out of the parked cars and licking at her stinging hand, which her salty tears had aggravated.

"Hi, Sarah," a deep voice spoke from the pavement. It was Stewart walking back from wherever he had been. His outward appearance was much as usual, slightly rugged round the edges but clean. He seemed entirely calm, not flustered in any way and though his face was pale, he did not look as though he had been crying. In fact he did not even look sad; just entirely normal.

Taking her cue from her cousin Sarah asked casually, "Hi Stew, where've you been?"

"Oh, you know, just walking." He reached her and held her tightly.

Sarah laid her cheek against his chest and felt his chin resting on top of her head. She could feel his heart thumping and knew his apparent calmness was a facade. "I'm really sorry, Stew," she pulled away to look up at him, brushing away stray locks of her hair that floated irritatingly in her eyes.

"For what?" he asked.

"Well, Archie of course, you know…?"

"Yeah, I know. He died." Stewart smiled.

"You okay?" Sarah was filled with concern for her baby cousin. He was clearly in denial; his eyes were bleak and he looked completely bemused.

"I think so," Stewart shrugged, his smile vanishing as he headed towards the house.

With her back to the traffic, Sarah sat on the wall again and watched her cousin disappear into the garage. Her thoughts tangled as she tried to organize her position in her mind. She did not know what to do. What if the airline forfeited her flight for not showing up? Right now she had to be here, although there was not one part of her that wished to stay. She wanted to run away from it all, bury her head in the sand and pretend it wasn't happening. At that very moment all she wanted was to cease to exist, but the opportunity to die back in her flat had passed her by. Sarah wasn't sure what had happened to her as she'd hung out of the window teetering on the brink, but whatever it was she knew she had made a choice. She would not kill herself, not now, no matter how deep her grief. She also knew that however far she ran and however deeply she buried her head, it would not change the fact that Archie was gone.

Everything in Sarah's life, in all their lives, had seriously altered yet nothing seemed to have changed around her. The sun still blazed in the sky when it should have gone out; the traffic still crawled by the curb when every engine should have died. Even the birds in the trees continued to sing sweetly on that beautiful summer's day, yet every single one of them should have fallen silently from its perch. The world kept on turning, time kept ticking and no matter how hard Sarah tried not to, she kept on breathing.

Stewart emerged from the garage a few moments later with a rum and coke in hand. He came to sit beside Sarah and they both stared listlessly at the house. "The Davies are on their way; should be 'bout an hour Mum said." Stewart put his arm round Sarah and gave her a squeeze. "What time's your flight then?"

"Twelve. I've cancelled. The airline's calling me back, hopefully to rearrange the date," Sarah crossed her fingers between her legs.

Stewart nodded. "Hels is on a flight out of Sydney tomorrow morning."

Sarah did not know how to respond. Thinking of the pain Helena must be enduring was too much. She wondered how James's family was coping. His mother had never recovered from Mal's death – and now this. Sarah gritted her teeth determinedly holding back her tears. She held out her hand, "Can I have a sip of that?"

"Sure," Stewart passed her his pain-numbing drink of triple rum and a dash of coke, and watched as she swallowed the lot. He got up from the wall and strolled back into the garage, re-emerging seconds later with a bottle of gin, tonic, rum and cans of coke. Settling himself down again he lined them up around his feet and re-charged Sarah's glass.

An hour went by, with Stewart and Sarah attempting slowly to annihilate both the gin and the rum. By the time the Davies arrived they had dented both quite considerably. The remainder of the day whirled by in an intoxicated blur. People came and went, flowers stayed, piled high on a patio table. Dusk came and moths flittered beneath the patio light. People drank and talked in subdued tones, occasionally someone laughed; some slept; others just sat and didn't move at all. Some cried and hugged; others were sick or busied themselves in preparing unwanted food, all trying to deal with their grief in their own tortuous ways. Most mourners left at sundown, but the family all stayed, anxious to support Robert and Joanna in their time of need. At some point on this deplorable day, Sarah learned that her flight had been rescheduled for a month's time.

It was around half-past eleven when she staggered her way upstairs to Helena's tiny box room. Halting halfway up in a drunken stupor, balancing both feet on one stair, she lost herself in the array of photographs lining the walls.

"I'm not whole any more, Archie," she whispered, staring at his service photograph, looking fabulous in his uniform. "My heart has been split in two; it has been ripped out of my chest and completely and heedlessly tossed away. What do I need that for, hey?" Tears began to track her face again. "But I promise that for as long as I can, I will travel this world for the both of us. I will trek the outback, I will swim the reefs. I will climb every mountain and roll back down each one of them with you in my heart."

Sarah gasped for air as she whispered at Archie's unchanging grin, her lips pressed to the photograph. "For as long as I can I will laugh and sing with our family; one day they will smile again. I will smell every sunflower I pass and think of you. Every breath I take, I shall be jubilant for I know in my heart that is what you would want. I will live each day as though it were my last and, Archie, each day I will pray to the stars in the heavens above me that somehow, someday, somewhere we may meet again."

As she turned away, her eyes fuzzy with tears and the effects of alcohol, Sarah saw something glinting on the stair tread. Bending towards it, her head swimming, she overbalanced and shot out a hand to grab the banister, narrowly stopping herself from falling. Curious to know what it was, she reached down and her hand closed over it. Swaying, Sarah opened her fingers.

Shining in the palm of her hand was Archie's St Christopher.

"How did this...?" Gasping with shock, her mind reeling, she gazed down at it remembering the day she had given it to him. Then something clicked and his words came back to her '... only in the event of my death should you open that letter.'

CHAPTER TWENTY TWO

A FALLEN STAR

Archie, Felicity, Emrys and Kriss rounded a bend in the river, which had been their focus for what seemed like forever. All Archie could see was mile upon mile of rugged countryside stretching into the distance, the sluggishly flowing river cutting a way through it. They walked doggedly beside it, sometimes under trees, at others out in the open enjoying the late afternoon sunshine, towards the distant horizon that seemed no closer however far they walked.

Footsore and weary, they came to the end of the tree line, rounded another bend and there at last, in all its heart-stopping magnificence, their goal was before them. Golden and gleaming, just as Archie had first imagined, it spanned the widest part of the river, its shimmering aura propelling outwards and upwards arching into the sky. It was a spellbinding sight and the four travellers ground to a halt, jaw-dropped, silent, awestruck.

"There it is. We made it!" Archie broke the silence at last.

"Now there's a sight I never thought I would see." Emrys' face split into a grin of pure joy, heartfelt gratitude standing in his gray eyes as he looked at Archie, who responded by leaping forward and throwing his arms around the centaur's neck.

"Let's get you across it," piped Felicity, buzzing forward. Emrys and Kriss began to march towards the bridge. Preoccupied, Archie hesitated, gathering his tumultuous thoughts.

"Come on Archie!" Kriss bellowed, grinning with excitement. Still Archie did not move. Kriss waited for a moment, a puzzled frown replacing his grin. Slowly he walked back. "What's wrong, Archie? What are you thinking? Whatever it is, stop. We are here. You simply have to cross."

"I can't help but think, Kriss, my mind won't stop," Archie was panicking, his face drained of colour, his gaze darting this way and that over the water.

"What is it, what have you thought, tell me?" Kriss pleaded.

"I'm sorry; it just p-p-popped in," Archie stammered, searching the air for help.

Emrys and Felicity had hurried back to him and were privy to the exchange, each of them burrowing into Archie's mind for a glimpse of his thoughts. "What popped in?" they asked in unison.

"You didn't!" Felicity read the information immediately, throwing Archie a knowing look. "Oh my God!" she exclaimed. "What a prize idiot."

"I'm so sorry, Fee. Lillian said it would be bad," he admitted, "but I never imagined it would be this bad. Help me." He stared at Felicity not knowing what to do, begging the star to make it better. Running his fingers through his hair until it stood up in a crest he looked like a startled hoopoe.

"Well you certainly conjured up a good one this time. I didn't realise your imagination was so, err... Jurassic!" Felicity said, shaking her head in despair. "I can't help you, Archie. This one's beyond me I'm afraid."

"What is it?" Emrys shouted in frustration. "What have you conjured? I'm not getting it at all."

As he spoke, the wind got up. Everywhere went dark, the sky turning rapidly from blue to inky black as storm clouds raced across the sun. The waters of what had been a tranquil scene began to frolic; rapids appeared and in seconds the river was a boiling fury, swirling into a giant whirlpool that sprayed and roared, bubbled and foamed. "What is it?" Emrys' voice rose to a terrified shriek as he gazed, stunned at the river.

Out of the water an almighty beast was surfacing. Two crusted and clawed reptilian feet emerged from the depths attached to a titanic body that reached up and up, lifted higher and higher on two scaly lizard legs. Out of its vast shoulders grew three necks. Three sets of beady green eyes peered at them out of three snarling carnivorous heads, each with slavering jaws lined with tusk-sized, razor-sharp teeth. The gargantuan, loathsome creature towered over the four terrified travellers drenching them in water with its enormous tail that slapped onto the river and thrashed powerfully from side to side.

"What is it?" Emrys bellowed again. His appalled friends were mute as they watched the beast rising above them. "Archie, Archie, what have you done? It's a dinosaur with three heads," the centaur squeaked, as they all back-peddled frantically, Felicity dragging Archie away by his lion's hide.

"No. No, it's worse than that," Archie screamed, as the monster rose up, stretched its necks, widened its mouths and breathed fire, shaking out from its back a gigantic set of jagged wings that blocked the entire view of the river.

"BACK EVERYONE! GET BACK!" Bellowing, Kriss turned on his heel and sprinted as fast as his legs would carry him back towards the tree line. Emrys, mesmerised, was rooted to the spot. Felicity took flight, dragging Archie up into the air. Glancing back she saw Emrys' hesitation, saw the beast's flaming breath reaching out to him and she panicked, lost her grip on Archie's hide and screamed as he plummeted to the ground.

"Emrys!" she screamed again, in a voice so surreal and high-pitched that Kriss, who was almost back to the trees, heard her and stopped dead. He saw Archie fall from the sky and land a short distance away. Kriss was on him in an instant, "You okay?" he yelled, skidding to his knees beside Archie and searching the sky for the star.

"Fine," Archie yelped, catching his winded breath and getting to his knees. Wincing, he too looked up to search the heavens for Felicity. "Where is she? I can't see her."

"Oh my God," Kriss gasped, "she's going back for Emrys."

Felicity, seeing Archie was alive and on his knees and that Kriss was with him, had spun round and was buzzing back through the overcast sky. Wondering how she could possibly carry Emrys' bulk she lowered her light, both to conserve her energy and so as not to attract the attention of the fire-breathing monster below her.

Her shrill cry snapped Emrys out of his stupor. He backed away so quickly he tangled his hooves and almost fell, staggered, picked himself up and began to gallop, head down, flat out. But it was a mere step for the fiend that hunted him. As it lumbered out of the water exercising its wings, Felicity swooped down, snatched Emrys' wrist and flew up into the air. With her wings beating on her last reserves of energy and her heart only barely taking the strain, she flew faster and faster, grappling for height, her hands locked in Emrys'. Behind them came an almighty roar. Seconds later a massive blast of heat scorched Felicity's wings. And like a stone she fell.

"I can see Emrys, they are coming, let's keep back," Kriss yelled at Archie, herding him towards the curve in the river. They sprinted into the trees and took cover, not realising the three-headed monster was no longer in pursuit.

"Can you see it?" Behind a large tree stump Archie, panting, bent over clutching his middle.

"How can you not see it? Its size is phenomenal. What did you think when you were fabricating it? Whopping beyond all proportions?" Kriss barked sounding angrier than Archie had ever heard him.

"I'm sorry," he whispered in shame, "so very sorry. One minute in my head I was over the bridge and home then the next, it was just there."

"What exactly is it?" Kriss stepped out from behind his tree peering through the shadows for Emrys and Felicity.

"A one-hundred foot, three-headed, green-eyed, fire-breathing dragon that never sleeps," Archie explained, as he joined Kriss. "It guards the bridge day and night," he continued quietly, sick with anger and disgust at his inability to stop the thought that had popped into his head as he gazed up at the bridge. God knows where it had come from; some long forgotten book he had once read or horror movie he had once seen. That it was out of the Dark Ages was a racing certainty. Why the hell hadn't he conjured up St George to go with it!

"What you have created is monstrous," Kriss stared in awe from the safety of the trees. He turned back to Archie and glared, "You uncontrollable, stupid, stupid young man. How are we ever going to get even close to the bridge now? Answer me that!"

"We have to slay it," Archie replied in a hoarse whisper, catching sight of Emrys trotting chronically lame towards them.

"And how exactly do you propose we slay a monster-sized, three-headed, fire-breathing dragon that never sleeps?"

Archie made no reply. He watched as Emrys approached, huffing and puffing, clutching his chest, one side of his dog-collar twisted up round his ear. Archie strode to meet him. "Are you okay? Where's Fee?" he asked, searching the land behind the centaur. "I can't see her, where is she?"

"She's… she flew with me. I cannot imagine what it must have cost her," Emrys panted, his face drawn with pain.

"Where is she?" Archie repeated.

"It breathed fire at us and... I fell... back there," Emrys gasped.

"Where?" Not stopping for a reply, Archie shot forward. He stared in the direction from where Emrys had come, willing Felicity to appear. He could see the dragon resting on the river bank in the distance, unmoving, its wings folded back. It was watching and waiting, smoke puffing from its nostrils. The star was nowhere to be seen. Scared witless for Felicity, Archie ran back to Emrys. "What do you mean you fell? Did she drop you? Did Hope fall too?" Archie searched Emrys' face, but saw no answers there.

"I'm sorry, Archie, I don't know," Emrys struggled to breathe.

Kriss put an arm around the centaur's shoulders. "I think you may have broken a rib or two, old friend, and by the looks of it you have sprained a fetlock. Even with only one eye I can see you're in a sorry state."

"One moment I was there face to face with that... thing, then I was running, then I was flying, then I was falling out of the sky and then I was running again," Emrys looked down at his hooves. "And against all the odds here I am." Looking up he caught Archie's gaze and held it, "Hope saved my life, Archie. Whoa; easy, where are you going?"

Archie had bolted out of the trees and was sprinting towards the dragon. Kriss shot after him, grabbing his arm. Archie shrugged it free. "No, Archie," Kriss said urgently, "no, not yet, just wait a minute. You aren't thinking straight." He snatched hold of Archie's arm more forcefully this time, attempting to halt his demented friend. Archie again slipped out of his grasp, but something in the big man's voice got through to him. Deep down he knew he could not take the dragon on single-handedly, he was distraught and panicking.

Running his fingers through his hair Archie turned slowly to face Kriss and Emrys, who now stood at the big man's side. Looking from one to the other he roared, "Where is she? WHERE IS SHE?" he roared again, this time at the sky, waving his hands frantically above his head. It was not as dark as it had been; the black clouds appeared to be dispersing. The sun was hanging low in the sky and an eerie light lay on the shadowed land. A rush of anger swept through Archie as he stared out at the desolate terrain. "Do you suppose she's simply disappeared on us again? She wouldn't, would she? Ahh," he cried out in torment, "Why do I feel like this? I don't even know who she is."

Swinging away from his anxious minders, he viewed the fading landscape taking stock of what he could see. Behind him the woodland rose steeply to a ridge of hills. The river flowed to his right; the dragon was some 800 metres upstream, guarding the bridge, which Archie knew was there but could not see. Nor had he been able to since his mind had conjured a reason not to cross it, for in the dim reaches of his brain he knew that is what the dragon represented. "...there's an enormous part of you that doesn't want to cross..." Lillian's words came back to him. Even now, he did not understand why, he knew only that he was still not ready to take that final step. He looked to the left. Here was unexplored territory, a no-man's land of wild, burnt grasses stretching out featureless to the horizon. There was nothing to see. Archie's shoulders slumped, but as he was turning away a white smudge on the river bank caught the periphery of his vision. He swung back, "There," he announced suddenly, pointing with a trembling finger.

Kriss and Emrys stepped up beside him and peered along his finger. "Right there," Archie jabbed the air.

"What are you going to do?" Emrys' gruff voice sounded in his ear. The centaur was clearly panicking. "We won't get near her, the monster will annihilate us all."

"Hush a minute, Emrys," Kriss laid a hand on the centaur's arm. "Let him think."

Archie was thinking hard, delving into his mind. He thought about Grace and the yellow aura she had given him to help him clarify his own and others' actions and to use as a shield. He remembered what she had said about his enormous strength of will. He thought about Lillian in her underwater cave and the foresight she had given him, along with her warning to filter his thoughts. He remembered the lion he had faced and slaughtered whose hide clothed him and credited him with extra strength. It came to Archie that if he really believed he and his friends were safe from the terrifying creature he had conjured then they would be.

"It won't touch us, don't even look at it," he told them. "Just trust me." So saying he began to chant, "Aura bright, propel my yellow light," over and over until his glow encompassed all three of them. Then, for the second time today, he focused solely on Felicity. Willing her to be alive yet knowing it was impossible for her to be dead he began to run, his feet pounding over the tufted grasses, Kriss and Emrys at his side. As he ran, he thought of all the times Felicity had saved him: the simple glass of water she had plucked from the air on the day he arrived in Transit; the night when the moon had first tried to trap him and the very first time, when he was a small boy under the ice-bound lake. She had even saved his life this very day, behind the waterfall. He remembered her smile, her giggle and her unending stream of tears. He remembered the willow crown she had made for him, which he still had in his pouch. And he remembered her kiss. Thinking only of Felicity and erasing all other obstacles from his path, Archie bounded towards her. Neither he nor his friends once looked at the dragon.

The fallen star lay crumpled on the river bank like a dishevelled flag, unmoving and lifeless. Reaching her Archie crashed to the ground beside her. She lay face down in the mud, her aura gone and her fragile wings burnt to the stem; all that remained was the blackened wispy skeleton of one and a stump of the other. The remains of her white satin gown clung to the curves of her body, melted into her skin. Her once curling blonde hair was singed black, frazzled to her scalp.

Archie did not hesitate. With a heart-wrenching cry he gathered Felicity into his arms and stared down at her. Though tarnished in mud from her head to her tiny feet, her face was pale and unblemished, her eyes wide open stared up at him, her lips were parted and silent.

"She's gone," Kriss whispered, putting his hand on Archie's shoulder.

Fists clenched, Archie squeezed Felicity's lifeless body. Consumed with red rage, his jaw ridged, his teeth gritted, he began to beg, "Wake up, please wake up. Oh, Fee, don't be gone. You are my hope, my guide, remember? Please, please wake up. I need you. I need you so badly." From his glazed eyes, tears of passionate fury poured down his face onto hers. "You were all that reminded me of home," he whispered, burying his face in her neck and sobbing like a child.

After a moment Archie's anger eased and his mind snapped into focus. Scooping up Felicity's delicate burnt remains he strode back towards the trees. Aware of the dragon's scrutiny, Emrys and Kriss followed, trusting Archie's word and with solemn faces steadfastly looking the other way.

Once in the shelter of the wood, Archie laid his burden down on the soft mossy ground. "Make her better, Emrys," he demanded. "You have every remedy known to man in that brain of yours. You can make her better, I know you can. Please help her," he implored, glaring at the centaur.

Emrys, appalled, stared straight at Archie, "She's gone, my friend!"

"Gone, gone where? How can she be gone? We are all gone, for God's sake!" Kneeling on the ground beside Felicity, Archie beseeched the centaur, "It's not possible."

"Look at her, Archie." Kriss came up beside him. "Just look at her. Her light has gone out. Emrys is right I'm afraid, the star is dead."

"Don't say that. She isn't dead, she can't be. There's no such thing as death. You told me that, Emrys, so now tell him," Archie yelled, distraught, his rage bubbling up again.

"In every phase an end has to come," Emrys said, a single tear dripping down his seamed, stubbly face. "The star has moved on to her next phase, my friend." He sighed, "Our sky will not be as bright with her gone."

"So that's it then?" Archie glared hopelessly at Emrys, "You've given up on her, haven't you." His fingers brushed against something entangled in Felicity's burnt hair. It was the willow crown. She had not taken it off since she had woven it only hours before. With tears scalding his cheeks, Archie felt for his own crown, pulled it from his pouch and placed it on his head. It rested there perfectly. He had accused her of wanting to make him look silly. He did not feel silly at all. What he felt was an urgent and desperate need for her forgiveness. He gathered her into his arms again, cradling her tiny damaged body against his chest.

"I'm sorry I couldn't find you, Fee, in this mangled mind of mine. I'm so sorry. I'm sorry I couldn't get us across the bridge. I'm sorry for trying to force you to talk when it was obvious you couldn't. I'm sorry for creating a monster that burnt your wings. Oh, God, Fee, don't be dead, please don't be dead." Archie sobbed uncontrollably, his teeth chattering with grief and shock as he clung to her, never taking his gaze from her face, which even in death was hauntingly beautiful. "I'm sorry you were forced to live a life looking down at me from the heavens dreaming of what might have been," Archie whispered in her ear. "I'm so sorry for… for everything.

"Now it is my turn to make a promise to you. I believe you live on - how can I help it after all that has passed?" Archie dashed away his ceaseless tears against his shoulder and began to rock the corpse cradled in his arms. "I will see you again, Fee, even if I have to search every level of this infinite and parallel universe, I promise I shall find you. I know you're out there somewhere. I swear to you, I shall not rest until I find you, not for a single instant. I don't know who you are or why I don't, I know only that I love you." Gently he laid her down, kissed her forehead and shut her eyes and, as with every time he had ever touched her, the strong feeling of déjà vu swept over him.

"Ahh!" He sprang back, "What does that mean? Why do I feel this has all happened before?" Frustrated beyond measure he threw himself at the waters' edge, kicking at the river. "I don't understand a single part of it."

Whilst Archie had made his regretful tribute to the fallen star, Emrys and Kriss had retreated a short distance away and bowed their heads, but now they both moved to his side. "Do not despair, Archie," Kriss said, "you will understand in time." He looked round at the clearing, "I think we should camp here for the night and be thankful the Moon is not out to witness this tragedy. She will be furious tomorrow when she rises anew and learns one of her stars has gone out."

"Sod the bloody Moon. I hate her. Imprisoning Felicity all these years; trapping her in grief and forcing her to watch as I lived life after life without her, slowly forgetting her. I hate the Moon." Archie stamped his foot and fisted a nearby tree trunk, bursting open the skin across his knuckles.

"Easy, Archie," Emrys said. "The heart never forgets. Hope is still there in yours, somewhere." Shaking his head the centaur murmured to Kriss, "Let's leave him alone a while, gather firewood and scrape together something to eat, shall we?"

Kriss nodded, "Could you just let us have some more comfrey and mushrooms, please, Archie." Wordlessly, Archie retrieved the mangled medicaments from his pouch and handed them over. With sympathetic murmurs of gratitude, his two friends moved into the thickness of the trees, leaving him alone with his grief.

Drowning in an overwhelming sense of desolation, Archie wanted nothing more than to be by himself. Felicity lay higher on the bank, still and cold. He was forced in that bleak moment to accept that she was gone and had he not already been dead, he would have wanted to die too. Standing with his feet in the river he fingered his crown and looked down into the water, lost in his thoughts.

Kriss and Emrys worked silently in the trees, intermittently checking each other's war wounds, both feeling the loss of a dear friend; both acutely aware that beyond the shelter of the woodland there lingered an insomniac fire-breathing monster, mercilessly guarding their only route home.

CHAPTER TWENTY THREE

A MESSAGE IN A BOTTLE

"It's looking better I think, there's no bleeding," Kriss gently padded Emrys' puncture wound with more puffball mushrooms and comfrey then ran his hand down to feel the centaur's tender fetlock. "At least it's not broken," he said as Emrys flinched. "We've been very fortunate, my old friend." Kriss's own wounds, though sore, were no longer quite so painful and the swelling was considerably reduced. His investigation of the more badly damaged eye had revealed a deep gash only millimetres from the eye socket; he was lucky not to have been blinded. Renewing the dressing, he said, "Surely if Archie created such a monster with a mere thought he can destroy it just as easily?"

"You are right, but it is not a matter of Archie simply imagining it not there. He cannot reverse the thought and whilst creating it was effortless, eliminating it will not be so easy. He needs a battle so he can rise to the challenge. That is his way. We must help the process, Kriss, now, tonight, we must devise a plan to slay the beast victoriously and then physically follow it through. Grab some of those if you please. Leaves as well as flowers," Emrys pointed in the direction of a large patch of bright yellow dandelions ripe for picking and eating, "then we'll get back."

"It will be a pure revenge on all our parts after what has just happened," Kriss remarked in a melancholy tone, gathering dandelions and placing them into the centaur's misshapen hands. As he did so he spotted something that gave him an idea: a broken branch, long and straight much like his staff, but more slender was lying among the flowers. Picking it up, he tested its balance. "Emrys, what do you think?" he bounced it on his shoulder, flinging up his arm and pretending to launch it like a javelin.

"It's worth a try, are there any more like it?" Together they found six lengths of timber that could be pared down to create lances. Now all they needed were some sharp flints to use as a paring knives, and there were plenty of those scattered on the woodland floor.

"She's free now," Emrys said, as they gathered enough for the task. "You know that don't you? I'm happy for her. She can move on and once Archie remembers her and crosses over he can move on too… until they meet again."

"Do you think that's likely? Kriss hefted the would-be spears across his shoulders as they strolled back towards the river with their finds.

"That he'll remember her? I hope so."

"That they'll meet again."

"Ah," Emrys shrugged, "who knows what lies in store for any of us, my friend? Archie and Hope are like one book ripped into two halves, no matter where their pages are scattered their story must end together eventually. But the guilt Archie feels right now for creating the creature that killed her must be indescribable; if anything even worse than his grief."

The two old friends walked in sombre silence through the trees. Almost back to the river they saw Archie squatting at the water's edge. "What is he doing?" Emrys muttered moving quickly, Kriss at his heels. There was a loud smash of breaking glass. Puzzled, they looked askance at one another then hurried down to the river bank.

"What are you doing, Archie? Are you okay?" Kriss called as they approached, throwing a stricken glance at the dead star as they passed her by.

"I saw someone." Archie pushed himself onto his feet and turned towards them, "A stranger. That same figure I saw before on the other side. It's shadowed me ever since I arrived in Transit. It's dressed all in black, even its face is hooded and it comes and goes like an apparition. Every time I near the river I see it lingering over there."

"Yes, but what was that noise we heard, it sounded like glass shattering?" Beneath the bandages Kriss's forehead creased automatically into a worried frown making him wince as he studied Archie's heartrending expression, the wild glittering eyes, the pale, taut face smudged with dirt.

"I found this bottle," Archie, looking lost and bemused, nodded to the smashed glass littering the ground at his feet. "It floated over to me. I watched it cross the river from that side to this like someone posted it. I think it must have been the stranger." Moving away from the broken shards he sat down abruptly as though his legs would no longer support him. In his fingers he clutched a tattered piece of paper.

"Well then, somebody probably did post it." Emrys peered over Archie's shoulder. "What does it say?" All three looked down at the sheet of paper in Archie's hand. He began to smooth out the crumpled page on his a bare knee. "It's too dark, I can't see," he said.

"Then take it over to the light," Emrys pointed smartly to a spot beyond the trees where the evening sun was bouncing off the river and casting long shadows on the bank. A slight mist was rising off the water.

Kriss nodded with approval, flung down the wooden shafts, yawned and sat down, leaning his back against a tree. "Good idea," he murmured.

"It's quite a long letter, Archie," said Emrys, " and since it's meant for you, you'd better read it to yourself and then tell us what it says afterwards; that is, if you want to." He settled down beside Kriss and started munching dandelions.

Archie did as they suggested and walked out of the woods. Holding the stained and creased sheet of paper up to the light he began to read, gasping in shock as he recognised the handwriting. In the top left-hand corner was the name and address of the sender:

Miss Sarah Walker

Hope Hall Boarding School for Girls

(Some rundown old mansion in the back of beyond – I hate it here)

HP11 2AF

His eyes widening, Archie saw that it was indeed addressed to him and as he noted the date his mouth fell open.

Mr Archie Fletcher

23 Eversely Avenue

London, N21 9PF

19 January 1992

Dearest Archie,

Well, I've been here two weeks now and I've not heard a dickybird from you. Do you have any idea how hideous it is living here? You're so lucky to be in the land of the living, at home with Auntie Jo, Uncle Robert, Hels and Stew. You may as well lock me up in prison and throw away the key. I've not spoken to a soul since I arrived, not that I'd want to, the girls are too busy gossiping amongst themselves, they're all old friends from old schools. It's so cliquey it makes me want to puke (and no I haven't been gorging on chocolate again!). I have to take etiquette and deportment lessons after school with a couple of old crones, as well as extra lacrosse training. Like going to school isn't a chore enough.

The headmistress is an old battleaxe. I'm a real outcast and everyone here knows it. Some of them try and talk to me but never for long, as soon as someone better comes along, I'm ditched! My tutor's okay, I suppose, she called me 'The Bridge' in my tutorial today, whatever that means. She said I connected with every group that had formed in our year from the 'cool group' to the 'geeks'. I think she's trying to be kind, attempting to make me fit somewhere in this hell-hole.

What can I say, I feel helplessly abandoned. I know Mum and Dad love me but they don't know me at all. I don't want to be moulded into something I'm not. Can't they see it will only push me away in the long run? I just want to be at home, Archie, like you are. It's not fair. I cried on the phone to Mum for an hour last night and she still won't come and get me. All she can say is, "You'll thank me one day, dear," or "They'll be the happiest days of your life". Well I can assure you I will not thank her, nor do I desire to recall a single instant of my being here. I hate it, Archie, and I miss you terribly. I just want to come home.

You are in my heart wherever I go. Please write.

Forever

Sarah

Archie finished reading and stared unseeing at the river swirling at his feet. He was utterly dumbfounded. How had this got here? He had never seen this letter before. Then a memory blasted into his brain and he was back in Woods Eves, sitting round the dining table one Easter, years ago, covering for his cousin.

"It must be the letter my cousin Sarah sent our Nanny in Wales by mistake," Archie guessed out loud as he ran back into the woods. "It was meant for me, but I got hers. Sarah had mixed them up," he explained to his friends who listened avidly. "But I don't understand how it got here."

"Ahh… Sarah," Emrys' ears twitched and his eyes sparkled, "that name is for a real lady, one of great beauty. It was a name given to her by God. A name that He may change at His will." Focusing back on his audience, he explained, "Genesis, Chapter 17, Verse 15, as I recall. Sarah, as she became – she was called 'Sarai' before God changed her name - was Abraham's wife." Emrys' attention wandered to the river, his brow furrowed in thought. "Now it seems to me that the name of another real lady is repeating over and over in my mind: that of

'Brenda'. Does that name mean anything to you, Archie? It was she, who asked me to wait for you, I'm sure of it."

"That was my Nanny Fletcher's name. You and she were old friends. She died of cancer when I was seventeen..." Archie swallowed. "We'd been staying only weeks before for the half-term holiday ... it was Halloween ... It wouldn't have been long after Sarah wrote this letter..." he fell silent remembering watching his grandmother waving them goodbye as they drove away, all of them aware it was probably for the last time.

"It is still her name, Archie," Kriss smiled, "because if she was the one in possession of the letter and she is over there," he nodded across the river, "who do you think posted it?"

Archie did a double-take. Kriss's expression was one he had never seen before, the big man actually looked cheeky. "Nanny?" Archie turned to stare over the river. "You're saying my Nanny Fletcher's just over there?"

"It's the only explanation, isn't it?" Kriss continued to smile. Archie gawped across the water, a spike of elation rising in his chest to think that a part of home, and such a dearly loved part, was only a stone's throw away. But as good as that news was he was too filled with grief to draw much comfort from it.

"She's waiting for you, Archie. Let's not disappoint her, eh?" Emrys chipped in.

"No; of course, but why has she sent me this?"

Emrys opened his mouth to speak, but Kriss shook his head and laid a hand on the centaur's back to keep him silent. "That's not for us to say, Archie, read it, and then read it again. It is up to you to balance your own heart, we cannot do that for you."

"I don't understand guys. Why won't you help me? I know, because you've told me ad nauseum that it's my lesson to learn, but I'm at a brick wall here, the pieces aren't fitting for me. Won't you just give me some guidance? Please?" Archie begged as he began to re-read his letter.

Emrys gave Kriss a look and without uttering a word said into his mind, 'Just a little nudge eh? His love is blind.'

'No, Emrys; he has to work it out for himself,' Kriss thought back, nodding to Felicity's corpse and unobtrusively tugging at Emrys' elbow. Without a word the two of them got up and began to edge slowly away leaving Archie to ponder.

"Emrys!" Archie's voice halted them in their tracks. "You said 'Sarah' was a name given by God, in Genesis, right? And that He could change it?"

The centaur turned back, praying with all his heart that Archie had struck gold.

"Might he have changed her name to 'Hope' or even to 'Felicity'?"

Jubilantly, Kriss swung round and slapped Emrys' rump, his eyes twinkling.

"Maybe this time he did," Emrys grinned, but Archie, far from being pleased was both confused and frightened. He sank to the ground beside the river.

"Sarah ... my twin-cousin Sarah ... is Fee?" Archie turned pale, he felt sick. "That Fee ... up there ... lying dead? They're the same person? I don't understand. Did Sarah die too? Has she now died again? And Fee? Are they both dead? But how-"

"Easy, calm down," walking forward Kriss attempted to pacify Archie, placing a hand on his shoulder and giving a gentle squeeze. "Your cousin Sarah did not die, she is fine, still living her life on Earth. She's the same indefinable and fickle Sarah you knew and loved," Kriss reassured. "Well done, though. You did it. You finally found Hope."

"Yeah, but she's dead, Kriss, what good is finding someone when they're dead?"

"As good as any other, believe me," Kriss assured. "Hope is free now. She will be delighted. She can move on and so can you."

"Why couldn't I see it? They are so similar in so many ways," Archie thought aloud. "That explains the déjà vu. Every time I touched Felicity it felt familiar, as though it had happened before. And it had ... only she was Sarah ... or was she Fee?" He was still utterly confused.

Emrys bowed his head to Archie's ear and whispered, "And your relationship with Sarah was...?"

"Special," Archie said without hesitation. "So special; she was special; we were special. Never like that… err, you know ..." he flushed and dropped his gaze, "but we were great friends. Our families always called us the 'twins'." Archie smiled, his eyes distant, his gaze resting on Felicity's broken body at the top of the bank.

"Yes, you were special," Kriss agreed, crouching down to run his hands through the water. The sun was sinking leaving a warm and lazy glow, the day drawing to its close. The river dazzled before them like a million diamonds sparkling at once.

"Let me get this straight," Archie said, shaking his head. "Sarah, my cousin, is still on Earth, yet Felicity is a star in space and Transit. How the hell did she get to be in two places at once?"

Kriss smiled, "Like you said, she's special and in her time as a star she has become even more intrepid and bright." He looked up at Emrys, "Sit down, old friend," he ordered. The centaur promptly laid himself out on the bank beside them.

"I have known her a long time, as you know," Kriss said. "The day Sarah - that is, my friend Sarah who was forced to marry Joseph - took her own life she became a star of hope and has watched over you ever since, Archie. As I told you, she was banished to the heavens but wanted desperately to walk the Earth with you one more time," he paused, considering.

"I know all that," Archie said quickly, anxious for Kriss to get to the point.

"Every soul has a certain lifespan on the Earth-plain," the big man continued. "They go there to learn many lessons, mainly about personal responsibility. Each path walked is varied. Choosing to understand that the human soul continues eternally is a very hard concept to grasp, many choose not to understand it at all and simply live their lives out. It's difficult, especially when you have the added complication of trying to accept the different views of others and dealing with the wrath of mother-nature. With each life you live, you move up the scale and into another phase."

Archie nodded, listening carefully to everything Kriss was saying, idly rinsing his hands through the cool water and watching the mist rising off its surface. A faint snore came from behind them and despite himself he smiled at Kriss, who smiled back. The sun was now below the horizon, its lingering warmth and the sound of the bubbling river were soporific and Emrys had fallen into a doze.

"Hope could see from afar your final life cycle approaching," Kriss went on, "so defying all the odds she decided to walk the Earth one last time, with you."

"She hoodwinked two other stars so she could sneak back down," Archie remembered. "She told me about that."

"That she did, Saiph and Chara," Kriss chuckled. "She split her soul temporarily in two, one half remained in the heavens to guide and wait for you; the other half threw itself at the next gateway to Earth. The day you were born, so was she. Did your mother tell you of your birth?"

"About the voice she heard and the rainbow? Yes; I always thought it was a figment of her imagination. I know different now."

They both fell silent; thoughts of admiration for the fallen star's unconditional love and the risks she had taken occupying their minds. For Archie, things were becoming clearer as he began to fit all the pieces together. Try as he might he could still not recall a golden cornfield, but rolling down the mountainside with Sarah was one of his most treasured memories; a moment of pure magic that he would never forget. To think of it now made him smile and in his heart he knew without any doubt that Sarah and Felicity were two halves of one entity. He had been privileged in life and in death to share, however briefly, the existence of both. For the first time a sense of peace began to steal into his senses.

"So what now?" he asked after a time.

"Hurrumph! Now, we slay the dragon and get you over that bridge," Emrys stated, waking from his doze.

"What about Fee, we can't just leave her?" Archie's mind spun at the thought of having to dig a grave. "What happens to the star part of her soul?"

"Ah," Kriss smiled. "It has united with its other half. Sarah may not feel it now, but she is whole again. And she has chosen to live out her life on Earth, so now it is your turn to play the waiting game."

The evening drew in; above them the sky was moonless and cloudy. As the cloak of darkness fell, Kriss laid a fire striking a spark from two dry flints to light it. Between them the three weary travellers managed to avoid the pending situation of Felicity's body, each silently content with having her close by through the night. They fed on dandelion, Juneberry and watercress salad and as they ate, Kriss and Archie peeled the bark off the shafts of wood, smoothing them on rocks and using flints to chip each tip into a wicked point. Soon they had six serviceable spears. The wind picked up considerably whilst they worked, fanning the flames of their fire and chivvying the river into bubbling more forcefully.

Emrys encouraged them to begin preparing mentally for their plight tomorrow and as they baked their spears over the fire to strengthen the wood, their conference proceeded. "Do you remember how you created the Chinese breakfast purely by your desire for it, Archie?" he began.

"Yes," Archie said, thinking back to when one wish had become reality.

"The only way to get rid of it was to eat it, right?"

"Yes again. It was as real as you and me. I couldn't make it disappear," Archie agreed.

"Here we have a similar situation," the centaur's mouth twitched, "fair to say on a slightly larger scale," he said drily. "We have to see ourselves triumphant moving on with this quest just as you did with the lion, Archie. It's all about mind over matter, we can do this. The power of thought, positive thought, can be magical," Emrys said.

"I don't think I'll be able to get my hands round this beast's neck somehow. And I didn't believe then that I would be able to kill a lion with my bare hands," admitted Archie without shame.

"No, but I did. So I put the thought into your head and you made it happen. Be positive, Archie. Remember, this time you have us behind you and the power of all our thoughts to help you. It won't be easy, in fact I have no idea how we can conquer such a beast." Emrys shook his head as he pulled a spear from the fire and ran feeble fingers down the shaft. "We must be clear in our minds, and confident. Try to think up a way to avoid, distract, divert or better still, kill it. We must put our minds together and think," he flustered.

"That's what got me into this mess. Now all I keep thinking of is the dragon's strengths!" Archie exclaimed in despair.

"What about your own strengths? What about your faith and self-belief? Think of them now, for it is they that are being tested here."

Emrys continued to lecture Archie and Kriss throughout the early darkness and once satisfied their plan was worthy he allowed their minds to rest with sleep.

CHAPTER TWENTY FOUR

HOLD YOUR NERVE

The sun had not yet risen. Thick, dense cloud raced across the starless inky sky. The three warriors were woken brusquely by torrential rain, their campsite and fireplace now a boggy swamp. Drenched and buffeted by a shrieking wind they scuttled to salvage their spears as the rain pummelled down. With the river flooding rapidly towards them, the water rushing over their feet, they scurried closer to the tossing trees. No one spoke as they peered through the darkness at the encroaching torrent. Forced to retreat they squelched their way up into the woods and onto firmer ground. Looking back, all they could see was swirling muddy water. The river bank had completely disappeared.

"Felicity!" Archie screamed. Heedlessly, he dropped his spears and clambered back through the trees, his willow crown was knocked off by a low hanging branch and disappeared in the darkness, his feet sinking into the mire.

"What are you doing?" Kriss roared through the driving rain, his voice flat and muffled by the downpour.

"Fee," Archie hollered in distress. "We left her behind."

"The river has taken her. There's no point, Archie. You're sinking. Get back here." Kriss scrambled after him and lunged for Archie's hand, but he had rapidly sunk to his waist and Kriss could not reach him. "Grab this," he yelled, leaning down to lower a spear across the bog.

Unable to assist, Emrys remained well back watching the scene play out before him. Archie was now up to his armpits, the sludge sucking him down as he grabbed the spear. Kriss, holding firmly onto a tree root with one hand, hauled at the spear shaft with the other. The cords stood out on his neck as with brute strength he slowly pulled Archie to safety.

"She's gone," Kriss uttered, as he unwisely relaxed for an instant to recover. His bandage had fallen away in the struggle revealing the dreadful bruising and gashes all down one side of his face. His eye flicked open, crusted with dried blood. There was no time to do anything about it: as he spoke the ground in front of them fell violently away taking the trees with it. "MUD SLIDE!" he yelled. "Get back!"

The sound of falling cracking timber was deafening as the land on which they stood shifted forward. Emrys had already climbed further into the trees, running from the rapidly widening river. Archie and Kriss scrambled to follow, slipping and sliding as the unstable ground gave way beneath their feet and plunged into the wild water below. Using the doomed trees and their spears for purchase they kept just ahead of it, hoisting themselves higher and higher through the woods, until the trees thinned and there were no more left to hang on to. Out in the open near the crest of the ridge, battered by the wind and rain, panting and exhausted, the trio watched the flooded river find its level, the gushing water taking with it everything in its path.

"It's an ill wind that blows no good," Kriss gasped, thinking positive. "This darkness is exactly what we need; a cloak to hide us as we make our move." He looked from

Emrys to Archie for approval. Both nodded; neither spoke, their terror standing in their eyes. "Then let's go."

Nothing more was said about Felicity's body being washed away by the tempest. To Archie it seemed on reflection somehow fitting that the river should have taken her. Better than being buried in a pit and covered with mud. He and Kriss took the lead, each carrying three spears. Emrys, unarmed, brought up the rear as they traversed the ridge. Mindful of the altered terrain they fought their way obliquely down the slope beyond what had once been the tree line. Lightning cracked open the sky affording them a brief view of the surging river and the dragon lying in wait, too immense to be affected by the torrents swirling round its feet. Then it vanished, plunged into darkness once more.

"If we can't see it, then it can't see us, right?" Kriss, aware they were all in a state of nervous tension attempted as always to be a calming influence.

Emrys, his face set in a perpetual frown plodded onward, but Archie was even now unable to control his thoughts, 'Unless someone forewarns it!' In despair he zapped the thought immediately, hoping no one had heard. "Over the bridge; I see myself over the bridge," he gabbled, striving frantically to cover his mistake and praying the bridge would appear to him again now he felt ready to cross.

Slowly and tentatively they shuffled closer and closer to the river and the beast that awaited them. The sky turned from inky black to charcoal gray; somewhere behind the thunder clouds the sun was rising. With every step they took it grew lighter and there was nothing they could do about it for there was nowhere to hide. When they were no more than a hundred metres away from the watchful dragon, an agonisingly familiar noise pierced the storm. Wide-eyed the three petrified warriors halted and gazed at the sky, listening. The ravens were back. Archie closed his eyes as the screeching drew closer.

"I'm sorry," he muttered, the unrelenting rain drowned his words, but his expression spoke them loud and clear. Kriss glared at him then swung frantically round trying to spot the birds before they attacked. Shaking his head sorrowfully, Emrys simply stared down at Archie as the ravens swooped in. Masses of them circled above, squawking and diving, but not one aimed to attack. Their noise heightening they shot forward towards the dragon like hundreds of black sirens vibrating through the air.

"They're going to warn it," Emrys spoke calmly looking straight at Archie.

"I know, I'm sorry, my brain just won't shut down. I…" Archie's voice trailed away in an agony of self-disgust.

The centaur nodded, "It doesn't matter. They would have come anyway. Whenever the Moon is out or there's a battle to be had the ravens will fly. Do not blame yourself."

"Archie, get moving," Kriss yelled, hefting one of his spears into the throwing position. "We go first. Emrys, stay close to us and do what you can. Now! Run, we've no time left." Kriss rushed forward. Archie leapt to his side their feet sliding on the slippery, shale-strewn ground. A cacophony of ravens could be heard over the storm, which showed no signs of breaking. The three intrepid warriors sped towards their vast target, the monstrous creature's silhouette looming before them.

And behind it, shimmering in the gloom: the bridge.

"Keep low if you can," Kriss threw back at Emrys, attempting to duck and weave as he ran, his red cape flying out behind him. There was nothing in their path to hide them. Their headlong dash across open ground was suicidal and yet not one of them had a negative thought in his head. Each one focused on the task in hand: Archie, fired by the reappearance of the bridge, fixed his mind solely on getting his feet onto it. Emrys concentrated on Archie, aiming to keep his thoughts from straying, and Kriss visualised the forthcoming battle and stabbing the beast in its black heart.

The ravens were circling the dragon's heads. Three blasts of fire shot into void. The scavenging birds drew back screeching. "Keep moving, stay low," Kriss yelled again. "We can and we will do this." He lengthened his stride, one spear poised for throwing, the other two held firmly at his side.

Warned, the dragon watched them come, necks waving, heads lowered, green eyes pinning their position. It lumbered from the river and stood on its hind legs to face them, swiping wicked claws at the air.

"Archie, propel your aura," Kriss bellowed.

"Aura bright, propel my yellow light," Archie gasped, forcing out his energy as his yellow shield appeared. "Please God keep us safe, please God keep us safe." The shield widened to encompass his friends. "Over the bridge, let's get over the bridge," he chanted. "Mind over matter, come on legs, run."

Illuminated in a bubble of yellow light, they charged. The dragon opened its mouths and flames shot towards them licking round the protective aura that sheltered them from its heat.

Straight through the beast's legs they grafted, running beneath its great dripping body. Kriss speared a giant ankle as they passed it and the beast roared in anger. The ravens shrieked and flustered in the commotion, swooping down to attack, rebounding off Archie's glowing armour.

"Keep running," Kriss bellowed. "We're nearly there."

Unscathed but riled, the dragon spun round and took flight, its wings beating the air above their heads. Like a jumbo jet it crash-landed in front of them engulfing them once again with fire. The shield held strong, but Archie's panic was beginning to overthrow his positive thoughts.

"Don't think, Archie," Emrys' voice hollered filled with dread. "Hold your nerve." Recharged, Archie propelled his aura out further, launching a spear at the dragon's thigh. It struck hard. The beast bellowed and pulled its leg into the air as the trio once again darted beneath it.

"Spear it again," Emrys screamed. Halting, Archie and Kriss turned and each flung a spear at the dragon's back, both struck true, one in the tail the other in its flank.

"Keep running," Kriss prompted, gasping for air. They turned and laboured for the bridge. It was only strides away.

Lungs burning, legs like lead weights, heart thumping with fear, Archie stumbled breaking their shield his aura shrinking to a fuzzy glow around his head. Emrys broke away, turned in panic to see the dragon rotating back towards them. Two tiny spears stuck out of its bulk like pins in an elephant, but its eyes were rolling in pain and it seemed for a second to hesitate.

"Archie propel…" Kriss shrieked in horror.

"No! It's injured, spear it again," Emrys insisted. "Spear it now, with all your might."

Although their minds were free from obstacles and the bridge well within their reach, not one of them could think of stepping onto it while the fearsome creature was still standing. Archie faltered; they each had just one spear remaining. Their only means of attack seemed utterly ineffective against this gargantuan beast; of no more use than twigs. "Do it, Archie. DON'T THINK! Hold your nerve," Emrys roared.

His eyebrow raised in query, Archie looked at Kriss.

"Aim high," the big man ordered impulsively, grinning at his companion. "Go for a throat." Archie nodded and grinned back, euphoria suddenly spiking his chest and firing his limbs. He was hurdling fences, rolling down a mountainside, running to beat the wind. He put back his head and laughed out loud. Behind him, Emrys drew a silent breath of relief and moved past to stand out of their way.

The two javelin throwers looked up and up towards the skies where the dragon's three heads snarled and drooled in fury as it gathered itself for a full blast of fire. Side by side, they took aim. Each attuned perfectly to the other they strode forward as one accord and on the final delivery stride turned sideways. Legs braced fore and aft, biceps bulging, they drew back their spears and summoning all their power unleashed their weapons into the air.

Spinning through space the spears flew as directed towards the gullets of two hideous heads. And then the elements stepped in. A blast of strong westerly wind impelled the wooden shafts more forcefully and the sun pierced through a break in the clouds to spear the dragon's eyes with a brilliant shaft of light. Its middle head shunned downwards pulling its other heads with it. Dazzled, the dragon failed to see the two handcrafted wooden spears, each now targeting an eye on two of its heads.

They struck like darts to the bullseye, severing two optic nerves. The dragon bellowed in agony throwing itself backwards, blinded by spears and tears of blood.

CHAPTER TWENTY FIVE

WE ALL MOVE ON

"It's not dead, but we've blinded it. That's good enough, let's go, let's go," Archie hollered at Emrys, who was nearest the bridge. The centaur watched for an instant as his two companions charged towards him through the torrential rain, waving him on. With joy in his heart he kicked up his heels and ran onto the bridge.

The dragon, unable to see with two of its heads but with all other senses alert, heard the hooves clip clopping onto the sturdy gold platform. Enraged and in torment it swung round, spread its wings and using one like a giant whip slapped it down on the bridge just in front of Emrys, stopping him in is his tracks. The bridge shuddered; Emrys stumbled, bouncing from balustrade to balustrade. The dragon rose into the air preparing to strike again.

Archie and Kriss jumped onto the platform, slipping and scrambling up the bridge to join their friend. "Keep going," Archie screamed, his arms flapping to shoo Emrys on. "Don't stop, Emrys, you're nearly there, we're right behind you. Keep going." The centaur did not look back, his four legs bounding into action hammering on the floor of the bridge. Galloping flat out, he thundered over the apex, slid a couple of metres, gathered himself and soared into the air - and with that leap Emrys was the first one home.

The infuriated dragon swooped down to the bridge redoubling its efforts. Archie, dripping wet, shut his eyes as a giant wing hurtled towards him. It missed him by inches, smashing down so hard in front of him that a hairline crack ripped across the apex of the bridge. Archie was thrown flat on his face. He clung, spreadeagled, one hand gripping each quaking balustrade. Over the noise of the hammering rain and the screeching ravens a loud and ominous creak sounded from below.

"Keep going," Kriss screamed, storming forward and pushing him onward. Archie, who had briefly lost sight of his target, refocused quickly, let go of the balustrades and threw himself across the damaged apex. The bridge groaned and shifted, the crack expanded and the entire structure slewed and began to buckle.

"RUN! Run for your life!" Kriss yelled, gesticulating wildly.

Archie started to run, hesitated and glanced over his shoulder, skidding to a halt when he saw that Kriss was now stranded on the wrong side of the widening gap. "Jump it!" Archie shrieked, but as he spoke he felt the bridge shift downwards, the struts beneath his feet splitting asunder and collapsing into the swirling torrents below.

"Just get over," Kriss bellowed, making no attempt to jump. "Don't worry about me, get yourself over." Archie did not move. There was not a single part of him that could leave without his friend. It was not in his nature. Helplessly he grabbed the buckling balustrade, his feet rooted to the spot.

The dragon came again, smashing its other wing on Archie's side of the bridge. The section immediately before him collapsed instantly and he slipped and slid down the now vertical slope. He grabbed at a strut, his hand clutching thin air. Slowly he tumbled over the edge and like a ragdoll hitting a brick wall, smacked into the heaving water.

The déjà vu that had dogged Archie's existence in Transit came back to haunt him with a vengeance. Submerged, winded and disorientated, he kicked and struggled against the torrential river. Still conscious, lungs bursting, he fought to see through the murky water and glimpsed a shadow disappearing beneath him as he battled upwards, pulling, pushing and driving to the surface. Breaking through, fit to explode, Archie gulped in a deep breath of air. Unable to focus, he felt something clutching at his legs, as though a giant hand had grabbed him and was wrenching him downwards. It could not be happening. Not again. Had everything he had been through been simply the kaleidoscope of images that occurs at the moment of death? Were they all merely figments of his overactive imagination? Had ten days been ten minutes? Was he back in the sea amidst the wreckage of the plane, about to drown and die all over again? Or was he trapped in a never-ending cycle, condemned to repeat all those heartrending experiences over and over again. It was unthinkable, but it seemed so.

Thrusting and twisting, grabbing and heaving at whatever had him trapped, Archie wriggled free, kicked out and once more began his fight for the surface, but the hand caught hold of him again. No; not a hand, but a set of claws. 'The dragon,' he thought, kicking, bending and grabbing at the colossal tightness encircling his legs. He tried to wriggle free, but the razor sharp talons pierced through his skin every time he writhed. Inch by inch he was dragged down to the riverbed. He began to lose feeling in his legs, but this had not happened before. Archie knew then that he was still conscious and he was not back in the sea but in the river. Hope rose in his chest: 'Aura bright, propel my yellow light, aura bright, propel my yellow light,' his mind repeated over and over. 'Help me Grace, Lillian, help me anyone. Please!' Archie stopped struggling, his eyes still open. The foggy water filled his head. The current was as strong as the grip that held him. Archie closed his eyes, vanquished; he could not hold his breath any longer. 'I can't fight any more. I can't win this battle, I give up. My mind has won.'

'You do not need to rely on gasping for air to fill your lungs, Archie. Breathe.'

He felt a feather-light touch on his hair and the gentle stroke from a small hand. Obeying the command he opened his eyes wide and drew oxygen from the water into his bloodstream. Lillian, the Keeper of Secrets, smiled, 'This underworld is no place for the likes of you, Archie Fletcher,' she whispered into his mind.

Archie winced in new found pain; the panic of drowning had subsided, but his legs were numb and the grip had transferred to his torso. It was as though he was being slowly crushed, bone by bone. 'Help me,' he thought.

'You have the strength to fight this, Archie. Fight it now.'

'I can't, it's too tight.'

'You can and you will.'

'How?'

'Just follow your guide… follow your heart.'

'She's gone.' Overwhelmed by a spike of raw grief, Archie closed his eyes.

The river bed began to tremble as a giant quake sundered the earth. The water grew cloudier, the disturbed silt dispersing as another earthquake ripped up clods of mud and broken rocks. The dragon let go. With only his arms to use, Archie dragged his numbed body through the shaking water. Above him he heard a terrible, distorted wailing. As he gained the surface, the colossal beast hit the water with an immense splash and in a mighty surge the river swirled into a massive whirlpool.

'It's down,' Archie thought, as he was dragged back into the water, pushed and pulled this way and that, smacking like a piece of flotsam into the dragon's body, helpless to avoid it as the rapids spilled over him and his useless legs. As the monster's girth was followed through by its three enormous heads, Archie was struck hard, one of its open jaws driving him downwards and pinning him to the bed of the river. He opened his eyes to find he was caught inside the beast's mouth, caged by its unbelievable teeth. He felt the presence of Lillian and in the corner of his eye caught a glimpse of her wispy stature illuminated by her aura.

'Get up, Archie,' she ordered sternly.

Get up? He could no more get up than fly to the moon; he did not have an ounce of energy left inside him. His hair, which had grown somewhat during his time in Transit, floated thickly around his lolling head. His eyes rolled as the circulation started to pump round his legs. The pain was excruciating.

'Follow your guide; follow your heart,' Lillian said again.

'How can I follow her; she's gone. Don't you know? She's gone and I have a creature bigger than a dinosaur pinning me down tight inside its jaw. How exactly do I get up?' Archie knew he was whinging, he didn't mean to, she was only trying to help him, but this time her help was an intense frustration for there was nothing he could do.

'You're so shirty, Archie Fletcher! How many times do I have to tell you Hope will always guide you?'

The jaw locking Archie widened slightly, the cage of teeth now trapping him less tightly.

'Goodbye, Archie. Follow her; it's your only way home.'

'Come back, don't leave me,' Archie pleaded, watching Lillian's wraith-like figure fading into the darkness. In utter despair he focused on the blip of light, which he assumed was her ebbing aura. He waited for it to vanish, but the blip became an orb and the orb grew.

Wonderingly, Archie's mind exploded, 'It can't be!'

But it was. As the sphere of light expanded, Archie glimpsed the figure inside it. Her wings spread, her aura brightened and she giggled. Through the bars of his cage Felicity's lovely face looked down on him, then it seemed to blur around the edges and it was Sarah's face, even lovelier. And in the depths of her shining eyes Archie saw a field of golden corn. And at last he knew her.

'It's you!'

'Of course it's me, Archie. Forgive me, I have made a choice to live and see the world, but wait for me. Our time will come. Know that I will love you for eternity. Follow me now; it is time for you to go home.' She reached a delicate hand through the bars of monster teeth and caressed his cheek.

He did not hesitate. Flipping onto his stomach, he barged with all his might at the widest gap in his spiky confine. The tooth broke, grazing Archie's shoulder and ripping a gash in his lion's pelt as he squirmed through the narrow opening, his blood flooding into the water to mingle with that of the dragon issuing from its mouths.

With a final push Archie won his freedom and reached out for Sarah, but in that instant her orb vanished and he was alone in the darkness once more. He did not know what he felt at that moment: a sense of loss, certainly, and yet his grief had dropped away from him and he knew with an unshakeable certainty that Sarah was his soulmate; that the two of them were separated only by time and eventually would be reunited. What he had to do now was somehow summon the strength to get back to the surface and go home, but his body and mind were beyond exhaustion. He pushed off weakly, using the dragon's body as a springboard, but the water was in turmoil and very, very deep and though Archie thrashed around and tried to rise to the surface, it was beyond him. Without Lillian's presence he was no longer able to breathe under water. Starved of oxygen, he began to drift back down to the riverbed.

He was plucked from the depths by two gigantic hands.

Gathering Archie to his chest and cradling him like a child, Kriss surfaced and lifted him high into the air.

Astounded, Archie drew breath and gaped up at his friend. "What's happening? You're… you're g-g-growing! You're a g-g-giant," he stuttered, unable to believe his eyes. Kriss made no reply. His huge legs began to stride across the river towards their desired goal.

Stretching himself to peer over his saviour's shoulder at the defeated dragon, Archie gasped with fear. Two eyes, shrill green, looked back at him from one head. The wounded monster was not defeated at all, but lay primed and peeping out of the torrents waiting for its chance.

"We have to finish it," Archie bellowed, thumping his tiny fists against the giant's vast chest. Kriss marched on, his recovered staff like a telegraph pole, his now enormous red cape flapping in the wind as it whipped at the waters several metres below. "What's happening to you, Kriss?" Archie yelled, glimpsing far beneath him the small portion of the bridge that remained standing, sloping down to the other side. The remainder, completely demolished, had disappeared into the depths.

It seemed to Archie, awestruck, that either Kriss was still growing or the dragon was shrinking. It was not long before his friend could simply cup him in one hand and Archie felt as if at any moment his head would brush the clouds. He wrapped his arms round the giant's little finger and yelled up at him, unsure if Kriss could actually hear him. "Finish it! Don't leave that part of me behind. Squash the beast, God damn it!"

Kriss lumbered round, raised his enormous staff high into the air and struck down, piercing the dragon's body. Archie felt the vibration in Kriss's hand as the earth far, far below, trembled beneath him. Swiftly, the giant marched onwards. "I am taking you home," he boomed. "I will not be distracted. It is time."

Deafened, Archie watched the other side draw near, but the sadistic waves were whipping round Kriss's legs. The mortally wounded dragon had one last trick to play. It rose from its watery grave, a single malevolent head still snarling. Surging out of the river it lunged, toppling the giant into the water.

"NO!" Screaming, Archie was flung from the safety of Kriss's palm into the air. "Aura…. Oh… au…" he wailed, his eyes wide as he witnessed the world hurtling towards him. He could see neither Kriss nor the dragon, only the tormented waters below him, which he was rapidly - too rapidly - approaching. This time he knew there could be no rescue and he wept for the generosity of his friend who had tried so hard to get him over the bridge, but ultimately had failed.

In freefall, Archie closed his eyes, feeling the rain on his face as he plummeted headlong towards the river and his inevitable end. And then he heard music: the sun, which from the start had been on his side, was coming once again to his aid. A shaft of sunlight had found a gap in the thunderous skies and was bending into a bow. Archie felt his fall begin to slow as though gravity had failed. Then he felt a pull swooping him sideways and down towards the shattered bridge. A mellow energy had taken hold of him. Streams of colour spilled before him and as he composed himself staring at his feet, he landed on a rainbow and was submerged in a spectrum of intense colour. He had seen its like only once before.

"Grace?" he whispered in awe. The rainbow felt solid enough to walk on, but he could see it was not, for his feet were swimming through the multi-hued bow. And she was there, holding out her hand to him.

'Go now, Archie. Your heart is balanced. It is your time.' The Angel of the Rainbow spoke soothingly into his head as she took his hand and guided him gently down her rainbow onto the remains of the golden bridge. Shaking, Archie grasped the balustrade for a final time. He turned to see the rainbow evaporating; Grace vanished and the music stopped; the sun had done his work and black thunderclouds loomed once more to cover his liberating rays.

"Goodbye," Archie muttered under his breath as he stared out across the wide river he had battled so hard to cross. "Goodbye all. Mum, Dad… Hels, Stew… goodbye." His eyes filled with tears that flooded down his face. "Maybe I'll be honoured to bump into you again one day in another world, another adventure - another parallel universe."

Archie went to step off the bridge, but turned back one last time and whispered into the atmosphere, "Thank you all of you who helped me. Thank you." As he lowered his foot to the ground, his head swam and he felt suddenly nauseous. He was not sure if it was shock or the strange odour that lingered on the damp air; one he kind of recognised but couldn't quite place. The rain had eased to a light drizzle, but the ground was sodden and the bank Archie stepped down onto was slippery with moss. Mint bushes grew in wild profusion along the river, which was no longer raging. The aroma was pungent, but fresh and distinctive masking the other smell and Archie's nausea began to subside. Out of the corner of his eye he saw a normal sized Kriss squelching his way up the embankment towards him. Sobbing with relief, Archie reached for the not so very big man's hand and yanked him through the clustered mint onto level ground.

"How did you DO that?" Archie gasped, only then noticing that his friend's wounds had disappeared. Kriss looked exhausted, but his skin was without blemish.

"Thanks," Kriss spluttered, sucking in a harsh breath. Wiping his muddy hands across his ripped tunic he grinned, tapped a finger to the side of his nose and said, "If I told you, you'd be as wise as I am. Where's Emrys?"

"I don't know; I haven't seen him, I've only just got here. Did you finish it? Is it dead?" Archie questioned eagerly, searching the river for any sign of his dragon.

"It's dead!"

"Thank you, Kriss," Archie smiled apologetically, patting his friend's shoulder, "you're a saint." The words were no sooner out of his mouth than the strangest thought occurred to Archie. Sopping wet and surrounded by the refreshing smell of bruised mint, both men stood and stared at one another, Kriss with one sardonic eyebrow raised. Archie's hand strayed to his neck and a wide smile spread across his face revealing a newly chipped front tooth. "You ARE a saint. You're my lost St Christopher!"

Kriss's gaze remained locked with Archie's, "But you never really lost me," he said with a broad grin. "The night your plane went down you died with me wrapped round your throat. You shifted into Transit without me, but when you took your last breath I was given the privilege to serve you and try one more time to keep you safe and get you home."

"You were here to protect me as Saint Christopher? Sarah gave me that pendant."

"I know. She has it back now, but the sentiment of her gift remains with you. So if you ever need a hand crossing the river again, I'll be here."

"Thank you," Archie said simply, feeling inadequate, not knowing how he could possibly express the rush of gratitude he felt for this unassuming gentle giant who had been his friend, his companion in arms and his protector.

"It's been a pleasure… nay an honour." Kriss reached out and shook Archie's hand.

"Hello," interrupted a voice from behind, startling them both. They turned abruptly, their backs to the river, facing the voice and new territory. "I have been waiting for you." Before them a large figure peered down at them, it was cloaked in black satin from toe to chin. A black helmet encased its face and in its gloved hand it held a clipboard.

'Oh my God, it's Darth Vader!' was Archie's initial, spontaneous thought. The stranger did not chuckle as Kriss did.

"No, I am not Darth Vader. You have no battle here with me. But I am who every man fears. They call me 'Death' and I am he to whom all must pay their due," the apparition swelled at his own importance. His voice was neither cold nor hostile, but monotonous and calm. Only his appearance was severe and intimidating. "Please state your full name."

Archie looked across at Kriss, who gave an encouraging nod. He hesitated, dumbstruck. "He knows who I am, mate," Kriss muttered in Archie's ear, nudging his elbow and snapping him out of his trance.

"Archie Fletcher," Archie's voice, whilst deep, seemed childlike in his own ears. Never in his wildest thoughts had he envisaged talking to a man posing as death itself.

"Please state where you have come from," Death stipulated, drizzle dripping down his helmet and onto his clipboard.

Archie's eyes widened in confusion, "I came from London on the Earth-plane. I am the son of Robert and Joanna Fletcher, of 23, Eversely Avenue-"

"And why are you here, Archie Fletcher?" Death's monotone interrupted.

"Because my aircraft crashed," Archie replied bluntly.

The forbidding apparition consulted his clipboard, "Why has it taken you so long to find me? Your Company arrived ten days ago."

Archie hesitated, unsure what to say. Knowing he had to find the answer for himself, he delved restlessly into his head thinking, 'Why am I here?' His mind felt scrambled and the answer he found though true seemed rather lame. "I got lost," he said shortly.

Kriss rolled his eyes skywards and again nudged Archie's elbow.

"Err... I had some things to do." Archie could not believe the utter drivel that was coming out of his mouth. Beside him, Kriss snorted.

"Ten days? You must have had a lot to do," Death retorted drily.

"Yes, it's been ... err, busy."

"You spent ten days in Transit and you are not sure why? There must be a simple explanation?"

Archie was petrified, he could not think. Every answer he found seemed ludicrous and he knew he needed the correct reply or Death might send him back into Transit - to face what? He shuddered to think. "I was lost," he gulped, "but others were too. Emrys and Felicity; they needed me to help them."

"And did you help them?"

Archie hung his head at the mere thought of Felicity's corpse being washed away. "I did my best."

"Ah yes, and that is all one can do," Death agreed mildly. "What lesson have you learnt during your Transit?"

"Lesson?"

Death nodded slowly, "Lesson," he repeated sternly.

"This is important," Kriss whispered, "think, my friend."

"To control my thoughts," Archie said hesitantly, praying possibly he could be right.

"Your life will never be boring, Archie. With an imagination as free as yours, your soul will endure a never-ending adventure. Taming your thoughts in Transit is very wise since all realities are optional there," Death paused like a frozen statue, "but that was not your lesson."

Archie lowered his head thinking hard, lost in memories of yesterday. Anchored somewhere deep inside him a silent kiss struck a chord suffusing him with tenderness. His eyes misting he said softly, "My lesson was to find and forgive a lost star."

"And did you?" Death demanded.

"I forgave her," Archie swallowed, "but I found her too late and now... she's a dead star," he whispered.

"You must surely have learnt by now, Archie Fletcher, that we do not die. We merely transform our energy - our spirit - into something else. Felicity, who has been both Hope and Sarah in her lives, is not dead. Indeed, she is very much alive. And because you finally found her she is no longer banished to serve the Moon."

"Is she here?" Archie's optimism came oozing out of his pleading eyes.

"Nor is she here. She made her choice. Did she not tell you so?"

Archie nodded dumbly; he had hoped she might conceivably have been teasing him. It would be just like her.

"She is safe," Death's tone sounded vaguely sympathetic as he tucked his clipboard under one arm and gazed at Archie, his eyes glinting behind his helmet. "And you will see her again, but first you must wait - just as she waited for you."

The apparition's homily ended abruptly as the bushes behind him came alive with rustling. The strangely familiar odour Archie had smelt earlier wafted strongly towards him. "What is that smell? Emrys, is that you?" He eyed the jungle of waving foliage and from its midst there emerged a beautiful face, a face so real and so recognisable it was as though time had rewound over two decades. She looked amazing. Aged in her prime, dressed immaculately in an elegant and vivid purple dress, was Nanny Fletcher.

"Chicken pie, potatoes and fresh runners from the garden," she beamed at her grandson, taking him in her arms. "I'm here to meet you and I knew you would be hungry." She reached up on tiptoe and kissed Archie adoringly on his forehead. "Let me look at you. Ah yes; you are a man. Sorry I'm late. It's not like me at all. I'm just extraordinarily busy. You'll never guess who I've just bumped into charging through the jungle with his horse? Reverend Emrys Nevett - would you ever believe it?"

Overwhelmed, Archie clasped her to him laughing hysterically. "Oh yes, I would!" he spluttered on her shoulder. How could this be happening? She felt solid, so very real and yet she was undoubtedly dead – as indeed was he. It was all too much for Archie to take in, but for the first time in what seemed like months he felt suddenly and incredibly happy.

Unperturbed by Death's regal stare, Nanny Fletcher wrapped one arm firmly around her grandson's waist and hurried him away into the lush thicket. "We must get you something else to wear," she said, wrinkling her nose as she led him along a narrow winding trail between colourful shrubs and waving palm trees.

"Where's Granddad?" Archie asked excitedly, his heart thumping so loudly it was like a drum beat pounding them through the jungle.

"You'll see. So many are waiting for you," Nanny chattered cheerfully, beating down foliage from their path, "James made it across safely. He's with his brother… oh, what's his name?"

"Mal?"

"That's it. Gosh that was over a week ago now." She stopped a moment and looked up at him. "And with James came this dish of a man," she grinned, "William Clift - but don't tell Granddad I said that!"

Archie winked, laughing at the absurdity of it. His grandparents had been the most devoted couple in life and were likely no different in death. "Your secret's safe with me, Nanny," he grinned, his heart swelling with gladness that everyone was safe.

"So all is well, Archie, and tomorrow a new sun will rise and it will be for you," Nanny Fletcher squeezed him proudly. "Yours was a phenomenal Transit - historic, the greatest transformation ever seen. You've done something no one's ever done before. Oh, but the adventure's only just begun, dear Archie, just you wait and see."

EPILOGUE

My story closes at the crossing of the man called Archie Fletcher. It is, at this present moment, the most important day in Archie's life, crossing from the Fletchers' world back into the Parallel. I finish at the start of his new life because his adventure here on Earth and in Transit, was so heady and rapid it would be a travesty to miss any part of it. In his short life and his phenomenal Transit, a collection of marked memories developed a stem for yet another unknown future. Unfortunately for those he left behind, the private and cherished memories of times gone by, stored deep within our hearts, are all we have left to cling to. Archie's story was a fleeting journey of raw hope and unconditional love. Yet parallel to that it is the fateful story of one boy's courageous imagination and a flicker of the man he momentarily became. His life on Earth was a lightning odyssey that will fire his family for eternity and as the sun rises on each new day without him, time unrelenting for even an instant, there is a knowing deep within us all that the adventure of life must go on.

A NOTE ON THE AUTHOR

Born in North London in 1978 and raised by both parents, together with her older brother and sister, Claire Kinton quickly discovered her passion for writing, her creativity nurtured early by the late headmistress of her second primary school.

As a deeply passionate writer, Claire has the natural ability to write from her heart, gifted with twisting powerful real life events into poignant, even funny but always unforgettable novels.

Claire Kinton currently lives in Lincoln, England with her husband and three children. She is the author of

The Game Trilogy:
Dead Game
Waiting Game
End Game

You can join Claire on Twitter @Claire_Kinton
Or on facebook www.facebook.com/Claire.Kinton

www.clairekinton.com

Find out more at:
www.ghostlypublishing.co.uk
And connect on Facebook at:
www.facebook.com/GhostlyPublishing

If you liked this book, you'll love:

Waiting Game

The awesome new sequel to the People's Book Prize Shortlisted "Dead Game".

Living in despair after the tragic death of her cousin Archie, Sarah Walker finally succumbs and embarks on her long-awaited trip around the world. Landing herself in a dingy Thai soi, she runs into a forgotten rogue from her past. Terrified, Sarah flees and in doing so, finds herself in a ghostly world with warped satyrs, dual-headed snakes, and a wicked witch who plots to enslave her; trying to piece together the jigsaw of her past in time; the true meaning of friendship is at stake. Waiting Game is a dangerous journey but it is a fragile heart that travels it. Compelled to move on whether she wants to or not, Sarah's scars run deep, but just how far will she go in an attempt to find Archie?

Lightning Source UK Ltd.
Milton Keynes UK
UKOW042210030313

207085UK00001B/1/P

9 781909 587083